I0780883

THE BLUE BOTTLE TREE

NANCY HARTNEY

The Blue Bottle Tree by Nancy Hartney
Copyright © 2024, Ozark Hollow Press

Paperback ISBN: 978-1-958783-26-9
Hardback ISBN: 978-1-958783-28-3
EBook ISBN: 978-1-958783-27-6
Cover Design by Emma Unger.
@Unger.Creative
Behance: https://www.behance.net/emmaalyssa
Blue Bottle Tree Sketch by Graham Hawks
Published by Ozark Hollow Press
PO Box 4573
Joplin, Missouri 64803
Lia Wu, Publisher
Ozark Hollow Press Edition 2024
Printed in the USA

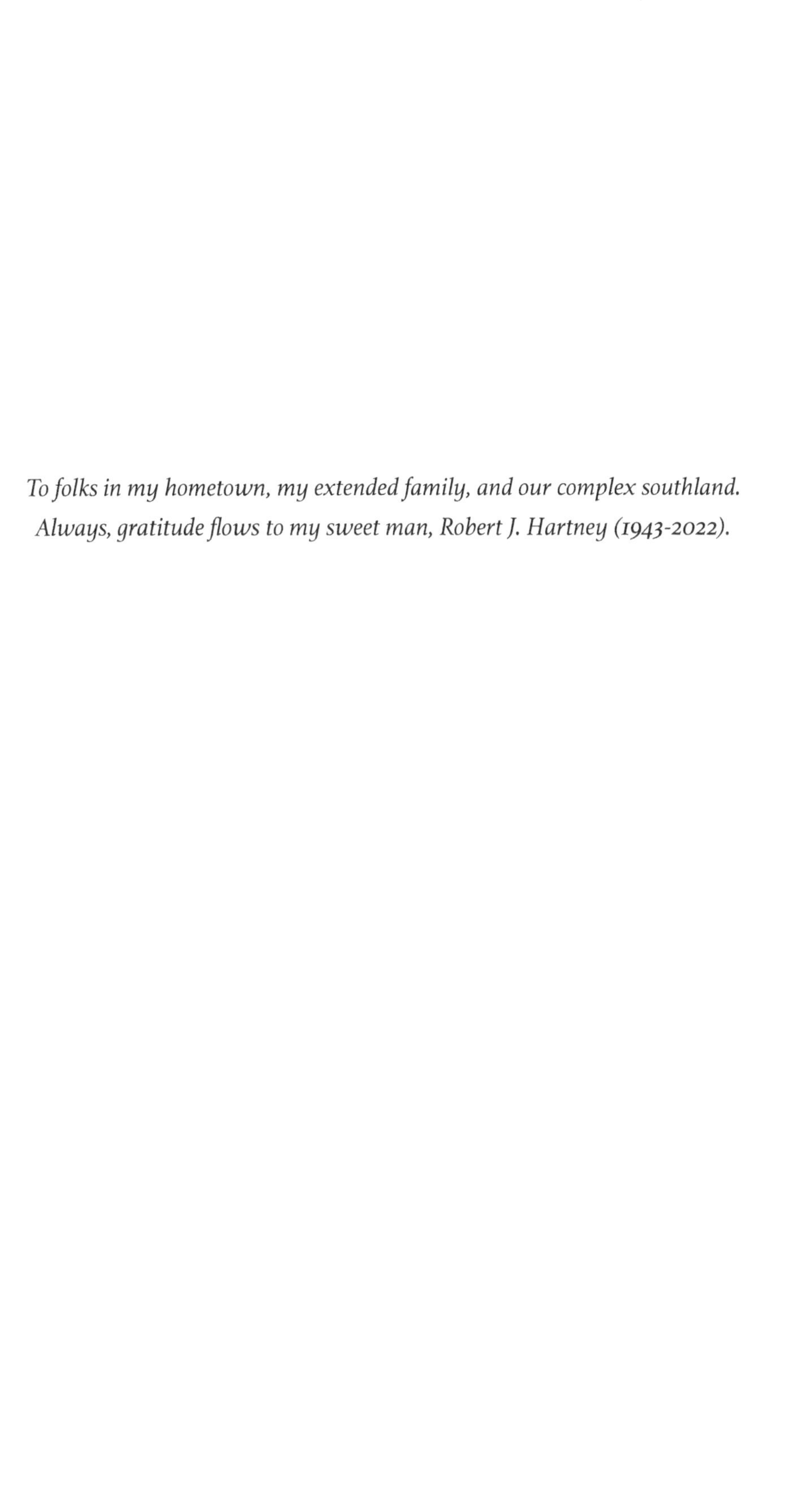

*To folks in my hometown, my extended family, and our complex southland.
Always, gratitude flows to my sweet man, Robert J. Hartney (1943-2022).*

CONTENTS

CHAPTER ONE
LETTA DAVIS

LATE IN THE AFTERNOON, chores finished, Letta Davis gathered her cane pole, coffee can of wigglers and started toward the river. She hummed under her breath, glad for an afternoon to herself.

Using back roads, she walked barefooted along the oak-shaded track, puffs rising with each step, dust warm against her feet. By the time she got to her fishing hole, an eddy favored by catfish, the sun had started drifting toward the tree line. Willow-sweeper fingers dipped into the tea-colored river and sycamore lined banks.

A string of catfish, tied to a tree root, floated along river's shallow edge nearby. A late breeze rustled through leaves, creating a mosaic of shade and light. A conjure woman, her back crooked, sat on the bank and watched Letta approach. Her hickory-tinted face and dust-colored clothing merged, almost invisible, into shadows–there, yet not there.

Letta nodded to the elder in greeting.

Closing her eyes, the conjure woman spoke in a voice like paper crumpling. "I know you. You one called Letta. You work for them

Butlers. That man owns this here town." She spoke through a near-toothless mouth, moved a wad of coarse snuff around with her tongue.

"Uh-huh." Letta reared back and scowled at the woman. Her recollections touched again over her time with the Butlers. Years fraught with stress. Thoughts she only summoned during those nights when moon hid its face.

She settled down on a fallen log, uncoiled her fishing line from the cane pole. "Uh-huh. I that one. I work for them Butlers a long time. My momma worked for them ahead of me." She baited her hook and, with a flick of her wrist, popped the line into the water, watched the cork settle in a still pool. "Got time today. Looking to catch a mess of fish for supper."

"That man Butler you work for, he rebuilt this here town," conjurer said. "Now he strangle it. Like he strangle you. He's got that wife dying from the cancer. That boss woman gonna ask you do somethin'. You'll wanna do it but can't. Not yet. She'll pass over soon. Bottle tree won't protect this family. White time hang heavy." Conjure woman spat a stream of brown juice off to the side.

Letta knew conjure woman had wisdom beyond this time, this place. Knowledge stretching back to Old Ones from Africa. Nonetheless it surprised her the woman knew so much about her. Out of respect for their ways, Letta had stuck blue bottles on dead tree limbs in the Butler yard to catch any malicious swarming haints. Had placed a bottle tree next to her own shack and painted shutters blue to ward off evil. She listened to sister crows with their warnings. Recognized shades crossing times.

Still sweating from her walk, Letta shivered. She had not expected to see this conjurer, had not expected to have her afternoon disturbed with anyone prying into her business. Annoyed, she sucked her teeth, felt the woman's fading eyes take her measure.

Mud and musty cattail odors hovered over the river. A fish jumped upstream, creating concentric circles, increasing into larger circles as they rippled downstream. Several crows that had perched along a tree branch cawed loudly and took flight.

The woman pointed toward disappearing dark forms. "They telling us times changin', be dangerous. Bottle tree not gonna catch evil around that Butler man. Round his big house. Too many ghosts. Too much evil." She stood stiffly, stretched her knotty frame, and climbed higher up the bank. She sat on a protruding tree root near Letta and recast her line.

The two settled into silence, lost in separate thoughts. Occasionally, one or the other slapped an errant mosquito and shifted about, while chewing snuff and watching their corks float.

The crone leaned over and gripped Letta's shoulder, knotted fingers digging into her flesh. "Leave that house. Leave them Butlers. Haints telling me hard times a'coming. Blood be on you and that household."

Letta jumped at the touch. "Uh-huh." She shrugged the hand off, careful to remain neutral-looking, yet respectful. "That Butler sister, Susan Pea, be back next few days. Things get easier when she gets here."

"She come back, but ain't easier with that man, nor that cancer woman. Butler sister ain't carin' for that blind girl, neither."

Letta knew conjurer only slightly. She knew of her powers, her gift from Old Ones. Although her afternoon peace was disturbed by crone, Letta listened. Ancient tongues spoke through conjurer, gave her knowledge and wisdom not known to others. Now the woman sat and spoke of days ahead.

"That cancer woman and her sister only do stuff in them white-woman ways. Still leaves all work and mess on your doorstep. Cookin'. Cleanin'. Fetchin'. They frown and watch over you shoulder. Give false freedom."

"Naw." Letta stared down at her hands, calloused with broken fingernails, holding her cane pole. She had spoken without conviction and wondered what business the woman had taking up the afternoon, speaking of sorry things to come. "What you talking on?" Letta's voice wavered between respect and uncertainty.

"You ain't got nuthin' left over to do caretaking for own family." Conjurer paused and put another wad of snuff behind her lower lip. Silent, she stared across the river, wiggled her fishing pole, and spoke with a voice echoing from far away, from the past. "That Butler man never ever lift no finger to keep that sawmill accident from your man. He *let* that cable cut him in two pieces."

Letta blinked to clear her vision, continued to stare at her hands, nostrils flaring. Hands that scrubbed toilets, hoed okra, and pulled weeds. Shelled peas. Mopped floors. Chores completed before she walked home in the dark, bone tired, to her own children. All those days, she struggled with keeping her three in school. Struggled with loneliness. Struggled with revenge held tight in her heart. "Been most two years since my man cut dead. That Butler man never once said no kind words about his passing."

Conjurer grunted an acknowledgement.

They sat silent again, continued to fish.

Letta rebaited her hook, wiped sweat off her forehead. Gnats worried around her eyes and ears. "Years been hard," Letta said. "Susan Pea gets here, she take over care of cancer woman, that blind girl. Give me chance to let up some. Finish raising up my boy Elijah and my Merry. My oldest, John, he in Army. Gotta wait till that Army allow him come home. Yessah. I be able to let up some."

"Ain't no white woman gonna allow no letting up for our kind. All's they think is more work. Stay in you place. Mark my words, more. Never less."

Letta jiggled her pole slightly, sat quiet, and continued to pick through her thoughts.

Conjurer spoke again in a scratchy voice. "You still under that Butler thumb. Only thing gonna change, you got three white women you carin' for. Three, not two." She spit a stream of juice and waved gnats away. "Hard days behind. Harder times comin'. Like that there Bible tell, blood be wages of sin. More secrets them Butlers not wantin' known, comin' real soon."

Letta did not respond. The woman's words fell against her ears like a beating heart. At that precise moment, a cloud passed before the sun and darkened where Letta sat. She shuddered at the sign.

Conjure woman humphed, then spoke again, her voice scratchy. "White people think they know us. Say all us look alike. Say we breeding like rabbits. Say we can take hard work. Humph." She spat and lapsed into silence.

Sun sank still lower until, finally, crone stood, gathered her pole and bait. "Old Ones say blood gonna spill before the days turn cool. Mark my words, blood gonna spill." She pointed a crooked finger at the string of fish. "Take that mess of cats. I too tired to clean them. Besides, you ain't got no time to catch supper a'fore dark."

Letta sucked her teeth and nodded thanks.

The woman hobbled into the weeds and down a narrow path parallel to the river. She disappeared into the shadows, pole bobbing slightly with each step.

Mosquitos hummed louder, drifted around Letta's ears in clouds. She wiped her face with an old handkerchief and flapped at buzzing insects. She glanced at the sky, watched the summer light slant low, felt the promise of darkness hang in the air. An owl hooted from a down-river cypress.

Stiff from sitting, she stood with a grunt, tucked her line around the pole, tossed bait into the river, and gathered the string of catfish from the shallows. Taking a deep breath, she started home, thoughts still churning.

A chill descended.

CHAPTER TWO
SUSAN PEA BUTLER

IN SMALL-TOWN SOUTHERN MINDS, New York City personified race mixing, night clubs, Yankees, and perverts. Promiscuity reigned and gonorrhea was a gift given across class and race lines.

Susan Pea, despite her Southern heritage, had taken a northbound Greyhound within days after graduation. High school gym coach had hugged her tight, scribbled an address on a piece of paper. "Barbizon Hotel. Go there. You can do this. Be independent."

With news of Eve's changing status and Letta's unusual phone call for help, Susan Pea reluctantly pointed her ancient Pontiac toward Georgia.

She left the big city, drove south through Philadelphia and Baltimore, radio stations playing Ricky Nelson's lily-white dribble or Sinatra's crooning for cheek-to-cheek dancing. Further south, Memphis and Atlanta country stations bawled out Elvis Presley. Simon and Garfunkel sang "The Sounds of Silence." Johnny Cash pledged "I Walk the Line." Rockabilly-soul-blues spiced the air with a unique energy. She drove, smoked, and flipped through stations.

CHAPTER THREE
SUSAN PEA BUTLER

SUSAN PEA CROSSED the Georgia state line May 1970 and drove straight through Lee Town into Bainbridge, her hometown. She turned from Highway 84 onto Broad Street, slowed, and looked at stores and offices, Willis Park Hotel. A pecan tree stood alone at an intersection next to the Baptist church marking another turn. Homes lined streets, their front lawns dotted with fallen leaves, wet from the night's rain. Not particularly appealing, Bainbridge appeared to struggle between a lost past and current times.

At the edge of the city, she turned on the old Quincy Road toward the Butler mansion.

Pulling into the family driveway, she shifted the rusted Pontiac coupe into first gear, turned the engine off, and stepped out. Acid churned through her stomach, causing her to belch up something clumpy, sour. Her throat burned. Sweat outlined her armpits in a ragged semicircle.

Leaning back into the hot car, she popped the glove compartment, found a stray rubber band, and wadded her stringy brown hair into a limp ponytail. Not pretty, but cooler on her neck. Once slender, now plump she stretched her forty-eight-year-old body and grimaced. Her fair flesh rusty with freckles.

At the edge of the yard, she stared at the oak tree, a witness to the puny human flow beneath it. Drooping branches and weeping moss strings had formed a silent touchstone during her growing-up years, shading her Butler years of glory and angst as it had done for previous generations.

Sighing, she started toward the house. With each step, another memory materialized. "Long damn drive to this backwater, humid sink-hole," she mumbled. "Lordy, lordy, I left this sweltering place in a huff and am returning under a cloud. Everything changed, nothing changed. How can that be?"

Mutt, family junkyard rescue, rushed out baying at the strange vehi-cle. He sniffed around her and the car with the attention only a part-beagle can give to odor. Satisfied, he trotted to the house and hopped up the porch steps. She followed at a walk.

Pride-of-the-town mansion, now gone to seed, stared at her with hollow eyes. Susan Pea shuddered, craned her head up, looked at the second floor. Wisteria, once a small twig near the porch, had grown, climbed along the ledge, and covered this portal to the past in purple. She took a deep breath and resumed walking.

Letta Davis rose from an open-slat porch swing and rested her gnarled hand on the railing. She stood a moment, watched.

"Hello, Letta." Susan Pea stopped near the porch steps.

"Missus Susan." Letta nodded, her face blank, her speech deeply accented and drawn out. "Been 'pecting you since yesterday. Missus Eve gonna be pleased you finally come back home."

"It's good to see you again. I only wish circumstances were differ-ent." Susan Pea cocked her head sideways, shaded her eyes. She spoke with a quick, clipped Northern accent, something deliberately acquired over her years among the Yankees. Her voice also carried that gravely quality too much smoke and alcohol lent a person. "I've missed your common sense."

"Humph. Go on with you now." Letta dismissively waved her hand. "I know you think I'm too opinionated. 'Specially since I'm hired help. But person got to have they own mind. Go way best for them."

"Why, Letta, are you trying to tell me something?" Susan Pea teased as she climbed the porch steps, her regard for the woman palpable.

"Uh-huh. Lot of these here years done gone by since I last laid eyes on you." Letta, a thin woman with too large feet and a gap between her front teeth wide enough for a round toothpick, had lived her life in south Georgia. Wiping her hands on her apron, she flapped it upward, fanning her face. Her gait uneven, she limped to the porch edge. The Butler housekeeper and nanny for thirty-five of her fifty-six years on earth, her face betrayed nothing.

"Don't reckon I can tell you stuff you ain't already learnt in that big city." Letta sucked on her teeth and continued. "New York City. My, my. Here, summer heat and sweet ice tea say all what gotta be said."

They fell silent and, as if on cue, absently looked across the yard, lost in separate scenarios.

In the distance, a car backfired. Boy-shouts filtered through the trees from a distant, vacant-lot baseball game. A crow cawed and disappeared into the trees.

"How is Eve today?" Susan Pea broke the silence. She respected and loved her sister-in-law despite her hesitation to return home. News of Eve's cancer had gnawed at Susan Pea. Close friends in high school, often making plans to graduate, get jobs together, and live in Atlanta, they had nonetheless grown apart. With Eve in the final stages of her life, Susan Pea drove south.

"She still got cancer. Weak most days but doing okay." Letta blotted sweat from her narrow face before continuing. "She perk up considerable last few days when she know you on the way. Come on in the house." She turned and took several steps toward the front door.

Susan Pea followed. "I'm grateful for your help these last months, especially with Eve. She's needed something besides those austere nurses Major hired. My brother has never been the most thoughtful man. Nor kind."

"Yes, ma'am. He sure a blunt man. Gotta be careful of him." Letta smoothed her apron and sucked her teeth again. "Still and all, I glad you come home before cancer eat up Missus Eve."

"What does doctor say?" Susan Pea's voice quavered with guilt, thinking she had not been the best of friends nor kindest of sisters-in-law.

"He says she only got a few months. Give her what she want. No need worrying." Letta nodded several times, her face wrinkled as she scrutinized the now current Butler matriarch.

Susan Pea swallowed hard and asked, "Where's Janie?"

"Janie? She in class right now. Missus Eve keep a special teacher for her most times. Give extra lessons. That little gal may not be able to see good, but she smart."

"Has Eve talked with her about dying?" Susan Pea spoke directly, did not mince words.

"Uh-huh. They talk. She know her mama gonna cross over soon."

"We can shoot a rocket to the moon but can't stop cancer. What's the world coming to?" Susan Pea took a deep breath and sighed. Conflicted thoughts crawled through her mind.

Letta spoke in an easy drawl. "Janie say that her mamma's room smell like Clorox and wet cotton. Say it sound too quiet. Got no lively vibrations." She continued, her words laced with plantation phrasing of south Georgia. "Them stairs too much for Missus Eve. Janie tells us fix up downstairs library for her mother. Put her in middle this old house, you know. Got Missus Eve's books. Got big windows. She look right out, see trees, azaleas. See them birds. Janie call birds name by the fuss they make."

As if aware of discussion, sparrows, perched along several limbs of a dogwood, bustled among themselves. The women studied the birds silently, glancing after them as the cluster took flight.

Letta continued her report. "Well, Missus Eve get up of a morning, sit on porch while Janie eats her breakfast." She pointed to a porch rocker with a cane-laced bottom. "Janie go out, tell Missus Eve good-bye. Go on to school. Missus stay there till she tired. Won't eat much. Spend time reading them poems, napping. Sometimes she writes." Letta spoke slow. "Seems only yesterday she be up and around real good."

Susan Pea agreed with Letta, added her own musing. "She was the town beauty. Spirited. Way too gentle to be married to Major."

"Uh-huh."

Susan Pea reflected on intervening years. Eve had married out of high school. Had a baby born with limited sight. Later lost her husband in a car accident. Susan Pea moved north. They had drifted apart.

A car whizzed by on the street. The driver waved. An orange, one-eyed tom cat sashayed across the yard, tail flouncing, headed toward the dog kennels. Humidity hung heavy.

Letta held the screen door open. Susan Pea took a deep breath and stepped inside the shabby mansion. Letta followed. The screen banged hollow against the door frame behind them. They stood, side-by-side a moment, seemingly lost in thought.

Susan Pea took several steps into the foyer, mouth open. Despite her resolve to remain composed, her eyes glistened. Memories tumbled against her, some battering, bruising, and others pleasing. The place resonated with feelings. "It's only an old house. Not a shrine." She gasped, realized she had spoken aloud.

CHAPTER FOUR
SUSAN PEA BUTLER

Susan Pea paused in the foyer while Letta turned and slid pocket doors open to the main room. Dust motes whirled in a shaft of light. Several over-stuffed chairs in rose and green florals graced the area. A teal striped sofa and floor lamps with Tiffany-style shades cozied up the room. Eve had chosen warmer decorations when she wed and moved into the mansion years prior.

Susan Pea ran her hand along the piano. "Eve played beautifully. Major always managed to marry women with musical talent."

"Janie play piano, too," Letta said. "She hears a song once, she remembers it. I'm proud of her music. Missus Eve proud, too. Sometimes, of a Sunday, when Missus feeling good, she bring Janie to play at *my* church."

In her bones, Susan Pea knew caretaking her dying sister-in-law would demand a delicate balance—and she'd need all her strength to pull it off. Her stomach knotted at the prospect. She craved a cigarette. Pausing, she took a deep breath. Caring for Janie would be a conundrum. Surviving under Major's thumb, her niece could only expect coldness and isolation caused as much by her limited vision as his attitude. Eve had been the saving grace, holding divergent family members together. But now she was dying, creating a catalyst for change. For everyone.

Letta's drawl broke into Susan Pea's thoughts. "Come late afternoon and evening, Janie home and reads to Missus Eve—sometimes she uses them braille books. Sometimes she tells stuff she remembers."

"Good. I'm glad," Susan Pea said. "Up until all this happened, Eve and I stayed in touch by phone, usually only Christmas. She told me Janie spent time with her during the afternoons. Read to her, played piano. Talked about birds." Susan Pea turned in a slow circle, breathed in the room, touched a picture frame of Major and Eve together.

"Eve came to the city not long after her diagnosis. Must have been three years ago."

"Yessum, I know. She tells me. That trip back years ago, good for her, too. She say it better you not live here. Major ain't able to control you. Least ways, not as strong."

Letta, still talking, ran her hand along furniture and fluffed several throw pillows. "You gonna stay here? I fixed that old room upstairs for you. It aired out and ready."

Susan Pea, lost in memories, startled at Letta's announcement. "Oh. I don't know. Where does my brother stay?"

Letta explained sequence of events with Major's moves. When he fell out with his first wife, he rented an apartment downtown, left the mansion. After remarrying, he moved back into the mansion, his new wife, Janie included. With Eve's diagnosis of cancer, he moved out again. Found himself a mistress.

"Well," Letta said, "He mostly stays in his town place. Or he stay with his woman friend in Albany."

Susan Pea raised an eyebrow. "Doesn't surprise me. Major never tolerated sickness or anything he considered weak. Even as a kid."

"He only comes by this old house ever now and again. You ought not to worry none 'bout seeing him here." Letta continued talking in slow, measured beats. "He checks on them dogs most days. Yessah, loves his hunting. He 'specially like that old dog. Gunner. Ever once in a while, he come in to see Janie and Missus Eve."

Susan Pea sighed, felt tension across her shoulders. She hadn't seen or talked with her brother since he sent her North. The entire episode had been hateful and deeply hurtful.

Letta cocked her hip and watched Susan Pea's face change.

She swallowed hard, took a deep breath. "But, since he's not around, staying here will be convenient. Thank you." She blinked back thoughts, turned, and moved toward the converted library suite. Tapping lightly on the open door, she stuck her head inside.

A breeze ruffled yellowed window sheers. Sunlight dappled across the floor, shifting as tree leaves twirled outside.

Eve sat in an overstuffed, floral chair, feet resting on an ottoman. Her pallid face was deeply creased. Once lush hair lay thin and lifeless, and now, a nondescript color. Bones and blue veins protruded along the back of her hands. The room had a sickly-sweet odor.

Susan Pea blanched at her sister-in-law's appearance. Swallowing, she stepped into the room and mustered a cheerful tone. "My good-ness, Eve, you have on lipstick. And you've painted your fingernails."

Eve laughed, a happy sound that eased tension. "Well, I needed to dress up for your homecoming."

"I think coral becomes you. It screams defiance. I love it." Susan Pea spoke in a complimentary tone and watched Eve's face light up.

"I think it's rather pretty myself." Eve extended her arms, and, beaming, beckoned Susan Pea toward a chair. "You've made it. I'm glad you came before I must leave. Time grows short. At least that's what doc tells me." A faint smile played along her lips, her voice light, almost bubbly. "It's been a long time since we've been together. Not since New York. Come here. Give me a kiss."

Susan Pea stooped, kissed the woman who hardly resembled Eve she once knew so well, and pressed her cheek against her dry forehead. A numbness engulfed her. She caught a faint whiff of *Joy*, Eve's favorite perfume.

"Leaving will have to wait. You and I have got too many things to do." She walked to the window, discreetly wiped a tear, and placed her hand on the sill. "Shall I close this, or do you want air?"

"Leave it open. I like light. And fresh air." Eve motioned to Susan Pea. "Come prop me up higher so I can see those birds better. You know how I need my wild things."

"Your wild things?" Susan Pea exhaled and reared back, beaming. "Why, those wrens are independent spirits if Lord ever made any. They're too quick to belong to anyone." She adjusted pillows and helped Eve straighten her position. "Letta tells me you and Janie have talked about all this mess."

When no response came immediately, Susan Pea sat on the ottoman, leaned forward, took Eve's pale hand, and waited.

Eve watched Susan Pea's face for several seconds before responding. "Many times. She knows I'm going. I had hoped to see Janie graduate and settled at the university." She patted Susan Pea's hand, spoke in a flat monotone, "I could have left peacefully knowing she was there. Doesn't look like I'll have time now."

"Janie's to go to the university?" Susan Pea's mouth flew open. She blinked several times. "I had forgotten. Of course, she's going."

"Yes, I've made arrangements. Letta helped me." Eve smoothed her bedjacket. "They have an ornithology program she can enter."

Susan Pea recognized a familiar tightness in her chest. She stood still. "Well, Letta's here. I'm here now. We can call on Andy. Among us, we'll see to getting Janie settled at the university."

"Andy's in the Army. He's rarely here," Eve said. "Truth be told, he's never forgiven Major for refusing to identify him as his son and heir. Besides that, he's never quite forgiven me for being his stepmother." Eve's face sagged. She lifted her hands, then let them drop to her lap.

Susan Pea sighed, dragged a wooden straight chair from the corner, and sat beside Eve. "What can I do, honey? Tell me what you need most."

"Stay here with us. Keep me company. I need adult, non-pitying conversation. I need someone strong to help these last months." Eve leaned forward, groaned at the movement, and stared straight ahead. "We used to be so close. I've missed you."

Susan Pea smoothed errant wisps of hair off Eve's pasty face and tucked them into place.

Several decades previously, Major had banished Susan Pea north. The scent of scandal trailed behind, even among Letta's people. Susan Pea felt an acute crush of years in-between when Eve married, was widowed, and then, without preamble, married Major. Susan Pea had felt horrified, angry at everyone.

"Know what I want?" Eve's voice, more rasp than words, broke through Susan Pea's reflections.

"No. What do you want?"

"A bowl of peach ice cream. A small one. A coming-home celebration. In your honor. After all, Georgia's known for its peaches."

Susan Pea rose. "Why, I can't think of anything better. As hot as this afternoon is, we need something to cool us off. Besides, aren't us women known as Georgia peaches?" She laughed, held her arms wide, and bounced as she left the room.

Minutes later, Susan Pea returned, placed a bed tray across Eve's lap, and fluffed several of pillows. They settled down, ate slowly, savoring teaspoons of the cold treat.

Eve took several bites, placed her spoon on the tray, and studied

Susan Pea's face. "You must promise to take care of Janie. She's so vulnerable. Curious. She wants to be a woman, but she's still so young. She's naïve."

"Oh, honey, don't worry. I remember a thing or two about being young and entering womanhood. How old is she now?"

"Sixteen, almost seventeen. A little over a year and she turns eighteen. She'll graduate high school, too."

"She and I will get along fine. No worries."

Eve leaned forward, her bowl of ice cream in her lap, and reached for Susan's hand again, held it in a weak claw. "Major is the one to watch. He's got no conscience. He's a vulgar man. Mean."

"You married him," Susan Pea said, her voice accusatory. Taking several slow breaths, she realized she had never quite gotten over the shock of those nuptials.

Eve, her face blank, spoke as if from a distance. "Yes, I did. I made a devil's bargain and now you are my sister-in-law, my only family, because I made those vows. He promised to take care of Janie for life."

Susan Pea sank back and stared at Eve.

Eve continued talking. "Major may not allow Janie to go away when time comes. Help her leave here. Promise me."

Frowning, Susan Pea touched Eve's face. "You know I've always loved you. Even when I knew we wouldn't be able to express it in the way I would have liked. Eventually I made a close friend while I lived there. We both kept our femme identities." She swallowed hard, gathered her emotions, and stared at Eve. "But never mind, I'll take care of Janie—family ties or not. And furthermore, I'm not anyone's patsy. Don't forget, he's my brother. I can handle him."

"You can't run off to New York again. You'll have to stay put for Janie." Eve moved her ice cream dish to the chair arm and spoke quietly. "Promise me you'll care for her. It won't be easy. Nothing with Major is easy."

Susan Pea placed her bowl on a shelf above the roll-top desk and grasped Eve's thin hand, tracing protruding veins and delicate bones. "I promise with all my heart, I'll guard and support Janie for as long as I live."

"I've set up as much as I can, but need you to be sure it happens," Eve said. "Lab director—Pieter DeGroot—is a good man. He'll help mentor her. Janie wants to be on her own, so this will be a good first step. Letta knows about him."

"Ah," Susan Pea moistened her lips before speaking. "Well, it's always nice to have at least one good man on your side." She gave a half-hearted shrug and closed her eyes a moment.

"One other thing—when I go, bury me under our oak. You hear?" Eve pulled herself half upright and croaked.

"I can't bear lying next to him for all eternity. I've had enough in this life. No need to carry it into the hereafter."

CHAPTER FIVE
MAJOR BUTLER

HALFWAY THROUGH MAY and the Bainbridge community was sweating toward June. The Butler household routine varied only on Fridays when Major, on his way to work the pointers—sometimes with his trainer Wes, sometimes not—occasionally thundered into the mansion.

Late one Tuesday afternoon, sky steel colored, Major dropped by unannounced. He parked the Lincoln and clomped toward the house. Letta watched him from a kitchen window, bile rising in her throat. Tendons stood out in her neck, her pulse visible. She gripped the edge of the sink to still her hands.

A big man, he strode purposefully up the walkway, his face a roadmap of sun and stress wrinkles, hands liver spotted. At fifty-something, he still sported a full head of hair with only a few grey streaks at his temples.

Usually, he preferred staying in his town house, bought years before in reaction to the first Mrs. Butler's infidelity. Now, visits into the huge mansion were infrequent, and even less so into his wife's presence.

Letta swallowed several times. Her legs trembled and she continued to grip the sink's edge. Most often, he stayed Saturday and Sunday in Albany with his woman friend.

He stopped near the porch steps, opened his pocketknife, stooped, and cut zinnias from the flower bed, crushed stems into his paw of a hand, and carried them inside. Letta grimaced at his boorish behavior but remained silent.

He ignored Letta and went directly into the library, now Eve's room. Standing in the doorway, he took a cigar out of his pocket, placed it unlit between his teeth.

"I see you're still here among us living."

"Yes, dear husband, I'm still here."

He flopped the flowers on the dresser and boomed toward Letta. "I've brought flowers for my sweet wife. Come in here and fix them in some water for your mistress. They are not dead either."

"Yessah." Tall, straight, she walked in with a blue vase, arranged the zinnias, and placed the bouquet on a side table. She glanced at him, her eyes narrowed.

He did not acknowledge her.

"Thank you, Letta. Please stay. In case I need anything while Major's here." Eve stretched a hand out and struggled to sit upright.

Letta stepped beside the bed, adjusted Eve to a sitting position, and patted her mistress's arm. "Yessum. I stay."

They made eye contact.

"She's got no business here." Major growled and glowered at Letta. "No need in her staying."

"I want her here." Eve's face paled. She glared at Major and wadded the bedsheet edge in her hands. Silence became a visible fog. Even the birds outside laid by.

Letta froze, narrowed her eyes, and shoved her hands into apron pockets. She swallowed several times before she spoke. "Missus Eve tell me stay. She's apt to need me help her, bring something." Still scowling, she crossed the chamber and sat in the corner rocker.

Major removed his unlit cigar, rolled it in his fingers, sighed heavy, and turned back toward Eve. He watched her for several full minutes, sighed again, and replaced the cigar, still unlit, in his mouth.

A grim smile settled on Eve's face. She spoke with more croak than voice. "Yes, still among the living. It's because I *cherish* our marriage vows—until death do us part. I want to stay as long as possible, dear husband." Her smile grew thin, bitter. "We'll keep our love as a tribute to all *happy* marriages. But don't worry, Susan Pea or Letta will call when you're free again."

He groped in his pocket, pulled out a lighter, lit up, and took a drag, his cheeks hollowed. He allowed the cigar to burn a few moments, took another draw, and blew smoke upward. He twisted the fat stogie in his fingers and thumped it with his forefinger. Ash fell on the rug.

"You don't mind if I smoke, do you?"

Abruptly, he stalked to the window and stood silent, his back to her. When he turned, his body sagged and his face crumbled, as if mortar flaking from a brick wall.

"What happened to us, Eve?" Major asked. "We used to talk about books, hopes, dreams. We made love late into night. Somehow, it all changed." He shook his head, fumbled with the cigar.

She stroked the bedsheet, her answer barely audible. "There were too many wounds to overcome. For both of us."

"I suppose you're right. Simply too much." He closed his eyes, took several deep breaths, and opened them again.

Ghosts of Major's first wife, her abrupt unexplained departure floated quietly nearby. Denial of Andy's parentage. Loss of family fortune. War, his return.

Eve's voice quivered. "Our hurt runs too deep." She paused, blinked, and then glared at him again.

Major fingered the cigar, stood rigid. He walked away from the window toward the bed and its sunken figure.

He had been ruthless when he came home from the war. Had run over everyone and everything. Re-establishing a Butler prominence was all that mattered. Nothing was sacrosanct. He had married Eve as a part of that. Major drew on the cigar again.

She had agreed to grace whatever lifestyle he chose, be it state office as his hostess or town patriarch championing the handicapped. Finally, she had demanded he educate Janie, make sure she had lifetime status, and income. A fair exchange.

At one time, she had made him a better man. He coughed and fumbled with his stogie. "Love fades. Grows silent. Regret sets in," he said, his voice husky, jaw muscles twitching, nostrils flared. "I miss us and our short time loving each other. I miss what will never be again."

Outside a Greek chorus of birdsong rose. A discrete fragrance of lavender scented the air. Somewhere deep in the house, a loose screen banged against a window.

Eve stirred and spoke softly. "Really, Major? Don't go sentimental now. Not after all these years. Not after Andy. Not after Janie. True, our first years together left us breathless. But then, one year and another and another stacked up until they became a hurtful series."

He swallowed twice, Adam's apple bobbing, stood beside her bed. Carefully, he leaned over, adjusted the sheet covering her diminished body, and smoothed the lace trim.

"I regret denying Andy. I regret our lost time. I regret my *special* fondness for Janie." He walked back to the window, stood again in silhouette.

The rocking chair whispering, Letta closed her eyes. Times had been more peaceful in the mansion before the household declined into angst.

Major's callous disregard for others was palatable. These final days between him as patriarch and Eve as his wife left everyone exhausted.

Letta opened her eyes, laced her fingers together. Sadness welled up. Revenge continued to grow in her soul.

Eve stirred. Her voice had a monotone quality. "Fondness can be confusing. Especially for a young woman. She only needs your money and this house, your status. Nothing more."

"You have been a woman to match me. You have kept your bargain. I wish I could have worked it out better."

"Yes, if only." Her eyes stung, grew moist. "I think Letta's bottle tree attracted more haints than it chased."

Letta humphed and crossed her arms, hands clasped around her elbows to hide her trembling. She rocked. "Bottle trees from the Old Ones. They ain't from no Baptists."

Major frowned at her, grunted. He stared off into space, thoughts drifting. "I've always been unlucky with women in my life. I was so young when Mother died. Susan Pea, too. We never learned how to love." He motioned with his hands as if to conjure words needed. "I almost had it with you, but somehow it disappeared. I'm unlucky that way."

"Luck has nothing to do with it," Eve said. "We've both lived the life we chose—and made our bargains with the devil. You need to set a date with him. He's waiting, you know. Boatman's ready to row you across." She sank back into the bed and closed her eyes. "We *both* need to set our departure dates."

Letta, from her corner, silently bowed her head before she rose from her rocker and silently left.

Finally, as if nothing further need be said or done, Major took several steps to Eve's bedside, removed his cigar, kissed her on the cheek with a tenderness he had not shown since their first years together.

"I loved you. Once." He walked out, his tread reverberating heavy on wooden floors.

Eve looked out the window. Sparrows continued their business. A mockingbird called, its quick notes in imitation of another winged cousin. The clock ticked too loudly, laboring through minutes toward an unknown final hour.

CHAPTER SIX
WOMENFOLK

JANIE TAPPED INTO THE KITCHEN, plunked down, and laid her walking stick near her feet. She rested her elbows on the kitchen table. Susan Pea watched as sunlight, shining through the window, glinted off Janie's tangled curls, burnishing her red hair with gold. She grinned, dimples curving into her cheeks. Freckles hiked across her nose.

"I like having you home, Aunt Pea."

"Well, it's sort of good to be back after so many years." Susan Pea glanced up from her pie making. She shifted flour and placed a round of dough on the pastry sheet, allowing it to rest while she selected peaches.

"Mother used to read me parts of your letters. Now you can tell me in person." Janie wiggled with anticipation. "You have the best stories about big city life."

"Really?" Susan Pea murmured and allowed her mind to roll back the years.

She had lived in the Barbizon Hotel her first eighteen months. At a Hungarian restaurant nearby, she sat at the bar and tried a martini. Her first. Later, she ate dinner, and watched others until the place began to empty. She paid her bill and walked to a used bookstore, open despite the late hour. This city never slept, didn't even doze. Sometimes, too lonely to stay in her room, she wandered Greenwich streets, listened to African jazz *artistes* playing music from their souls—entering and leaving by the backdoor. Music often laced with drugs. The city opened a window on foods, exotic smells, and other nationalities. Not exactly coloreds, but not white either. A human melting pot. And below it all, she realized the gritty underbelly of Southern segregation skulked. Still, this city suited her. No longer anchored to a defeated region still singing "Dixie," wrapping itself in bed sheets and Confederate flags. She had found herself.

Barely into her arrival at the Butler mansion, Susan Pea struggled to balance changes. Eve's dying. Letta's silent judgement. Janie's emerging young adult adolescence. Major's looming presence. Susan Pea's confidence waned and waxed as she struggled with expectations—hers and those of others. Home had its benefits but also levied heavy obligations.

"Tell me," Janie repeated, her voice sharp with questions.

Susan Pea paused at Janie's second request, glanced briefly at Letta and took a deep breath.

"It's like any other big city. Atlanta or Memphis—just bigger and more complex. It's segregated, but not so rabid as here." Susan Pea paused. "It's more crowded with people from various ethnic groups. You hear all kinds of accents. See some kooky-dressing folks. My neighbor upstairs was from the Midwest. She always dressed in layers, even in summer. Every layer was different. Either a check, a stripe, or some bright, knock-off orange."

Janie cackled at the image. "Sounds mixed up."

"Oh, she was. She talked nasal-flat and smoked cigarettes. I asked her about that once, and she said she could never smoke in her little Nebraska town. She was making up for lost time."

Susan Pea continued peeling peaches. "Traffic makes you dizzy. Taxi drivers constantly honking. Diesel exhaust fumes overpowering." She paused with her peeling. "Now that I think about it, it's similar to New Orleans, but without humidity and river odors."

"What do you mean?"

"Well, people mix in New Orleans, but it's still segregated, not rigid, sort of loosely segregated. New Orleans has more shrimp and okra with their cooking. New York uses more European cooking styles."

Janie scooted her chair closer. "This is so cool. Tell more."

Susan Pea cocked an eyebrow and sliced peaches, juice dripping sticky between her fingers. "They don't put much stock in our ways."

"Like what?"

"Oh, wearing gloves to church on Sunday. Or to a funeral. No white shoes after Memorial Day. Always say nice things about people, especially those deceased. Church celebration of Lord's Acre Day."

"Humph," Letta said. "Pay you to remember them things. South got a dignity ain't like no other place." Lips still pursed, Letta cutting shortening into flour, added cold water sprinkles, mixed, and shaped dough into a pie plate. She crimped edges and cut strips for a lattice top. "South also got stuff she hides."

Susan Pea rolled her eyes at Letta in agreement.

Letta half smiled.

Janie, unable to see any eye banter between them, said, "Keep telling."

Letta sucked her teeth and worked the dough.

"Well, Northerners are a tad stand-offish, cool. They talk faster, more clipped. They mostly say what they want straight out, not sliding around edges way folks do here." She worked silently for a few moments. Janie's face changed from puzzled to a grinning acknowledgement.

Baking usually took the entire morning and part of early afternoon, concluding with a cinnamon-scented kitchen and pie for dinner. Sometimes Letta made several loaves of yeast bread when through with pie baking. Today, she listened silently, and with so many peaches, continued her pie making.

"Everyone fears communism and Russians in both places," Susan Pea said. "Southerners are more fanatical about those things than New Yorkers." Her voice was even and thoughtful. "Seems kind of crazy since Korea ended years ago. About '53, I think." She paused and added in a quiet voice, "President Truman integrated the Army a year after Korea ended. Although, I don't think it's working out that way."

Letta, finished with her dough and pie making, began clearing counters, wiping table. She perked up at the mention of an integrated Army. "It ain't happened like it supposed to. My John in Army. It tough on him. I had to tell him about his pappy while he in that other country."

Susan Pea stopped peeling. "Your husband's dead? I didn't hear. What happened?"

Letta slid several mixing bowls and baking accouterments into the sink of soapy water. She stared at Susan Pea a long moment, lips set in a hard line, and cleared her throat. Her hands in dishwater, she spoke in a voice full of lead and grief. "An accident. *Them men at mill tolt me*. A cable come loose. Cut him half in two."

"Oh, good Lord, that's horrible. I didn't know."

Susan Pea stopped her peeling, leaned slightly forward toward Letta. "I'm sure you miss him. Children must miss him, too." She picked up another peach and peeled it.

"Army not let John come home for his own pappy's home-going." Letta, eyes glistening, continued washing dishes.

Susan Pea fell silent, her mouth open. She shivered. "I *am* sorry."

Letta pursed her lips, her jaw muscles protruding. She did not reply.

"If John couldn't come home," Susan Pea said, "that means he must have been in Vietnam. Maybe around the time of Tết?"

"Yes, he done been there most two years. Volunteered." Letta thrust her chin forward. "He writes me ever week. Not many sons do that for they momma. He's a good man."

"Andy was in Korea," Janie interrupted, eager to add to the conversation. "He told me it was cold and muddy and he's glad to be out of that country."

"Major's son? Your stepbrother? Eve didn't tell me," Susan Pea said.

"He came here about six months ago, in January. He went back and is at a medical base. In Germany, I think."

Silently, Susan Pea reflected. "Korea was bad. Vietnam has shaped up worse. Politicians say that if Vietnam falls to communism, all of Asia goes. Of course, it's hard to trust what they're talking about."

She added spices into one bowl of peaches, stirred, dumped it into a pie shell, and passed the filled concoction over to Letta.

"No matter where you are, if you're honest with yourself, you go back to your home roots. They shape you." Susan Pea wiped her hands on a dish towel.

"That's true," Letta said. "Roots shape you." She stopped washing, took a clean pie plate, and sat it on the counter. She stood still, appeared to reflect on their conversation. "John gonna come back here. I tell him no. Tell him I manage without him. He says he come anyway. He man of family now."

Susan Pea refilled a cup of coffee. Janie drank her juice. Letta continued her dishwashing. Each retreated inside their own musings.

Susan Pea added spices to the next bowl of sliced peaches, laced them with butter, and filled three additional pie crusts.

Letta dried her hands and wove pie lattice-tops. As she finished, she popped each into the oven. Some she sat aside to bake later.

Susan Pea explained while cleaning flour and dough scraps off the table, "They don't have trees like our southern live oaks that drip moss and spread out with enough shade for a whole family. Think about that oak out front. It's two hundred years old. I'll bet it could tell some tales." She paused and reflected on the ancient giant. "Honestly, I missed trees and vine-ripe tomatoes most. Those hothouse things they sell up there have less taste than cardboard. I even missed boiled peanuts."

"Boiled goobers!" Letta thumped her leg. "Them salty things smacking good!" The three fell to laughing.

Wiping her eyes and catching her breath, Janie said, "But talk about snow. What's it like?"

"Oh, honey, beautiful sometimes with tree bare branches, reaching up with those skeletal fingers." She raised her arms and spread her fingers, automatically mimicking the trees although Janie could only see a rough shadow of the gesture.

Letta snorted and shook her head.

"Storms come roaring through," Susan Pea said in a drawl, "and it seems the whole area gets gray. On sunny days, especially frozen ones, sun feels really warm. I think it's psychological. Doesn't matter, it still seems warmer with sun. Those days, wind blows, and diamond snow makes the air magical."

"What's diamond snow?" asked Janie.

"That's a fine snow the wind picks up and blows into the air. You would probably feel it on your skin like tiny pin pricks. Others see it like a thousand diamonds sparkling in sunlight. Absolutely enchanting."

"Hum. Like pin pricks." Janie cocked her head and then asked, "Did you miss being here in Georgia?"

"I missed your mother. Missed getting to watch you grow up and getting to know you better. And Letta. Missed talking and baking with y'all. I even missed Andy, that handsome rascal. He breaks hearts with those dark eyes. Mesmerizes all the girls. Even when he was in school."

Letta busied herself with pouring sweet tea. Condensation glistened on the glasses. "Lots good things in South," she said. "Neighbors. Folks you know all your life. Working together. Going fishing. Church dinners on the ground. All day gospel singing." She placed a glass near Janie's hand and said, "Gatherings for church singing."

The girl picked up the glass of tea and ran her fingers along the sides, through wet droplets, and took a sip.

"We've got fireflies too," Letta said, her voice sounding far away.

Susan Pea reflected on those tiny blinking insects of summer. Although short lived, she thought them magical. She paused and gazed out the window, watched a bee float toward a flower.

Susan Pea turned toward Letta. "It's true, the South holds treasures and dangers." She chuckled and placed her hands on her hips. "Where else could it be fun to bake pies together except in the South? Yep. I missed you both. And sweet tea."

Letta wiped her hands on a dish towel. "Yes, ma'am, and I hear tell folks in the North don't drink sweet tea."

Janie took a swallow. "Oh, y'all, you're teasing again." She replaced her glass on the table.

"No, she's not teasing." Susan Pea shook her head. "Here in the South, sweet tea is tradition, culture in a glass. It's almost a religious duty to drink the syrupy stuff."

Letta cackled. "That's right, 'specially in this here heat."

Susan Pea play-shoved Janie's arm, creating a round of giggles.

Letta danced in sunlight streaming through the window and hummed.

Janie acknowledged collective sounds, teasing, and then took another long swallow of tea.

"I can't imagine a life without sweet tea. What else to tell about the big city?" Janie smoothed her hands along the tabletop, dabbled her fingers in a condensation puddle.

"Well, it's so old, history leaches out of every building and along all the streets."

"Older than the South?" Janie asked.

To Susan Pea, the city's past seemed one long stream of people, soldiers, ships, planes, the Lincoln Highway, railroads. One big area divided into sections called boroughs, each distinct. The Irish came to escape the potato famine. Starving Italians flocked to the city escaping World War I. Puerto Ricans fled the Spanish-American War. Southern Blacks ran from Jim Crow harshness.

"Janie, I wish you could experience different things about city living. Foods, rich smells, people, and noise cacophony."

They mulled over their conversation separately. Finally, Janie sighed and said, "I wish I could try it all, but only if I can wash it down with sweet tea."

Letta got to hooting again.

Susan Pea crowed and leaned back in her chair. "If you ask for tea, they'll bring you a cup of hot tea."

Janie scrunched up her face. "You'd think they'd know better."

Susan Pea fell to laughing until she had to wipe her eyes. Letta did a dance shuffle beside the kitchen sink. Janie, caught up in glee, almost tipped her chair over backwards laughing.

Janie righted her chair and cocked her head. "Is it true Aunt Pea you got your nickname because you got lost one time. When Mother and Letta found you, you were in the garden eating green peas."

Susan Pea gave a throaty chortle. "Yes, it was something like that."

"Her eating those raw things was quite a sight," Letta said. "Folks been calling her Susan Pea ever since."

Once again, they got to laughing.

Janie wiped her eyes and asked, "Where did you live?"

"Well, when I first got there, I lived at a hotel called Barbizon."

"A real hotel?"

"Yes. But for single women only that wanted to live and work in the city. Rooms were tiny, but we had a restaurant and gym. I made some good friend there." Susan Pea sat still a moment, remembering. "Major paid for it in the beginning."

"Then why did you leave?" Janie asked.

"I wanted to be independent of Major. I earned my own money, so I moved."

"Do you think I'll ever get to live in a hotel? Travel?" Janie asked.

Susan Pea cocked her head sideways. "Maybe."

Cinnamon and nutmeg fragrances filled the room, knitted the women together. They continued to talk while pies baked.

Letta finished washing the mixing bowls, drying them, and wiping down the counters. She dried her hands and stuffed on kitchen mitts, opened the oven, and checked the pies. Nicely brown and bubbling, she pulled them out and carefully placed them on trivets. She'd take one home to her children, leaving several for the Butlers' dessert.

Letta turned back to the sink, drained dishwater, sighed, and sat in a kitchen chair. She flipped her shoes off, fanned herself with her apron. "What y'all want for supper?"

CHAPTER SEVEN
EVE BUTLER

With Susan Pea's return, the old mansion creaked with additional sounds. And with shared stories and conversations, laughter reverberated within the walls. Eve relished the additional commotion.

One Wednesday morning, Eve heard a shower running somewhere in the house. Perhaps the upstairs bathroom that Susan Pea and Janie shared. The water stopped and there were noises of water taps on and off, a toilet flush, and door opening. Footsteps. Another door slammed. Finally, footsteps down the hall, Susan Pea's lighter step on the staircase. No tapping cane. Janie must still be asleep.

Eve twisted, listening.

Morning sounds had catapulted her back to the early days when she and Major shared a bed, before deceit, anger, and cancer had eaten into her being.

Those days, she had loved him, loved his sheer animal magnetism. They had taken pleasure in each other's body. Relished time spent talking about classical literature, Greek mythology, political affairs, and what she hoped for Janie. Those weeks spun into years, morphing slowly into something less satisfying.

It had been years earlier, on a fifth anniversary trip to Savannah when she'd lain listening to a similar shower. The hotel, rather pleasant, had been situated near one of famous town squares. She recalled listening to the shower cut off. The bathroom door opened, clouds of moisture floated out, and a silhouette stood framed against the light. Major. He dried himself, wrapped a towel around his thickening waist, and walked barefooted into their shared bedroom, his manhood pushing against the towel.

Holding her, he slid his thumb along her arm. He leaned into her, bent her head back, searched for her mouth. He grasped a small breast in one hand, held her, and smothered her slenderness with his bulk, becoming increasingly rough with his love making, insistent they produce a son. She found herself mired in regret, the weight of her 'I do' vow pressing onto her chest until she gasped for breath.

He had been blunt with his expectations. "Hear me good, you and your blind whelp are in my house living with the advantages of my name for one reason—you are to deliver me a son. I'll not allow the Butler name to sink into oblivion. You have one obligation. Keep the Butler name alive."

Startled, she had said, "You have a fine son you have chosen to alienate and abuse. You don't need another soul to mutilate."

"There is no certainty he's my seed. That's why that faithless whore's gone and you're here." He stalked across the room and lit a cigarette. Stood long minutes staring out a window at the gardens below.

"Trust your own eyes. Andy's got your jaw. Your coloring. Anyone that *looks* at him can see you. Thank the stars he doesn't have your mean heart."

Susan Pea stuck her head in the doorway, jerked Eve back to the present moment. "Good morning, Eve. Did you sleep well?"

Eve watched Susan Pea walk into the room. "I slept off and on. Now I'm worried I have spun a deeper agony for y'all."

"What do you mean?"

"I've asked you to come home, help me die." Eve took a deep breath, puffed her cheeks, then blew air out, struggled for the right words. She shook her head. Lingering doubts over Major's trustworthiness to allow Janie a life of her own continued to plague her. A second plan seemed necessary. Just in case.

"I hope I have done well for Janie." She blinked, allowed her mind to continue to spin, as she held her hand out to Susan Pea. "For now, let's go to breakfast."

Susan Pea helped her sister-in-law out of bed and toward the kitchen.

While cancer was no blessing, it had rewards. Eve's womb remained empty.

CHAPTER EIGHT
SUSAN PEA BUTLER

YEARS EARLIER, when Eve was first diagnosed, Susan Pea had resisted returning home. Reluctance to face her past, her brother. She had been reduced her to offering Eve solace over the phone, finally invited her to the city. Eve made one trip north before her disease got worse. Susan Pea's guilt at withholding her in-person presence mounted until, finally, circumstances snatched that decision from her. Eve was dying. She needed Susan Pea to help with Janie. Susan Pea had returned south.

Once back home, despite all her newfound independence, Susan Pea realized she was slipping into her old rebellious, spoiled role. The stigma of being called difficult, whispered about, and ostracized for her "different" nature lingered. Now a few days after Mother's Day, she and Janie sat in the porch rockers side-by-side, watching the sun go down. Letta brought iced tea.

Janie turned toward Susan Pea. "Is it hard to be here? Especially since I've heard others say you and Major don't get along."

"My brother and I never got along. Even as children. He's a selfish man. Unforgiving. Hard."

"He says really derogatory things about New York and how you live there. Why is he so upset?"

"Probably because the city gives me too much freedom from here. He resents that. Doesn't understand nor even wants to understand."

"He said that he sent you there."

"True." Susan Pea, silent, rocked a few moments, and looked again at Janie. "But bless his nasty little heart, I've got to hand it to him, he's pulled us out of bankruptcy and re-established our community standing." Susan Pea's voice softened. She stared at the old oak, listened to town sounds drifting toward her. Sighing, still looking across the yard, she spoke in a neutral voice, "New York is an exciting place and there are certain freedoms I miss about that life."

She thought about her all-female hotel. Sweet girls fresh from some Kansas farm. Self-sufficient gals from New Jersey. A scattering of southern strays. They all rented rooms.

Her love of Southern literature and food never diminished while she choked on the stench of segregation, the hypocrisy of McCarthyism politics.

She knew denizens of cheap walk-up flats, tourists interested in the Empire State Building, and shopgirls earning a paycheck called independence.

Letta padded toward them, brought iced tea to cool the evening. Her face, deeply lined, reflected fatigue. She sat in the swing, half listening to the conversation. Mutt napped on the porch near the top step. A plumber's van drove by.

"Andy says that you go with women," Janie said.

Letta cut her eyes sharply at Susan Pea, grunted, and kicked the swing into motion. She sucked her teeth. "Ain't wanna hear no more this talk. Men muddle stuff up."

Susan Pea paused in her rocking. "Your brother Andy? When did he have time to tell you such things?"

"Remember, I told you he was home on leave. He said there's a lot of things he thought I ought to understand about family. Now that I'm older." She blinked and cocked her head to the side.

"He probably had a lot to say. I'm sure he's listened to gossip around this old town and to what Major has to say."

"Yeah, some of that." Janie paused, then spoke in a clear voice, "He said you were one of those 'hard-to-handle women, a difficult one. Not like most women'."

Susan Pea took a deep breath. "Go on. What else did he say."

"He said you were not the kind to marry a man."

They fell silent a few moments.

"You've got a point," Susan Pea finally said. "Relationships between women are different than those between men and women. Both are important. Difficult in their separate ways."

Janie rocked forward, head tilted. "Is it better being with a woman than a man?"

"What? Who told you anything about anything?"

"Andy called you 'a spinster aunt.' Said you *liked* women instead of men. He called you a lesbian."

Susan Pea choked, gulped a swallow of tea to get her voice back. "He doesn't know me or understand. Besides, what do you know about lesbians? Or sex?"

Janie sat up straight. "I know stuff. I can't see well, but I know things about sex." She repeated in a louder voice, "I know a lot of things."

"Is that so?" Susan Pea lit a cigarette and leaned back. Her chair grumbled made the porch boards creak. "Tell me, Miss Know-it-all."

"Oh, tongue down your throat kisses. Boys complaining about blue balls. Wanting to touch me in private places and see how I react."

"Wherever did you learn such things?"

"Around school. Girlfriends tell me stuff. Sometimes boys say things. Mostly, they are curious about me since I can only see shadows.

It's like they don't think I can hear and smell. Or feel either. Boys are dumb. Especially those at school."

"Really?"

"Being blind is a kind of blessing in disguise."

"How you figure?" Susan Pea's voice took on a tender tone.

"I do all that other stuff better than them. I can hold hands with a guy, slide my hand up his wrist and tell if he's fat or not. Mostly, I try to see how he treats me. I can smell pretty good, too. You know if some guy's sweaty. Or maybe doesn't wash every night."

"Good grief, girl. You're a savvy little thing, downright precocious. Are you dating?"

"Yes. No. Not sure you'd call it dating," Janie said. "I hang out with my friends at dances. I wish I could see how I compare, how others see me."

"What do you mean?"

"Well, since I started my period, started wearing a bra, I keep changing. I don't even really know myself anymore."

"Who helped you with those things?"

"Mother helped me with my period. Took me to buy a bra. She said girls should know how to take care of their personal needs. That was before she got so sick. Since then, she doesn't talk about boys and stuff. Sometimes I don't know what to think." Janie remained silent before, holding her hands out as if weighing her next words. "Am I more or less like everyone else my age?"

Puckering her face, Letta kicked the swing into motion and sipped her tea.

Susan Pea took a quick look at Letta, turned back to Janie. No one spoke for several minutes. Only the swing creak and the rockers swish filled the void.

Finally, Susan Pea spoke . "What do you want to know?"

"Well, start with how I look next to the other girls."

Susan Pea glanced at Letta again, turned back to Janie. "You are a beautiful young woman. You have lovely curves and magnificent red curls. When you smile you have dimples. Your hands are graceful with long fingers, just right for playing piano."

Janie twirled a hank of hair around her finger.

"Your mother should be talking with you," Susan Pea said.

"I know, but she doesn't. She's too sick and I don't want to bother her."

"I think she'd rather handle your questions. After all, I'm only your aunt."

"That's why I can ask you." Janie grinned. "You've done lots of interesting stuff. And as my aunt you don't have much control. Besides Letta won't tell me and Mother's too sick now."

At her name, Letta spoke gruffly. "Ain't right for me to be telling bout that stuff to no white girl." She sucked at her teeth for emphasis.

Susan Pea shrugged as if Janie could see the movement

"You mind getting us some lemon for the tea?" Susan Pea gestured toward Letta. "Always need to balance sweet and sour."

Letta frowned, heaved herself up, and padded inside. She returned with a small bowl of sliced lemon. Susan Pea squeezed a few drops into her glass, plopped the slice in.

She stood and braced her hip against the porch railing. "You'd never know it by looking at me now, that I had every male heart on a string back then. Had a perfect hourglass shape. Now I'm afraid it's somewhat Rubenesque."

"What's that?" Janie said.

"In a word, fat with interesting curves." Susan Pea chuckled to herself. The school times had been exciting. Still, her angst with exploring her sexuality, living under the Butler name and its attending gossip, had taken a toll.

"You still got that shape, Missus Susan," Letta chuckled and slapped her knee, "but these days, it's covered up. Yes, ma'am, covered up."

Susan Pea snorted. "For your information, I've turned it to an advantage. Men tend to move out of a big woman's way."

Janie fell into a fit of guffaws. She and Susan Pea continued until they gasped for breath. Letta cut loose and hooted along with them. Mutt raised his head, thumped his tail, and added a woof. Then, in his canine wisdom, he put his head on his paws and fell into a doggie doze.

Wiping her eyes, Letta kept chuckling as she rose and strode inside. "I got work to get to."

Janie and Susan Pea continued talking, lost in mutual enthusiasm. They did not appear to notice Letta's leaving.

"I want to play some sport," Janie said.

"Honey, you do other things with your talents. You play the piano. By ear. You hear a tune, and you can play it without fault. You identify birds by their call. You read braille. Do you know anyone else can do those things?"

"Well, no." Janie twirled a hank of hair around her finger. "Know what's the absolute best?"

"What?"

"Wes." Janie cocked her head and twirled a finger around a strand of hair. "You know, going out with him to work the dogs. He takes me whenever he works them in the back pasture."

Susan Pea leaned forward and blinked. "Wes? Does your mother know?"

"Mother said it was okay so long as he only took me to the kennel yard and the training area. I don't tell her whenever we go to a real field location."

"How do you know what's happening?"

"Well, sometimes he tells me. He'll set me up on the edge of a field before he lets the boys out. I can hear them snuffing and rustling around. When we take Mutt, Wes puts a leash on him and tells me to hold him. Mutt gets too excited, wants to bark." Janie shifted in the chair, leaned forward slightly, and spoke rapidly. "I hear it get still when the dogs point. Then there's a great whirring explosion, a wild sound. Sounds like wind snapping a flag or cotton cloth ripping."

"Doesn't noise bother you when he shoots?"

"Yes, sometimes." Janie continued, her voice rising in excitement. "In the summer, he shoots blanks to train the dogs. He only kills when I'm not along. He does it to teach Otto to retrieve."

Susan Pea watched Janie's face become more animated, heard excitement in her voice.

"I know he shoots live rounds when I'm not there. I think he loves the woods and those creatures, too. Still he kills them."

"Major hired him to train his bird dogs," Susan Pea said. "Wes sees matching skills as a challenge between him and the wild things. It's part of that ebb and flow of woods, of life. He respects those pointers, their drive to follow what they were bred to do. I think he tries to balance those things."

"Major sees hunting differently." Janie's voice grew faint.

Susan Pea watched her niece's face change, grow thoughtful, her brow knitted.

"He *wants* to kill. Says it's a way to keep score. He talks about birds flying, how they drop. He hands me dead birds when he comes back from hunting. Their heads flop. They're so still. The doves feel small. The quail are chunky, bigger. I cry when I hold them." Janie's voice caught and she swallowed hard.

"I think that's why Major hands you those birds. To upset you."

"He's cruel." Janie sat silent a moment, her index finger moving in circles on the glass as if reflecting her thoughts. "Major makes fun of me. He says I'll not cry when I eat them."

Janie rocked slowly, head bowed, face scrunched. "He used to hand them to Mother. Tell her to cook them. She hated that." Janie shook her head. "Letta would clean and cook them after Major left."

Susan Pea shifted, rattled ice cubes in her glass. "Seems ironic that doves are peace symbols. He killed those, too.".

She stood and stepped toward Janie, kissed the top of her head. "I grew up here, knew Wes and many of the Lee Town people at one time." She fell silent mulling over the complexity of her brother, Wes, and southern penchant for violence.

CHAPTER NINE
JOHN DAVIS

THREE YEARS prior to Susan Pea's return, Letta and her son John had sat at their kitchen table drinking coffee. They talked. At nineteen, he wanted more than Bainbridge had to offer. A young man, eager to explore, torn between family and a desire for his own adventure.

Letta's husband snored, his drunken breath filling their bedroom. She rose from the table and closed their bedroom door, sat again. Those days, her hopes had died in direct proportion to his drinking. He'd never taken up with other women, told them he was not free, had a family he needed to care for. She loved that in him despite an occasional slip. His easygoing nature eventually died under the weight of prejudice and harsh work. Her heart had slowly fractured.

"Son, me and your pappy love you. But there ain't a future here. Look at him now—he drinking." She gestured toward the closed door. "Always coming home bone tired. Can't even raise his manhood no more. I love him. He's a good man. Been a good father." She wiped her nose. "Too late for me and him. We living with false freedom. Got no other place to go. But you different. You young and got a life ahead. You need to *leave* here. Find a future in some other town."

His fisted hands on the table, John shook his head. "I can't leave with Pappy drinking. He don't earn enough from that stingy Butler mill to make ends meet even with you working. Y'all barely scraping along. Besides, Merry and Elijah still need raising."

"Pappy, me, and young'uns get by okay. Especially since they finish up schooling soon." Her voice took on a frayed quality. "We got folks, you Aunt Mae and Uncle Elbert—up in Cleveland. I sending Elijah and Merry up there soon I can. Me and you pappy make it alone." She reached across the table and patted John's fist. "You a man. *A Black man*."

Letta stood, tied her apron, smoothed it, and sat down again. She stared off toward the closed bedroom door, thoughts adrift. "Leave here before one of them honkeys decide on mischief. You hear me—*leave* here." Her voice rose an octave. She thumped the table with her forefinger. "White man don't rule you. You your own man."

"I think on it, Momma." He stood and straightened, tall and angular, handsome. "I hear about those men out in California. Black Panthers. They stand up for *all* they people. They work for their schools, kids. Taking back control over they community." John coughed deep from his chest, frustration stinging behind his eyes. He swallowed, blinked back rising moisture, and partly shoved his chair under the table, scraping it on the linoleum.

Letta spread her hands open on the table and responded slowly, "Maybe they got right idea. Maybe not. All that strutting round makes white folks jumpy. Still and all, I ain't wanting you and my babies to stay under thumb of folks still mad they lost the Civil War. Parading around in bed sheets, waving Confederate flags. Torching our churches. Don't want y'all growing up with them sorry choices." She leaned over, and with her hand, swept crumbs off the table.

John bowed his head a moment, slid the chair further under the table. "I know, Momma. I just don't know what to do."

"*You* got choices. You man growed now. President Truman fixed Army so's you can join up. Now they taking our kind too. *Go join up*." Letta said, thumped the table again for emphasis, her voice rising. "Leave this sinkhole. See what you find if you look away from South."

She sighed and spoke more softly, "Me, Pappy, Eljah, and my Merry —we all manage for a while longer. You oldest. Go first. I send young'uns later after you get settled." She thrust her jaw forward and watched John. Her face reflected long days of worry.

"Missus Eve and Janie onliest ones I think on." She sat still a moment. "Missus gonna die soon. She done got Janie set up. Lordy knows Susan Pea take care of her own self. Me and your pappy only need make it a little while longer. Then we leave, too."

John gazed off, saw the present laid out before him. "Them ridge runners be looking for me to work at that mill. Take heavy work, dangerous stuff."

"There's another truth," she said. "Life don't give up easy. I scared, son, but I figure out how to handle this. Figure what needs to be done to get you safe gone. I conjure, think on this heavy work. I listen for what bottle tree warns about."

"Major ain't gonna let none o' us leave here. He needs our sweat and labor. Thinks we owe him something."

"Ain't gonna ask him." Her voice rose in anger, needle sharp. "You leave now, before too many them stump jumpers gets in habit using your bent back. They used your pappy, broke him. Looking to work you like a mule too. Keep you under thumb."

John fumbled a moment with his hands on the chair back and focused on his Momma's face. "I ain't wanting to leave y'all here."

"You be a warrior like our Mandinka people. Ancient griots tell of them fighters." Letta thrust her jaw forward. "Reckon you needs join up with Army soldiers, be our warrior. Make yourself a new way out of what our Old Ones teach." She humphed, realized a cold panic slicing through her breathing. She closed her eyes, struggled for control, and shoved fear down into soles of her feet. "Ain't no shame in doing best for you own self first. Later you help those come behind." Her voice held a weariness reflecting pain, maybe hope.

Standing slowly, she turned away from John, wiped sweat off her face with her apron. "Folks been packing up, sneaking off, leaving for North since that big war ended. They go next county over. Go in night-time. Catch a ride if they can. Walked if need be. Some tried to go north but didn't make it. They body left here hanging, but spirits set free." She sagged, felt bone weary. "Hard to stop water running downhill once it starts."

"That hell-forsaken mill," John said. "All it do is keep boss man rich. Pay my pappy enough to guzzle his *life* away. Not enough for him to do better for us, for you."

She whirled toward John and spoke in a sharp, rapid hiss. "He doing best he knows how. He make way better for y'all. He trying." Glaring at her son, she wiped her hands on the apron, her eyes reflecting agony and sweat of three hundred years. "Do what I tell you. *Use* that Army as your way out." She banged an iron skillet on the stove, lit a burner and set a pot of black-eyed peas to boiling. Leaning across the table, she pulled the light chain. The bulb glared harsh, swaying slightly from the motion of Letta's pull. "School end, I send Merry to her auntie up in Cleveland. She can finish school up north. End of summer, I send Eljah next. Me and your pappy stay. We cover for y'all. Major think I'm bound to him. But I got my ways."

John swallowed hard, Adam's apple jumping. He turned away from his momma, walked outside, and sat on the top porch step. Sizzle of frying potatoes and smells of bacon lard floated out the screen door.

The last of day-down dissolved as night draped heavy across John's shoulders. Frogs called for mates, a monotone without passion. Mosquitos began swarming. Small creatures rustled in leaves. Off in the distance, an owl hooted.

JOHN HAD HOPPED A GREYHOUND NORTH, joined the Army, asked for infantry duty. Vietnam. He raged when sonsobitches assigned him to a supply unit as a cook. He fixed breakfast and dinner, drove a field mess truck during dry season, worked rear kitchen during monsoons.

In December 1969, a telegram from Letta: *Pappy dead.*

Army denied John leave to travel home. Fears of his going AWOL undergirding their decision.

At night, alone behind his bunker, he sobbed. Angst backfilled the hole left by grief. Determination and self-discipline had taken deeper roots.

Vietcong insurgency changed, morphing into a larger struggle, required more men—from both sides. John extended and volunteered for *combat*, transferred to *infantry*. He slogged through rice paddies, swatted mosquitos, and realized a growing self-confidence tainted with bowel-gripping fear. Heard the whup-whup-whup of helicopters. Sweated. Got bored. Felt adrenaline highs. Men shipped in and men processed out. Some walking, some in body bags. Their faces—yellow, black, red, white, and brown—obscured by plastic bags or distorted with tension, simplified their differences, made things more *equal*. Men were needed, regardless of color.

Unbeknown to Army brass or dogface grunt, the war was burning toward Têt.

CHAPTER TEN
FALL RECEPTION

A YEAR BEFORE HER DEATH, Eve had mustered her strength and set additional plans for Janie in motion. She commandeered Letta to drive her to the University of Georgia in Athens. Her invitation to the Fall Harvest Reception presented a solid chance to meet Pieter DeGroot.

"I'll not stay long. But I need your help. Please." Eve, unable to manage alone, needed Letta to accompany her and do the driving.

Letta balked. "Missus Eve, you know ever state trooper between here and there gonna stop us. Ask us what we doing. A Black woman driving a white lady. Besides, I don't have much practice driving no car."

"I need you. I'm not strong enough to go alone. Besides, I'd consider this a personal favor." She touched Letta's arm briefly, her eyes beseeching. "That reception is my best opportunity to meet Professor DeGroot. I still need him to agree to take Janie."

Just as opposites attract, Janie's science teacher and Pieter DeGroot years prior had spent their graduate time at the university as roommates and lab buddies. Consequently, as DeGroot's peer, he had advocated on Janie's behalf.

"I've got her admitted," Eve continued, "and everything set up with the biology department. People tell me DeGroot is the best. They say he's a gentle person." Eve fumbled with her wedding band and, lost in thought, left the room.

Letta listened, mumbled under her breath. The drive, after all, was only a couple of hours. Missus Eve had always been kind. Now she was sicker. In the end, Letta acquiesced.

They left early the morning of the reception.

Still grumbling, Letta sat behind the wheel, squirming against her chauffeuring duties to the university, two hours distant.

"I owe you this one, Letta," Eve said and climbed into the car. She wore a gauzy dress, bright with floating flowers, looking her feminine best.

"You look right fine in that frilly dress," Letta said. "Didn't know this here shindig mean to dress up fancy. I still nervous bout this driving."

She shifted, checked for traffic, and pulled out of the driveway toward Athens, glancing sideways at Eve.

Eve, hands fluttering to smooth the skirt, smiled weakly. "University throws these dressy events annually and gives it a fancy name. It's supposed to be a thank you for donors, but it's a time to pry more money out of everyone."

"Yessum." Letta spoke mechanically, her face glowing with perspiration. Driving was hard business and required attention.

They drove in silence for forty minutes before Eve cleared her throat. "You might as well know the real story. Once Janie is admitted, her grades and study habits will carry her. But being blind is a handicap. Most people are not accustomed to giving her a chance. If I can swing accommodations and wrangle a support position for her, she'll do great. Especially with her auditory memory for bird songs."

"Yessum." Letta drove silently, focused on the road. She relaxed after an hour and half-watched the scenery.

Months earlier, Eve sent a desperate message to Susan Pea to come home. Reluctant to return south, Susan Pea had met Eve in Manhattan spring, 1967. They shopped and talked and planned together, realized again their special bond. Finally, Susan Pea had agreed to return home —soon. When Janie would be closer to graduation.

The fall reception allowed Eve to nudge her plans along, to finalize them. "I can't leave things up to Major. I don't trust his *intentions*." For long minutes, Eve watched farmland glide by as Letta maneuvered toward Athens. The old car purred, a comfortable familiar transport. Pickups, long haulers, and passenger vehicles hurled past. Letta stuck to her protracted pace, nervous lest she attract attention.

"Lucky for me," Eve said, "Major's busy thinking about those dogs and hunt season. You know how men are. Oil their guns. Get dogs trained up. Collect gear. They can't think of anything else."

"Yessum, Major keeps them guns clean—he loves 'em. He hire that trash Wes to do training, take care them dogs." Letta adjusted the car center mirror. "What you got to worry 'bout?"

"Him. Major. I fret about him constantly. About what happens to Janie when I'm gone." Eve's voice quivered, then took on a severe tone. "I want her to be safe and have a full life."

"I reckon that Major can jump sideways any minute." Letta reflected briefly on her own daughter's limited options: Black, southern, poor. She closed her mind against judgement.

"Thankfully," Eve said, "he's off making sure all farm leases are ready. He can't abide not being kingpin, the perfect shot, with dogs trained to practically serve quail on antique platters to his hunting guests. He's always got to top everyone."

"Yessum."

Eve was quiet for a few minutes. "If I understand correctly, it's the twenty-fifth year of this program and they are making an extra effort to keep various degrees well-funded."

"Yessum."

"Besides, it works out better—especially on this little issue—if Major doesn't go. He doesn't agree with me."

"Yessum. What you reckon that professor man like?"

"I understand he's middle-aged. Balding. Janie's teacher said that he's introverted, sort of nerdy. Students call him Doc Pete." Eve settled further into the car seat. "He's got an auditory catalogue he's started. Once he develops it, it's going out to all college and ornithology research centers. It'll be a perfect project for Janie."

"Janie smart. She pretty girl, too." Letta sucked her teeth and shifted.

"She gets too full of herself sometimes and tries to rush into adulthood." Eve frowned, her fair face fearful. "She's willful. And, too knowledgeable about some things and yet so naïve about others. Especially relationships. Her girlfriends lead her on. I'm not sure that's good."

"Yessum."

They drove on in silence. After a while, Eve dozed, a peaceful look on her face despite her sallow complexion.

Letta gripped the steering wheel until her knuckles protruded. She drove the speed limit, her nerves still a-jangle.

Eve's cancer would flare again later that year, a reminder she would not live to see Janie graduate high school and enter college.

When Eve entered the reception, she gradually became conscious of a knobby man quietly watching her. He did not approach, but continually stationed himself nearby, within hearing range, as she chatted with various department heads, faculty, and state agriculture officials.

After half an hour, Eve floated toward the man, her hand extended.

"My name is Eve Butler. I understand you oversee the avian labs. Your department head tells me you are developing a catalogue of birdcalls—only one in the region."

The man flushed from the neck up, his birthmark, splattered along his left jaw, glowed red. He stuttered a moment, fumbled with his hors d'oeuvre plate, steadied himself, and shook her outstretched hand.

"*Ja. Ja*, I'm Pieter DeGroot. Labs for graduate and undergraduate students fall under my wing." He half-smiled at his pun and shifted from one foot to the other, all the while carefully balancing his hors d'oeuvres.

She chuckled softly at his wit and Dutch-laced English. "You have a sense of humor. How pleasant among academic types. I'll bring my daughter Janie to meet you." Eve watched as his birthmark transitioned from rose to red. "She will be entering the university next fall. She's got a finely tuned ear for birdcalls."

"*Ja*. Does she plan to study birds seriously or is it with her a hobby?"

Eve laughed aloud and lightly touched his arm. "God love you, but you should *never* call her a hobbyist. She's quite serious about her birds. Frankly, I'm amazed at her uncanny ability to distinguish between calls and decide whether it's a mating song or a territorial dispute. Or if they are simply fussing over food."

They chatted amicably for a few minutes until Eve glanced at her watch. "Oh, goodness gracious, the time has flown. I must be going." She extended her hand again and purred, "It was most pleasant to have met you."

"Bring your daughter to visit campus soon," Pieter responded.

"Yes, I will." Eve tilted her head. "I have a meeting with the biology department next month. I'll bring Janie then."

WEEKS later the departmental chair dropped by Pieter DeGroot's graduate laboratory.

"I noticed you met Eve Butler at the reception. You two had a long conversation."

"Who?" Pieter glanced up with a quizzical look.

"You remember. She's Joshua Butler's wife."

"Joshua Butler?"

The chairman flinched, his voice exasperated. "He's one of the old-guard families in the state, most often referred to as Major—a sort of nickname because of his war service. State game boys listen to him about regional hunting. A big contributor to research in general with emphasis on game birds and wing shooting. He regularly invites his cronies to hunt which farmers love since he pays well for after-harvest privileges across their land."

Pieter scratched his forehead a moment. "Now that you remind me, *ja*, I remember Eve Butler. She talked about her daughter. Janie. *Ja. Ja.* She's to enter the university next year. Study ornithology. *Ja*, I remember."

"Her daughter's considered blind," the department head said. "I think she has extremely limited sight, kind of a tunnel vision. Mrs. Butler has set up a research fund contingent on her daughter's special needs being accommodated. She might fund something more permanent. Depending on how things go."

The department head walked around the lab, studied a spotting scope, ran his hand across a box of banding tags, and fingered a recorder. He glanced out the window and turned back to Pieter.

"What with those Russians launching space probes, the administration is keen on more science and math students. Besides, there's trouble brewing in Southeast Asia. Whatever happens will affect our young men and our enrollment numbers. We'll need all the funds we can get. Follow up with Mrs. Butler, will you?"

Several days later, on his way out, Pieter DeGroot noticed a young woman near the parking lot edge. She tapped along with a cane and stood with her head cocked, twisting toward the sound of warbling birds.

He slung his briefcase into a dented station wagon and walked over, drawn as much by the young woman's rich curls as her apparent interest in birds.

"Hello." Pieter crossed his arms and eyed her with curiosity. "May I help you? Are you lost?"

She turned slightly at his approach. "No. My mother's inside talking to some professors or something. I'm a birder. I'm not lost. I like following bird calls. Besides, I enjoy walking. It's good exercise." She continued tapping along the parking lot. "By the way, did you know you can only see straight ahead, but you can hear in all directions at once?"

"*Ja*, I did know that." Pieter followed a few steps behind. "What else can you tell me?"

Janie thought a minute, then continued talking. "If you learn bird-calls, you can know what's around the moment you step outside. Doesn't matter where you are—a parking lot, at your house, or in a field."

"*Ja*, that's right. Frequently foliage hides birds and people don't even notice. But when a bird sings, you focus on the sound point. Maybe identify the bird."

Janie turned toward Pieter's voice. "A bird is telling you what it is every time it sings. A real musical ad."

"You must be Janie Butler." Pieter smiled as he recognized her.

Surprised by his statement, Janie turned to the sound. "How do you know my name?"

"An old classmate recommended you."

"You must mean my science teacher," Janie said. "Mother and he talked. If you are Pieter DeGroot, he thinks your program will be a good match for me."

"*Ja. Ja.* I met her. I recognize your red hair and that cane. My name is Pieter DeGroot. Students call me Doc Pete."

"Hello." She bowed slightly in his direction. "Most people recognize me by my cane. And my red hair. Sort of an identity card."

"Your mother tells me you plan to enter the university."

"Yes, I hope to. And, live in a dorm. It'll be my first time out on my own. I'm excited." She tapped a few steps away, moving closer to bird noises.

"You are quite the song sleuth. A regular birder-by-ear." Pieter, hands in his pockets, rattled his car keys.

"You're nervous," she said softly.

Pieter snorted and rattled his keys again. "How could you tell?"

"You're rattling stuff in your pockets."

"Your mother said you were precocious." Pieter grinned at Janie's chatter. "I believe her."

Janie chuckled and continued following the bird noises. Goosebumps skittered up her arms.

She tapped along the paved edge, occasionally stepping off onto grass, and tilting her head toward a bird call. Pieter strode a few steps beside her.

A campus transit bus screeched to a stop at the parking lot entrance and, with a pneumatic wheeze, opened its doors. Students funneled off and on, their voices loud then faded as they drifted off their separate ways. An impatient car driver honked sharply at the bus and slow sprawl of students.

"I wish I could see birds. Their colors and feathers."

"I can describe a bird's body shape. Colors. Flight patterns."

"The bill also because that determines what it eats."

"Yes, of course. Perhaps you and I will work together if you come here." Pieter, unconsciously, rattled his keys again.

"You're still nervous." Janie said and continued walking. "I think Mother's in a meeting about my enrollment right now."

"Must be with the dean and my department head. They're keen to set up a scholarship." Pieter stopped and glanced back toward the stone building. "I saw Mrs. Butler go in as I was leaving." He cocked his head to the side. "Why don't you and I join them? We can all finalize details together."

Janie beamed. "Okay. You can tell me more about available classes. Where I might work."

Often awkward and shy around new people, Pieter blinked several times. "Of course." Her inability to see lent him courage. She'd not be put off his birthmark. His voice took on a solid tone.

Falling into step with each other, they chatted and strolled toward the building.

CHAPTER ELEVEN
SUSAN PEA BUTLER

THE ONE-EYED CAT sat near the puppy yard entrance, licking his paws. The sun had barely begun to warm the day when Susan Pea opened the kennel gate leading to the outside runs and yard enclosures.

She relatched the gate, stood a moment, listened to excited yelps, drank in the earthy blend of dog musk and humidity. She admired the fine-tuned bodies.

Major had redesigned the kennels shortly after he had returned from Europe. Dogs, alive and eager, gave him something positive to focus on. He could see construction and progress, instead of cities in rubble, beyond hope. Most of all, it helped erase the lingering stench of war death in his nostrils.

A state-of-the-art complex, kennels consisted of a concrete slab covered by a galvanized roof with open sides, which kept the entire complex cooler during savage summer heat. The runs abutted the barn. A cutout dog door led inside the larger structure which mitigated sharp winter temperatures.

Each pen contained an inside sleeping platform, outside run, and slatted loafing bench—all separated by chain-link fences, permitting dogs to see each other but not scrap over feed.

A grass enclosure divided the feeding pen, providing adult canines an outside open space, from the puppy compound. The whelping room did double duty as storage for feed and vet supplies. It gave off a pungent medicinal smell. Straw bales were stacked along the barn aisle. The entire complex was fenced off with walkways leading from one area to another.

Wes Smith's head snapped up at the metallic creak of the gate opening. He grimaced, twisted the faucet off, and wiped his hands on his pants.

"Wes, I'm glad you're here," she said. "Janie told me you still worked for Major."

"Yeah. Where else would I be?"

He finished wrapping the water hose around a metal keeper. "Kennels got to be cleaned every morning, year-round. I'm out here at least once every single day. Usually more."

She sauntered toward Wes, her southern belle flirtations flipped on high. "Good to see you again after all these years."

"I heard you'd come back." He stiffened at her appearance. "Guess there are some things you can't leave behind." He cocked his head, a sly grin playing along his face.

Despite the early morning hour, his unshaven beard shadow made him appear virile, as if he had come from some warm bed directly to the kennels. She could practically smell testosterone.

Her eyes flitted over him: lean despite his forty-plus years, dark hair with no signs of grey, hands rough from outside work.

"Doesn't Letta's son Elijah help you?" Susan Pea said.

"Sometimes. He comes after school most afternoons."

"Of course."

Winged-game bird hunting, always a gentleman's sport, helped

Major as he recovered community standing and family prestige. At least the sport's patina steadied the family, while he recovered the fortune his father, assisted by his uncle, had squandered through drink.

"I'd like to see Sadie's puppies. What are they, about three weeks now?"

"Yeah, eyes opened about a day ago. They're walking. Still wobbly. Fat. Sadie and pups are down yonder." With a nod, he gestured toward the concrete walkway far end.

"Show me, will you? You know how I enjoy babies." Coy-like, she fluttered an eyelid.

He paused a moment and glowered at her. "You know with these kennels. Why do I need to show you?"

"I forget." She cleared her throat. Gave him a colorless smile. "Besides, you might have changed things since I've been gone."

"Nope. Everything's the same. At least in the kennels." Wes stood hip cocked, regarded her up and down, licked his lips, then shrugged. "Guess there's no getting rid of you any other way," he said halfheartedly, and leaned down to finish wrapping the hose. "Watch where you step."

Susan Pea admired the way Wes's jeans outlined his butt as he bent over. She couldn't help herself.

She followed his lead as they walked toward the puppy pen. Although gone many years, one thing that had not changed were dog pen smells. Stink rose thick despite the hose-down. It would be hours before the sun dissipated the heavier odors and dried the puddles, with the entire process repeated the next day.

Sadie whined and sashayed toward the two. The dog wagged her tail side to side while her babies scrambled around. Susan Pea opened the gate to the adjoining larger whelping enclosure and walked ahead of Wes, leaving him to close it. Sadie and her puppies were nestled inside the sheltered portion.

A merry jumble of pudgy bodies tumbled about. Susan Pea stooped and picked up a brown-and-white male with a dark saddle across his shoulders. "He's a carbon copy of old Gunner." She inspected the squirming pup, checked the toes and feet, pushed his lips back, and inspected the gums.

"You nailed the pick of the litter. Major wants to keep a dog-pup and a bitch-pup from this litter. Probably that one you're holding." Wes wiped his hands on his jeans again.

"Let's hope he carries his sire's talent." She stooped, replaced the wiggling pup, and chose another, an orange-and-white like Sadie, the mother. "Have you named them yet?"

"No, not yet. I think Major intends all names begin with a 'G'—he figures this is probably Gunner's last litter with Sadie." He scooped up the spotted dog-pup, stroked it a moment, and returned it to the jumble.

Sadie sniffed among her puppies, licking them, her tail wagging, and doggie happiness on her face. Babies rolled against each other, pink tummies flashing and legs flailing air. She lay down. Puppies scrambled over each other for a teat nursing. Sadie seemed relaxed.

"How many females do we have this time?"

"Out of seven, we've got four. Bitch you were holding is top pick, even over males. You have an extreme talent for just knowing which ones are best right off," Wes squinted at her. "Or you're just damn lucky and happened to pick up top two of the litter."

"It's not luck. Remember, I've been around hunting dogs most of my life." She turned slightly. "I understand you have a young hunter this year."

"Otto?" His eyes lit up. "He's going to be a top one."

"What are your plans with him?"

"Why?"

"Curious, that's all."

Wes appeared to mull over options, then said, "I think he'll go competition field trials, probably gun-dog pointing and retrieving."

"Competitive trials and the hunting field? You're ambitious." Susan Pea watched the man's face grow intense, animated yet focused.

"Wins at the big ones can put me on the map for sure," he said. "If I add training and stud service, I can build an entire kennel based around Otto. He's young, but I think he's got the right stuff."

"What about females? Especially if you want to breed and hunt purebreds." With a final stroke around Sadie's ears, Susan Pea stood with a blank face and waited for Wes to respond.

"I've got some connections and ideas," he said.

"Old-timers say figure out the breed you need, then pick the litter, not the pup. Good bit of advice there." Susan stuffed her hands in her pockets. "Is Major interested in these long-range plans?"

"Don't know. Haven't talked yet."

She raised an eyebrow. "Major always says you are first and foremost a dog man. A top one. How do you hope to convince him?"

"Swap Otto for wages," Wes said.

"You mean buy Otto? With work? Branch out on your own?" she said her voice carrying a note of awe.

"Yeah. Move to Midwest. Branch out. Have my own kennel." He hesitated a second.

"Getting out of Georgia would minimize any potential competition and conflict with him." Susan Pea glanced around the kennels. "But, on the other hand, he might not want to lose you."

Wes ignored her statement. "I've got my eye on an outfitter service. Midwest would open a completely new range of birds—pheasants, grouse, water birds. Major's not interested in that part of the country, nor that game."

"We've got grouse here too."

Wes snorted. "Mostly in the uplands. Hard hunting for a young dog in training."

"Humm. Yeah, maybe so." She stood a moment, surveyed the yards. "By the way, you still live over in the Lee Town area?"

"Yeah."

She stooped and played with puppies a moment before standing again and stretching her legs from the squat. What Wes had said and how it might work intrigued her. She spoke her thoughts aloud. "I respect your dog skill, your *country* eyes and *country* instincts. Your plans sound interesting."

Wes grunted an answer.

"Everything hinges on that shorthair," Susan Pea said. "Establish the outfitter scenario first. Go field competition circuit after that. Start a breeding line... hmm... might work." She allowed her voice to drop as if approving his plans. The thought of him moving to another state appealed to her.

"Something like that." He turned, his movements quick and edgy.

"You'd have to think about moving. Too many old ghosts around here."

"You should know. About ghosts." He clenched his jaw, glanced at Susan Pea over his shoulder, and bent to pet Sadie's ears.

"Yeah, I know about getting out of town. Know about ghosts, too." She frowned at the man—his precise movements, work calloused hands, and veiled facial expression.

Southern men loved their hunting dogs, guns, and whiskey—in about that order. Wes really wanted Otto. With only a little manipulation, she could have Wes by his balls.

"Maybe I can help. You and I both know Major is not going to want to lose you. There'll have to be something in it for him," Susan Pea watched Wes's face. Lines around his eyes deepened. "If you want, I can help," she said. "Or do you think you can handle everything on your own?"

His eyes narrowed into hard slits. "I'm a loner. I'll think about it."

"Are Gunner and Otto still in the last runs?" she asked. "I'll look at them. Finish your chores. You're a working man." She waved her hand dismissively. "Besides, as you so eloquently pointed out, I know my way." She walked down the aisle without waiting for an answer.

Shoulders rigid, lips pressed in a narrow line, Wes watched as she moved toward the runs.

She stopped in front of Otto's pen. No doubt about it, he was a fine-looking shorthair. Solid brown head, saddle back, two feet tall at the shoulders, maybe more, bright dark eyes, and dark speckled body. Webbed feet. Floppy ears set high on his head. She admired the dog's stance and apparent curiosity. She compared him to Gunner, appreciated both dogs as textbook examples of their breeding.

She browsed the row, examining other dogs in training with a critical eye. Most hunters around town placed their gun dogs with Wes. Training fees went to Major. Goodwill tips to Wes. Her mind spun as she left.

Fingering the Pontiac keys, she slid behind the wheel, mindlessly started the old eggbeater, and drove toward the grocery store. Spoke her thoughts aloud. "No doubt about it, Wes is ambitious. He'll require a short leash."

With luck, she could control Otto—and the man would follow. Working closely with Wes would require some finesse with Janie still living there. The girl's face brightened whenever he was mentioned. Much too old for Janie, but as the first testosterone-driven male to admire her budding sexuality, she was deeply attracted. After all, he was only matched against curious, clumsy teenage boys. A wolf among dogs.

Susan Pea caught herself chewing her nails. She jerked her hands down, realized she gnawed them into the quick, and grew embarrassed by their shabby appearance. Better to stoke up the cancer sticks instead. She pushed the lighter in, fumbled for her pack, and jiggled out a Lucky Strike—a nasty habit. The cigarette lighter popped out, she lit up, her cheeks hollowing on the first pull.

Her mind spun back to Wes, and ownership papers. The cigarette did little to take her thoughts off his intentions. After all, it was not like he could just take the dog. Ownership papers were necessary. She'd known greedy men and women. They shared a common characteristic: grab what you can when you can. Even if it's out of another person's mouth. Tomorrow never comes.

Wes personified his kind with one exception—he was a master at planning several moves ahead.

Distracted, she circled the town square twice, then drove to the Winn-Dixie several blocks past the courthouse. Locals might not see it, but after her years away, she recognized the town's steady slide into decay. The Old Guard with it. She pulled into the store parking lot, navigated around potholes, and parked next to a Ford pickup.

Crushing the cigarette, she climbed out and walked toward the store, barely glancing at the truck, its hood held fast with a bungee cord.

CHAPTER TWELVE
SUSAN PEA BUTLER

Susan Pea rose early to a watery-blue dawn, air still cool from the evening. She felt rested, eager to start the day, to see how the dogs worked in the field, how they responded to handling. She planned to accompany them on their daily training—without having disclosed her intentions to Wes.

Odors, rich and brown, met her as she entered the kitchen. Even as a child, she had loved the smell of morning coffee.

"Mornin', Missus Susan. You up bright and early." Letta bustled about making biscuits. "Breakfast be ready in a minute or two."

"No need," she said and took a mug out of the cupboard. "I'll just grab coffee and eat later. I'm going out with Wes this morning."

Letta's eyes narrowed. She frowned. "I worry 'bout you out with that man. He might train them dogs good, but he not one to be trusted."

"Doesn't sound like he's changed since I knew him back in the day."

"Cat don't stop killing birds. Habits is habits."

"I know, I know. Still, I want to see how he works that dog."

"That man trash." Her voice sharp, Letta opened the oven and popped in a pan of biscuits. "Whatever he says, you double check."

"I'll be careful," Susan Pea said. She stepped outside on the porch and watched early light sluff off night. If there was anything to love about the South, it was morning with a vague promise of... something. She finished her coffee, left the cup on the porch rail, and walked to the kennels.

Wes was already tending the dogs.

"Sun's barely up," she said as she approached Wes, "and already day has a wet blanket feel. What time did you get here?"

"If the sun's up, then I'm running late. Why?" Wes did not look at her but continued filling water buckets. The kennel pulsated with energy as the dogs ate and snuffled around the feeding yard looking for any extra kibbles.

"Curious. That's all," she replied.

"I'm a working stiff. Not like you." The insinuation lingered as he filled water buckets.

"Letta told me you're still working at Joe's auto parts store." Susan Pea watched Wes for a reaction. There was none. She pressed him.

"Major can be miserly with paying hired help," she said. "Kinda odd since he loves his dogs. And his hunting. You'd think he'd be more generous. Especially for a top dog man."

Wes grunted, turned his back, and continued to fill the remaining water buckets.

She fell silent, busied herself with puppies. They tumbled about, a merry hodgepodge of pink tummies and floppy ears. Puppy odors rose, filled her nostrils.

Wes finished his morning routine and growled at her. "More to the point, what are you doing here today?"

"I'm going out with you. I want to see how the shorthair handles."

"Otto—Otto's his name." Wes snapped, his teeth clenched and jaw muscle popping.

She slipped her hands into her jean pockets, smiled to herself at having riled Wes. "Yes. Of course. Otto. Thanks for reminding me." She stood a moment. "Are we taking Gunner, too?"

"Since you're going, I'll just work out back. Use the training arena. Never hurts to have a tune-up on basic stuff."

"No." She spoke forcibly. "He needs a solid workout. Let's put both dogs in the field under genuine conditions. I want to see them in action."

Wes froze. His face scrunched into a frown, eyebrows knitted together. As quickly as he clouded up, his face changed, morphed into a blank slate.

"Major know you're going?" he asked.

"He doesn't need to. Besides, I want a better handle on the dog before I back you. You did say you want his papers, didn't you?"

"What the hell. I never asked for your help. In fact, not sure I want *anything* from you." Body rigid, Wes slowly inclined his head, picked up a rope lead, and moved toward to the pointers.

He glared, remained silent, weighed options known only to him. He acquiesced with something close to a snarl. "Okay. We'll take my pickup. Gonna work Frog Bottom Creek area."

"Isn't it a long drive? I remember it being rather remote, isolated in fact. Trappy." She felt a fleeting apprehension about the drive and place.

"Not many go there if that's what you mean." He turned to her, cold, eyes crinkled. "Want to change your mind. Stay here?"

"No." She was abrupt. "I need to see what that dog has. I'm a fair judge of hunters myself."

Wes snorted, strode to the Ford, dropped the rear gate, signaled both dogs up, secured Otto first, then Gunner, in their crates. "Only got one orange vest. You wear it. Stay a bit to the side and behind. Don't signal or talk to the dogs. That's *my* job."

"I've hunted before. I know the routine."

"Follow it," Wes said. "Especially since it's your first time with *me*. And Otto."

"What about guns?"

"I've got a side-by-side in the pickup. Don't need anything else."

"Don't I get a gun?" She stopped, held her hands out, and then dropped them to her sides. She swallowed, felt her face flush warm.

"I'll take care of whatever comes up." His voice had a splintered edge. He stared straight ahead. "We're not hunting today. Training and exercise only. I carry a gun in case an emergency comes up."

"You expect anything to come up?" Her belly knotted. Saliva flooded her mouth.

"You never know when you're out in the woods. Anything can happen." His eyes narrowed, lips fixed in a tight line. Sweat beaded in his neck creases.

A prickling crept along her arms. Frog Bottom lay to the west off Highway 310 and thirty miles down a washboard-rough dirt road before becoming a weed-choked track. The area was wild, rough, even for seasoned hunters. She'd only hunted the area twice and knew it a place a person could easily get lost. *Was Wes trying to intimidate her?* Damn him, she was determined to see Otto work—and prove her mettle.

Neither she nor Wes talked on the drive out. It jarred her teeth roots. Several times she caught him watching her out of the corner of his eye.

He parked in an oak's shade on the edge of the track and stepped out.

Susan Pea opened her door, stepped out, and paused to appreciate the meadow and overgrown beauty. Common broom sedge, waist high and already a tawny brown, swayed in a light breeze. Creeping fescue matted the ground. Pine trees ringed the area, murmured with turpentine-scented breath. Nothing compared to the open countryside and the sweating heat of the South. The ubiquitous juxtaposition of death and life in the wildness surrounding them. It never failed to fascinate her. Even today, her worries about the remoteness were swept aside.

Wes dropped the tailgate.

She startled at the metal-on-metal clang, the spell broken. For a moment, the meadow lapsed into silence.

He climbed into the truck bed and focused his binoculars on the east end. "We'll run a line to left of that tree stand and back along the bank." He gestured vaguely toward the creek. "If a covey's moving, it'll be there. We're late. It's eight, which means birds should be finished with their morning forage. Another hour and they'll drift toward shade looking for a clear patch where they can fluff, dust off." He unloaded the dogs and jumped to the ground.

"Hup boys, look 'em up. Find 'em. Find 'em." With two short pips and a wave of his hand, Wes set the pair off. They ran parallel for fifty yards, then began a serpentine pattern.

A consummate outdoorsman, he had a predacious beauty manifested in his long stride, lean form, and melding with his dogs. He carried the shotgun broken, two shells showing.

Susan Pea followed.

Taut muscled, Otto moved to the right, floating effortlessly over the ground. With his solid-colored head, brown-ticked body, and docked tail, he was the model German shorthair. Gunner stood a moment, head up, nose twitching. He worked in slow, deliberate sweeps, his whiptail held high, moving with an elegant boldness and grace.

The dogs, all business, scoured through tangle, intent on bird scent. Twice, the pointer stopped, investigated a patch of ground, and, finding no line, continued working. Both times, the shorthair paused, watched the older dog, and without a positive point, moved on. Both dogs maneuvered yards ahead of Wes, running loops through the grass.

Susan Pea made a mental note to double check the shorthair's willingness to honor a point, hold steady especially to shot. One thing for certain, he glided over the ground like a canoe through still water. Strong, he had the right bird instincts. With careful training, he could be what Wes hoped. And best part, all she needed to control Wes, was to control what he wanted most—those ownership papers. With those in hand, maybe, just maybe, she could manipulate Wes away from Janie.

They neared the creek bank and a single male bird ventured out, his black-brown-beige head bobbing as he fed. Several females scuttled through grasses toward a briar patch, choosing spots surrounded by stickers, natural protection from predators. The covey followed the lone quail's lead in dense underbrush and brambles.

Wes trailed them with his binoculars as the whites continued pecking and scratching in the grasses. The dogs scoured, nose-to-ground, back and forth sweeping the field. Wes varied his path—walked straight, angled slightly left, and worked a twist-and-turn pattern. Gunner, the old hunting pro, diligently scoured the weeds, while Otto part-cavorted and part-settled around clumps of fescue. Closer to the pines, the young dog froze on point. The old pointer honored. Wes nodded to himself. Overanxious, Otto broke point, dashed toward tall grasses and briars. The covey exploded, an abrupt staccato whirring, brassy vibration fading in thin morning air.

"Whoa. Whoa." Wes signaled Otto. "Damn." He eased up to the dog and snapped on a slip-leash. Stooping, Wes gently repositioned him, and repeated his "whoa" command.

Susan Pea put her hands on her hips. "Major won't tolerate that in front of his hunting buddies."

"Let me worry about stuff. You just stay outta the way." Wes part-snarled, part-spoke.

"No problem." Susan Pea raised her hands in mock surrender. "But if you expect Major to keep this dog, he'll have to show more steadiness."

Wes spun around toward her, irritation radiating off in waves. "By end of season, Major will swap my wages for Otto."

Susan Pea shook her head. "I don't see that happening.

"Maybe." He smiled, an acerbic twisting of his lips, pleased at surprising her. "On the other hand, I *might* marry Janie and he'll give me Otto as a wedding gift."

Her mouth flew open. She stopped mid-stride. "What gives you any idea she would even *have* you? You're *common*."

"She doesn't see me like that. She sees me as a hunk, a real stud. Why not marry her?" He snorted and turned back to the dogs. "Think about it—I'd be your nephew-in-law." He laughed, a raucous, grating sound. "You look completely pale. Possibility scare you?" He brayed again.

Susan Pea flinched at the sound, aghast at the words, and muttered under her breath. "Nephew-in-law. I can't believe it. Man's got brass balls." She continued her cautious trailing of Wes, her ruminations spinning out of control.

Wes pushed toward the trees along a sagging fence row, deadfall collected in the tangled wire. The trappy ground made this a treacherous place to cut across.

Nearing the fence line, Gunner pointed, head held straight toward a patch of weeds and foreleg bent for the next step. Otto honored.

Nodding at the canine teamwork, Wes eased into gun range and moved slowly; hat brim pulled down, covering any facial shine, he waited with the gun low. In a smooth motion, he brought the stock to his cheek, swung the muzzle toward the birds as the covey broke in one pulsating knot. Wes focused on a lone white, led it, and fired.

Otto stood steady, head movement following the quail flight path, then swiveled toward Wes as birds disappeared. The shot and whirr of wings left the dog looking back and forth between man and sky. A clear miss with no bird to retrieve.

Wes whistled the shorthair to his side. "Good boy. Nice job. We'll get them next time." He rewarded the shorthair with a chin scratch and pats before signaling break.

Gunner stood steady. Pleased, Wes cradled the pointer's head with one hand, patted him, and released him also. He reloaded the shotgun, draped it broken over his arm.

The piercing whine of a bullet and concussive shock startled Susan Pea. Her ears rang, she crouched low, mouth gone dry, eyes wide in a fight-or-flight reflex. A second bullet whizzed past, thumped into the tree trunk near her head, scattering bark splinters into her face. She could see the wound in the trunk, ginger-colored and clean.

The shot had not come from Wes. "What in hell?" She shuddered.

Wes immediately snapped the shotgun closed and scanned for dogs. "Whoa, boys. Stop. Whoa."

Both dogs froze, heads up and ears cocked. A flock of grackles rose from a thicket and whirled, a single entity circling the area. Silence quivered in the empty sky.

Wes pivoted toward the blast.

A square figure, partially hidden by shadows, filled the entire space between two saplings. With the sun behind him, his face remained obscured, but, clearly, he held a rifle at waist level.

Susan Pea, several yards behind, rose from her crouch, and stood immobile in the broom grasses, hands at her side, fists clenched. She could hear her heart's racing cadence.

"What are y'all doing here?" The man stepped from half-light of the oaks into the open, his thick drawl slipping through air. "It ain't bird season. Y'all could've got shot."

Dressed in faded overalls, he appeared harmless, wearing a plaid shirt with pearl snaps, sleeves rolled back a turn, and a Cardinals baseball cap. He part-stalked and part-waddled toward them, negotiating uneven ground cautiously.

"Training. Working my dogs." Wes spoke with a deep drawl, his voice bass, pulsating with anger.

The stranger continued talking and moving his bulk forward. "Not a field you likely to hunt. Too dense."

Wes coughed slightly, stood with legs splayed as the man approached. "Got good briar cover. But that doesn't matter. Like I say, I'm training."

"Didn't expect to see no people out here today. Especially no woman." The man stopped.

Being shot in a remote section scared her. Sweat beaded up on her face. Her palms grew slippery. Breath came in gulps.

Wes held the shotgun in the crook of his arm, muzzle level, and glanced toward the man's Remington rifle. "Deer hunting? Kinda out of season too, aren't you?"

Leaning slightly aside, the man spit a stream of tobacco juice and smirked though a brown smear. He slapped the barrel across his palm, allowing it to bounce slightly, and lowered the muzzle.

"Yeah. Only checking to see if'n any game out here." He spat a third time, his drawl becoming more pronounced. "Man hires me to scout out his leases. He's an impatient sort. He won't hunt nothing slow. Needs action. Good game. A sure thing."

"What's the idea of popping off in my direction?" Wes, muzzle still level, jutted his jaw forward, gritted his teeth.

"Didn't see you folks. Especially little lady. Sun got me in my eyes.

No harm done." The robust man shifted and cradled the gun in his arm, finger around the trigger guard.

Wes spoke low, his voice edged with menace. "Don't want my dogs hit by mistake. I'd likely get upset about that."

"You'll never find a more accurate shot or careful hunter than me. That's why folks hire me. Pay good money, too. For my *specialty*. Know what I mean?"

"Yeah. I understand *specialty*. This what you got?" Wes gestured toward tree wounds, hand sweeping the field. "If this is careful, I'm not interested in sloppy."

The man lifted his cap, ran a hand through a buzz cut, and replaced the cap. "Humph. No harm done."

He swiveled his head and glanced up at the sky. "Well, sun done got up too high. I'll head on back since it looks to be a hot one today." He glanced at the dogs. "You got a fine pair there. Be a shame one of them got shot by someone careless." He lifted his cap a second time, resettled it on his head.

Wes stepped sideways, eyed the stranger, nostrils flared. "I might be tempted to kill anyone hurt my dogs."

"Well, no sense making threats," the man said and shouldered his gun, leaned slightly forward, and spat in the weeds. "I need outta this here swampy heat anyway. My truck's parked other side of yonder pines stand. Besides, all this carrying on has scared everything off." He turned his back and started out through briars and grass tufts, picking his way toward the far tree line.

Eyes narrowed, face in sharp profile, Wes watched the man's retreating bulk.

Voice high with anxiety, Susan stepped toward Wes. "Do you know that man?" She blanched and swallowed hard, her throat jumping with the effort.

He lowered the shotgun muzzle, did not answer immediately, and instead called the dogs. "Here boys. Kennel up. Gunner. Otto. Kennel up, kennel up."

At his shout, both dogs bounded forward. Wes gestured toward the truck. The dogs scoured grasses as they made their way across the field. Staring straight ahead, he answered Susan Pea. "Don't *know* him. Seen him around. Lives over toward the southside."

"Lee Town? Same place you're from?" She spoke in an accusatory tone. "What the hell? You still live there?"

"Said I didn't know him."

"I thought you identified with all those crackers. With those peckerwood, tobacco-chewing, mouth-breathers," Susan Pea said.

Wes squinted at her, jaw muscle working, voice bristly. "Meaning what?"

"Thought y'all ran together." She scowled at him.

"Damn your vicious bitch heart," Wes whirled and stepped toward her. "You come driving back here to play high queen redeemer and think you can change up everything? Well, you're up against more than you even considered."

"You sonofabitch. You rank right up there on the top rung with those bubbas, even if you did learn to read. I'm no fool, and I've got a bit more pull than you." Susan Pea leaned forward, spittle flying from her mouth, her teeth almost snapping. "Be *very* careful. I know more is going on here than meets the eye."

"Like the hell what?"

"Maybe Otto gets *lost*. Maybe you hand him off to be held for later pick-up," Susan Pea's face twitched with accusation. "Maybe this whole thing's something you planned all along and that's why you didn't want me to come along today."

"You think you can play rich-princess-bitch with me? Don't even try. I said I didn't know him." Eyes narrowed, Wes stepped away from her. "I'm no idiot. What the hell good is a dog with no papers!"

As if choreographed, they backed away from each other, breathless and glaring. They stomped back to the truck, she slightly left, following him. Her thoughts had spewed out in an angry deluge, sweeping away any chance of a quiet resolution.

He carried the shotgun. Closed.

She'd seen his kind before, dirty fingernails and all. Harm erupting off him, like skunk stink. The sonofabitch was lying.

CHAPTER THIRTEEN
LETTA DAVIS

LATE MIDDAY ONE WEDNESDAY, Letta settled into her rocker with her favorite shelling bowl and an empty basket for pea pods. She sighed heavy, took several deep breaths of honeysuckle-colored air, and realized, once again, June afternoons on a shady porch jawing made even Georgia humidity pleasant and work agreeable.

Janie, with her heavy cane, tapped outside and sat beside her. "What are we having for supper?" Mutt plopped down under shade tree.

"Now that you here, you get busy and help, we'll have peas for supper. Put your hulls in here with mine." With her bare foot, Letta scooted the bushel basket between them, slightly touching Janie with the rough weave. "Day smelling sweet like it do, both us shelling, we'll finish these in no time." She moved the rocking chair into a slow sway, relishing the motion and company.

On the top porch step, Janie took the bowl, nestled it between her knees, and repositioned the basket for her hulls. She sat in the sun, closed her eyes, and lifted her face to its brightness.

"Letta, what does red taste like?" She twisted back toward Letta.

"Girl, red's a color. Got no taste." She snorted at such whimsy.

"Andy says color does have taste. Sometimes sound." Janie began shelling, albeit slow. "Once, he put cayenne pepper on my tongue. Said that's how red tastes. Then he whistled high, sharp, said red sounds like a whistle."

"What else that boy tell you?"

"He gave me a peach still sun warm." The girl continued her chatter, barely shelling any peas. "He said it tastes like pink looks—pleasing, a summer breeze."

"He tell you that? Well, what does he know anyway? He still a whippersnapper. Cause he in Army don't mean he know stuff." Letta humphed and continued shelling the blackeyes. She watched Janie. Sweet, blind girl with her perplexing white people ways.

"For a stepbrother, he treats me special. Mother says he practically dotes on me." Janie said. "He travels different places. He tells me about how people talk, things they do, and how they dress. I'm glad he comes home occasionally."

"You pretty full of you self." Letta's teasing voice spidered. She continued thumbing out peas and dropping empty pods in a basket. Wrinkles gathered around her eyes. She often worried about the girl's future, how her creativity would fare in a seeing world, especially with her mother dying. Occasionally, she thought tenderly of Eve despite the racial chasm between them. She continued shelling, her chair taking on a lazy rhythm. Her years in the Butler household had always been conflicted. She cared for Janie in the way she did all growing things.

For her part, Janie's behavior fluctuated. Letta attributed that to her teenage years and listened now with a well-honed ear.

Janie spoke again, interrupting Letta's thoughts. "He said you can feel color, too. Yellow is like winter sun, a gentle, slow warmth.

Summer's sun is orange, it makes you sweat. It can hurt you, like a stove burner, good for cooking, but you must be careful." Janie stopped shelling a moment, lifted her hair with both hands, allowing air to cool her neck. A breeze stirred across the yard and rattled the bottle tree, a delicate glass-on-glass tinkling.

Years prior, Letta had started a bottle tree at the mansion, stuck glass containers on dead branches of a stunted crepe myrtle and taught Janie to move her hand along stubby branches. She had explained as they stuck bottles on the bare ends, the bottles would guard against malevolent spirits.

The family referred to the bottle-laden tree, standing in the backyard, as Tiny Blue. It had defined the yard's edge as long as Janie had lived in the mansion.

"Mark my words," Letta said, "them bottles catch haints. Keeps them away from door. They likes sparkling glass so they gather round, climb inside, burn up. Paint porches blue cause haint don't cross water. Color blue scares them."

An errant breeze caused the bottles to tinkle. Janie turned her head toward the sound. "You can freeze water into an ice cube that sounds happy in a glass of sweet tea. Summertime, you can wipe your face with ice, make it chase heat. Your fingers can stick to an ice cube. Pulls your skin when you try to drop it. It's two things." Pleased with her cleverness, Janie beamed.

"Well, I reckon that's right." With a soft swish-thump, swish-thump, thump Letta rocked back and forth, grinning at the observation. "Haints dart inside less you paint shutters blue. They cause mischief."

"Letta, you know all sorts of things. What would I do without you?" Janie's voice had a lilting quality, almost teasing, but not quite.

Letta stopped rocking. "I know more than folktales and superstition." She thought about the Old Ones and storytellers that kept her people's oral traditions alive.

She continued talking, "I know about people, too. People can be blue. Feel sad. Could be they lost something. Maybe a person. Maybe a treasure they loved." Her voice became moody.

"Now that Missus Susan home, you got all people you need, you got family. She take care you and Missus Eve." Letta resumed rocking. "Family brings most joy. Sometimes they be ones cause most hurt."

"Like now, with Mother dying," Janie said.

"Yessum."

Janie cocked her head toward Letta, her brow puckered in puzzlement. "I know Mother's dying, so it will not surprise me. But, I think I'll still be blue when she's gone."

"I expect so."

"I've never lost anyone. I don't know what death is like." Janie's voice trailed off.

"You gonna be sad when she passes. Could be you sad-blue now. Blue cause she not able to help you like she once did. Sad cause she not be here much longer." She took a deep breath. "Folks can feel blue thinking 'bout future. She stopped, sat still a long minute. "Don't help to know about future."

"No matter," Letta continued. "When someone dies, you gotta look around, pick up pieces that broke apart. Hold on to memory. Call they name. Keep going." She picked up a pea pod, tossed it back into the basket unshelled, her thoughts cluttering one against another. *Her husband gone. Her mother gone. Constant struggle to keep her children safe. Daily effort to keep her thoughts to herself.*

"People are the same, yet really different." Janie paused and ran her fingers through the shelled peas. She shifted her rump on the step, edged the bushel basket over, and continued with her work.

The chair ceased creaking as Letta paused, considered a response. "People like them colors we talk on. Takes all kinds to make world, keep it moving. Look at you. You can't see. You put spice in this old household cause you notice stuff in a different way."

"Like you," Janie said. "With all your Black ways. You think different, act different. You're bossy, but you aren't in charge. Still, you're *wise*." Janie's face scrunched with her conflicting thoughts.

Letta chuckled, delighted with Janie's insight. "I be in charge more than you think. But never you mind that. Truth is, all us people different. Like Tiny Blue," Letta leaned toward the bottle tree, "has all kinds shapes. Can't have a haint tree with only one or two bottles."

"Tell more."

"I control my own self. I be my own boss and make my own decisions. I try to care 'bout others. Sometimes, they care back." She rocked slow, watched shadows shift. "I know even when a person leaves this place, go live some other place, they still got roots here, can't never leave *everything* behind. Folks remember them. Remember feelings."

"Will that happen with me?" Janie asked. She shifted her rump on the step, hoping for a more comfortable position.

"Course it will."

Janie straightened her blouse across her stomach. She ran her fingers through shelled peas, sat silent.

"Even you move away, can't never leave Georgia. Can't untangle them roots." Letta recognized the tug of past and present living within her. She ruminated. "Haints living in them bottles don't weigh nothing. Nobody can see them. Lots of them live in small places. Haints is really thoughts. Folks conjure them up. Some good, some evil. Haints can come from ancient knowledge or from now thoughts. They spread out among us. Time come ripe, haints call a person. Person hear them calls, think on what haints saying, and before too long, they cross river."

"What river?"

"River separate life and death. God-fearing folks like to call it River

Jordan. Other folks call it River Styx. Don't matter the name, still gotta cross over when you die."

Even though Janie could not see the gesture, Letta pointed toward the bottle tree, sliding her chair forward and leaning slightly. Porch boards creaked. "People sorta like haints. They get drawn to something. That thing might end up hurting them. Can't undo hurt."

Letta smacked in an audible pout so Janie could understand. "You can hear haints moan and wail. Some folks lock all they feelings away. Don't do no crying. Don't wail. But hurt gotta come out. Come out when it ain't expected. It come in all kinds of shapes."

"Well, people might act that way when they're sad," Janie said, her tone smug. "But the bottles only make a sound when the wind blows. It's air. No spirit's inside. You're superstitious. Besides, people are smarter than haints." She patted her stomach, shifted her position yet again.

"You mighty sassy for a blind girl." Letta, despite Janie's lack of sight, pointed her finger at the girl, shaking it as an admonishment before resuming her shelling. "How you know it be wind? Haints likes to ride on them winds. Come round when you don't know they be near, Missy-know-it-all."

"My science teacher. He blew across a Coke bottle, and it made a whoosh sound. Besides, I can feel the wind blow and that's when I hear those bottles," Janie said.

Letta humphed. "Haints crawl into them bottles early of a morning. Sun comes out, heats them bottles, haints burn up. Need heat you gonna make stuff change." She paused and repeated, "Need *heat* you gonna make stuff change."

A bird fluttered into the chinaberry tree, twilled several high notes, and flew away. The far-off sound of a train whistle floated toward them, died on the wind.

Janie sat her bowl to the side, tucked her legs under her chin, and leaned back. She listened to Letta despite teasing the woman about her folk customs. "You always seem to know things *before* they happen."

Letta grunted. Her foot in two worlds. She reflected on second sight, shivered at ghosts that materialized before her, trailing anger like smoke.

"Why do haints crawl inside if the sun burns them up?" Janie asked.

"Bottle tree stand like it do between earth and sky, between living and dead," Letta said. "Spirits like that sparkle. They drawn into the bottles. Besides, tree pretties up yard. What else we gonna do with that old bush anyways?" Pleased with her practical use for the shrub and empty bottles, Letta raised an eyebrow.

They sat for a time, lost in separate thoughts. From the yard fence, a cardinal sang. Janie's head swiveled toward the sound.

Letta paused a half-beat and tested Janie. "What kinda bird that?"

"A cardinal. They sing in a string of notes. They're spirit birds, too."

"They's real pretty in winter," Letta said. "The only color round when it turn cold, sitting in bare trees. You do real good telling birds. Most folks only know a bird when it sits in plain sight, out on a limb."

At seven, Janie first showed Letta her predilection for birds. She had sat on this same porch, her face scrunched, and commented on bird calls. Letta had praised and encouraged her.

"People recognize each other by their speech," Janie said, "by the way they talk."

"Suppose that be truth of it," Letta replied.

"That's the way I tell the birds apart."

Silence ensued for a moment.

Letta continued to rock, her chair singing against the porch boards. "Some birds good when they come round. Some pesky. Crows smart—always have a lookout warn if trouble coming. One leaves, they all leave. Crows bring news from other side."

Janie sat her bowl aside, stood, and stretched her arms up. She braced on the porch rail, hands on her hips, steadied herself, and ran fingers though her tangled curls. "Well, I'm tired of shelling. I think I'll walk down to the gas station and get some chewing gum. I'm out of Juicy Fruit."

"Well, little missy, finish up these here blackeyes first if we gonna have them for supper. You know how you mother likes them."

"I've got my mouth set on that gum. You don't mind finishing up alone, do you?"

Lordy, child shouldn't be traipsing around by herself. How could Letta watch her, keep mischief away, and take care the house all the same time? She had her own family, her own daughter.

Her lips in a straight line, Letta acquiesced. "Nah, don't guess I do. You go on. Take that cane and Mutt. Make that dog stay right with you. Get you gum, come straight back here. I go with you, but I needs finish shelling these here peas for supper."

"Letta, you forget, I'm in high school. I'll be going to college in another year." Janie thrust her chin forward, a determined look on her face. "I can go places alone without you."

"You ain't so big you can get uppity. Mind what I say. Don't hang around them worthless men riffraff at that store. They only good to pass man-gossip around." Her gnarled hands thumbed out a row of peas in one zippering motion. She stopped a moment and pulled the bushel basket closer for her hulls. A breeze set the bottles tinkling.

Janie lifted her hair again, held it on top of her head. Still balanced against the porch railing, she pivoted toward Letta's rocking. "If the bottle tree captures bad spirts, why is Mother dying? Why didn't the bottles catch her cancer? If the haints fear blue, why did they come into our house?" Her voice quivered.

"I don't know child. I don't know." Letta sucked her teeth, frowned.

Janie dropped her hair, picked up her cane, touched it on the top step, tapped her way down, and confidently strode along the sidewalk toward the country gas station several blocks away. Mutt, tongue lolling out, trotted beside her, occasionally stopped to investigate a patch of weeds or piece of debris.

Letta watched Janie until she disappeared around the corner, worry lines deepened across her forehead. *That blind girl only a few years older than my daughter Merry. Maybe I ought go with her, keep them men away.*

She dug around in her apron pocket, pulled out a tin, and placed a moist pinch in her lower lip. She sucked on it, wadding it around with her tongue, and mumbled to herself. "That girl not woman growed and already she got a swell to her belly. Can't be I only one see that there bump. White people don't take to that kind of trouble too good. I ain't say nothing. Let them white folks discover for they own self."

She shook her head, resumed rocking, thoughts splintered between her white-Black world and the old ways.

CHAPTER FOURTEEN
LETTA DAVIS

Letta set the lunch tray near Eve, unsure if she was awake or sleeping. Light laced across Eve's diminished body, played on her closed eyes. Letta adjusted the paisley bedspread quietly and placed a newspaper near the tray. Wiping her hands down the faded apron, she turned to leave.

"Stay, Letta." Eve stretched her hand out, eyes still closed. Her voice barely audible, she faltered before she gathered strength from some unknown source. "Stay. Only a moment. I need to ask you to do something for me."

Sorting through a shoebox of possibilities, Letta remembered crone's foretelling of an unwanted request. A request that would bode an unfolding of other events and needs. Dread lay wool-wet in her thoughts. She feared Major. Felt a sad compassion for Eve and Janie. Thoughts churned through her soul, contradictory and agonizing. Finally, she answered in a soft voice. "Yessum. I stay."

Eve cleared her throat. "Major has been complacent in too many things. He came back from overseas unbalanced, too accustomed to death. He's strangled with his own sense of power. He got rid of Andy's mother and married me."

"Yessum." Letta reflected on the strange disappearance of the first Mrs. Butler. Nobody had seen her go. Nobody knew anything. Letta walked across to the window, fingered the lace curtain, gazed through wavy glass.

"I think he married me hoping to undo his first marriage. Hoping to exonerate those bloody war memories."

Letta remained silent. Her thoughts skimmered over the first Mrs. Butler's disappearance and the intervening years caring for Andy, managing his adjustments. Her own family's needs. Years of bone breaking work by her husband at the sawmill.

"Lord says everything has a time." Eve's voice a croak. "My time is coming. You and I still have things between us. We keep stepping around those things that divide. We pretend they are not there."

Letta twisted her fingers together and stood utterly still, a blank slate blending into elongated shadows against the wall.

"Your son. The oldest." Eve spoke in a low voice. "Major wants him at the mill."

Letta remained silent, loath to speak.

Eve closed her eyes, face ashen, and lay still. When she spoke again, it was barely audible. "Your son..."

"His name be John." Letta cut Eve off, her voice tree bark rough. "That's my John you speak 'bout."

"John," Eve said. "Yes, I remember. Tall. A square jaw. Kind eyes. John. That's a strong name. Biblical." She paused for breath.

"He a good man," Letta said.

"I didn't hear about your husband's death until several weeks after. Did you try to tell anyone what happened?" Eve asked.

Letta stepped back, spoke with a grimace. "Tell what? Tell that my man drink he self to death? Tell that them peckerwoods allowed to treat him like a dog? Tell that ever one watch him whipped into two pieces then don't say nothing? Major allowed that." She choked back her hurt, continued in a taut voice. "Naw. Don't say nothing. Major a hard man."

"What did you do?" Eve asked.

Clenching her fists, Letta held revenge tight by its tail, sniffed the air, smelled the devil's sulfur. She spoke slow. "I see my granny-woman, that crone. She listens to the Old Ones, tells me what's gonna happen, what needs doing."

Eve's breath, came in raspy gulps.

The desperate sound pulled Letta back. Her mouth stretched into a cynical line. Her face twitched. She held her peace.

"Where is John now?" Eve asked.

"He doesn't live here no more."

"Isn't he in the Army?" Eve asked. "Like Andy? Seems we always shove our best men toward killing."

"Not gonna stay in no Army now." Letta retrieved a tin of wet tobacco from her pocket, changed her mind, and slipped it back in her apron. She folded her hands, stared through Eve.

Eve paused, appeared to gather her strength, and spoke faintly. "When I'm gone, ask John to end this misery. Ask him to put it all to rest." She coughed, her throat jerking with the effort.

"I ain't understand what you mean," Letta said. "I'm a Christian woman. I do what's right."

"I know your people have your shadows, your ways, your wisdom. You have *other* ways to find justice. We have the gossip mills, sometimes the sheriff, and the law. Of course, we bend and twist things to suit our ends. Your other world can be more useful since it is hidden."

Eve pointed in the direction of the antique dresser. "A key. On the back of the mirror. Locker at the Athens Greyhound bus station. I put it there." She spoke in gasps, breath seeming to fail her.

Letta studied the dresser and snorted. It had been in the mansion as long as she could remember. Crackled varnish, sitting in the same spot for years like some grand dame. Over time, that dresser presided over each new Butler bride's deflowering. Some not even brides.

Eve struggled to speak. "Bus station. Find the locker and open it. There's a letter for you. Ask John to finish everything. Finish things for y'all, for me."

"That asking a lot of a Black woman. A Christian woman. Lord done said vengeance was His. I can't go against Lord."

"I know. Susan Pea's coming home soon. She'll be here to help you." Eve struggled to speak. Struggled to breathe.

"But you have people and ways I can't get to." Eve twisted slightly on the bed, her face sallow, her voice world weary. "People talk. They say John's a sharpshooter."

"I ain't wanting my son ever again set foot in this swampy, mean land. It stinks of rot."

"He's the only one capable, only one with skills. And he's a *good* man."

"Stepson Andy capable, too. He white. He come and go without nobody asking questions. Nobody lynching him cause his skin dark. South's a whore."

"The Army is Andy's career," Eve said. "He can't step outside the bounds."

"You ask my John to step outside them bounds." Snappish, Letta frowned at Eve.

"Yes, I suppose I am."

Letta gritted her teeth until the jaw muscles protruded under her skin.

Eve twisted with a spasm of pain, pulled at the sheets, and closed her eyes. She panted and gasped, her face blanching.

Letta did not respond to Eve. She let her thoughts course over young men that slinked north on dark nights, out of harm's way. Thought about those that cringed before white mobs. Remembered again strange fruit hanging high. Some she knew personally, others she only heard tales of before a white mob took their lives. And, the girls, the women, jerked into an abyss of pain and self-shame by some pale skinned man. John, his own man now, would choose his path separate from her. Only the Old Ones could shield him from danger.

Reopening her eyes, Eve sank into the tangled bed. "No matter what he decides, or you decide, take the envelope. Take it for you and your family." She coughed several times, clutched the sheets, and spoke with a new urgency. "Major belongs to the devil. Needs to go."

Outside they could hear birds fluttering among tree branches and in the azaleas, their chirruping spirited. The morning smells, still sweet, hovered in the room. The two women, each thinking their own thoughts, were silent.

Finally, Letta crossed her arms and glared down at Eve. "Done said it plain. Don't want my John involved. He got his own row to hoe."

Eve closed her eyes. "Doesn't matter how. John or another way. You *know* how to handle things."

Distant neighborhood sounds coiled around the open window. The house moaned in the mid-morning heat, creaking with age and accumulated sin. The striped feline slipped into the room and sidled against Letta's legs. She glanced down, bent, and stroked it, watching as it arched against her hand. Cats reminded her to be independent, stand on her own feet, to accept the other side of life. She stood, straightened herself, and fluffed sheets around Eve's shoulders again.

The woman lay silent, hands fisted in bedsheets, her eyes following Letta's movements until she left the room. Only a slight rise and fall of lace-trimmed sheet indicated life still lingered. Her time grew near.

Stepping out on the veranda, Letta stood a moment in the light. Mutt, lying under the porch, twitched in his sleep. The mid-day sun radiated heat and energy for growing. Each thing possessed a dual purpose, nothing one-sided. She began a slow stroll around the garden. Flowers planted around the edge of her herb knot were wilted. With no rain for over a week, foxglove drooped. Zinnias and marigolds grew straight, their color fading. Iris, their sword-shaped leaves erect, graced the yard. Weeds, in bar ditches and along bogs, grew abundant, their seed heads already grown heavy.

Letta touched the plants. "Lord sends rain for my flowers in His good time." She picked off a few withered leaves as she walked.

She tapped Little Blue as if to awaken anything inside. "You suppose to trap them haints. Reckon wicked ones slip out once in a while. Can't be helped—sometimes things not work like they supposed to." Pausing, she pulled grass runners out of the rose beds, knocked soil off, and tossed them. "I live off sweat and gristle of my ancestors. Momma always tolt it be better for next generation." Letta shook her head. "She was always hoping."

Letta raised her face to the sky. "Crone woman conjure payment from those that got debts that need paying. She do it in her own good time."

CHAPTER FIFTEEN
SUSAN PEA BUTLER

"Letta?" Susan Pea hollered over her shoulder. "What happened to the screen in Eve's window? It's gone." She leaned across the frame and shooed birds away. They fluttered onto azalea bushes and tree limbs. "They've left squirts all over the place. Did you realize the screen was gone?"

Eve, eyes closed, her voice scarcely audible, groused, "No need to call Letta. I asked her to take the screen. I enjoy their company." Eve appeared tiny beneath the quilts. Skin, once as luminant as a sea pearl, now translucent blue, strained against her facial bones. Her body shrinking, limb by limb.

Susan Pea stood with hands on her hips and surveyed the room. "Janie told me she was feeding a squirrel in here. I didn't believe her. But, with the screens gone, of course they'll come in too. They get bold when it comes to food. I believe her now."

She leaned over and patted Eve's hand and pulled a chair close. "I brought some poems for us to read."

Eve gave a weak nod. "Who?"

"Poet Maxine Kumin. She lives on a farm in New Hampshire."

Eve nodded again.

"She's fond of wild things and the woods," Susan Pea said. "Favors farm animals, especially horses and sheep. She writes about her relationships to them. Sometimes she's called a regional poet, a sort of Granite State Robert Frost." Susan Pea settled into the chair and opened a slender book.

Eve sank deeper into the bed, her breath shallow, strained. Her arms had grown chicken-wing thin. Susan Pea read. The poet's words meandered pleasantly across the room as Eve drifted into a restless doze.

Sparrows chortled on the sill. A jay in a nearby tree, too cautious to perch closer, rudely squawked. Off in the distance, a dog barked.

Closing the book, Susan Pea sat long moments, watched her sister-in-law, a friend who had accepted her with all her foibles and strengths. Both women had carved their own separate but linked niches. Now, time grew short.

Susan Pea ruminated. With Janie to care for, Eve had no choice but to remarry after her first love's death. Her eyes stung and tears began to form as Susan Pea stood and kissed Eve on the forehead, silently wishing her freedom.

Quietly, Susan Pea glanced back at the lace curtains, at her friend, and left the room.

With Susan Pea's May arrival, the household had settled into a routine. She rose early and brushed Eve's hair, helped with her toiletries, and several times a week, assisted with a bath. On this particular June day, Eve, with her sister-in-law's help, donned a bright blouse, spritzed *Joy* on her neck and shoulders, and put on coral lipstick—all in an effort to keep her spirits up Afterwards, leaning into each other, they joined Letta in the kitchen where they sat around the table.

Eve cradled a cup of green tea, occasionally sipping it. Letta made sourdough biscuits, and, while they baked, drank coffee with Suan Pea. By the time they finished their first cup of coffee, Janie, fresh from her shower, joined them.

Letta rose, put her cup on the counter, and began to fix over easy eggs for Janie.

"I am going to work the dogs this morning with Wes," Janie said. A resounding silence ensued. Letta stopped. Susan Pea sat her mug down with a thunk.

Extending her hand to Janie, Eve tapped her daughter on the arm with a forefinger. "You can only go with Wes in the training field near the kennels. No jaunts off into those leases. They are too wild and too dangerous. You could trip and break a leg. Or something."

Janie shrugged at her mother's comment. Letta sat a plate of eggs before Janie, who began to eat with relish, sopping her biscuit in egg yolks.

Letta humphed. "Young woman ought not be out with no man gallivanting around anyway. Alone. Specially no older man who is womanizing trash. Folks talk."

Taken aback by her audacity, Susan Pea and Eve scrutinized Letta. The hall clock ticked off seconds, the sound pounding in the silence.

Eve touched Janie's arm. "Letta's right. You'll have to listen to your aunt and Letta. They'll be in charge after I'm gone."

Susan Pea cleared her throat. "Your mother's correct. Letta is, too. Kennel field only." A gray blanket of dread and self-doubt settled on her shoulders.

"When I go with Wes," Janie said, ignoring her mother's comment, "I work on my bird calls. I hear more sounds in the woods and along the creek than here."

"My sweet daughter, you have opened me to things I never thought about," Eve said. "You have given me an appreciation for bubble gum, bird songs, and pleasures of a hot day." She stroked Janie's arm. "I love you most dearly. Still, you need to listen—and abide by—what your aunt and Letta tell you. You are very young, brave, and have a great deal to learn."

They continued their breakfast in silence until the biscuits were consumed. Janie collected her cane and rose from the table. Mutt trundled beside her as she tapped out to catch her ride. She paused in the doorway and blew a kiss to her mother. "I love you, Mother. I wish you could live forever."

"I only want to live to see you a grown woman with your own path," Eve said. "After that, I'll be content. Here's an air kiss for you, too." She made a smacking noise in Janie's direction.

Fortified by tea and her time with Janie, Eve shifted to the porch, a fragile shadow, and sat watching the sun glint through the bottle tree, listened to the wind whisper secrets. She held a copy of Dante's *Divine Comedy*, occasionally caressed the cover, and fondled the page edges. She did not open it.

Classic literature had been her favorite, and the original element that drew her and Major together. In those early days, they'd read and debate the nuances of Dante's allegories. As time slipped by, their discussions grew argumentative. Dog-eared and underlined sections reflected changing thoughts. Now, her scribblings had faded, and page corners crumbled off. Still, Eve held the book in her lap and pondered over whether Major still read—or even thought—about the circles of hell.

She ruminated about her life with Major, how cancer had affected their lives, limited their time. She had not wanted another child, especially one with him. She often visualized the cancer, a deadly ally invited into her womb, enabling her to avoid his seed. It had given her relief, an ally that would release her from years of anguish, regret, and questions. But it also denied her seeing Janie grow into her own womanhood.

A Carolina wren hopped on the porch railing, a shifting reflection of Eve's musings. She had done what she could by marrying an ambitious man, albeit one of questionable integrity. If only she had secured Janie a better situation, she could leave without regret. As it stood, her daughter's welfare rested in the hands of Susan Pea and Andy. Sometimes Letta. All imperfect advocates, crippled by their histories, clinging to thin threads of caring.

While Eve sat outside, Susan Pea brewed a pot of strong coffee. Letta began clearing the table and running dishwater.

Susan Pea poured herself a cup of coffee, laced it with fresh cream. A special indulgence for herself. She gestured for Letta to follow suit.

The two lingered over their cups inside and kept a vigilant eye on the porch and Eve, allowing her time alone. They opined on the foolishness of men and how to handle the upcoming day.

Not until Eve stirred from the porch rocker, murmuring warnings in her husky voice-scratch for the haints to avoid anything blue, did Letta rise and begin the daily chores. Susan Pea joined Eve outside for the morning sunlight.

That evening, after Letta prepared supper and cleaned up at the mansion, she walked to her shack alone, in the dark, feet throbbing and back aching. Over the years, her toes had developed additional corns and her heart had grown heavier. She worried she did not have enough energy left to care for her own family.

CHAPTER SIXTEEN
WOMENFOLK

JANIE HAD SPENT the afternoon with her mother talking about the annual concert marking the end of school. She was to give a piano solo and sing two songs as part of the school's June closing. Gleefully, she had promised to give a pre-concert for family and friends as practice.

The morning of the special concert, Susan Pea threw open windows, allowed music to float out over the grounds. The aural calligraphy of bird calls set the stage for Janie and, ultimately, as she played, caused even nattering jays to pause and listen.

The day, a rehearsal for Janie's role at school, was a resounding success. Eve perked up, beaming, face full of color. Susan Pea radiated pleasure as she bustled about as designated hostess and proud auntie. The Episcopal priest and family doctor attended, outdoing the ladies with their enthusiastic clapping. The group appeared to pull energy from each other, relishing their shared conversation, jokes, and roles played within the Butler circle. Janie, like a napping cat in a sunny spot, basked in the group's praise.

Letta made a special lunch served buffet style in the formal dining room, for the gathering. Their comradery continued as they ate, traded friendly comments, and praised Janie. By early afternoon, the small group broke up, and went about their separate business.

Major had other obligations. He did not attend. Wes was not invited.

CHAPTER SEVENTEEN
JANIE BUTLER

AFTER THE GUESTS LEFT, Janie pulled a chair close to the bed, arranged herself, and held Eve's hand, traced protruding veins, petted paper-thin skin.

"I've learned some new poems. I can recite them for you." Janie's excitement at the poems was evident.

"New ones? That would be lovely," Eve said. "I'd like a few of old ones too. You make them sound special even when repeated over and over. I enjoy listening."

She released her mother's hand and resettled herself.

Reading had been a shared passion between Janie and her mother. When still a toddler, Eve had read to Janie, instilling a love of language, a reverence for how words reflected and enhanced life. Later, as Janie learned to memorize stories and read braille, she and Eve shared ever widening interests. Still later, they both found poems and settled on favorite poets for their shared afternoons.

Janie recited a new poem, her voice pirouetting across lines, while Eve drifted in and out of consciousness. Finally, she closed her eyes.

When Janie no longer perceived her mother's response, she moved closer, fumbled for the papery hand, and cradled it feeling its thin warmth ebb. Tears wet her face, dripped onto her lap, heavy as rain drops. She cried in a thin, child-like wail. Sliding off the chair, she slumped beside the bed still cuddling Eve's hand.

Letta, hearing the cry, stopped her evening chores. She stood at the edge of the makeshift bedroom, sensed Eve was no longer alive, knelt next to Janie, and gently put her arms around the girl. She rocked and hummed until Janie ceased sobbing and surrendered to the rocking.

"She gone, honey. Your mamma passed." Letta part-lifted Janie to her feet, part-held her, and helped her lie next to her mother.

Janie caressed her mother's face and cried until she gasped for breath.

Letta held Janie, patted her on the shoulder. Leaving the room, she muttered to herself, "I let that little girl say good-bye to her mama in her own way. I can't do no more for her now. Susan Pea be back shortly."

The striped cat jumped down from the windowsill, brushed against the bed frame, and disappeared into the house. A coolness settled as the light faded. Outside, an insect refrain intensified, rose, and fell, and rose again, sounds slipping through the open window.

Susan Pea gasped, her hand on her throat, and walked toward Eve's makeshift room. She stood in the doorway. Tears coursing down her face, she sat in the chair next to the bed until shadows stole high up, her hand caressing Janie.

The sun, sliding behind oak branches while crows gathered, sat on fence posts, and swooped into the grass hedges on the outer fringes of the yard. A signal crow set up such a racket, Mutt howled dolefully. By night the outside grew still. Eve, the linchpin holding the Butler family together as a unit, was gone. The disparate individuals, now adrift, grabbed at flotsam. Connections to the larger community were likewise severed. At midnight, Susan Pea rose, kissed Janie's cheek, and left the library, closing the door behind.

Janie stayed with her mother, tears spent, until a translucent dawn seeped into the room. She had dozed fitfully during the night, awaking when birds began their early hallelujah chorus, welcoming a new beginning. Exhausted, she slid from the bed and went to find Letta and Aunt Pea.

CHAPTER EIGHTEEN
FUNERAL

As BEFITTING the Butler family's community standing, a full choir accompanied by a pipe organ swelled out of the Eternal Salvation Baptist Church, the largest town edifice. Baptist preacher and Eve's Episcopal priest officiated as a team, moving between pulpit and altar.

Most of the county attended. Some attended fearing Major's scorn, while a few came out of morbid curiosity. Other folks appeared genuinely grief-stricken at Eve's passing and stood respectful of a life gone. They wept openly, dabbing their noses with cotton handkerchiefs.

Susan Pea, Janie, and Andy constituted a forlorn cluster in the front pews, knitted together in their misery. Grief numbed their thoughts, drowned out all but the moment. They fumbled wiping their noses frequently and held hands while pressed shoulder to shoulder. Janie hummed under her breath. Susan Pea sensed song vibrations flow among them, supporting them. Andy, home on leave, mustered efforts to remain soldier-like, his trim frame held rigid, dark eyes blood-shot.

Letta and her younger son, Elijah, sat stoic in the back pew, last row.

They wore their Sunday best. She with gloves, modest hat, and Elijah in a white shirt, wearing his pappy's tie.

Major, as a deacon, occupied a seat left of the central lectern. He gripped the chair arms until his knuckles became bloodless, sat immobile throughout the service, eyes locked on the stained-glass windows gracing the long aisle.

With the final amen, Major took a deep, rattling breath, rose, moved five steps from the sanctuary to Eve's casket. He removed his wedding band, placed it on the closed lid, and, staring straight ahead, strode out, acknowledging no one.

Sliding behind the wheel of his wine-red Lincoln, he cranked and drove toward Albany, home of his paramour.

A FAMILY RECEPTION, held in the parish hall, morphed into an overwhelming litany of condolences and platitudes.

Susan Pea, her face a mask, intoned, "Thank you for your sympathy," "Thank you for coming," "Thank you" until her voice collapsed into hoarseness, her strength ebbing with stress of acknowledging their kindness. Dazed, she silently touched the hands proffered to her.

Janie cried, without sound, tears coursing down her cheeks to drip onto her dress front. She clasped outstretched hands, unable to speak, thankful for the caring from school friends, teachers, and neighbors. Her young heart convulsed with sadness.

Standing in the receiving line, Andy continued until he found it unbearable. He stepped away and sought out Letta, working in the kitchen. She acknowledged him with a nod when he stepped into the bustle. She, and additional maids hired for the occasion, cooked, set out food, and washed dishes. Members of Letta's church community, they worked beside her, quietly recognized her sadness and her role in the family.

Her husband's death and his funeral had been a small affair, profoundly different from Eve's funeral. Her John had been denied leave to come to his own pappy's laying to rest. Andy, home for days with his stepmother's final days, emphasized Army's different consideration of the two men. Still, the Army taught John a new pride in himself, his skills, and his time out of Georgia. His letters home reflected that give and take of lessons, sometimes things he was not aware of.

Letta's community had gathered Elijah and Merry in their arms to rock and comfort them when her man was killed. For that, she was intensely grateful. And now, her people were working, taking care of Eve's laying to rest.

Baptist Auxiliary League women managed the ebb and flow between kitchen and fellowship hall, issuing directions in their shrill white voices—which bowl needed to be refilled and what plates to be cleared away. They directed the maids when to set out more fried chicken and deviled eggs.

Letta smiled ruefully, caught somewhere between being a family confidant and a household maid. She continued working, washing dishes, and rearranging food.

Evening shadows had dissolved into night by the time the last mourner departed, clean-up finalized, and the church closed.

ON THURSDAY, a fragile morning light cast gentle shadows over Eve's gravesite, moss strings dripped from the ancient oak. Susan Pea, Janie, and Andy stood nearby. Head on his paws, Mutt lay at Janie's feet.

Dressed in the same black sheath from Eve's earlier church service,

Susan Pea read several poems, her voice quivering—Walt Whitman, Emily Dickson. Fear, sadness, and defiance began a slow waltz across her thoughts. She had not planned on being left with Janie as her ward. Her shoulders tightened at the prospect. She took a deep breath, willing herself strength for the upcoming months.

Her young face swollen and bloated, Janie cried, not bothering to wipe away tears or mucus. Life seemed to be ending before it began. Hard choices crouched in ditches along her path. Mutt whined, his body leaning warm against her legs.

Letta—tall, enduring, silent—stood with her young son slightly apart, a few steps behind Janie. Neither Letta nor Elijah cried, they simply stood with bowed heads, clasping each other's hands. An aura of sadness surrounded them, mirrored by Sister Crow's flight as the final shovels of earth covered Eve's remains.

Wind caught moss strings, moved them in a slow dance. Sun speckled the ground in patterns large and small. Fresh dirt contrasted with the brown soil nearby.

Afterwards, no one spoke, each too grief filled. They drifted away separately, beginning to mull over life without Eve.

Janie sat in Eve's favorite chair on the porch and rocked, bereft. Mutt lay nearby.

Susan Pea wandered around the library, held three slim volumes of poetry, hugged them. She paused by the window and then sank onto the bed's edge, listless.

Andy, alone, leaned against the rough oak's bark and smoked.

Letta plodded toward her shack with Elijah. Lost in separate thoughts, neither spoke.

Major stayed in Albany.

During the night a steady rain, without lightning or thunder, soaked the grounds. Thus, did Evangeline Henderson Butler's mortal remains return to earth.

CHAPTER NINETEEN
MENFOLK

"DAMN IT TO HELL," Major bellowed as he entered the kennels, slamming the yard gate, stomping along the corridor toward Wes.

"What's got you all up in arms?" Wes instantly stiffened, grew wary. The atmosphere grew muddy.

"Eve interfering from the grave. She set up some meeting with that university man to come out. He's a disruption. What's his name?" Major's normally tanned complexion glowed red.

"You talking about that bird guy?" Wes said.

"Damn it, yes. That foreign man. Wants to talk about that stuff Eve set up. Hell if I feel like talking with some book freak." Major glanced and continued talking as he strode toward the end pens, paused, watched the dogs a moment. "Show him how the dogs work, flush a few coveys, go heavy on that conservation stuff, and get rid of him as soon as you can. Use Harry McKee's two pointers. Him and his kid can see how those dogs are coming along. Hunt the Corley Farm lease. Good cover there. Nice open meadow."

"Yes, sir." Wes gathered several leather leads preparatory to loading the dogs.

"Call the McKees," Major continued, "tell them to meet you there. You need to see what that place has to offer for this year anyway. Check it out." Major frowned and glanced at his watch. "Where the hell is that man? He's late."

Wes, face blank, watched his boss.

"Bring that .210 double-barrel shotgun for the Dutchman. Box of birdshot should be enough."

"Think we'll need guns?" Wes asked, aware that it was not hunting season and, even though they were going to be on paid lease, problems could arise.

"Private property. But just in case." Major waved his in hand in the air. "Always good to get stuff sized up, readied for the season. Besides, give you a change to see how that man handles a gun."

Wes shrugged. "Sure."

At Gunner's run, Major opened the gate, and sat on the slatted bench. He patted his knee, called the dog.

Wes picked up snap lines, turned toward the McKee pointers, both youngsters. "These two are coming along real nice. This'll be good practice for them." He doted on the dogs, but Major didn't hear, lost in his own thoughts.

Ten minutes later, a faded station wagon pulled into the driveway. Major scratched Gunner around his ears, gave a final pat, and reluctantly moved toward the front kennel gate. He considered the planned outing waste of time.

Wes, hip cocked, watched the boney professor settle his Dunmore fedora on his mostly bald head as he walked toward the kennels. He waved good naturedly as he neared them, introducing himself as he walked.

"Hello. My name is Pieter DeGroot." He spoke in heavily accented English and extended his hand.

Major stepped forward and clasped Pieter's outstretched hand. "Well, since my wife Eve wrote a check to your department for an endowment, I thought we should get better acquainted. She would have loved to have welcomed you. As it is, it's me. And my sister."

"*Ja, ja,* of course. I am pleased to represent the university in accepting the Evangeline Butler Ornithology Research Foundation honoring your wife. I believe your daughter Janie plans to study birds when she goes to University next year."

"Stepdaughter," Major said sharply. "Eve cooked up this deal. She had help from my sister. She'll join us in a few minutes."

"I was sad to hear of Mrs. Butler's death," Pieter said. "Accept, please, my sympathy. The research foundation will keep her memory alive."

Major's face quivered slightly and grew blank again as he looked Pieter up and down. At thirty-one and still a bachelor, Pieter DeGroot spoke of himself as a simple Dutch émigré who had originally taken a faculty position with the University of Georgia. Once settled in Athens, he had plunged into the university's biology program. His English was solid, except when nervous. Those times, he frequently lapsed into his native Dutch.

Southern tongues often had difficulty with Pieter. Most defaulted to calling him Doc Pete. Others called him Rosebud for the birthmark splattered under his jaw and down his neck.

Major cleared his throat. "I'll have to go along with Eve's cockamamie foundation. I don't agree. Nothing to be done about it now."

Pieter cocked his head and took a half-step back. "I understand you have kindly extended an invitation to hunt. I am looking forward to being out."

Regarded as an outsider, Pieter was tolerated by state game commission and locals since he worked with the university. Out of courtesy, they sporadically invited him on a weekend shoot. Pieter, for the sake of appearances, accepted occasionally.

Major waved his hand at Pieter's remark as if in dismissal. "I'll not be going with you. Wes has two other men, McKees, whose pointers he's training. He'll take care of everything. Their dogs are English pointers, got first-rate bloodlines, and strong potential to make respectable field dogs. McKees will meet y'all there. My sister Susan Pea will be going also. She can explain anything that you might have questions about."

"*Ja*, I had met Janie last year on campus when she came with your wife. Saw her again when Miss Susan Butler and she drove over late May. That was when I met Miss Butler. They are unique women." Peter pulled his gloves on, elbows jutting out at awkward angles. "Is Janie home today? I should say hello to her."

As if on cue, Susan Pea approached. "Good morning, Doctor DeGroot. I'm glad to see you again." She extended her hand with genuine warmth.

"*Ja*. It is pleasant to see you also, Miss Butler. I remember your too short visit earlier."

"Please, call me Susan."

"*Ja. Ja*. And you may call be Pieter. Like old friends."

Major drifted away.

Taking a deep breath, she continued, "I heard you ask about Janie. She's with her music teacher today. I'll tell her you said hello."

"*Ja*, that would be splendid."

Susan Pea chatted with Pieter and pointed out dogs in training as they strolled along the runs. "Did anyone tell you we'll be looking for quail today? Most folks around here call them bob whites or simply whites because of their three-note call."

"I know these birds. They are flecked brown, hard to see in brush. Their call is distinctive."

Wes watched them, then leaned over and spat. "I'll get those pointers loaded."

The Corley lease, more accessible than several other sites, was planted in row crops abutting piney woods and provided briar patches and ditch banks. Corn rows gave birds cover from predators, and, at harvest time, food. Prime quail habitat.

Despite its accessibility, the drive nonetheless proved jarring. They drove mostly in silence, glad McKees were to meet them and not share their ride over.

Once at the lease, the two men and Susan Pea climbed out of the jeep. Wes unloaded the dogs while Susan Pea and Pieter stretched and chatted. A few minutes later, a late model Ford pickup banged up the road and stopped. A cloud of dust settled over the small knot of people. Two men, one heavyset and loud, the other wiry, clambered out. Everyone introduced themselves and donned hunting vests. Wes handed the .210 to Pieter, shouldered his shotgun, and ignored Susan Pea. McKees each carried a gun.

The group walked twenty minutes across corn stubble. When one dog pointed, the second honored. Despite a strong point, the men still had to strain to see speckled quail ideally camouflaged in surrounding brush.

After several sightings, Wes leaned in toward Pieter, gestured toward the bird, and spoke soft. "Well, Mr. Professor, you take this shot." He inclined his head toward McKees. "Give these two fellers a chance to watch their dogs in action. If you do it right, those dogs will retrieve whatever you bring down."

Susan Pea stood several paces beside the men, lines around her eyes wrinkled into furrows. She listened as Wes coached Pieter.

His mouth dry and heart racing, Pieter raised the gun to his cheek, sighted. Susan Pea inclined her head toward him, offering unspoken assurance. Pieter pulled the trigger. Nothing. Blushing slightly, Pieter thumbed the safety off and took aim again, pulled the trigger.

The entire covey rose in an explosion of wings and whirring, their silhouettes soon dissolved in sunlight. Pointers bounded ahead, jumped above the stubble, and fell to sniffing, looking for a downed bird.

Pieter glanced at Wes with a sheepish grin. "I'm afraid I shot too early. The dogs will be disappointed."

Susan Pea walked forward, her Southern charm ready. "You're an academic, not a sportsman." She patted Pieter on the shoulder. "You'll have another chance. Don't worry. Everyone misses at one time or another."

Wes snorted, walked away, tossed words over his shoulder. "Wait until the dogs flush the covey, then shoot. Us southerners regard hunting, guns, and dogs as sacred. A man's sport."

Pieter's face grew warm at stress on 'man's sport'.

Wes took out a flask out of his pocket. "Here." He thrust the container at Pieter. "Take a swig. Might steady your nerves."

Pieter hesitated, shifted his feet, fumbled a moment, took a swallow, and returned the flask to Wes.

The more rotund of the two McKees stepped up, extended his hand. "Don't mind if I have a snort of that stuff. Wife's not here to frown." He belly-laughed, took a draught, then a second, and said, "Dogs held point. Steady to shot. They're working out."

He handed the flask to his younger companion, who took a long, deep pull. "Ah. Hits the spot." He smacked his lips, took a second pull and returned the container.

The group continued walking while Wes signaled the dogs ahead. A smaller covey scurried down field left of the dogs.

Pieter sneezed. Twice. Loud.

Birds ducked and hustled under broken corn stalks, downwind. The dogs lifted their heads, stood a moment, and continued their same line. The men frowned at Pieter, dark looks clouding their faces.

For Pieter, hunting quail held no appeal. They gave woods and fields personality with their three-note, bob-bob-white trill. Foxes, racoons, and possums balanced birds in a precise prey-predator reel.

Grateful today's hunt was game birds and not duck, Pieter moved forward. Chatter of duck rafts was pleasant, but marsh hunts were cold, wet, and uncomfortable, a stage setting for pneumonia. No doubt, men, shotguns, and *jachthond* skewed nature's balance to unequal, nonsporting.

Pieter didn't try to explain these things or his actions to others. He simply apologized. "*Ja*, I'm a bad shot. I did not hunt as a boy. Perhaps I would be better had I started at a younger age. As a man, I'm a bad shot."

At that precise moment, Pieter stepped into the scurrying periphery of a covey. Comparable to a grenade, a dozen or more exploded airbound and veered toward the pines.

Surprised, the younger McKee raised his gun to fire, but stumbled and sent his shot clipping off into grasses. The elder McKee danced out of the way.

Taken aback, Pieter hollered aloud as shot and dirt peppered his jacket. Susan Pea ducked low and, unable to suppress a giggle, watched McKee men flail about. Dogs bounded in the direction of disappearing birds.

Wes, his face dark, commanded the dogs. "Down, boys. Down." He gestured, brought the pointers under control.

"That dern well got my heart a going," McKee senior, color returning to his face, extended his hand. "Give me a pull on that flask." He sucked down two swallows of whiskey. "Always a good day when you don't get shot." He took another long pull on the flask, licked his lips.

The small hunting party began a slow amble further afield. After another hour, frequent pulls on the flask by McKees, and an empty bird bag, Wes, face dark and shoulders tense, called it a day. "Get these dogs back and taken care of. At least they did their job today."

Pieter apologized once more for his lack of shooting ability. And his allergies to dust. The tall man and his young partner, thoroughly mellowed with whiskey, but pleased with their dogs' performance, clapped him on the back.

"Bad luck today for everyone. Today was about dogs, not hunting. They worked really good. That's what I wanted to see. No harm, no fowl. No pun intended." Both McKees busted out laughing, delighted with his humor. They slapped Pieter and each other on the back. "There'll be another day."

Drinking the last of the whiskey, they shook hands all around, and wobbled toward their vehicles nonchalantly.

Susan Pea inclined her head at Pieter, knobby knees and all. She grinned. "I like your attitude."

Pieter beamed.

Wes leaned over and spat in the dirt, then loaded dogs.

CHAPTER TWENTY
WES SMITH

Despite personal misgivings, Wes met Major the week after Eve's funeral in a remote stretch of grassland along the Flint River Watershed. Not his choice, but he didn't intend to blow his chance to show off the shorthair by quibbling over the location. Even if it meant driving across the county and some fifteen miles down teeth-jarring washboard roads.

He realized most of Major's cronies favored English pointers or Brittany Spaniels. With that prejudice playing in his mind, it was weeks before Major agreed to draft the liver-ticked dog notwithstanding his natural hunting ability and tractable nature.

Despite having Otto in the kennels, additional weeks evaporated before Wes got the chance to work him in front of Major. The dog needed to be good enough to be kept in the kennel, but not good enough to pique Major's interest long term. Wes found himself balanced on a knife edge.

Parked near a sycamore stand, Wes worried, sensed sweat under his armpits, thought the area too tangled for a good trial. A mixture of woodland and open savannah would have been more reasonable. Dread slunk through his mind.

Loading the side-by-side with bird shot, extra shells in his vest pocket, Wes carefully double-checked the safety, laid the gun next to him, and dropped the tailgate. He leaned against it and waited.

When he had recommended purchasing the freckled German shorthair pointer as replacement for an aging Gunner, Major had grunted, rather vaguely, without comment. He chose not to face mortality—even by proxy in the form of his dog.

Forty-five minutes later, Wes spotted a rooster tail of dust from an approaching vehicle. A Jeep Willys pickup, a classy gentleman's choice, one step above a Chevy, took shape as it approached.

Major stopped the Jeep and parked. He stepped out, moved around to the passenger side, stuffed his vest with shells, unzipped the gun case, and slid the Winchester shotgun out. Turning, he ambled toward Wes.

Heavyset and bulky, Major walked with the rocking motion of a sailor on land. Past his prime, hands liver-spotted, he nonetheless oozed a predatory magnetism.

"Show me what that shorthair can do." Major placed an unlit cigar in his mouth.

"Yes, sir." Wes straightened, adjusted his cap. "Sedge is a bit thick here. Too close for good scent."

Major did not reply. He broke the double barrel, placed two unspent shells in, and snapped it closed. "We're here. Let's see what happens." He stood several yards away from Wes, eyes narrowed.

Wes fumbled with the crate latch, opened it, and released the dogs. He glanced sideways at the closed, loaded shotgun. Sweat lined his upper lip, made his face glisten. He struggled to remain neutral.

Dogs bounded out, jumped about a moment, and sat impatiently looking at the field. Otto whined.

"Let's get going," Major said.

With a quick whistle pip, Wes waved his arm in an arc across the field. "Get on, boys. Find 'em. Find 'em." Gunner and Otto whirled and bound over corn stubble, noses twitching.

For the better part of an hour, the dogs worked. Gunner serious, intent on his job. Otto flagging in spurts, lifting his head toward Wes, and spinning to follow Gunner's lead. Wes had trained toward standard field rules: Never rush training. Work a dog through an exercise several times, twice under same circumstances when possible. Vary settings.

Anxious, he glanced at his boss, attempted to gauge his reaction. Wes held his breath, realizing he wanted *good, but not too good.*

Major stepped around grass clumps, eyes scanning the trees. His gun, carried closed, rested light across his arm, muzzle pointing down, an unlit cigar clamped firm in his teeth.

The entourage walked for another half hour. Neither dog flushed a covey.

With his attention focused on dogs, Major did not look at Wes. "Throw your canvas chunk into those grasses yonder. I'll fire. Need to see how Otto reacts to live fire."

Wes tossed the decoy in a high arc above the two dogs. Shotgun boomed as the decoy hung in the air, began the fall, landed in the sedge. Grey-blue smoke trailed across the field, thin and spectral. Otto pounced on the canvas bundle, toyed with it a moment before he held it soft in his mouth, and trotted around to sat in front of Wes. The acidic odor hovered, slowly dissipated.

Major watched Otto—and Wes. He rolled the cigar in his mouth. "Butlers have owned and used classic pointers as long as I can remember." He broke the shotgun, put spent shells in a pocket, and reloaded. Snap it closed. Again. "This one will be the first time we've even considered a shorthair. A gentleman's dog should always be a complement to the hunt. He'll have to show me something more solid if he's to stay in *my* kennel."

Wes spoke, his voice steady. "He's collected and firm even when it's windy. He didn't cower with the shot. Held steady. Retrieved. I haven't worked him much with live fire." Wes thought to himself. *Balance. Keep it all steady. Train against his playfulness and develop his innate, bred-in-the-bone hunting instincts.* "I'll keep working him."

"Best get on with it." Major chewed the unlit cigar, spat out tobacco shreds. "My kennel. My dog. My say-so."

A gust kicked up, bent grasses low. Wes stood silent, scanned the field before finally turning to his boss. "Yes, sir."

"Set up a hunt, first day of quail season," Major said. "You'll need to work this boy so I can see stuff he's got. Otherwise, he goes back. I'm not interested in being embarrassed in front of my friends. Not interested in anything but perfect performance. *My* number one rule: bring in bag limit every time." He held up his index finger and repeated, "*Every* time."

"Yes, sir."

With a curt wave of his hand, Major dismissed any further demonstration. Wes whistled the dogs in. Major made a point of checking his load, then carried the side-by-side unbroken.

At the vehicles, Wes called dogs forward, snapped on leads, rewarded them with head pats, water, and signaled them into the crates. Still panting, they jumped gracefully onto the pickup, flopped down in their crates, and stared out through the wire. Wes removed their leads and slammed the tailgate closed.

Turning, he noticed Major's shotgun, carried low and loosely pointed in his direction. A gnawing started in his chest. He stepped to one side. The muzzle, still held low, casually tracked along with him.

Sweat slid down Wes's backbone. His hands felt greasy, too slick. Thoughts a jumble, he struggled to keep himself calm.

Face blank, Major stared off toward the road. Without turning to Wes, his voice level, he said, "You're the best gall-damn dog man I've ever seen. Bar none. You have a feel for dogs, for hunting, and for game. You worked both dogs impeccably, even in this terrain. You love this."

Major leaned slightly forward, spat into the grass, and glanced up at Wes. "Sort of too remote. Is that what you said?" He placed his finger inside the trigger guard.

Wes swallowed, Adam's apple jumping. His shirt, sweat-soaked, stuck to his back. An errant breeze made him shiver. "Yes sir, it's far out. Too thick. Trappy. But quail like cover so there's always good shooting here."

"Not the kind of place most people would hunt." Major shifted the gun across his forearm, raised it buckle level, and continued in a flat manner. "Not a place most people would even *come* to. But it's one of my favorites. Especially when you need to get down to real business. You know, test the dogs."

Wes stood straight, eyes locked on his boss, breathing consciously slowed. Sweat in half-moons staining his shirt. "No, sir, most won't come."

"You know my daughter Janie," Major said. "I'd be displeased if anything *inappropriate* happened to her. You know, something to *embarrass* the Butler name. An incident *I* might not be keen on." He regarded Wes, lifted an eyebrow, and pulled his mouth into a thin, hard non-smile.

Wes shifted. *What did Major know? From who? Damn it to hell and back, he was no longer in the catbird seat.* Major's gun muzzle, still at buckle level, tracked with him.

"Like I say, you are one fine dog man. Your job is training bird dogs. That's *all*. Understand?"

Without lowering the gun, Major stood splay-legged, eyes hard.

Throat contracted and mouth too dry, not even moisture to spit, Wes stood rigid, still. Wind whispered through pines, soft and mournful.

Slow, deliberate, Major nodded, his finger resting on the trigger. The muzzle inched up, pointed slightly above midline. "It'd take quite a while for anyone to discover a body here," he said. "You know, should any *accident* happen."

A dark cloud floated across the sun, its shadow long, lingering. Silence echoed. A wind picked up and moved over grasses, bending them toward the ground.

The shotgun snapped open, the sound jolting, harsh. Wes flinched.

Major pulled shells and dropped them in his hunt vest. He placed the shotgun in its case, climbed into the Jeep, and, without a backward glance, drove toward the dirt road.

Not until the telltale dust cloud vanished did Wes move. He wiped sweat off his face, breath coming in rough gasps, realizing Major might actually kill him. The dogs scuffing in their crates the last thing he would ever hear.

A GRASSHOPPER JUMPED from one bent grass stem to another and a third before it vanished. The scent of resin and dust drifted across the weeds.

Late afternoon settled when Wes returned to the kennels. Shoulders still tight, he leaned against the barn door a full minute before he flipped on inside lights. Straightening, he twisted the faucet on, drank from the hose, and sloshed water across his face.

He put the two hunters in their runs and began his evening chores feeding Sadie, her puppies, and other dogs. He put a dish of kibbles down for the ginger tom, stroked him around ears and along its back. It purred.

No matter any outcome, he loved the feel of the woods, the buzz of the open fields, and his dogs. Hell, he even felt tender toward that one-eyed tom. He stroked the cat again, envying its independence.

The thought of Otto's papers played in his thoughts. To hell with marriage plans. Maybe Susan Pea was his best hope—but could he trust her?

CHAPTER TWENTY-ONE
SUSAN PEA BUTLER

THOSE FIRST WEEKS after Eve's death, days skulked by, leaving Susan Pea uneasy. The passage of time should reduce the ache she harbored—and her guilt at abandoning Eve. As teens in high school, they had become lovers, entered a forbidden world.

Eve, ever pragmatic, had accepted Susan Pea's advances and returned them without judgement. But Eve needed to escape her grinding poverty. She wanted a more established, socially acceptable option. Heterosexual marriage.

Within the space of seven years, Eve had married, delivered a daughter, and become a widow. Her husband, killed in an auto accident, had left Janie an orphan. Marriage to an older, well-heeled Major, her best choice.

Angry, feeling betrayed, a too-young Susan Pea focused on others—females and males, gays and straights—to soothe her crushed desires. In the process, she discovered crossing sexual lines could be accomplished on a variety of levels. Not until that fateful night in Atlanta and Major's abruptly delivered bus ticket, did she begin finding her own way.

With Eve's passing, a new morning routine took root. Susan Pea sat listless drinking coffee, while Letta busied herself with whatever household chore called first.

Distant and distracted even with Wes, Janie wandered though her days, lonely, unmoored. Late in the afternoons, she and Mutt walked around the kennel training field.

Susan Pea felt a certain relief after a few lost weeks, when Janie doubled down on work with her school tutor and the piano teacher.

Letta, watching from the kitchen window, felt a physical ache for both her daughter Merry and Janie. They needed help negotiating shoals before them. Merry, young and impressible, would have to deal with her skin color much as Janie would deal with her sightlessness. As a housekeeper, Letta dared not approach the waif. Threads between them unraveled, other bonds woven.

Neither could she hold and comfort her own daughter Merry. For the present, Merry was hidden in her auntie's cabin nestled miles deep in piney woods. Plans for travel north were almost at fruition.

At summer's solstice, a promise of rain hung in the sky, but failed to materialize. Hounds lazed lethargic in their runs.

Letta spent time tending the household garden, pulling weeds, muttering to plants, picking okra, shelling peas. When the heat grew too intense, she ambled inside to mop, do laundry, and clean.

Susan Pea gathered her thoughts and options, inserted herself into the household routine as reigning matriarch. Letta, having seen Janie throw up in a flower bed earlier, told her, creating an avalanche of confusion and hurt. She directed her anger at Letta. How did she know these things? How dare a housekeeper know before she, Janie's aunt, found out? Resentment swelled toward Letta. Afraid of caring for Janie alone, Susan Pea did not confront Letta. Rather, she criticized the woman. Dinner was served cold. She was neglecting garden chores.

Weeds had not been pulled. Okra was going to seed pods. Floors had not been properly mopped. Laundry was piling up.

For her part, Letta muttered to herself, avoided Susan Pea as much as possible. Often she worked outside in heavy heat to be alone. Kept her thoughts to herself.

Susan Pea had crinkled her face at the quandary, grew disgusted with Wes and the swell to Janie's belly. No sense picking at scabs. For better or worse, Eve should have been the one to handle this mess. Today, she stood at the kitchen window watching Wes as he strode to the kennels.

Light shards filtered through water spots on the kitchen window, spilled onto linoleum. Lifeless flies lay between the screen and glass. A rust stain marred the porcelain sink.

Mutt sat near the door, his tail thumping on pine flooring. The striped cat wandered in, wound around chair legs, and brushed against Janie.

Patting her lap, she invited the cat to jump. It curled into a circle and purred, claws sheathed.

Once Wes was out of her sight, Susan Pea made her way to the table, and sat opposite Janie, pulled her morning into focus. "Sweetie-girl, you don't seem to be feeling well. Is something wrong?" Her usually crisp demeanor and slow drawl took on a frayed edge.

"Why do you think anything is wrong with me? Mother just died. What was wrong was her cancer. Now I'm alone." Janie's voice rose a notch. She sat rigid in the chair.

"Well, you've thrown up several times over the last weeks. Letta told me."

Janie turned her head away from her aunt.

Susan Pea spoke in a calm voice. "A young lady does not usually heave every morning. She doesn't get picky about her food. She doesn't call fresh-baked biscuits moldy-smelling."

Susan Pea gently turned Janie's head back toward her, stroked her niece's cheek.

Janie caught her breath and pushed Susan Pea's hand away. "You don't know anything.

"I know that I suspect you are pregnant."

The girl's face changed in the imperfect light. "I'm not." Her lips formed into a pout. She shook her head.

Susan Pea, drawn to Wes once when she had sorted through her own sexuality, had seen him as handsome, a talented bad boy. She understood Janie's attraction. Tried to be gentle. "You are attracted to Wes. Could it be he's pulled you into this deliberately? Taken advantage of you?"

Janie's voice rose an octave. "What if he did. I'm almost grown. I deserve to be treated that way." Hands fisted on the tabletop, she remained unbending, tense. "Besides, Wes, thinks I'm different, special."

A shiver swept over Susan Pea. "You've got a lot to learn about yourself and men and life." Susan Pea sat back and propped her elbows on the table, spoke calmly, attempting to diffuse rising tension.

Janie sniffed, remained rigid.

Susan Pea stood, refilled her coffee mug, and leaned against the kitchen counter. Yes, almost grown. A striking young woman with those curls and dimples. I'll even admit you've got curves to set any guy on fire." She placed her mug on the counter and returned to the table. "But, I think it will be hard for you to raise a child. Especially if you must do it as a single mother."

"I'll not be alone. Wes will marry me. I know you think he's not our kind, but he loves me. Me. He doesn't pity me and worry because I can't see."

Susan Pea pursed her lips. Her mind spun. *He cares for that pointer and maybe the one-eyed tom cat, but that's the extent of his loving. For sure he's got no feelings for those women he has strung along.* She took a deep breath. "Do you believe him?"

"Yes! Yes, over and over again. I believe him." Janie sat erect, her head rotated in Susan Pea's direction. "I'll keep my baby, our baby. I'll love it. I'll raise it alone if I have to." Her voice grew jagged.

"How do you propose to do that?" Head angled, Susan Pea watched as Janie blinked, struggled to control her tears, gulped air.

"I know he loves Otto and cares for that one-eyed tom," Susan Pea said. "He loves hunting. But most of all, he loves himself. Himself."

"Me! He loves me." Janie jutted her chin forward.

"Wes is ruthless." Susan Pea's voice was flat.

"You're wrong."

"You know as well as I," Susan Pea said, "Major will fire him as soon as he even thinks you and Wes are lovers. He'll probably figure out a way to kill him." She tasted bile rise in her throat.. Without doubt, Major, with war blood on his hands, continued to be capable of murder despite his civilian status.

She harbored mixed feelings about Wes.

"No! He can't do that! I'm not going to tell Major. You don't either. He won't find out if you don't tell." Janie sat still. She blinked several times. "I need to talk with Wes first."

Susan Pea, hands shaking in disbelief, blinked several times. She watched Janie's face change from crying to determined.

"He says he's got one chance to make a name for himself," Janie said. "He can train field dogs for wing-shooting. That's why he works for Major. That's his way out of Lee Town, out of Georgia."

Susan Pea drew her breath, exhaled slowly. "If that's true, what does he plan to do with you?"

Eyes widened, Janie covered her face with her hands, hiccupping between sobs. She shook her head as if to clear cobwebs, blurted uncontrollably. "Supposed it's Major's. Would that make a difference?" Janie's bottom lip quivered. Tears coursed down her cheeks.

Susan Pea grew still. The house seemed to hold its breath.

Janie knew in an instant she had gone too far. She blew her nose and turned away. "What did you say?" Susan Pea fairly hissed at Janie. With no immediate answer, she pushed. "Are you trying to tell me something? Sweet Jesus, Mary, and Holy Joseph. Are you saying Major has been at you? When did he start this?" Frowning, she clutched her stomach to keep from heaving. She coughed, continued to hold herself.

Janie blew her nose, already raw from dripping. "I mean," she blew her nose again, shook her head. "I don't know. I just said that to see what you would do. I'm all mixed up." She wiped at her eyes, sniffed. "Would it make a difference?"

"You need to tell me the truth." Susan Pea eyes narrowed, her voice cracked. "Did Major ever lay with you? This is extremely important."

Janie fumbled with a Kleenex. Her voice sounded as if from a distance. "Mother got sick. She couldn't get out anymore. At first, he said I reminded him of Mother when they first got married. He said he needed me." Janie's voice was nearly unintelligible. "Said he didn't want to aggravate Mother with his man needs—she was too sick."

"Man needs?" Susan Pea fought to keep her voice steady. "Damn him and his purple cock. He's got a woman in Albany who's supposed to take care of that nasty chore."

Janie startled at the pronouncement, began to explain. "I told Letta. She called him evil. Said not to let him touch me. She said you'd come home and you would handle this Butler meanness."

"When did this happen?" Susan Pea's stomach churned.

"I don't remember. Maybe February before you got here." Janie snuffed.

Silent, Susan Pea took a deep breath, rage welled-up, made her face hot. Her thoughts raced in circles. *Damn his soul. He scares me.*

Janie hiccupped again. "Letta said Wes was a womanizer. She said Major was incestuous. I shouldn't have anything to do with either one. She said she was afraid for me, said I was too young and didn't know about men."

"She's right." Susan Pea's voice vibrated hoarsely. "Letta did call me. She was cryptic. Said I needed to get home to protect you. Help Eve with her dying."

They sat silent. A weak odor of honeysuckle wafted through on a breeze. The clock ticked loudly, striking off minutes before anyone spoke.

"Eve and I sorta stayed in touch over the years," Susan Pea said. "We talked on the phone, not often, but enough. When she came to visit in New York, she already had cancer. That's when she admitted she might need help keeping you protected." A vein protruded, pulsed along her temples. Susan Pea rubbed the throbbing with her fingertips. "I should have stayed in closer touch. Didn't want to think about coming back here, living here. I sure as hell didn't want to be around Major. Now I feel guilty."

"I lied about Major. He's tried but never did anything except touch me," Janie said. "I love Wes. *I want him.*"

Janie's voice pulled Susan Pea back to the moment. She shifted her weight. The chair creaked. The kitchen faucet dripped, echoed off walls.

"You don't approve," Janie said. "You flinched. I know what you're thinking, how can a blind girl have a baby? Especially when she's not married. People will talk." She sat back, palms flat.

"Suppose Major decides to kill him?" Janie gasped. "No!" She began to sob again, her hands shaking. "No." She clinched her fists, drummed them on the table. "No, no, no…"

Susan Pea caught Janie's fists, gently held them down with one hand. With her free hand, she wiped Janie's tears, stroked her hair.

"Aunt Pea, you have to stay here." Janie stopped her rant, jutted her chin forward, and straightened. "You gave Mother your word you'd protect me."

"Oh, Sweetie, I fear for you. Marriage and babies are not something to trifle with. They're not trading tokens, bargaining chips. Especially when you're dealing with Major or Wes. Neither man is what you'd call honest or family oriented."

"Help me. You can live here. I want my baby. I want Wes. You can help me. If you stay."

The house creaked and moaned with thoughts from previous Butler women. Secrets stacked in corners, interspersed with dust, no reprieve tendered.

"One of the last times Eve called me," Susan Pea said, her jaw muscles bulging, "she rambled on about blue bottle trees filled with haints. Said she couldn't protect you. Not against Major. Said Letta was trying to help but Major had done something terrible to her daughter. She needed to take care of her own first."

Janie put her hands over her face, sobbed. Susan Pea slumped in her chair, rubbed her forehead. The house grew quiet as if holding its breath.

"I'm so confused," Janie said. "Major never did anything but touch me. He only did it once. Afterwards he left. Letta told me he went to Albany, stayed with his woman friend." Janie wiped her nose with her shirt tail.

"I want a family since Mother's gone."

"But Wes?" Susan Pea said. "He's older than you, much older. Besides, he's low class and a womanizer to boot. He has no idea what faithful means. Doesn't know love or loving." She took a deep breath, her mind spinning over past weeks, and steadied herself. "Maybe Major would kill Wes. He may not do that, but he can make it difficult for everyone." Guilt gnawed bone deep. If only she had come back when Eve asked, Janie would not be in this predicament. Nothing to do but help clean up this whole affair.

The tiger-striped cat jumped down from Janie's lap and sauntered off. A green fly buzzed at the window, thumping off the glass. The low hum of a fan created white noise.

Janie sat up, gasped in realization. "Wait a minute. This house is mine since Mother's gone." She whacked her hands on the table edge, her face glowing. "In a trust. Mother made Major give it to me. Before she died. She told me it was to be mine."

Susan Pea cleared her throat, her mind still reeling. "I see."

"Wes and I can live here. We don't need Major." Janie's voice rose as she spoke. "I can buy Wes a kennel. You can live here, too."

"Doesn't Major control everything until you're twenty-one?" Susan Pea raised her voice, took on an anxious note. "He certainly kept Eve dependent, abused her emotionally. I doubt you get control of whatever is left to you in a will until you are older. Maybe longer."

"I'm not sure." Janie paused in her excitement, grew reflective.

"Before you make too many plans, let's find out specifically what he can and can't do."

Lost in separate thoughts, they sat still, neither moving for moments. Finally, Susan Pea kneaded her temples, spoke in a trembling voice.

"Once, you asked me about New York." Her voice echoed from a distant past memory. "I didn't run off on a whim. Major kicked me out." Her eyes burned at the memory.

"Kicked out? Why?"

Susan Pea glanced down at her hands.

Janie blinked, wiped her cheeks, and spread her fingers wide in a questioning gesture. "People say you wanted to be with women. Isn't that why you left?"

"Not entirely." The shame Susan Pea had experienced at being forced to leave played out in colors yet again.

Her lips tightened and her face wrinkled into furrows. She spoke in a tired voice. "I was rounded up at a house party in Atlanta. Noise complaint. Someone called the law. We were all underage, drunk, smoking grass, general debauchery. I dropped my brother's name, thinking it would get me off, but it just got me in more trouble. He told them to drive me home. He'd take care of things. They dumped me off at the house."

Janie gasped, disbelief ringing in her voice. "Dumped you off?"

"Yeah." Susan Pea considered again the deputies driving, their leering, dirty laughs, and lewd comments. Her face hot and pulsing, she had fluctuated between humiliation and defiance the entire distance between Atlanta and home.

Her voice faded to a whisper, an old hurt sharp again. "The month after graduation, he threw a bus ticket at me across the breakfast table. Said not to come back. He said no matter how big a basketball star I was, or how many times I got crowned homecoming queen, he wanted me gone."

"But you're his sister."

Susan Pea snorted. "Yeah, even Letta choked. Since I was his sister, he saw me as a blemish on the family name. He looks after his own interests first. Ha! Think about it, Letta's bottle tree only affects haints, ghosts, not those living."

Janie groped for her aunt's hand. Held it.

"Damn Major to hell, but I was so lost and alone," Susan Pea said. "Took a long time for me to find my feet. Leaving turned out to be like chewing gum. Keeps your mouth busy, but no real substance."

Tears glistened on her cheeks, dripped off her jaw. She smeared mucus across her face, her voice growing defiant. "At first, I thought I was lucky. Went to Queens College awhile, then fell into other things.

But, seemed like something kept trying to pull me back. If you stop and think about it, Big Apple's got no more tolerance than here. Just more people to spread it through. Harder to a get a job there. Especially for women. Or at least anything with a good salary. Racism and prejudice smother me in both places."

Janie squeezed Susan Pea's hand. "I'm sorry."

"Well, I did find my soulmate while there."

"Soulmate? What happened?"

"She moved to Boston when I left. We were complete opposites. I miss her."

"What's her name?"

"Theresa Scalia." As the name rolled off her tongue, Susan Pea stilled, her thoughts roaming back through the years. Their good times, sad events, and the synergism of the relationship.

"Tell me."

Susan Pea tucked an errant strand of hair behind her ear. Her voice caught slightly; she cleared her throat, and spoke from far away.

"Theresa was third generation Italian-Catholic, dark hair, and olive skin. We were quite a pair, what with me being Scotch-Irish, Baptist, fair, and freckled. She taught me about cooking and religion. I taught her sports and Southern literature. I loved cooking but never took to religion."

"How did you meet her?"

"We met at the 'Y' playing on a city basketball league. Got drawn to each other and went places together—Knicks' round ball games, Rangers' hockey, cocktail parties, street fairs, local concerts, coffee houses." The clock chimed twice, a relentless nibbling away of time. The house creaked and sighed with lost dreams and Butler angst. Outside in a faint breeze, bottles jingled, gleamed in sunlight. Haints floated free, mischief streaming behind in long, smoke-blue trails.

CHAPTER TWENTY-TWO
ANDY BUTLER

Johnny Reb's Pool Parlor, located on the rough side of Decatur County, was a hangout for white males as long as Andy could remember.

He stood at the door and reflected on that afternoon, at eighteen, when a fight had changed his life's trajectory. Years prior, it had been a day spindled on a testosterone-laced experience within these same dingy walls. Eve had still been alive.

Then, as now, he paused while his eyes adjusted from sunlight glare to dim, smoke-filled pool hall. The place appeared much the same, intervening years had not changed it since he last entered its portal. Odors of stale sweat, urine, and sour beer still dominated.

A half-dozen game tables aligned in stiff order, filled the dilapidated establishment. Wood stools along walls, rigid as soldiers, accommodated hangers-on and spectators. Next to the hallway door leading to toilets, cue racks hung on wall. A narrow bar dispensing beer slouched along the opposite end.

ANDY HAD ORDERED a beer that day. After his second round, he had pushed away from his stool and racked balls for solo practice. Selecting a cue stick, he leaned and bridged his stick across felt. The sharp crack of ball-on-cue ball ricocheted around the room.

A shaft of light sliced through the room as three individuals entered the pool hall. They stood a moment as a pack and then walked toward the pool tables.

"What do we have here? The great Bearcat football hero done come by. Or, should I say, the great Butler running back."

Andy did not look up. Didn't have to. He recognized the twang-accent immediately. Lee Town bullies. Rednecks. Memories of treading Bainbridge High halls still fresh despite the years, played out. Notwithstanding his football and in-crowd status, these three continued harassing.

He allowed balls to finish the break spin before he re-chalked. "I thought they took the last of the trash out long ago. Surprised to see ridge runner allowed back in here," Andy said, focused on the table, not giving them the respect of a direct look.

"That a fact?" shorter of the three responded.

Andy chalked his cue and bent across the table corner, positioned for his next shot. "Yeah. It's a fact."

"Out looking to see how other half lives?" a thin hawk nose fellow spoke. "Or are you looking for real snatch, instead of that cheerleader, cotton candy stuff?"

"I see you boys still wallowing in mud with other low life." Andy stood tall, placed his cue on the table, and, legs splayed wide, smiled. "Best part of you dripped down your mama's leg." His voice stayed flat.

The three exchanged smirks. The tallest spoke, his response sharp.

"Maybe you're over here pimping that bull dyke aunt of yours. Fat chance on any takers. We want real women in these parts."

Andy's mind registered raw steak when he slammed his fist into the tall one's face. Shock waves vibrated up his arm into his shoulder joint.

"You need to keep your fucking mouth closed." Andy spoke through clenched teeth and slammed his fist into the man's belly, grunting with effort. He drew back for another swing—never delivered. A pool stick thudded against his head, his knees buckled, followed by two swift gut kicks. A foot smashed into his hands clutched across his belly, breaking several fingers. A darkness descended as he lost consciousness.

He came to in the county drunk tank, dehydrated, on the floor. He rolled to his knees and tried to push cotton off his tongue. Ammonia odors seared his nostrils and metal-on-metal sounds clanked down the corridor. He held his hand before his face. Purple, swollen, throbbing.

A jailer stopped in front of the tank. "Hey, Butler, Major's wife is taking care of bail. Nice to have connections. Even if it is a stepmother."

"What happened to sumbitch egg sucker who did this?" He waved his hand and wiped his mouth across his sleeve. It stank of beer and was stained with dried blood.

"They left town on a fishing trip." The man smirked. "Who's to say what really happened? All's I can say is, Major sees you at his office four o'clock tomorrow. Good thing you got strings pulled for you."

"What the holy hell? They beat shit out of me, break my fingers, and I'm swimming in the drunk tank? What kind of deal is this?"

"Not my business."

"Do I get a doc for my hand?"

"Ask Major when you see him." Jailer walked away, disappearing down the corridor. The process, a bit convoluted and tedious, functioned well enough for him to make his appointment with Major. Sheriff drove him over. A bondsman met them in the office foyer. Sheriff waited outside, sweating in the heat.

Major leaned across his massive, mahogany desk, removed a half-smoked cigar from his mouth, and watched Andy as he walked into the office. "You've had it a bit too easy, living here as a Butler." Major's voice was neutral, even pleasant.

"I never asked for anything." Andy remained standing.

"No, you never did. Butlers that came before you fixed things, so you'd not want for anything." Major scowled at Andy. When he spoke again, his voice vibrated with anger. "What do they get? What do *I* get? You brawling in public. In a pool joint. And ya *lost*. To *trash*." He placed his cigar in a glass tray, lips curled in indignation, and leaned back. The leather chair squeaked in protest. He rocked a moment on casters, still angry.

"You've got no dice in this game. Not this time," Andy said. "You are —what do you call it—declining to represent me?" His face sweaty, hand throbbing, he frowned at Major.

"In the strictest sense, decline is correct. But you are in my county. And, without brag, I'm the best lawyer in this one-horse town. In fact, if I weren't a modest man, I'd say the best in the state."

Andy's mouth twitched. He shuddered.

"But today, let's say I'm handing out free *fatherly* advice, rather than legal advice." He rose, hovered near Andy a moment, and moved to a window overlooking town.

"I'm gonna need Vaseline for this." Andy muttered, anger coloring his words.

Major looked out the window a moment. "I'd prefer to call it a *choice*. You see, charges have been filed for public intoxication and assault with intent to damage a fellow human." His voice sarcastic.

"I didn't start that confrontation with those stump jumpers."

"You didn't finish it either." Major tented his fingers and spoke with a hard edge to his voice. "Contrary to your comment, I understand you threw first punch."

"Against three bullies."

"Well, no matter. You lost. In fact, right now, you are headed, as common folk are prone to say, down an open sewer."

"You got any idea what people are saying about your sister?" Andy asked.

The oxblood-dark leather chair complained as Major shifted his weight. "Doesn't matter what people say. She is no longer in the picture as she has been sent away. I have that ability, you understand me, boy? I will not have *you* be a smear on the Butler name."

Disbelief and frustration were written across Andy's face. Sweat greased his armpits and a headache bloomed in red swirls.

Major took a deep breath and spoke again. "I sent her north as soon as she graduated. *Sent.* She was, and is, a family smear."

The clock's distinct ticking echoed off office walls. Neither man spoke for long moments. Major pulled his chair closer rested his arms on the desk's polished surface. "You'll go before state magistrate when a date is set. He's known to forgive local transgressions whenever a young man sees his way clear to join his country in fighting communism."

He shifted again. "Let's consider a hypothetical scenario. Suppose you go before a court that is unsympathetic to able-bodied young men, fighting in a bar instead of serving their country. You have heard of that fracas over in Vietnam, haven't you?"

"You sanctimonious old bastard. You know I'm slated for law school." A fleeting glimpse of his law career vanishing under a conviction flashed before Andy.

"Are you saying you don't want to do your duty? Serve your country?" Major arched an eyebrow. "Don't cut me any slack. I can make my own way."

"Best control yourself. Contempt of court is not a trifling matter. Consequences can be steep."

Major slid a file from the desk side to center, opened it, signed several papers. He closed the folder and continued talking.

"Regrettably, you are the only Butler left to carry the name forward. That pains me. I am therefore persuaded to *give* you advice. I suggest you plead no contest to assault, throw yourself on court mercy, and join the Army." He buzzed his law clerk Thomas Alexander and handled the folder across. "Otherwise, I believe Georgia Department of Corrections has an open cell you could occupy." Major offered up a mirthless twist of his mouth. "Public intoxication and brawling, or honorable service to your country. Your choice."

Major scribbled his signature on a page, handed the file to Thomas. He took it and left as quietly as he entered.

"What about my hand?"

"The jailer said you might need a doctor. Army needs men with two good hands. I'll get a doctor to you as soon as you make your decision. You can let jailer know. He'll convey your answer."

REFLECTING ON DECADES-OLD EVENTS, Andy, by a stroke of fate, had shed his small-town Butler notoriety, entered a life of blood and guts and by-the-book discipline. He had joined the Army. Become a career officer.

Coming home for his stepmother's funeral brought the decades-old memory into focus. He hadn't thought of it recently. He flexed his hand, reflected on the two broken fingers now healed slightly crooked.

Although he hated Major and what he had done, it had been a blessing in disguise. He flexed his hand again. His angst still festered, felt hurtful.

He had seen the pompous old brute at the public funeral for Eve. Thankfully, he hadn't stayed for the family ceremony under the ancient oak. Andy had no intention of staying long, but Aunt Susan implored. "Janie needs us, all of us. She's alone in a way she's never been before. Stay."

In the end, Andy extended his leave. His aunt simply hugged him. "We're all needing to do things together. You. Me. Letta." She sighed. "Even Wes."

At mention of Wes, Andy grimaced, glanced down at his crooked fingers.

Noticing the grimace, Susan Pea said, "Let's not be rash. Not just yet. Wes and Major are knight and king in this chess game. You might be suspicious of Wes, even hold a grudge against him, but he's important to Janie. Major, too. Let dust settle first."

He had paused, glanced off, finally said, "Okay. For the time being." He flexed his hand again. Support was not something that came to Butler men easily. Nor did patience.

CHAPTER TWENTY-THREE
JOHN DAVIS

John had joined the Army a year after high school graduation. He rotated through bootcamp and shipped for Vietnam. He and Letta had planned his enlistment as a new beginning, away from Georgia.

Discharged months later as a sergeant, his two tours complete, John boxed his expert marksman badge away and returned his rifle to the quartermaster. Army regulations. Returning his rifle felt like returning part of his worthiness, part of his dignity. He loved the feel of that weapon, its lethal sleekness, its authority. Silently, he swore he'd always own a gun.

He had put great hope in the military, only to have it crushed when denied leave to return home for his pappy's funeral. Although his momma had not asked it of him, he veered homeward. With his pappy's death, he thought it necessary, felt obligated to assume man-of-the-family role.

He rode a Greyhound bus home. Drivers consistently gestured to the seats in the rear.

"Place for you back yonder, boy."

They always looked over his shoulder or stared at him in the mirror, never spoke personally to his face.

White resentment at his uniform became more evident the closer to Georgia he got. Getting off at various stops to stretch his legs, John avoided men clustered in groups. They idly watched him, chewed tobacco, scratched their crotches. Women crossed the sidewalk, subtly clutched their purses tighter, avoided walking too close. Remarks were made.

"Don't get uppity."

"That uniform don't cover up nothing. You still a spook."

"Remember your place. Stay with your own kind."

He knew signs, knew his place, and recognized when he crossed into the Deep South by increased, amplified expletives. Fury festered inside his chest. His stomach knotted. Color discrimination grew in the most unlikely places, followed him in various guises. Boundaries outside South were often indistinct, creating a false sense of equality. He only saw subtilties, like differences between purgatory and hell. Carefully, he assumed a passive face.

Northern cities gave way to heat and humidity, to undulating pastures, woods, and, occasionally, a rural church, middle of nowhere. Derelict farmhouses stared out through broken or boarded up windows. Along flat land, homes crouched among weeds and sagging fences. Strip malls appeared, fast-food joints, tractor-supply places, and dollar stores. Every town had a basic supermarket and a greasy spoon, mom-and-pop cafe, occasionally a faded Mexican restaurant. Potholes peppered main street. Neighborhoods looked exhausted. Poor. Even *whites only* places appeared worn down. Red dirt of Georgia, his rural home, lay as fractured as the day he had left.

John questioned his decision to return. He had few job opportunities to explore. Discrimination from law enforcement was rampant.

Only shabbiest of housing was available for his kind. From streets to courtrooms, justice was unequally applied.

On the other hand, his mama needed him for his earning potential as well as his emotional support. His brother Elijah, within a year of graduation, needed a big brother as role model. Male protection could always be used for his mama and his sister Merry. His closest family members had moved north and reestablished their lives.

Despite new laws suggesting equality among races, John had experienced some changes. Army had helped him with that. It had also instilled a new pride in himself.

Adjustments would be harder.

CHAPTER TWENTY-FOUR
SUSAN PEA BUTLER

HEARING her niece scuffing around upstairs getting ready for the day, Susan Pea yelled , "Breakfast is ready, Janie!" She wiped her hands on a dish towel and looked around fretfully. "I can't find my keys." Exasperated with herself, she hollered again to Janie, "I'll be back in a minute, honey. Pour yourself some milk. Biscuits and sausage today. Yours is on a plate on the counter. Butter is on the table. I'm looking for my keys."

"No worries, Aunt Pea, I've got it under control," Janie called back.

Backdoor thunked closed against the wooden frame as Susan Pea dashed out to check the kennel feed room.

Janie finished her routine and tapped down into the kitchen. She propped her cane near the doorway, felt her way along the counter, and carried a plate of biscuits and sausage to the table. Counting her steps, she crossed the room, opened the refrigerator, groped for the milk jug, set it on the table, and moved back toward cold air.

Sensing a presence, she hesitated, hand on the refrigerator door. She cocked her head, listening, then felt for the orange juice container.

She slowly closed the door. She stood still as if immobility could somehow make her invisible, her head tilted as she listened.

She sniffed, caught the distinct odor of cigar.

"Good morning, Janie." Major bent slightly and smelled her hair.

She jumped and gasped. "What are you doing here?" She jerked away, stumbled slightly, caught herself, and stood still. "Don't do that! Stop!"

Gripping her shoulders, Major guided her to a straight-backed chair at the table, pushed her to sitting, his hands lingering a bit too long, rough skin snagging slightly on her nightgown fabric.

Quivering, she sat ramrod straight, gripped the breakfast table edge, her knuckles devoid of color. Breath shallow, she shriveled under his presence, his looming.

Major bent again and rubbed his face through her hair, inhaling deeply. "You smell like roses." His hands slid over her nightgown, cupping her small breasts, fondling them. "Morning is my best time. No holes in the day."

"No! Stop it! Get away from me. I don't like that and it's not right." She pushed at him and began to whimper.

He paused, stroked her hair. "No need to worry. I'm your stepfather. You can trust me. Your mother always told me to take care of you. She even put it in our will." He continued to stroke her hair.

Janie twisted, pushed again at his hands.

Returning, Susan Pea paused, stared at Major's bent form, his hands moving over Janie's body. Listened to his murmured comments. Noticed cigar odor.

"What in God's name are you doing?" She stood in the utility room doorway, her scowling face crimson, keys dangling from her fingers, voice edging toward a scream. "You lecherous piece of slime."

Janie yelped in surprise.

Without flinching, arrogance writ large on his face, Major met

Susan Pea's eyes as he straightened, slid his hands down Janie's arms, and moved away. Turning toward the stove and coffee pot, he poured a mug, and leaned his rump against the counter.

Susan Pea stepped firmly between Major and Janie, her hand cupping Janie's neck, freezing herself and Janie in place. Without dropping her gaze from Major's face, she spoke to Janie, her voice firm. "Go upstairs. Finish getting dressed for school." Her hand still on Janie's neck, she gave Janie her cane and guided her toward the hall.

Susan Pea's whole being vibrated and sweat beads lined her face. She waited until Janie disappeared up the stairs before speaking.

"What do you think you are doing?" Eyes narrowed spittle flew into the air as she spoke.

Major, with a rancid lip twist, blew on his coffee and took a slow sip. "I'm having a morning cup of coffee. Do I need to add with two women that live under my roof, on my land, using my dime."

"For chrissake, she's sixteen!" Susan Pea said.

Major sighed. "I simply enjoy tasting honey from every source. You should know. Our old man taught us well. Runs in the family, sweet sister." Major raised an eyebrow. "I suspect that's why you swing like you do. Besides, she looks older than that. Turns seventeen soon."

"You have a sewage trap for a mind." Susan Pea stepped closer, white gobs collected in the corners of her mouth. She clinched her hands into fists, released them, clinched again.

"You're goddamn right old man taught me. Him a Christian, spewing righteous platitudes for *others* to follow. You'd think with all the women available, he'd leave his own daughter alone."

"Here, here. Let's be realistic. If not for Butler name, and me and my money, you'd be tricking on the southside of Dallas. Worse yet, in an Arkansas trailer park."

"He bought you with law school and legal practice. Threw in that sawmill as insurance. Dear old Daddy only demanded his next bottle and your silence, your acquiescence as payment."

"Living in a glass mansion means you can't throw rocks, dearie." He snarled, lips pulled back from his teeth and eyes narrowed. "Besides, by the time I got back from war, he had drowned in the bottle. He had no choice but to give me everything. You might say an early inheritance."

"Give? You took! You've carried on in his grand style with your hands on every woman within reach. You've been in manure up to your armpit since that time," Susan Pea said. "But *not* with Janie. I *promised* her mother."

"Janie's not blood kin."

"You took her on as a *daughter*. You do anything even remotely like this again, and I'll have law all over you."

"Law in this county is *mine*." He straightened, eyes blazing bright. "Besides, who's to believe you? Everyone knows you for a difficult woman, a *spinster*. Could it be you want her for yourself?" He smirked, manipulation rippling off his body in waves.

"I advise you, sister dear, best understand your place in this household, better than you have up to now. Especially if you want to continue living here." He turned his back.

Her legs wobbled, barely held her upright. Fear bubbled into her throat. She gripped the countertop, eyes widened, then narrowed.

Slowly, he sat his mug in the sink, inclined his head toward her, and glowered. "Coffee's a might weak this morning. I like it a bit stronger. Talk with Letta about that. Y'all take care of that." He walked out.

She steadied herself against the doorframe and struggled to breathe normally. Her promise to Eve rang in her ears. She had never understood about New York or the old man, or her brother.

Major—vile, despicable, self-serving. She wished him dead.

CHAPTER TWENTY-FIVE
SUSAN PEA BUTLER

Susan Pea leaned over the sink and vomited. She stood trembling, even after his car pulled out and reverberation dissipated in the distance.

She gripped the counter edge, heard Janie on the stairs, and hurriedly washed out the sink. Still trembling, she twisted away as Janie entered the room.

"Where's Major?"

"Gone."

"He scared me." Janie turned from Susan Pea, sniffing. "What's that smell?"

"Stuff gone bad in the refridge. I poured it down the drain." Susan Pea took Janie's arm and guided her toward the door, picking up the car keys as they left.

Outside, Susan Pea considered what the hell might happen if Major died. She'd have to manage the decrepit mansion alone. Letta could help. Janie and the university were all set up, hence no worries there.

She'd simply carry out Eve's plans. Devil's own question remained—how to get rid of the old reprobate? He needed to go.

Susan Pea opened the car door for Janie, slammed it shut, and walked around to slide into the driver's seat. She pushed the cigarette lighter in and tapped the steering wheel nervously.

"Answer me truthfully." Susan Pea's voice took on an edge. "You said Major fondled you once before. Has it happened more than that? Has he ever gone further? Truth, Janie." The lighter popped out. Susan Pea lit up and took a deep drag. "Well?"

Janie blinked, fumbled with her hands, and turned her head. "No. Maybe.I don't want to say."

Susan Pea struggled to control herself.

"It's all my fault. He said I was too pretty," Janie said.

"What the hell! Too pretty."

"He told me he was sorry." Janie's voice wavered.

Gripping the steering wheel, Susan Pea's knuckles pushed against her skin, her voice climbed toward hysteria. "That damn hypocrite needs shooting."

Janie sat stoic, silent.

"That's your mother's husband." Susan Pea lowered her voice. She thumped ashes out the window, crushed the cigarette in the over-flowing ash tray, and cranked.

"I told him it was not right." Janie wiped her nose, smeared wetness across her cheeks. "He said he wouldn't do any touching again. But he did it again this morning."

Susan Pea couldn't hear for a moment. Her ears rang. She took deep breaths. "Major is your stepfather. He's supposed to protect you." Susan Pea glanced sideways at Janie, spoke more to herself than to her niece. *What else to say? This seemed like a horrible rerun with her father. Every-thing was spinning out of control.*

Janie twisted her hands, and sat with her head bowed, snuffing. "He surprised me. What could I do?"

Susan Pea drove down the driveway, turned the street corner, and steered through town toward the high school. Silence, like humidity, became an unmovable blanket over her body, over her thoughts.

She pulled to a stop a few yards away from the school entrance. Neither spoke for a minute. Both stared straight ahead.

Janie snuffed and said, "I can't defend myself from him, Aunt Pea. I don't mean to be bad." Her words sank into a whisper.

"No! You're not a bad girl. Bad things are happening to you. Not your fault. He's responsible." Susan Pea reached across the seat and stroked Janie's face. "We are going to have to be cleverer in ways to keep you safe. Especially now."

"Safe?" Janie asked. "How, when he sneaks up on me?"

Susan Pea half-turned toward Janie. "I'll be hyper alert. Try to be around and available. When you're in school, be sure you can call for help if he comes around. Never get in a car with him or go anyplace alone." She grasped Janie's hand, held it, and slowly moved her thumb across its delicate palm. "He has no morals, Janie, and he'll take what he wants." Susan Pea continued to hold Janie's hand. When she spoke again, her voice took on an assertive tone. "Looks like he wants you. I'll be super vigilant. Get Letta to help. Andy, when he's here." Hands trembling, she lit another cigarette. "You are not to blame. *All of this is Major's fault.* You are not bad. We'll work together."

Janie bowed her head.

"You're already pregnant, Janie. I don't know if he knows that and is just trying to mark territory. Doesn't matter. He has no right to touch you. Ever."

Susan Pea pushed several strands of hair from Janie's face. She swallowed, the sharp aftertaste of vomit and its noxious burning choked her.

"At times when I'm with Wes in the training field," Janie said in a thin voice, "Major comes out. He stands close to me while Wes works with the dogs."

"What does Wes do?"

"He says dogs do their work no matter who is around. He says Major is his boss."

Susan Pea blinked, took a deep breath.

"He acts different around Wes," Janie said. "I can tell by his voice. You know, gruff. They only talk about the dogs. They try to act like I'm not there."

"Wes acts that way, too? As if you're not there?" Susan Pea continued to hold Janie's hand.

"He doesn't talk much when Major's there. He breathes faster. You know, sort of different."

"How?"

"They both act aggravated, grumble under their breath. I can hear them walk with big steps, all heavy. They don't speak much to me. Wes only gives commands to the dogs. They mostly make me stay near the truck."

"What does Wes usually do when Major's not around?"

Janie beamed and tightened her grip on Susan Pea's hand. "He encourages the dogs. He says 'find 'em boys. Find those birds. Look 'em up.' When it's us two, he sounds pleased when he talks. Now and then, he even stands by me, tells me what they're doing. He doesn't walk so heavy. He sometimes leads me on one of the wide field paths. Guides me with a rope so I don't trip in the grass. He tries to be careful."

"Good. That's considerate of him." Susan Pea squeezed her niece's hand and wished for another cigarette.

Janie paused, head cocked. "I can tell he's proud of Otto."

"How do you know?"

"His voice. It gets smooth, rippling, like water. And I can tell which dog is pointing by how Wes moves."

"Really?"

"When it's Gunner, he moves regular and gives a flush command sooner."

"And with Otto?" Susan Pea watched Janie's face.

"Seems he takes more time, moves quietly before telling him to flush. He asks Otto to hold point a smidgen longer."

"How did you learn all of this?"

"He practices a lot with Otto. He brings Gunner along to help train and give Otto confidence. He used to bring Sadie, before she had the puppies."

The school bell shrilled, and students milled lemming-like toward the entrance, their voices trailing. "I have to go." Janie swung the car door open and gathered her books.

Susan Pea frowned, stalled a moment. "Do you have your braille lesson this afternoon?"

"Yes."

"Wait inside until your tutor picks you up. I'll call her and tell her to honk for you. Inside, okay? Only go with her. She'll bring you home. I'll be there when you get home."

Janie sighed, leaned into Susan Pea, gave her a quick cheek peck, got out, and tapped her way up the steps into the building.

Susan Pea recalled having last seen Janie at her mother's wedding seven year prior. Reflecting on the memory, she marveled at the changes in Janie from a shy, stringy girl to an energetic, curious young woman. A wall flower now playing piano at school dances. A vivacious personality drawing attention from a circle of bright classmates. Independence and confidence more evident each day. No doubt about it, Janie had blossomed.

Steering the car into the traffic flow, Susan Pea drove back through town toward the mansion, thoughts of protecting her niece spinning. If only she could send Janie off to the university this year. Pieter DeGroot was not exciting, but he was kind. And, dull. Perfect to take Janie under his wing. His lab was a solid, safe place to work, bridging the gap between home and independence. Or, at least, more independence. The problem of a baby bloomed large.

CHAPTER TWENTY-SIX
ANDY BUTLER

"Janie, you hear that high keening—the one hanging in the air?" Andy held Janie's arm and pointed her north, his voice a rich baritone. "What is it?"

She leaned into him, her fingers tangled in his thick arm hair, and turned her head in the direction of his pointing. The April air was turning from cool to warm. This was Andy's first leave home in over a year.

"A hawk," she said. "Probably got fledglings in a nest close by. Did you know the male and female share feeding and hunting once the chicks hatch?" Her head tilted, she listened. "It's a red-tail out hunting. Maybe has a mate helping."

"I think you're right. A redtail," he said.

"Males are known to take a turn incubating." Janie twisted her head, followed the hawk's keening as it flew, circled.

"You might say they're real family men." Andy chuckled at his analogy.

They had stopped on the field edge, leaned backsides against the jeep pickup. Mutt sat on the dropped tailgate and shifted against her hip. She put a hand on his head and absently fondled his floppy ears. A westerly breeze kicked up.

"I like coming out with you." Janie nudged against Andy's shoulder. "You tell me things about the woods and creatures. Fields too. Wes doesn't talk much. He makes me stay mostly near the truck while he throws those canvas things. Whenever he pops off a noise pistol, he tells me."

"Does that bother you?"

"No, noise doesn't because he tells me and I'm ready. I like being with Wes. He treats me like an adult, a woman," Janie said.

"Really? A woman?" Andy folded his arms across his chest and leaned against the jeep. "What does that mean?"

"Oh, you know, grown up. He's interested in me." Janie shifted slightly against the jeep.

"Isn't he a little old for you?" asked Andy. "You can't see them, but he's got lines in his face and is starting a paunch."

She giggled. "No, he's not too old. Winkles are a plus. Gives him character. Besides, he's better than those school creeps."

"Creeps, huh?"

"Dimwits," she said. "They fumble around. Snatch at me or try to sneak a feel. Sometimes, I hear them talking with each other. They think they are so smart."

"Yeah, teenage boys can get sort of goofy," Andy said. "They're still exploring at this age. Caught between too young and wannabe-older-studs."

"Wes is smooth. He'll kiss me when we first get here. He holds my face and kisses really soft. But he gets busy with the dogs and sort of forgets about me until we start home."

Andy watched her face grow more animated as she talked. He leaned forward, gave her arm a squeeze, held it, and emphasized each word. "Wes is a dog man. He *should be focused* on dogs and hunting and not on your body. He shouldn't even bring you out when he's training." He released her arm and leaned back.

"But I want to come with him. I ask to come. He doesn't smell like those boys at school. He's more... you know... manly."

"You seem pretty enamored with him." Andy frowned.

"Maybe." Janie lifted her face to the sun. "You talk and still work dogs. I wish he would pay more attention to me."

"He's a trainer. I'm not a trainer. I come to be with you and let dogs exercise. There's a difference. Besides, I'm your brother." He pulled a blade of sedge grass out and chewed on it, continued to listen.

"Stepbrother," she said, gently correcting him.

Andy paused a moment. "Technically, that's right. But, I think of myself as a brother, not stepbrother."

She turned toward him and bumped his shoulder playfully. "Okay. Okay. You are a brother."

They fell silent. The red hawk keened again. Wind caught the notes and tumbled them across the sky until they faded. Dogs ranged along the perimeter, tails flagging while they investigated dried weed mounds along the tree line. Early afternoon settled across the field like a soft summer cloud.

Andy tossed the grass blade away and tapped her arm lightly. "I think I see where a rabbit has her nest. Could have babies there. Let's go see."

He shifted away and guided her toward a narrow path edged with thick fescue. "Keep walking in this direction," he said and gestured forward by guiding her arm. "Feel it? Use your cane. I'm going to ease ahead and see if I can pinpoint that nest."

"Oh, be careful. Don't hurt them. I'll walk slow."

Within a minute, Andy stood before her and nudged her with his elbow. "Here. A baby."

She touched his hand-bowl and wiggled her fingers. "Can I hold it?"

"Make a cup," he said.

Andy slipped a baby into her waiting hands. "Kits. That's what baby rabbits are called. This one has its eyes open, so it's probably about nine or ten days old."

Her mouth formed a perfect "O". With a fingertip, she stroked the petite form, miniature ears, and fairy feet.

"Tell me what you feel."

"It's an air kiss. Warm. Fur is a minuscule breath." She sniffed the baby. "So soft it could blow away. There's no smell."

"What else?"

"Motionless. Not struggling. Sort of hypnotized. Do you think it's scared?"

"Maybe. Baby rabbits and fawns don't have smell. Keeps dogs, coyotes, and foxes from finding them. They stay hidden while mother forages for food. Whenever mother's gone, babies stay very, very still. You said maybe scared, but I think it's Mother Nature's way of protecting them. Staying immobile. No smell."

She held the baby creature against her cheek. Mutt sat at her feet, watching, whining, and shifting. Silently, she fondled the kit and nuzzled its fur. "It's magical."

"Mama rabbits are called does," Andy said. "She leaves kits alone most of the day. Which is another reason they don't smell and stay so still."

Janie beamed, her face soft and happy. She handed the minuscule cottontail back to Andy.

"Hold Mutt," he said, "while I put it back. Don't want him to follow me and disturb their nest."

She leaned down, patted Mutt's head, and curled a finger through his collar.

Andy took her arm and pointed them back toward the jeep pickup. "You and Mutt walk straight ahead on this path. Feel it? It's not wide, but it's straight."

"Yeah. Okay." She tapped the path edges, testing width. "Will the doe come back?" Janie asked as Andy walked away.

"Yes, she'll come," he said over his shoulder. "There are three other nesting babies. They need each other for warmth."

She rummaged with her cane along the dirt and grass-edge, down the path back to the jeep.

"Wait for me there. I'll whistle the boys in."

With several short pips and a shouted 'kennel up, load up', Andy called the dogs, signaled them into the truck bed, closed their crates, and slammed the tailgate. He strode to the cab, signaled Mutt inside, and slid into the driver's seat.

Janie climbed in and shoved Mutt with her hip. She leaned across him and patted Andy. "Give me your hand." He extended his hand.

She traced around it carefully. "Your pinkie finger's twisted from that pool room fight. I thought it would be straight by now. Still got that bump on your nose?"

"Yep. Got best-looking boxer face around. Here." He guided her hand to his face.

She touched his forehead, moved her hand down and across his nose, broken long ago in a pool room fight. "What do women think of your rugged looks?"

"Most swoon, faint dead away. Once they come to, they don't think at all. They are captivated by my handsome profile and intense eyes."

Janie play-thumped him on the arm and rocked back laughing. She stuck her elbow out the window. "Don't tease me. Women don't just faint away. Besides, how many women do you have?"

"Little sister, I don't have any women. I'm married to the Army."

Andy pretend-punched Janie in return and they both doubled over hooting.

He cranked the engine, admired its throaty throb, and shifted into low. Windows open, wind ruffing through their hair, they rode in silence for a few miles.

"Why is Aunt Pea so crabby?" Janie asked.

"What do you mean?"

"Sometimes she talks with me, but sometimes I hear her talking low with Letta. They get quiet whenever they hear me coming. Seems they want to ask me something or tell me something, but they never do."

"You're the reason Susan Pea's here. She came back because Eve asked her to come," Andy said. "Now that Eve's gone, they are feeling extra stress. Susan Pea especially. I think they're only concerned."

"I'm graduating next year and starting my own life. I already have plans. They don't need to tend to me."

"Ever think you might need extra help?"

"Maybe. But Mother already set me up at the university in some bird lab. I'm moving away like Aunt Pea did. I'll live on my own."

"There's more to Susan Pea's moving than packing stuff up." Andy paused and watched Janie's brow crinkle before he continued. "What do you want to do at the university?"

"Mother made some sort of plans with a dorky-sounding man. I think everyone calls him Doc Pete. I'm supposed to help catalogue bird calls." Janie folded her cane and held it across her lap. "What did you mean about Aunt Pea leaving here?"

"She caused quite a stir. Left a few years before I went in the Army. Folks talked about her then and I'll bet they are still talking."

"Why?" Janie asked.

"People around here think only communists, liberals, and perverts live in New York and Boston. If anyone says anything about 'up north', others start a hollering match about the Kennedys, calling them Catholic rumrunners breeding faster than cockroaches." He snorted, smiled at the thought.

"Are they?"

"Maybe," Andy replied. "But I think people mostly fear anything they don't understand, anything out of the ordinary. Especially those who have lived all their lives in one general area, never had a chance to see a wider world."

"What do you mean?" Janie asked.

"Well, people here see Susan Pea as strange, unusual, too independent. Although, she was a natural beauty and a star basketball player. Went to State twice."

"Why do you think they act that way?" Janie said.

"Because it got around your aunt preferred women. I think the polite term now is 'spinster aunt'."

"Oh, you mean *that* kind of strange… like *queer*."

"How do you know about being called strange? Or queer, as you put it?" Andy asked.

"Kids at school talk. Sometimes, they say things to see how I'll react. Sometimes girls explain things to me. Boys act dumb, gather around, get rowdy, and say things. 'Wanna do a blow job?' or 'Come feel my dick.' Crazy boy stuff. It aggravates me."

"What do you do?" Andy asked.

"Everything they say is so exaggerated and then they laugh real loud. I just walk off. They're all knotheads." Janie placed her hand out the window, allowed it to wind wobble. She grew silent.

Mutt's long tongue lolled out, slobber drooled off and pooled on the seat. A rooster tail of dust rose behind, roiled in the aftermath.

Janie, her tone distant, said, "Some of girls are nice. They tell boys to knock it off, to leave me alone. When Mother got so sick and had trouble helping me with choosing clothes and doing my hair, some girlfriends would come by. They'd help match stuff up, hang things in my closet so I could find them, and figure out new ways to fix my hair. It was fun. We'd laugh. Talk about other kids, especially boys. I think Mother was glad to have them come."

Andy grunted an acknowledgement. They rode without speaking, bumping over sand ruts, and soaking in the woods. Heat waves shimmered in the air.

"Did you see where Aunt Pea lived? When she was at college?" Janie asked.

"Yeah. I went one summer before I shipped to Germany. She had a tiny apartment with two other girls. We all went bar hopping together."

"To a night club? A real one? With cocktails? Oh, tell me about it." Janie squirmed and pushed Mutt over against Andy. Mutt whined and scrambled across Janie's lap to sit next to the window.

"The others went back to the apartment around midnight, but she and I stayed out until sunrise. We ate peach ice cream for breakfast." Andy laughed, happiness bubbling in his memory. "Pea said it was our breakfast fruit."

"Ha! Breakfast peaches. What else?"

"Well, she had long fingernails, painted red." Andy whooped, slapped his knee. "She surprised me. When she lived at home, she bit her nails to the quick. I never understood, especially with her being a basketball star, why she was so insecure."

"Mother told me Aunt Pea made homecoming queen one year."

"That's true," he said. "She was a star athlete and smoking hot. Boys were all over her—those big boobs of hers." He chuckled. "She played around with a lot of those boys, teasing them on. But I really think she mostly thought about how to get out of this old town."

"I want to get out of here, too. Go to New Orleans. Or California."

Truck bounced over several deep ruts as they turned away from scattered woods and meadow, onto a graded road.

"Janie, you are a southerner, born and bred," Andy said. "You can't leave the South. It follows you."

"Letta says South is only good for gospel singing and breeding racists."

"That may be true. Still, if you're raised in a place, you understand it better than somewhere totally different. You don't want to end up merely an observer to life." Andy focused on keeping the rattling jeep steady on the graded road. He continued talking. "Well, if you understand a place and people, you tend to get involved with them. If things are too unusual, you might hang back and wait to see what's happening. You just observe. It can get to be a habit."

"Oh. So, if you wait to see what's happening, you never really get involved," Janie said.

"Something like that. You must mix and get involved if you want to understand people."

"You move all the time. Do you get involved?" Janie asked.

"My moving is different. I'm with the Army."

"But that makes you a full-time observer. You never fit in."

Andy took a deep breath, let it out slow. "Yeah, I guess it does. I don't really have a home except the military. And, men I work with." He patted her on the shoulder by way of saying not to worry.

They bumped along the washboard road. Wind curled through truck windows, scented slightly with heat and pine. Mutt whined, shifted against the window, and stuck his nose in the wind.

"You know I have to go back to base Thursday, don't you?" Andy said.

"Yes." She twirled a lock of hair around her finger. "Why did you even join up?"

"It's a long story. You know a fight caused these crooked fingers and nose," Andy said. "Major arranged my enlistment to keep me out of jail. A choice between Army and prison. Said it was necessary to keep family's name respectable. But what he really wanted was to get rid of me."

"How old were you?"

"I was eighteen when I enlisted. Almost nineteen. That was seven years ago."

"Do you like it?" asked Janie.

"Turns out, Army's best thing ever happened to me. Joke's on Major."

KOREA, winding down by 1953, still needed Army grunts for mop up. As troops left Korea, French hold on Indo China began slipping. Public attention switched to Southeast Asia and first waves of advisors entered country. Andy among them. By 1961, at the behest of politicos and military brass, advisor numbers climbed steadily. And jumped yet again. A heady time until flag draped coffins filled the bellies of cargo planes. Politics changed. Public swung divisive.

ANDY PROPPED his elbow out the window. Turning from the graded road onto state asphalt, they picked up speed toward town. Tires sang against the hard surface.

"Come on Miss Janie." Andy gave her a playful arm nudge. "Let's get lunch at Mockingbird Cafe. They fix a mean meat loaf coated in ketchup. They've got garlic mashed potatoes, too. What do you say?"

"I say yes."

"That's my gal," Andy said. "Not often I get to take a fine-looking woman to lunch. It'll make all the local boys jealous."

She laughed and floated her hand out the window, scooted over, pushed Mutt aside to share window space. He stuck his nose into the wind, ears flapping.

They returned home late, a pearl twilight floating in with their arrival. Janie fairly skipped into the house to check with everyone.

Andy replaced keys on the back door hook, hollered a greeting into the kitchen for Letta and Susan Pea, and ambled out to the front porch rocker to read *Post-Searchlight*. Never hurt to stay abreast of local news.

Janie plopped down at the kitchen table to tell of her adventures.

CHAPTER TWENTY-SEVEN
SUSAN PEA BUTLER

Standing on the porch step, Susan Pea watched Andy, his muscular frame bent at the waist, lean into the flower bed. He retched. Perspiration dotted his thin lips, snot ropes dripped off his nose.

"I feel guilty. I should have helped protect her." He spat and rubbed his eyes. "How could I miss it? I'm her brother. How did I not know that womanizer used Janie?"

"*Step*brother." Susan Pea handed him a handkerchief. "We all missed it. Get a grip. Guilt is no excuse for you gagging in public and whining." She oscillated between crumbling in fear and gnashing her teeth in defiance. "Wipe your nose. Save your sleeves."

"Surely to God, not with Janie. His own daughter," Andy said.

"*Stepdaughter*. No blood relation." Susan Pea snatched the hankie from his hands, crushed it into a tight ball, and stuffed it in her pocket. "We don't always want to see things right in front of our faces. All of us could have done better with helping Janie and Eve when it comes to Major."

"Amen on that," Letta said. "They had to live with him every day.

Same house." She crossed her arms over her stomach, stared across the porch. "I work here days, and I'm grateful to get home of a night. Even if it be late. Otherwise, I'd be troubled *all* time. Can't live in this here house."

Susan Pea cut her eyes at Letta. "Although Major is capable of anything, I don't think it was him. Janie stays away from him since that time in the kitchen. Fact is, Janie has, or had, a lover. I'd not put anything past anyone in this sinkhole town either."

Andy bent over again, arm muscles bulging as he held onto the railing. He spat into azaleas. "For chrissake, Janie's blind. She's sixteen."

Letta stepped close to Andy, handed him a dish towel to wipe his face. "Janie a bright girl. One way, she 'bout grown up. Other ways, she still a girl without no common man sense."

Andy mopped his face and gave the towel back to Letta. "We were out together yesterday. I didn't suspect a thing." Still leaning on the porch rail, he watched the street a moment, then shifted toward Susan Pea. "I'll say it plain out. I'll kill whoever got her knocked up. I'll do it with my bare hands." He gritted his teeth causing his jaw muscle to bulge. "I suspect Wes."

"Careful nephew," Susan Pea said. "There are those would kill him and pin blame on you. Besides, she turns seventeen next week."

"Whatever." He coughed, cleared his mouth. "She's technically still a minor, for chrissake."

"Look at the facts." Susan Pea held her fingers up and counted off her points. "Janie is a Butler by marriage, not blood. A stepchild. She's got inheritance and status simply because her mother made the devil's own bargain when she married Major. Eve recognized he was soulless, but she chose to trade matrimony for her daughter's financially secure future."

Andy shook his head.

"On the other hand," Susan Pea began counting on her fingers again, "it's not a good solution, but abortion is an option. That puts a fine period on everything. It's risky. Adoption is another option. But that means carrying this baby to term and no telling what might happen in meantime." Susan Pea stopped marking her fingers, lowered her hands. "No matter, you leave this thing alone. Janie wants this baby. Let her make the decision."

Andy sat on the porch edge, attempted to put his thoughts in order. "She can make whatever decision, but someone's gonna get his due." He rose and stood next to the wooden rail.

Uncertain, Susan Pea stepped closer to Andy and put her hand on his arm. "Give Janie her due, let her handle pregnancy part. After all, she must live with this the rest of her life." Her voice, still strong, rose a notch. "And I'm here. You're here. Together we can do whatever she decides, whatever is necessary."

"I here." Letta frowned, then volunteered her assistance. "Do most anything so long as I stay."

"Of course." Susan Pea turned toward her housekeeper, a question in her stare. "Are you planning on leaving?"

"Humph." Letta stood silent a moment, jutted her jaw forward. "Got a few things need tending before I leave." She stepped back into the porch shade, hand in her apron pocket. She fingered an extra tin she carried.

Skeptical, Andy moved away from both women.

"I'm a Butler," Susan Pea said. "I've got—what do you say— resources? I'm heir apparent as family matriarch and due part of the Butler estate. No question about my pedigree." She fluffed up like an old hen, crossed her arms, and settled heavy in the porch rocker. "No question about my legal rights either, especially in light of his efforts to disown you."

"Meaning?" Andy spread his hands wide and cocked his head.

"He never recognized, for certain, that your mother was faithful."

Susan Pea chose her words carefully and spoke slow. "He used that as leverage against *both* of you. That's why he denied you all these years." She nudged the worn rocker into motion. Porch planks creaked against the chair.

"That's old history. Besides, Janie's not his either," Andy said.

Letta, standing in shadows, sucked at her teeth. "I done heard more'n I want. You white people are too scared 'bout what others think. That girl got to live her life, make her own way."

Silent for a moment, Susan Pea sighed and spoke in a softer voice. "Major sees people as chess pieces. I don't think he ever actually loved *any* woman. Me included, his own sister. Maybe our mother, but only as an *idolized* figure years *after* she was gone. She died when he was barely eight."

Letta shifted, uncrossed her arms, and continued to stand against the porch rail. "Y'all need to keep in mind, in Georgia, girls marry at sixteen. She turns seventeen soon and, by time she graduates high school, she's eighteen. That makes her legal twice over."

Andy slumped forward, his head in his hands.

Susan Pea, silent, paused, stared at Andy. "Eve set Janie up with a university mentor. A Dr. Pieter DeGroot. Janie and I both have met him. So has Letta. For now, that's all that can be done."

"Really? You think that will work with some egghead?" Andy shook his head. "You expect her to just leave that baby with you two and go off to the university?"

"No. But I do think Major forgets it's chess queen who holds power," Susan Pea said and thumped her chest with a forefinger. "She's capable of moves in any direction."

"Goddamn it. We're not chess pieces. We're people," Andy said.

"Think about this," Susan Pea continued speaking in a controlled voice. "Major has a warped sense of right and wrong. His hands are in Sheriff's pocket, and he's got a choke hold on town council. He has total say at that mill, which employs half the town." She thumped her knuckles on the chair arm. "Don't forget his law practice. He doesn't need us." Exhausted, she shrugged. "We have to make him need us."

"Damn his soul to hell," Andy said. "Throw in his military years, especially during the war, and he demands total control, compliance, like some top commander."

With two white faces staring at her, Letta spoke quickly. "Ain't my place to say it, but he got his boot heel on lots more than y'all saying."

An uneasy silence settled among the three. Finally, Susan Pea took a deep breath and spoke in a steady voice. "He took on Janie on as a charity project. An example of his generosity. Eve paid dearly for that arrangement." Pulling at a hangnail, Susan Pea created yet another small wound. She castigated herself, vowed to continue smoking instead of nail biting.

"Nothing been said about asking Janie what she wants," Letta added. "She's wantin' to keep this baby. She thinks to stay right here and have *us* take care of this child."

"Are you telling me she's keeping the baby?" Andy said.

"Yes, what Letta says is correct," Susan Pea said. "I'm sure the father is Wes. But it's best that no one knows details at this juncture."

"Hell fire and damnation." Andy slammed his fist down. He pushed himself away from the porch rail and slumped onto the swing. It bucked side-to-side.

"Andy, I said it before, get a grip on yourself. Cussing on our front porch in a town as scandal mongering as this one is no fit behavior. Especially for a Butler."

Susan Pea stood, walked over, and sat next to him in the swing. She patted him on the knee. The swing settled into a minstrel's slow shuffle.

"You're a Butler. You can handle this. We both can." She dug her fingers into his knee.

"It's Janie we're talking about here." He wiped his nose. "She's only one among us that's decent or kind."

"Favorite nephew, that's not quite true," she said. "Good and bad exists inside everyone. Deceit is a human condition. We tell lies daily, small and big. We lie to ourselves. Especially a young girl in Janie's condition. In the end, everyone's got clay feet and no one's innocent." Susan Pea lit up a cigarette, took a deep drag, stood, and crushed it out on the swing, leaving a burned smudge.

"Still, I'll kill sonofabitch that got in her panties." Andy straightened, frowned at his half-sister.

Letta, propped against the railing in shadows along the porch end, shook her head. "Y'all oughtn't be talking loud out here. The trees have ears. Crows passing by, grab words and carry them all over countryside. Words, even thoughts, have power." She fanned herself with her apron skirt. "Ain't nobody innocent neither." Letta turned and walked inside. Screen clattered close behind her.

CHAPTER TWENTY-EIGHT
LETTA DAVIS

Stately pines cast their shadows long across nearby cornfields. Bloated storm clouds, marked by threads of heat lightning, melted into night. Dusk-tainted rain odors floated in the air.

The withered conjure woman and several gnarled figures sat around glowing embers. Those around circle held silent, blended without seam into dark. Letta watched the smoke grab their collective memories, twist them into a grayness running back through time to ancestral roots, and hoodoo traditions.

The conjure woman leaned forward, threw dried sticks onto coals, causing the fire to flare. She closed her eyes and spoke in a cracked voice. "Done tolt you, I know you. I know you sons, John and Elijah. Daughter Merry. They need leave here. Follow way north, where blue bottle points."

Letta squatted on a downed log, pulled a tin of wet tobacco from her pocket, and passed it around, an offering smoothing the way for her request. Long moments eased by before she spoke. "John home from

Army. He'll take my girl Merry, Elijah away from here. Like you tolt me, I tell him, blue bottle point way. Plans done made."

Conjurer poked at the fire again, her knobby hands clutching the stick. Sparks jumped into darkness and a flame blazed briefly with a rising wind. Pine smoke smeared turpentine odors through the air. Shoulders sagging beneath her cotton shift, crone closed her rheumy eyes for a moment, and then rolled them open again.

"What you doin' here now? What more you be wantin'?" She straightened and smoothed her garb.

Letta took a deep breath and exhaled slow. "I be fearing Major. Still, I gotta stand upright and live my life looking forward. Can't be scared all time."

The granny-woman fell silent, and then spoke, her voice convulsing from a distant place. "That Major man come back from over ocean not right. He *off*. He done got too used to killing." Flames mirrored on her face, vacillated, and flickered with a hidden power. A carnivore wind rose, became raw before it laid by.

Letta's hands trembled. She glanced behind her, eyes wide, whispered hoarse her hidden thoughts. "I need a wrongdoing set right for my Merry. Need it for others gone before, some coming after. Need blood payment."

A vixen's sharp bark cut the darkness. Sliced into their thoughts.

Crone grunted and spoke hoarsely. "That one that barked, she sly about it, but she kills for her kits. She don't be 'fraid of protecting what hers," crone said. "That son, John, he a man, got strength. Let him use it." She watched Letta with bloodshot eyes and spat into the fire. It hissed a response.

"John needs be safe, too." Letta's face knitted into a worry line across her forehead.

"Time cover over any deaths he might cause and put him right again with Old Ones."

Embers bristled and fire tongues sputtered briefly. Pine boughs whispered of movement elsewhere. Letta shuffled her feet, felt the weight of departed passions, waited on the crone to speak again.

"Thoughts have power. Gather them other thoughts from folks around you. *Use them.*" With knotted fingers, she threw dark powder into the coals, causing sparks to claw upward.

Letta's heart leapt with old granny's words. She sat silent, mouthed her dip, and gazed into the heat.

"Now I tell you, daughter," the crone pointed a boney finger at Letta, "my people send word to you as soon John and daughter cross that river, when they be safe in Ohio, beyond them nightriders." Crone smacked her lips and spoke gentler. "You Merry, one day marry a preacher man, be a wife, mother. She make you a grandmother. That girl be you legacy."

Letta knew that the woman spoke true.

Still, she wondered. "Will I live to see these babies?"

CHAPTER TWENTY-NINE
ANDY BUTLER

ANDY STOPPED inside the dim barn. Light salted his face. The place never changed. Peck's Feed Store Christmas calendar from 1949 still hung on the wall, decades out of date. Rusted license plates from an endless string of discarded vehicles covered space near the whelping room. Dust motes stuttered in the air. Memories, silent as a cat's shadow, floated out of reach.

He slipped into a pair of muck boots inside the feed room and walked to the outside runs, separated by woven wire and shaded by a hanger-style roof. He watched Wes hose down concrete runs, the spray sloshing waste into a septic pond behind the buildings. Major had built the entire complex after returning from the war scant years before his father died.

Sadie and her pups were loose while Wes cleaned.

"This year's puppies look good." Andy bent to scratch Sadie's head. Her tongue lolled out, the picture of a tired mama. "Gunner's offspring?"

Wes paused, glanced up, continued hosing the pen a minute before turning the water off. He stood, stretched his back. "Major can be a bit narrow-sighted, if you ask me." He wiped his brow.

"Yeah. Major likes his pure-bred pointers." Andy gave Sadie a final pat and stood.

Wes snorted, moved to the next series of runs, turned water on again, and continued cleaning.

"Where's Elijah? Doesn't he help with kennel cleaning?" Andy asked.

"Decided not to take them out today, so I sent him home."

Andy grunted an acknowledgement. He watched Wes a moment, sensing his own presence was an unwanted intrusion. He grunted again, picked up a squeegee broom, and began to sweep puddles of standing water into the gutter.

They worked in silence until runs were clean, water buckets scrubbed, refilled, and evening feed measured out.

"Janie and I spent the afternoon in the field yesterday," Andy said.

"Yeah?" Wes growled. "I thought dogs seemed a bit off this morning." His voice was devoid of interest in anything pertaining to Janie or Andy and their whereabouts. "What's it to me anyway?" Finished with morning kennel chores, he sat on a bench near the spigot and pulled off his muck boots, grunting with the effort.

"We were just letting them exercise. No training. But I got to thinking that it might not be safe for her to be out there while you're training, you know? You should have your attention on the dogs. She might fall. Run into a low limb or something." Andy leaned against a shaded spot on the wall.

"I wouldn't do it if I didn't think I could handle her."

"Handle her? Like a dog? Train her to be your sidepiece because you know she can't say anything to anyone? Especially with the likes of you? Janie's a girl." Andy pushed himself off the wall, fists clinched.

Wes glanced up at Andy. "It's not like that."

"Tell me what it's like then."

Wes stood with hip cocked a moment, shook his head, and turned his back to Andy.

"You sonofabitch," Andy snarled. "You don't care about her. Do you even bother to think about her in all this upheaval? After all, she just lost her mother."

"I'm simply giving her a distraction." Wes wiped his hands on his jeans, hung the mucks in a dry-holder, and slipped into his field boots and pulled on his hunting vest. "She'll be okay. Like I say, I can handle her."

Andy stepped in front of Wes. "I don't want Janie being handled. Being hurt."

"You got nothing to worry about with me. Remember, I'm just white trash from Lee Town. Don't y'all tell Janie to stay away?" Wes smirked and moved around Andy. "Tell you what, stepbrother, I'm the most man she'll ever have." He scoffed at Andy. "Besides, only need to be sixteen in Georgia to get it on legally."

"You prick," Andy said. "You fool around banging her and I'll cut your balls off. I'll jerk your filthy tongue out." His eyes narrowed. Face dark, he stepped closer to Wes.

"Easy, feller." Wes held his ground. "I'd suggest you think this through again. Maybe Janie wants a man."

Swaggering through the kennel gate, Wes paused, his hand on the latch, and turned toward Andy. "I'll tell you one other thing Mr. Army-Sharp-Shooter—*every* woman I've ever had on the mattress, *asked* for *another* round. What'll you think Janie will do?"

CHAPTER THIRTY
LETTA DAVIS

LETTA RECOGNIZED several things for certain—white women of whatever age were eager to taste the town's bad boy honey: Wes. She understood Butler family secrets that caused town gossips, white and Black, to smack their lips in relish. She studied on things, on various events. She tempered her assertive nature when she spoke with whites, kept her true thoughts to herself.

Gossip, fuel on which southern towns thrive, proved better than a weekly newspaper column for Letta. She listened with a practiced ear and said nothing. Whites treated her as invisible, mostly dismissed her even when she spoke up. Her church, a weekly source of natter and support, helped her braid various threads together.

She had heard of Wes's mattress experience, the golden fleece among town women. Heard of his divorcees, needing reassurance that they were desirable, sliding between whatever sheets were offered. Gossip swirled among her people of his quick poke before hubby got home, of his rough play with those that liked it. Heard of those bored married women who simply hid any bastard under their marital bed.

Most troubling to her ears were tales of appealing young, single women, he had left with a troublesome pregnancy, too often.

For his part, to be safe, Wes kept certain *connections* handy. Mostly midwives on the southside of town.

Today with everyone gone, Letta humphed and moved about the Butler kitchen, set biscuit dough out to sour and washed sticky flour off her hands, all the while talking aloud.

"White people think they *know* us. How can a person know another when they say you all look alike?" Letta used blank looks, mumbled answers, and downcast eyes whenever Major or another white, except women in Butler household, asked her a question. Especially those she did not want to answer.

"Gotta use what I know. Use things taught by first ones." She mumbled and went toward the pantry, lost in thoughts, finishing her chores automatically.

Over the years, she had grown fond of Janie and understood Eve's struggle with her marriage. Thoughts scoured through Letta's mind: her own mother raising a daughter forced on her by Major's father. That daughter—Letta's older sister—now locked Letta in a macabre waltz with Major. White power and his military training, his hands in the pockets of the sheriff and town council, and a disregard of county concerns, combined to keep him king of the heap. Major was worrisome. Still, foremost in Letta's mind were Merry and Elijah. And the Janus face of the South.

Late evening, days later, Letta walked to her cabin, checked on Elijah, slipped into her thin coat, and left for deep thickets.

CHAPTER THIRTY-ONE
SUSAN PEA BUTLER

IMPECCABLY DRESSED with a slight paunch beginning to show, Thomas rose from his desk as she entered the office. "Ah, Susan Butler. I heard you were back. Do folks still call you Susan Pea?"

"Hello Thomas," she said and extended her hand. "Yes, my nickname has stuck with me all these years, even in New York. I'm used to it."

"It's good to see you."

"Nice to see you are still with Major. My goodness, you've been here with him since your Duke University days."

Thomas moved from behind the desk and took her hand, held it between both of his. He had been with Major since those early days when he interned with his office. Major had hired him right after graduation as an apprentice clerk and, in time, used him as his sole law clerk.

Susan Pea noticed the firm grip, his smooth, too soft hands. He had taken on a few pounds, lost some hair, but still resembled the man she had socialized with years prior.

She thought him an able, legally correct law clerk, perhaps a little too honest. A capable man but lacking killer instincts. His pitch-perfect soprano voice made him a shoo-in for Sunday choir.

"I haven't seen you since high school. How have you been?" Thomas said.

"I'm doing fine. I moved back in May to take care of Eve and tie up some loose ends. Now that she's gone, Janie needs help settling some final property issues. You know how these things go."

"Yes, I understand." He motioned Susan Pea to a wingback chair. "I am sorry about Eve's passing. My sympathy to the family. She was an elegant and kind woman."

"Yes, she was." Susan Pea paused several moments before adding, "Thank you, Thomas."

"Please call on me. I'll do all I can to help." Thomas gestured toward the chair again.

She sat, crossed her legs flashing thick calves, and pulled out a cigarette. "Janie's going to need emotional support. I'm not sure I'm in the best position to help."

He offered her a light, placed a glass ashtray nearby, and sat in an overstuffed leather chair at an angle. "It will be difficult, I'm sure, but I have every confidence in you. Besides, I think Letta is still working for the family. She'll be a big help, especially since she has children of her own. Andy, too. Despite his military assignments."

"Yes. I suppose you're right."

"How is Letta?"

"She's much as she has always been. Getting up in age. I wouldn't know where to begin taking care of that house without her. I'm afraid, though, since I'm out of my depth caring for a teenager who thinks herself a woman."

"Of course. It's a certainly a conundrum for any mother and especially for you as her aunt." Thomas shifted. The leather creaked. "Major is not in now, but what can I do for you?"

"I need help with another thing." Susan Pea paused, flicked cigarette ashes off. "I think Eve's name was on the papers for a German shorthair pointer. Since she left her personal items for me to distribute and manage for Janie, I came by to pick them up. I'm considering drafting that dog to another owner. All the other legal matters can be settled later. Do you have those papers here?"

"Actually, I do. Mrs. Butler's attorney sent them over a week ago. I've already started the process to finalize her estate." Thomas, aware that Eve had named Susan Pea as executrix on Janie's behalf, nodded.

As his old friend, she realized he wanted to assist her in obtaining any paperwork to keep things easy.

"Let me get the folder." He rose and left the room.

Susan Pea glanced around. It had been years since her last visit to the office and she had forgotten how masculine in tone, yet sedate enough for a woman's taste: English countryside décor, forest-plaid chairs, burgundy leather couch, and a scattering of vintage botanical prints lining one wall. Indeed, upkeep of the family mansion might be imploding, but Major's office shouted money and style.

Thomas took longer than she considered necessary. She watched him closely when he returned with the folder.

"These have not been processed into the overall estate as of yet, so I will need to get them back if you do retain ownership." He placed the file on the desk, his hand lingering a second too long.

"I've missed seeing you." He stood at the desk corner.

Her reply was curt. "Well, I haven't been around for years."

"Yes, true enough." A hint of a smile crossed his face. "Our relationship was special when you were here. I've missed those evenings listening to jazz and talking."

She crushed her cigarette out and reached for the manila envelope, acutely aware of her chipped nail polish and yellow-stained fingers contrasting conspicuously against the richness of the desk. Embarrassed at her unkept appearance, she flipped through the papers, barely glancing at pedigree lines and ownership designation. Her face bloomed hot.

"Perhaps we can get together some evening and talk over old times." He cocked his head.

She pretended not to hear his enquiry. "Thank you, Thomas." She stood with as much charm as she could muster. "This will do for now. I'll be in touch regarding a final settlement."

"Of course." He took a step back. His voice had a cool quality as he half-sat, half-leaned on the desk edge. "Yes, I'll call as soon as Major is back. I think those documents need his signature as well."

She frowned. "Really? I didn't think he needed to know."

"The kennels and dogs have always been his purview. Part of an agreement before Eve and he married. House and grounds were meant to go to her, but not the kennels." Thomas remained propped on the desk edge. "As a point of clarification, Major owns the mill and this legal practice. I think most of your share of your father's estate was given as part of your living expenses in New York."

"Oh. I see. So, I shouldn't expect anything further?" Susan Pea's voice rose in a question. She caught herself and added, "Well, of course not. Major would plan it that way. Naturally, as wife, Eve leaves all her share to Janie." She glanced down at the file.

Thomas nodded quiet acknowledgement.

"Otto belongs only to Major?" she asked.

"Yes. He must agree to anything done with that dog."

She slid the packet of papers into her handbag. *Thomsas may be needed more than initially thought.* She allowed her tone to soften slightly. "Maybe we should get together and talk. About old times, of course. Listen to some notes. After all, we've been *friends* for a long time." She had not been drawn to him, but now with his usefulness more apparent, she found him an acceptable companion. Maybe even an enjoyable one.

"Yes, I would enjoy that." Thomas pushed away from the desk, took a step closer. "There are a lot of new jazzmen out these days. More playing in Atlanta every year. Big names coming through."

She tilted her head and looked down, took a deep breath, and glanced up . "Maybe we should plan a long weekend and hear them." She twisted a lock of hair around her finger and smiled.

CHAPTER THIRTY-TWO
JANIE BUTLER

Entering the barn, Janie walked down the aisle and stepped into the feed room. The wooden floor creaked as she turned and closed the door. Her heart pounded and a wild adrenaline pulsed through her. She could smell fresh straw, pungent dog chow, and feel heat from the sunlight spiraling through the window.

Soundlessly, arms came from behind her, hands moving up and down her arms. A face she knew by touch, familiar, now buried into the crook of her neck, nuzzling her curls, inhaling her fragrance.

She turned. Wes kissed her palm, her fingertips, her eyelids. He pressed her down on spongy bags of feed, huge, overstuffed pillows with lumps. A country hide-a-way in sight of the mansion.

"What if someone comes in?" A question and test of sorts. He pressed against her.

"Aunt Pea's at Winn-Dixie, shopping." Janie slid her hand across his jeans. "Besides that, she sends Letta home early on Wednesdays. I'll be back inside before anyone knows I've been out."

Fingers twisted in her hair, Wes pulled her head back and covered her mouth with his, released her hair. His hands roamed across her face and around her breasts. Wes traced her lines, moved his hands over her body, He began and ended with her face, cradled it in his hands, gentle—*almost* affectionate.

He murmured about her beauty, taste of her freckled skin, and clean odor of meadows that lingered in her hair. He kissed her neck and nibbled her ears, blowing hot, soft breath into them.

Eyes closed, Janie spoke soft. "No one knows I'm out here." She flicked her tongue across his lips, kissed his neck.

"Aren't you worried?"

"Not really. Besides, I want to be with you." She continued to nuzzle him, blow softness into his ear.

"Stop teasing," he said. "I'm aching. I positively hurt. I need you."

She closed her eyes.

He kissed her throat. "That's my sweet girl."

She pulled slightly away. "Shouldn't that be 'sweet woman'? I'll turn seventeen soon."

"I thought you were already seventeen." Wes held her at arm's length.

"Well, I'm almost seventeen. You still like me, don't you? No matter how old I am?"

"Sure. You know I do. Sixteen or seventeen—doesn't matter. You're different. Challenging."

Janie smiled and snugged against him.

"Well then, here's an early birthday kiss to my special birthday *woman*." He gently tangled his fingers in her hair, pulled her head back, and gave her a long, deep kiss. "A made-to-order present for you. No matter when your birthday is."

Trembling, she softened against him, an arm around his neck, and returned his kiss.

He pulled her toward him, ran his hand over her stomach, felt the swell to her belly. "Your pregnancy's beginning to show just a little."

"I know. I feel some changes. Do you think the baby knows?" Janie said.

"How sweet." Gently, he pushed her down onto the feed bags, pressed against her. "I've almost forgotten how sweet *you* are."

"Your only girl now. Right?" Insecure, she always asked the same question. He did not answer but continued to caress her.

Later, pulling clothes back into place, Wes said, "Come with me Saturday. We'll take Otto out. We can spend the whole day."

Janie shook her head. "Aunt Pea will never agree."

"She's your aunt, not your jailer. Don't ask."

"She's my guardian now that mother's gone."

Wes cocked an eyebrow.

"Letta will fuss." Janie drew back from Wes.

"For chrissake, she's your *housekeeper*, not your babysitter," Wes said, his voice growing gruff. "You want to be called a woman? Act like one. Make your own decisions."

"You're like the boys at school. Always pressuring me."

"Sweet girl, I'm much better than those clueless wimps. Come here. I'll show you."

Janie blinked and moved against him.

CHAPTER THIRTY-THREE
LETTA DAVIS

LETTA POURED herself a cup of coffee and watched as Janie entered the kitchen, opened the refrigerator, rummaged about in the interior, and pulled out the orange juice pitcher.

"Janie, what you doing up so early? It's Saturday.".

"I know. I'm going out with Wes to work Otto."

Janie poured juice, her index finger resting slightly inside the glass, gauging the amount. She returned the pitcher to the refrigerator, plopped down at the kitchen table, and slid her hand across the surface to her glass.

Letta reared back and frowned at Janie. "You aunt know this?"

"This is not the first time I've gone with him to work the dogs, Letta. It's no big deal. Really." She took a sip of juice as Letta nudged a plate of freshly buttered biscuits under her hand. A small smile spread over Janie's face at the gesture. "You're too good to me, Letta."

"Humph. You need to stay right here till Missus Susan come down."

"We've already had this planned and I'm going. Besides, this is his only Saturday off for the month."

"That man's gonna drag you into more trouble. He's no count."

"Oh, Letta, people like to talk about him," Janie said. "He's exciting and adventurous and independent. Others want to be like him but can't. He says I'm *different*. He says I have a spark like none of his other women." Janie beamed, remembering the conversation. She took another bite of biscuit and chewed thoughtfully. "Besides, just because you are good to me, doesn't mean you can boss me."

"Humph. You still need to wait on your Aunt Pea to come down." Letta frowned and poured herself more coffee. "You running too wild. You already be in trouble."

Janie gulped the last of the juice. "Can't wait. Gotta go." She shoved the plate aside and hurried out the door, Mutt trailing.

Letta watched from the back porch as Janie made her way toward the kennels.

Wes's old pickup sat near the gate, motor thumping, Otto already loaded in the back crate. He popped the horn once to attract Janie his way and swung the door open. She veered to the noise, clambered inside and scrunched over to allow Mutt room.

Letta mumbled her thoughts as she watched Wes slam the truck into gear and throw gravel. "No telling what he say to her, much less what that peckerwood be doing. That girl not understand she playing dangerous." Twisting her hands together, Letta picked up a dish towel and turned away from the window as the truck crunched down the driveway.

Susan Pea walked into the kitchen in time to see Janie and Wes turn onto the main road, Mutt sitting between them. Frowning, she bent to look out the window more closely. "Where's she going?"

Letta, her face creased with worry, pointed in a vague gesture. "Janie say they gonna work them dogs. Ain't proper, her out with that man." She sat her mug down with a clunk.

Susan Pea glared at Letta. "I know she's pregnant and I'll take care of things." She picked up her cigarettes from the table. "She's not your daughter and you need to mind your place." Silence coiled up, heavy and angry between them.

Letta scrunched her eyes narrow and willed her face blank. She placed a cup of coffee before Susan Pea.

Snappish, Susan Pea shoved the mug away, causing it to slosh on the table. She stared at the puddle. "Oh, Letta, I'm sorry. I didn't really mean that. I'm at a loss. What a tangled web Eve has woven, and I just can't seem to find a way to unthread it." She lit a cigarette and inhaled deeply. Tears welled in her eyes.

"Humph." Letta folded her hands, drew back slightly. "Good thing Missus Eve gone before all this here trouble come busting up." She struggled with her place in the household, knowing she had to let white folk deal with Janie and her pregnancy. Things like this brought shame on the household.

Susan Pea shook her head and stared out the window again, as if the answer lay on the road. "I've talked with Janie several times. It's not as though she has the ability or the time to get around with any other boys. Wes is the father." Susan Pea crushed out the unsmoked cigarette and picked up the coffee mug. "I don't know what to do. Have you said anything to her?"

"Naw. I try to not be hearing stuff go on around here. I know talking to y'all 'bout that girl ain't my place." Letta crossed her arms, tilted her jaw upward, and stared at Susan Pea. "I keep my eyes down, don't see stuff. Nothing but trouble if I do."

"Okay! Okay, but has *she said* anything to you?" Irritated, Susan Pea stood and leaned against the kitchen counter, her face furrowed with lines. She took a swallow of coffee and immediately jumped to spit it out. "Oh, hell. I burned my tongue." She blew on the coffee, attempting to avoid another scalding.

Letta frowned, then wiped up the table spill. "Janie never pay me no mind. That girl think I don't know nothing except old wives' tales."

Susan Pea took a deep breath, cradled her cup in both hands, blew on the hot liquid again. "She's told me the girls at school tell her to "use what she's got.""

"Well, she's used it," Letta said. "No two ways about it, Janie in trouble. That Wes might be poking around in Janie's panties, but he after more than snatch. You mark my words."

Susan Pea leaned on the table, hand on her forehead. "I know. He wants that dog. Wants a kennel of his own. He needs Butler money and influence to do all that. He's too smart and ruthless for his own good."

Silently, Letta turned back to her kitchen chores.

Susan Pea sat staring out the window, lit and began smoking another cigarette.

CHAPTER THIRTY-FOUR
JANIE BUTLER

AT THE FIELD TURNOUT, Wes got out of the truck, slammed the door, and strode to the back. He dropped the tailgate. The dogs, eager to get going, scratched at the crate doors.

Janie scooted over to the passenger door, opened it, and waited until Mutt hopped out. She closed the door, stepped to the wheel well, and propped against it. Sighing, she lifted her face to the Indian summer sky.

"Can you believe what a glorious day this is? Still hot, but you can feel a change coming."

"Like what?" Wes spoke impatiently, his attention riveted on the field.

"Musky odor of leaves. Crunchy sounds when you walk. Sometimes, the air has layers. Sort of cooler near your legs and warmer on your face. Days are getting shorter."

"Yeah. In another few months, it'll be quail season. Need to work these boys more often."

"Not Gunner. Major says he's a finished pointer. Best in the county,"

Janie quipped, her voice happy with her grasp of the dogs and their training.

Wes snarled at her. "Drop the Major stuff. I'm the trainer."

"What does it matter?"

"Because *I'm* the trainer. Understand?"

She paused, shrugged, and, pouting, lapsed into silence.

"Gunner's solid because he's older," Wes said. "Got more experience. Besides, he was mostly trained when Major got him, years back. He never did any of the work, any of the real training. Otto's young, just now coming into his own." Wes turned toward Janie and said, "I'm the *only one training* him."

He unlatched the crates and signaled the two dogs out. They ran around him, sniffed, licked at Janie's hands, and danced in tight circles, anxious to start. "Come on," Wes said. "We need to get going."

He draped a lanyard across his shoulders, stuffed the truck keys in his pocket, and handed Janie a nylon line attached to his belt. "Stay close. You've been here before. Besides, I'll let you know if there's anything different." His voice took on impatience and eagerness. "Don't pull. Pay attention and stay on the path. It's wide and mostly clear." Wes ambled ahead, signaled the dogs with short pips, all the while keeping the line snug.

Senses heightened, Janie tapped along behind, one hand on the line while Wes walked ahead. Occasionally, the grass tangled around the heavy cane tip and sometimes her feet, making her do a jig to free herself. She'd jerk the line taut, regain her footing, and follow. Wes paused a half-step each time and continued his easy pace. Using her wood cane and the line, she negotiated changes in direction or an occasional bobble without difficulty, growing more confident as they walked.

"We're a good team," Janie said. "I trust you with all my being."

Wes did not respond.

Weeks earlier, on one of their trips to the lease, he had explained the surroundings to Janie while she held his arm and moved carefully along deer paths. He talked about the dogs, and touched her frequently, shrewdly guiding. She, in turn, slyly rubbed against his body, inhaled his manly odors and tangled her fingers in his thick arm hair. He whispered in her ear, breathed softly into her tangled curls, and drew her close, telling her to speak softly and not distract the dogs. Often, he had gently kissed along her neck and remarked how fresh she smelled.

Today's trip, with just the two of them, should end up the same as previous visits. She shivered with anticipation.

Wes stopped walking. The line slackened.

Feeling the sag, Janie paused and cocked her head. Birds chirping. Dogs rustling through broom grass. Breeze rising. Air cooling slightly. She inched her hand up the line until she touched his sweaty back, sensed muscles through his hunting vest.

She knew he felt affection for her, thought her pretty, daring, smart. She wanted him to say he loved her. Do more than keep her on the hook. As it stood, his plans were solidifying too fast without room for her.

"Being out with you and the dogs makes me feel special," Janie said. "But do you ever think about anything but those dogs?" Her voice petulant, she hugged him from behind.

"Like what?"

"Like me. Like us."

"Yeah. Sure. That's why I brought you."

Standing on her toes, she stretched across his shoulder, slid her hand along his cheek, stroking his whiskery stubble. "You didn't shave this morning." She laughed, placed her hand on his shoulder, and stepped beside him. "Know what? I hear the birds scuffing and singing and know the field is still peaceful."

"Yeah."

"Night creatures go to bed, and day things wake up. That's how I tell when the light changes. By the bustling. The smells." She fondled his hand, laughed aloud.

Wes relaxed slightly under her touch. "Yeah. I notice those things too. The dogs are quick to sense things. I watch what they are doing." He hugged her from the side. "I try to focus mainly on what the dogs sense. How they react." He stood a moment, and then continued walking, feeding the line out between them.

Feeling the slightly cooler air, Janie realized she was in the shade near an oak she had enjoyed on previous outings. She called it a grandmother tree.

"Come on. Let's sit a while. The shade is nice." She tapped through the grass and held her hand out to feel the rough bark. Dropping the line, she plopped down next to the trunk, laid the cane beside her. She did not collapse the cane; it was too easy to get small wads of grass stuck between the metal fasteners.

"I think you miss a lot because you *can* see. Come. Sit here with me." She patted the ground beside her.

"Really? What exactly do you think I miss?" He did not move.

"Sometimes I hear a rabbit scream," Janie said, "and I know a hawk must have caught breakfast for her fledglings."

"Not necessarily, Miss Smarty Cane. Maybe it was a coyote that caught that rabbit." He moved closer and leaned down to poke her in the ribs. She giggled. He poked again. She poked back. They fell to laughing.

He pulled her to standing, grasped her around the waist, and began to whirl.

She looped her arms around his neck and, with knees tucked against him, surrendered to his spinning, turning faster and faster.

Delighted, she hung on. "You're making me dizzy." Head back, she entered his playfulness before tucking her face onto his shoulder and holding tight until, breathless, she squealed, "Slow down! I won't be able to walk straight."

He slowed, placed her on her feet against the oak, and said in a rich bass, "You're something else." He kissed her on the forehead. She leaned back, face upturned, and beamed.

"Hand me my cane before I tip over."

They both gasped for breath.

Janie grasped her cane and raised her face to Wes. "Just think, I'll be going to the university next year and I'll be on my own. A student and a working woman." She beamed.

"You've told me often enough."

"I've got a mentor. His name is Pieter. Pieter DeGroot. I'll have to call him professor or some such thing, I suppose."

"You told me that, too. I met him at the kennels. Not a good shot. Besides, he's a foreigner. Not after a little snatch, is he?"

Janie play-pushed Wes on the arm. "No. Besides, Aunt Pea and I both think he's like a grandfather." She laughed and pushed at him again.

"Off to college? What are you going to do about the baby?" He placed a finger under her chin. "You can't hide it forever."

"Everyone at the house knows. Except, I'm not sure about Major." She rested her face against his chest, marveling at his heartbeat, held his hand, kissed the callouses, and breathed in the canine odors and man-sweat. "We can get married. Major will let us live in the house. You'll be in charge of the kennels."

"I don't think Major will allow me to live in that old mansion, married or not. He's certainly not gonna let someone else control those kennels."

"I'll get him to." Janie snuggled against Wes and stroked his chest. "Aunt Pea might decide to go back to New York. She likes the big city with all the people and hustle. She's too bossy anyway." Janie paused, reflected, and spoke again. "Letta will stay and help, I'm sure. She'll take care of the baby. And me. When I need her." Confident, she hugged him tighter. "But I'll be in charge."

Wes stepped back, held her at arms' length. "So, you'll be in charge. The princess of all she surveys. You sound mighty sure of yourself." He raised an eyebrow, bent to kiss her lightly on the cheek.

Janie cackled. "Yes. I'll be in charge. Me." She tossed her mane back and, hands on her hips, stood firm before him.

"What about your university job? All the bird stuff?" he asked.

"Oh." Janie paused then said, "I can do that later," she said. "After we're married, and I have the baby."

"Suppose Letta doesn't want to stay. Doesn't want to take care of another baby. What happens?" He slid his hands around her waist and spoke, a rough edge crowding his words.

"She's always been with us. She doesn't have any other place to live."

He pulled her tightly into his body, seeking her undivided attention. "There are a few other things to consider if you are serious. About you and me."

She stepped back, paused, and then burrowed against him, cheek on his chest. "Of course, I'm serious, Wes. I love you. You're the only man I've ever *really* been with."

"The only way I can see any of this working, even with the university, is you get rid of it." He nudged her belly with his hip and watched her face.

She stepped back. "What? Get rid of...?" She stuttered and blinked in rapid succession, unable to form the words. Her face took on worry wrinkles.

"I know someone who can take care of that little chore for you. *For us.*"

"Chore?" Janie slid her hands protectively across her stomach. "Are you talking about an abortion? I don't want that. I want this baby."

"I have Otto and a training kennel to think about. I don't want a baby. No family." Wes studied her face, his eyes narrowed.

"I love you." She tilted her head back. "The baby is part of that love." Her hand still covered her stomach, caressed it. "Why can't we have this baby?"

"One step at a time," Wes said. "Take on the wedding and wife part first. Be satisfied."

"I'll be a good wife. We'll have a wedding and all, but I want the baby, too."

"Major will splatter all over if he thinks we'd been rolling around together—especially in his town. Probably have me shot."

"No. I can make him listen. He thinks I'm his pet now, with Mother gone." Anxious, she slid her hand along his shoulder and down his arm, seeking his hand. "Besides, he's never around. Mostly he stays in Albany, with his other woman."

"We need to have a long engagement." Wes cuddled her and said in a flat voice, "Get the town on our side. We can't do that with a baby. Especially if it comes too close to the wedding. Folks speculate, talk shotgun marriage, and *that* would really send Major ballistic."

"I don't care about that stuff," Janie said.

Wes ignored her comment, continued talking. "We marry, wait awhile, and have a baby later." He propped his chin on top of her head, stroked her back. "That should keep tongues from wagging. Major tries to break us up, and he'll be the subject of town gossips. Maybe even lose business connections."

Janie squirmed against him. "No. I want this baby. Major will let us get married if I tell him we're having a baby."

"Don't do that." Wes held her shoulders, hard, and pinned her against the tree.

Janie flinched, face draining to ashen, gasped for breath.

"That man doesn't listen to anyone," Wes said, his voice cold, bristly. "He acts in his own best interest. Makes it a point of pride to protect the Butler name. That's why we need to wait."

"He'll listen to me." Janie's voice resonated with confidence, even as tears welled up.

"We'll get engaged. Announce it to the town real proper like. You get settled into your job. Start your degree. I'll get things going for us here, *then* we'll get married. There'll be nothing that old man can do."

"*No!*" Janie, voice quivering, shook her head violently. "That's months away. And that way, we couldn't even live together. Double no."

Wes ignored her outburst. "Besides, Major will be more likely to give me Otto if we line things up first. Make a wedding present out of him."

"But, you love me, don't you?" Janie asked.

"I've got feelings for you," he said.

"Feelings? What kind of feelings? Tell me," Janie said. Her voice carried a high note bordering on panic.

"Curiosity. Affection. You're an intriguing lay," Wes said.

"Don't you love me?"

"Of course, I love you. But be careful. Don't force the issue, girl." Wes spoke sharply. "You had your reasons for spreading your legs."

"No! I did it because I love you," Janie said.

"Not hardly. You love the attention. From a *man*. The real reason is that sex feels good. That's why you do it. You're as lustful as any other bitch." Wes leaned forward and nibbled her ear. "We both like the *danger* of being together. Possibility of discovery."

Janie nuzzled into his face. "But you said I'm special. You said I'm different from any other woman you've ever had. And I love you." Desperation coated her words.

"Are you using this baby to manipulate me?" Wes asked. "I've had this pulled on me before. Besides, you're trying to make Major do more for you, now that's your mama's dead. Make him do for you out of guilt? You have your own reasons. You are as conniving as the rest of us."

"No! I love you. You must love me, too."

"I told you how I feel. Let's do this right."

She stood still for a heartbeat and then lunged toward his voice, her hands clawing for his face. He sidestepped her clumsy attempt, held her wrists, and squeezed her tight until she gulped.

"You've got to marry me!" Janie screeched, voice high and panic-stricken. "Aunt Pea and Letta already know that you're the father. I'll tell Major and there will be no backing out."

Wes elbowed her, pinned her tighter to the uneven tree bark. "He'll not put up with you saying it was mine."

Janie squirmed and flailed until he loosened his hold. He held his face next to her ear. "They both think I'm low-level, white trash. They have no interest in me being part of the *great* Butler family. They certainly don't want to think about *me* in *your* panties."

She jerked away, stumbled slightly, covered her face, and sobbed.

"Major is not one to allow any loose talk or chance blackmail from me or any other swinging dick. He'll have me done away with as soon as he thinks I've already tapped you. Gotta do away with this one. Fast. We'll have another."

"No. I'm not doing it that way." Janie's voice ratcheted up several notches. She shoved against Wes.

"If you want it that way, then I plan on clearing out as soon as I can get my hands on Otto."

"Clear out? I thought we were getting married. That you loved me." Sobs rattled out of her throat. She fumbled for his hunting vest, hooked her fingers in a pocket, and pulled him toward her.

He yanked her hand away, pinned her arms, and spoke hoarse. "I'll help you get rid of this baby. We'll talk up an engagement. Do it my way. Get Susan Pea so she must support us. Otherwise, you're only another convenient piece of patch."

She twisted a hand loose, stretched out a claw toward his face in an attempt to scratch him, and wailed. The noise bumped against a tree, another, and another until the pine needles muffled it into stillness.

His hands in her hair, he twisted her head to the side, whispered into her ear, licking and nibbling. "Get rid of it. Afterwards, we can marry. You being blind is going to make things hard at first, but we can get used to stuff. Then think about another baby. I don't need a wife and some brat dragging me back. Especially one that can't really see."

Janie began to cry even as she sought his lips. He continued to pull her hair, forcing her face up, and returned the kiss. Braced against the tree, she wrapped a leg around him. Pissed, heartbroken, desperate, she threw her body into him, intent on changing his mind.

He stroked her thigh, kissed her on the lips.

A MASTER at stringing women along, Wes found pleasure in variety. Until he grew tired or manipulated them to *his* ends. Janie was turning out to be more of a problem than he imagined. Her insistence on having this baby was making life unlivable—fast. He wanted Otto, not a troublesome woman and baby. He needed time to think.

He'd trained Major's dogs for years and kept his eyes open. When Otto appeared and ignited new ideas, he rooted around in his opportunist soul for a ticket out. Now, with Janie almost seventeen, he thought her ripe for the plucking. A perfect pawn.

Major's first wife, Lacy Anderson Butler, had disappeared. The man then exploited his housekeeper Letta Davis to raise Andy, and, without announcement or even a hint he was thinking about it, remarried several years later.

Eve Bulter, wife number two, had arrived at the mansion with a girl-child from a previous relationship. Within three years, after a town brawl, Andy joined the Army at Major's instigation and left. Major had focused on rebuilding the crumbling Butler empire. The hunting kennels were his nod to the genteel South.

Wes snorted. He ran his hands up and down her arms.

She tried to kiss him again, seduce him with her body.

"Think about it, Major's son-in-law." He whooped, head thrown back, laughing. "You think he'd try to make me change my name to Butler so's he doesn't lose his throne?"

CHAPTER THIRTY-FIVE
LETTA DAVIS

On the border between the cultivated field and tangle of woods, two wrinkled women and a wizened dwarf sat in the fragile glow and passed around a bottle. A red rooster lay on the ground behind them, eyes blinking, his feet tied with twine. In the navy shadows beyond the trio, a form moved, and another. Voices rose slightly. A grunt emerged.

Letta stood in the navy darkness at the edge of the thicket and watched the campfire smolder. Beating at the underbrush with her stick, she created a series of soft snaps, sounds like bird bones breaking, and walked toward the knot of people. At the edge of the gathering, she squatted on a downed log, took a long, deep breath, and pulled a tin of moist tobacco from her pocket. She passed it around, an offering appeasing the Old Ones.

The conjure woman poked the glowing coals with a bent stick and closed her milky eyes, spoke in a quavering voice. "What need you gots for me now? I tolt you to send them three—Merry, Elijah, and John—north." Her eyes flashed open.

Night sounds rose and eased by before Letta spoke. "I done what you say. All the plans set in place. Will send my children off when time grows ripe. Then wait for word to come back they be safe. Like you done tell me."

"Hum." The crone pointed a finger in Letta's direction. "You and yours be safe when y'all gone. Time grows ripe soon."

Letta looked at her scarred hands, rubbed them together.

Embers reflected in the conjure woman's eyes. Arms resting on her knees, she spoke again. "You a used-up wife, dry inside. No more babies. Husband gone. What you want of me this night?"

"Only got one more thing needs tending." Letta hesitated, rose, took the woman's vein-knotted hand, turned it palm up, and placed two thick, gold coins in it. They gleamed in the moonlight.

The conjure woman clinked them together, rolled them over and over. She closed her fingers around the orbs and placed her fist next to her heart. Silence lengthened. Finally, she stretched her arm out to rest on her knee, hand turned up, open. A fierce glow emanated from the gold. "Coins be old. Older than my time. They speak of blood."

Letta spoke slow. "They buried by those in the days before freedom. Blood spilled on them in the time of chains, but they stay hidden. Blue bottle tree, sometimes Old Ones, watch over them."

A thin boy darted out of the dark, snatched the coins, and faded into the shadows.

The woman nodded. "What be you wantin'?" Her voice quivered in the manner of the elderly.

"A man needs cross over to that other side." Letta stretched her arms out, warmed her hands at the fire before she sat back on her haunches. "I done what you said. I listen to them crows. Old Ones. I plan. I bend with the wind."

Somewhere in the pines, an owl hen hooted and spread her wings. Phantom-like, she lifted from the branch to drift silent across the cornfield, hunting food for her fledglings. Near the briars, the shadow of a fox moved, dissolved. Life and death shifting, balanced one against the other.

The old woman's voice crackled. "Revenge be on your heart. You needs own it. You know this man?"

"I know him," Letta said. The words seemed too loud, reverberated against her own ears. She watched the coals, felt the heat.

"Why he got to go?"

"The man has lived enough," Letta said. "Ever' thing he touches shrivels and dies. He used up all his goodness. Now, he got no soul."

The crone scratched in the dust with a stick, cast several bird bones, seashells, and a twisted stick in the embers' dark glow. She closed her eyes. Time crawled by before she spoke again.

"You be killin'you own line if'n you seek vengeance." Her eyes flashed open.

"*His* daddy forced on *my* mother don't make him nothing to me." Letta spat into the ashes. It hissed in response. "*Man needs to go.*"

The owl hooted a second time, flew on silent wings through the pines. A burning knot ruptured, the sound spiraled up with smoke, freed the acid burnt smell.

"You elder sister cause that man. I know what you ain't say. Seed come from this man's own father. You best think on this."

"I done dwell on it. Time and time again. This man evil. His own flesh and blood, his own sister, want him go. I know her thoughts, gather them with my own." Letta sat silent a moment, then spoke without anger, her voice flat. "He need to join his daddy. They can serve together in hell."

"The devil be out walkin' tonight. The Evil One and this man struggle at the crossroads. Man don't know it yet, but *he want* to go." The woman pointed a crooked finger at Letta. "Still, y'all needs think on it. Needs to *want* it. Thoughts strong. Ill will come loose from a person, fly unattended. Haints catch them thoughts. Use them."

Letta laced her fingers together and watched the rooster struggle against the twine, then grow still. The wind brushed through the pines, moaned, and died.

The crone's voice grew hoarse. "When that man cross over the river, each be free. Families be released. Balance come 'ween good and evil, birth and death. Tell no one. Not the wind or the crows. After that man cross, you choose you path careful. Never speak again of him. Remember it all."

Silence settled. A shooting star appeared against the darkness, its burning trail cutting through the dark before vanishing. A vixen's sharp bark rose among the trees.

The hoodoo crone rattled a bag of bones, spoke knowingly. "Look in them road ditches for white flowers grow on hollow stems. Smells of carrots. Got purple spots on them stems."

"I know this plant," Letta said. The tall parsley-looking plant congregated around her thoughts. She sniffed the air. Saw springtime leaves, seed heads bending heavy, long roots digging deep into the soil.

"Do like I tell you. Collect them for man that gotta go. Devil dance a gig, smack his lips when he sees that man coming."

From beyond the circle, the sound of clinking coins grew loud. Distant lightning stirred. A storm collected in the west, the scent of rain built. Gloom grew thick.

"Coffee. He like coffee," the crone said. "Strong coffee."

Letta spat a last stream of tobacco juice into the ashes. With effort, she rose from her squat, limbs heavy and tired, and disappeared into the night.

CHAPTER THIRTY-SIX
LETTA DAVIS

First thing the next morning, Letta sent Janie off to her lessons and handed Susan Pea a grocery shopping list. "We be needing these things. You do better with shopping than me."

As soon as Susan Pea was out of sight, Letta stood on the back porch, shaded her eyes with her hand, her head turned toward the kennels searching for Elijah's thin form. Her last child, a quiet boy, almost ready to step into manhood. She needed to send him north in the next few days before people got restive. With fall coming, people forgot about Blacks, started thinking about bird season.

The air took on an electricity, a change not seen, but heard in the footfall of the town's men, in the way they caressed their shotguns with oil-soaked rags. Even the hunting dogs sensed the change.

She stepped off the porch and ran her hands over the lower tiers of her bottle tree. The glass rattled like hail on a tin roof as the colors fluctuated on the dewy grass. She continued her quick pace to the kennels, hands fisted in her apron pockets.

"Elijah. I be needing you." Her voice too quick, anxious.

"Yes, Momma." The teen popped his head up, concerned. His mother rarely came to the kennels—for any reason.

"I need you to fetch me something."

"Yes, Momma. I here. I finish up with these here dogs." He turned the faucet off, dried his hands on his pants, and hurried toward her.

"Go down to that bar ditch run alongside yonder bog." She pointed. "Fetch me some water parsley."

Elijah stared at her. "Water parsley? That tall weed grow in them bogs?"

"That be it. The one with white flowers. Stems be green with purple spots. Smells like carrots. You seen it."

"Why you want that stuff?"

"Never you mind." Letta's voice waivered slightly. "Look for them white flowers and purple-spot stems. Cover up. Use gloves. You pull up the whole plant—maybe three or four. Lay them on the porch at home." She wiped nervous sweat off her hands.

"Aw, Momma, I can't pick nothing with them work gloves."

Letta grabbed Elijah by the shoulder, her fingers digging into the soft tissue. "You do as I tell you do. Don't let nothing touch you." She shoved him slightly and released her hold.

Elijah rolled his shoulder, allowed the shadow of a frown to cross his face. He stood a moment, cocked his head, and said, "I done mostly finished. Reckon to go on now."

"All right. Get moving." She waved her hand dismissively.

"Yes, Momma." He blinked several times and set off at a trot down the dirt path.

Letta's day moved slowly, her thoughts a constant jumble. She felt guilty at sending Elijah to fetch the water parsley, yet she'd be missed if she went. Susan Pea's return from the store annoyed her, made her anxious. Still, Letta continued to *feel* the dark thoughts of those around her. Toward evening, she heard a crow caw, tell her the shadows were waiting. Tall weeds with leaves, seed heads, and roots intact, lay near the threshold of the front door when Letta arrived home that night. The yellow glow of the lantern clearly outlined their shape on the porch. Her aches dissipated. Blood thrummed hard through her body and she nodded satisfaction. "Time be passing. All things ready when the leaving hour come."

CHAPTER THIRTY-SEVEN
ANDY BUTLER

ANDY, held his steaming coffee, stood at the edge of the back porch. He half-turned and hollered back into the kitchen. "It's almost nine o'clock. Wes ever been this late before?"

"I never seen 'em late, even a little." Letta stepped out onto the porch.

Andy knew she disliked the man and had little interest in his whereabouts. He also knew she kept track of Wes as a result of Elijah's hours there, despite his patent disregard of her son's work.

"He's usually here before sunup, isn't he?" Andy's shouted question was rhetorical since he already knew the answer. He sipped his coffee and continued to look across the yard to the kennels.

Letta simply grunted her response, wiped her hands on the dish-towel, and turned back into the kitchen.

Andy lingered a moment longer, finished his coffee, and left the cup on the porch railing. He ambled toward the kennels.

Sadie sat politely at the puppy-yard gate, tail thumping. The little ones tumbled around her.

Andy cocked his head. "No breakfast yet? Well, let's fix that." He opened the gate, grabbed her dish, and ducked into the feed room.

She danced anxiously around the yard and fell to eating as soon as he placed the bowl before her. He refilled the water bucket.

Finished with the mama dog and her puppies, Andy turned to the adult males. Gunner sat at the gate, whined, and shifted from one foot to the other. The old pointer ignored the kibbles Andy put down, instead scratched at the gate. Andy frowned and eyed the other runs.

Otto's run stood empty. Gate closed and latched, as if Wes had taken only the one dog out. Dogs in the other runs paced and looked askance at Andy. Water buckets were either empty or only half full. Taking one dog out for training was not unusual, but leaving the others without their morning feed was not like Wes.

The August sun had climbed high, dragging heat along behind. The one-eyed tom was already settled in a patch of dappled sun, seemingly content to clean his whiskers. Gunner continued to pace and whine. He did not touch his kibbles.

Something felt off. Andy's stomach knotted. His throat tightened. He scanned the barn drive for any sign of the Ford pickup. Nothing.

Slowly, he searched the area, found odd tire tracks where they cut across the grass. He knelt and ran his hand over the flattened grass. The surrounding area still glistened with condensation. Whatever vehicle crushed the grass came after dewfall, in predawn hours. Tracks showed a vehicle pulling off the gravel drive, onto grass, and back onto gravel. Andy's neck hair prickled. Worry gnawed at him.

He clumped up the back steps into the kitchen. "Letta! You see anything out of sorts when you got here?"

"No, sah," she replied. "Can't say I did. Still a little dark while I was walking over. Sun come on up and was in my eyes time I got to the house. You not up when I got here. Ain't changed my habits." She rolled her eyes and turned back to her work.

"Odd tire tracks, but I'm not sure they were from Wes. Kennels still dirty and the dogs don't look like they've been fed. I'd swear one's missing. Did you see his truck when you got here?"

"I don't rightly remember." Letta paused, worry lines bunched around her eyes. She sucked at her teeth. "Don't reckon it was here, now I think on it."

"Break like this in routine can't be good, a missing dog and a latched gate."

"I never pay no mind to them kennels. I come in and started coffee. Fixing biscuits."

"What about your boy? Wasn't he supposed to be here cleaning the runs?"

"Elijah?" Letta looked sharply at Andy. "You speak of Elijah. He home today. He be here this afternoon." Aggravation played in her voice. "Y'all Butlers should know and call my boy's name after all these years. He be gone soon and you people hardly recognized his existence. He deserve to be called by name."

Andy turned, did not acknowledge her aggravation. He snatched up the jeep keys and started out the backdoor.

"Want I should call anyone?" Letta wiped her hands. "Need to get Missus Susan up?"

"Not yet. Let me see if he's out doing some early training and simply running late. I'll see if I can find him."

"Major not want you taking his jeep. He'll not want you charging around after Wes. He give that feller lots of rope, what with them dogs and all."

"I know," Andy said. "Still, I should be back soon. Don't tell Susan Pea. She'll only worry and want details. Which I don't have." A creeping anxiety rose, sent shivers up his neck and onto his scalp.

Mind whirring, he drove west out of town, remembering Wes favored the Corley Plantation lease, especially when working the shorthair alone. Bobwhite were plentiful and surrounded by scrub woodland and dotted with open fields, a solid training site. Heat and humidity, best handled predawn or near dusk, may have prompted Wes to leave early. Maybe he deferred feeding and kennel cleaning until full daylight when he got back. With hunt season looming, the kennel pace had picked up.

The drive, relatively short on gravel roads, took only thirty minutes. Andy guided the jeep into a sand-track pullout, took binoculars and a whistle from the glove compartment. No sign of any other vehicle. Not likely he would find anything here unless Wes entered the field from the northeast side, fifteen miles around on a twisting dirt road. If Wes was out there, Andy should intercept him midway. He'd probably see Otto first, because the dog typically ranged ahead.

Andy could not shake the feeling Wes was up to something. He started through the tangled grass. For the better part of an hour, he tramped through low scrub, flushed one covey, but found no sign of either dog or man. Sweat strung his eyes and gnats swarmed, their incessant buzzing around his face an irritation. His anger at Wes mounted as he flapped at the insects.

At eleven, Andy looped back to the jeep, gave a last scan, and drove twenty twisting miles to Flint River. Sweeper branches dipped into an amber-colored flow and sunlight glinted off open, wet stretches before sand bars gave way to steep banks and occasional white-water chutes favored by canoeists. High water debris on banks complicated footpaths and take-outs. He relished the area's challenge, recognizing its haunting beauty. Perfect for deer, quail, and foxes. And dumping anything unwanted.

Andy searched until one o'clock. Sweat soaked his pants and plastered his cotton tee across his chest. He stopped at a gravel bar, knelt at river's edge, peeled his tee off, splashed his face and neck, and dashed water up his arms. He sat on a tree felled in a long-ago storm and tried to puzzle out what could have happened. He realized Wes could be anywhere along the river or on any of several different leases. No choice but to head home, counting the morning's work as simply an error in communication.

The sun was sliding toward late afternoon when Andy pulled onto Highway 310 toward Bainbridge. Six miles down, a Georgia state trooper appeared behind him, flashed patrol lights. Andy pulled onto the highway edge and watched the officer in his rearview mirror. The officer made a radio call before he slung the cruiser door open, walked toward the jeep pickup.

The patrolman leaned on the open window.

"May I see some identification, please?"

Andy presented his driver's license and military ID.

"Mr. Butler says you took his vehicle without permission."

"Major's a controlling sort, rather domineering. But if you've been with Sheriff long, you already know that."

"Yes, sir. Only doing my job and following orders."

Andy snorted and shifted, tapped the steering wheel with his thumbs. After all, there was no direct connection between state patrol and county sheriff except a cooperative relationship.

"Did you have permission to take this vehicle?"

"No. My father owns it. I'm out looking for our hired man, our trainer. He didn't show up this morning. Our German shorthair pointer's missing. I think there's a connection. I should have realized Major'd pull a stunt like this."

"Do you have a weapon, sir?"

"I took a deer rifle when I left this morning." He squinted at the officer. "Mind telling me what this is about?"

"I'll let Sheriff explain. Right now, I'm taking you into county courthouse for a stolen vehicle. Step out, please, sir."

"I told you, it's Major's and I'm his son."

"Step out of the vehicle. Now."

Susan Pea bailed Andy out two days later. As an active serviceman arrested by local law enforcement, Andy was finally escorted to his Army base for holding while case jurisdiction was determined. A mounting frustration gnawed on him at the tangled web propagated among Georgia Highway Patrol, Decatur County sheriff, Military Judge Advocate General, and Georgia State Game Service.

Andy could barely contain his fury as he and Susan Pea walked across the base parking lot. She unlocked the Pontiac, stepped back a moment at the blast of hot air before sliding into the driver's side.

He moved around the car and climbed in, rolled the window down. "Why the fuck would Major have me arrested for looking after his interests? Especially for a dog he doesn't care about. Unless he's involved with the disappearance. His hand is all over this stinking mess."

Susan Pea finished buckling her seatbelt and pulled out into traffic. She pushed the lighter in and lit up. She sighed and shook her head. "Nephew, you have fallen into a deep pit of no return. For someone that's supposed to be tactically smart, this is a non-smart move."

Andy clinched his jaw, the muscles pulling taut under his skin. He propped his arm out the window. "Damn sonsofbitches. Both bastards —Major and Wes—need to be stretched out cold and blue." He stared straight ahead, continued to grit his teeth.

She looked over at Andy. "I don't care if you do kill both, but be quiet about it. And smart. This isn't one of your long sniper shots to brag on. Roll your window up. Air conditioner's on its last legs."

Andy complied and fell silent. They circled the town, drove the long way around while both cooled down. The Pontiac air conditioner hummed but did little toward cooling. As they neared the homeplace, Andy spoke from a distance. "Janie know anything? She might know something since it involves Wes."

"I haven't asked her yet. She should have gotten home from school while I was bonding you out. I'm not looking forward to this."

Andy looked at his aunt. Felt a twitch of guilt. Even if Janie knew nothing, it would fall to Susan Pea to tell Janie her lover had disappeared. And, while it would remain unsaid, the man likely favored that dog over Janie.

CHAPTER THIRTY-EIGHT
ANDY BUTLER

CRISP BEHIND A MILITARY DEMEANOR, the army advocate sat rigid before Andy. The interrogation room, stark and almost empty, amplified every harsh sound.

"What rights do I have? Exactly?" Andy nervously brushed his hand through his hair.

"In your case, as an Army captain, active duty, Uniform Code of Military Justice prevails. As it stands now, murder violates both civilian and military law. We've got an Army man accused and a civilian crime. We've got two jurisdictions, both with trial rights. We'll need to formally untangle legality first and settle on an exact charge. Or charges."

It had been a week since Wes's disappearance and a half day since his body had been discovered. Hikers had come across his truck and found a gruesome bloated body slumped along it, covered in flies. Word had it there was one, very neat bullet cavity to the forehead. Upon inspection, the exit wound left a crater in the back of his skull. Contents from the head splattered all over the door panel in a bloody bones-and-brains Rorschach image. The empty dog crate sat in the back.

Sweat greased Andy's armpits, leaving damp rings. "Do I have any say on these trumped-up charges?"

"Captain, the charges are serious and appear to have some credence." The advocate twisted a pen between his fingers, put it down, and flipped open a manila folder.

"Your Ranger record is spotless and exemplary. You have gotten good reports and earned promotions since your initial enlistment. That's good news. Enlisting under a bit of a legal tangle goes against you. Arrest for using your father's jeep without permission is not good. And, of course, your lack of alibi doesn't help."

"With all due respect, Colonel, this is a setup."

"I'd agree, except for your fingerprints."

"Of course, my prints are all over everything. All over the house. I've been staying there a few weeks while on bereavement leave for my stepmother. I told them I took the gun."

The advocate drummed a pen on the desk, stopped, and stared directly into Andy's face.

"It's known you and Wes had conflict over your stepsister. I believe she claims to be carrying his child, which constitutes motive. Rifle gives us the weapon. A full day without any witness or other alibi gives opportunity. We also have a body."

"Sir, with all due respect, I didn't kill that sonofabitch. I didn't pull the trigger."

"If I understand correctly, your father unloads and cleans his firearms after every use."

"All true, as far as it goes. Anybody needed killing, it was him. But I didn't—did not—kill that perverted bully." Andy sat rigid, hands on the table. His gaze did not deviate from the man before him.

"Your aunt has hired a civilian attorney. He should be here tomorrow. We'll start sorting through procedures on all sides. Military and civilian legal systems are intertwined, yet independent. In your case, as I explained earlier, both systems have a claim."

Andy dropped his gaze to the file before the two men. He brushed a hand over his face.

The colonel closed the file and pushed his chair back. The sharp grating underscored the tension and dangling questions.

"Everything you've mentioned so far sounds legitimate. But it is also circumstantial." Andy glared at the man standing behind the table.

"Possibly. But your prints were all over the cartridge in the rifle." The colonel paused for a moment. He collected his papers and thumped the file on the edge of the table. "Your saving grace, or worse luck, depending on your viewpoint, may be that the killing bullet hasn't been located yet. It seems to have travelled through the victim and probably ended up on the road in the dirt. Maybe the woods. That open field has been hunted for years. And other vehicles have driven that road before and after the shooting. Place is a regular shell repository." The advocate had no facial expression. He stuffed the file in a briefcase and called the guard.

Susan Pea had quickly hired an attorney. He was a contradiction. His clothing stated elegance. His appearance screamed pugilist. He wore a double-breasted pinstripe suit with a purple Hermès tie and contrasting pocket square. He had a pronounced chin and a nose that deviated slightly left. Broken capillaries in his face signaled his love of drink.

"I didn't do it," Andy had said at their first meeting.

"I believe you," the lawyer replied, his voice a whiskey and smoke gravel. "Keep in mind that what I think has no bearing with the judge. But we're going to clear this up and see you walk."

Andy visibly relaxed, coming as it did from what appeared to be a street fighter. That is, if the man could keep alcohol use and the defense separate.

The lawyer lit a cigarette and began. "Here are the facts: Your old man wasn't home. You took his gun. And his jeep. You suspected foul play with or by the kennelman Wes. You have had a solid career in the Army, no rap sheet, and commendations. Most townspeople wanted to see Wes dead. Lots of possible suspects, including killers for hire." The attorney opened his briefcase and clicked a ballpoint pen several times.

"Now, tell me what you know and *what you don't want to divulge.*" He moved his chair closer and stretched his hands out. "Tell me, in detail, what you did that day. Including your thoughts." He settled, pen poised over his legal pad, and waited.

CHAPTER THIRTY-NINE
FUNERAL

Susan Pea balked at allowing Janie to attend Wes's funeral, fearing it would exacerbate emotional upheaval and create a whirlwind of scandal.

Janie howled and fought Susan Pea.

Letta remained stoic. And silent.

Janie screamed until hoarse before bolting through the kitchen door and disappearing outside.

Later, Letta found her on the feed room floor between bales of straw, having cried herself into hiccups. Wes' favorite tomcat, on top of the stack, watched the girl with his one eye, tail wrapped round his feet, tip twitching. Letta scooted the cat away, plopped down, put her arms around Janie, and rocked.

"Wes was going to marry me," Janie said. "We were going to run the kennel together."

"Oh, child, that man talk don't mean what you think it does. It only talk."

"You don't understand. He really loved me." Janie wiped her nose on her sleeve and turned in Letta's direction. "He might not have said it like that, but I know he did. *Me*." She spoke as much to herself as to Letta, patted her chest emphasizing her declaration.

Letta, dry-eyed, remained on the floor, holding Janie until her tears subsided. She part-lifted Janie to her feet, helped her to the straw bale, and sat next to her. Letta stroked the girl's hair, petted her forehead until the shadows shifted inside the barn as dusk gave way to night.

"Let's go get you cleaned up," Letta said. She stood and pulled Janie to her feet. "Nothing more can be done now. What's done ain't gonna be undone. Not even if you crying you eyes out." Arm wrapped around her waist, Letta guided Janie out.

In a soft voice, Janie said, "Where's the cat? Wes's cat. Do you see it?" She felt along the bales, until she touched the cat. It purred and preened under Janie's hand. "It's mine now. I'll take care of it."

Sensing the girl's intention, the savvy creature darted off before Janie could pick it up. She began to cry again, dissolving into gulps.

Placing hands on Janie's shoulders, Letta guided her out of the barn. "We come back, get that willful thing later. Right now, you and me gonna see your aunt. She crying and worried her own self."

"I'm not talking to her. I hate her, anyway." Janie pushed back from Letta's hold. She tightened her grip.

Janie continued to cry and talk. "She's always calling Wes trash. I don't want to talk with her. I guess now that I'm having his baby, I'm trash, too."

"Now, now," Letta said. "People say hurtful things when they upset. Besides, she only family you got left."

"No, she's not. There's Andy."

"Army man can't be no family." Letta grimaced, thinking about John. Thankfully, he was not career. "Come on. You got to come inside. Can't stay in no barn."

Two days later, Lee Town residents, remembering their homeboy, turned out more numerous than fleas on a dog for the funeral. They hung about in clusters and gossiped, each telling what little they knew of events. What they didn't know, they filled in.

Susan Pea and Letta stayed home with Janie.

Major appeared at the last minute as Wes's employer.

CHAPTER FORTY
SUSAN PEA BUTLER

At her core, Susan Pea did not have heart to set foot in Eve's room after her death. Neither she nor Janie could bring themselves to attempt cleaning and returning the room to its former library status. Not until Letta had completed yet another perfunctory dusting, moved books around on shelves, tossed left over medicines, and gotten rid of the walker, did Susan Pea brace herself and commandeer Janie, did they begin. Bereft, both moved as if in quicksand.

After a half hour, Janie waved her hands in the air. "I don't know what to do. How to act. What to *feel*." She plunked down on the bed, and sobbed.

"I understand," Susan Pea said. "We'll do this together, one step at a time."

Janie rose from the bed, looked around the room, and shook her head in confusion. "I can't think. Can't make decisions. Right now, I'm just too sad. First Mother, now Wes murdered, and Andy all tangled up. He's my brother and I love him too. What should I believe? Who to believe? I'm too lost."

With tears in her eyes, Susan Pea put her arms around Janie and kissed her forehead. "We're going to get through this together. You hear me?" She hugged Janie hard and held her hand.

Janie fumbled with the Kleenex box, continued to sniffle and cry.

"For right now, let me take you to your piano teacher's. Y'all can play your mother's favorite music. Maybe find something new. Okay?"

Susan Pea hugged Janie while she cried quietly, moved around as if sleepwalking.

"I'll work through this first round of sorting and deciding. Put everything that's personal aside for you later."

"Okay."

"I can probably handle most with Letta's will help anyway. She knew your mother and knows who needs what things." Susan Pea sighed deep, absently ran her hands over Janie's shoulders.

"I don't know what to do anymore. I feel so alone," Janie said. She wiped her nose on her sleeve.

"Oh, baby girl, go spend the afternoon with your music." Susan Pea hugged Janie. They swayed together a moment before she stepped back and held Janie at arm's length. "I'll save Eve's real treasures for us when you feel up to it."

Returning from dropping Janie at her music teacher's, Susan Pea found Letta and Elijah taking the bed upstairs to Eve's old room. They worked quickly, put on fresh linens and replaced the floral spread with a plaid one.

Downstairs, Susan Pea straightened stacks of books and papers and wandered out, still unable to focus. Finally, she settled down to sorting through personal items.

Letta and Elijah finished upstairs and began working quietly around Susan Pea, returning the library to its original state.

Sunlight meandered across the floor. The room seemed to breathe in relief.

The following day, after Janie left for school, Susan Pea donned old jeans and a denim shirt, plunged into cleaning closets and chests of drawers. That chore went faster than Susan Pea expected. Nonetheless, it still took most of the morning.

At noon, Letta stuck her head in the door. "Missus Susan, time to stop pawing through them clothes and stuff. 'Specially them newspaper scraps. Dry your eyes and wipe your nose. Come eat lunch. You know'd this day coming. Bear up."

Susan Pea sniffed, struggled for self-control. "Truth is, I don't have much of an appetite."

"Yessum. Well, you come on and eat anyway. Done fixed up a mess that chicken salad you said you had up north. Ain't never heard tell of it before." She clucked her teeth in annoyance.

"You made it with cranberries and walnuts for me?" Susan perked up, pleased that Letta would do something just for her.

"Ain't got no walnuts. Used pecans," she called over her shoulder as she walked from the cluttered room into the kitchen. "Room cleaning done waited this long, leave it go another hour."

Susan Pea stretched, arched her back to relieve the muscles, and moseyed into the kitchen with several items flung across her arm.

"I finished all the closets and most of drawers and separated everything, but I need to go back through some stuff with Janie. I put things she might be especially interested in aside."

Letta took a deep breath. "That good. Girl be wanting keepsakes."

Susan Pea continued talking as if Letta had not spoken. "Maybe that red, silk top—Eve wore it when she spoke at the Ladies Auxiliary Ball several years ago. Janie will need something dressy for graduation. Maybe this would be a good remembrance."

"Miss Janie can't see red," Letta said.

Stressed, Susan Pea barked at Letta. "We'll *tell* her it's red. Besides, that silk top has tucks. She can feel them." Susan Pea folded the blouse and stacked it neatly with several other items.

"Yessum. She can feel." Letta reflected a moment, hands shoved in her apron pockets. "I recollect we talk one time and she say color got taste. Say red like cayenne pepper. I tell her that blouse look like that pepper taste." She smiled faintly, remembering their afternoon shelling peas weeks ago.

Susan Pea stood in the middle of the room, stretched a second time.

Letta stacked crackers on a plate, stirred chicken salad and added more mayonnaise.

"Janie can make more memories in her red-pepper blouse. But what am I going to do with all those other clothes?" Susan Pea swept her arm toward the cluttered room.

Letta picked up two glasses and began pouring iced tea. She spoke slowly as she moved around the table. "Most of them dresses and suits best go to secondhand store on Broad Street. Winter stuff you send over to them churches on westside. Sunday meeting dresses and shoes go to churches, too." She scooped up salad and arranged it on a plate. "Dress jackets be good for church ladies. Coats go to cleaning women 'cause they walk to work. A few smaller sweaters and coats I take over to southside schoolhouse for kids."

"The school? Those things will swallow them. The arms are too long and shoulders too wide," Susan Pea said.

"Them kids grow into them." She stopped her kitchen tasks to stare at Susan Pea. "Why you ask me what to do, you gonna argue about it?"

"Damn you, Letta, don't be so cantankerous." Susan Pea's voice carried a note of irritation. "I didn't mean anything by that comment. You know these people. I don't. I need your help."

"That's right. I know them. You don't." Letta sucked her teeth and continued glaring before finally tucking her ruffled feathers. "You in charge. But I telling you that girl don't need no clothes. She got her own stuff. Give them clothes where they do most good. Give her keepsake stuff she can feel, hold. Special things she pass down to her own babies someday." Letta gestured toward the chicken salad. "Sit down and eat."

Two glasses sweated on the table. More parched than hungry, Susan Pea downed a tall glass of iced tea and refilled it before taking a bite. They ate in silence until she pushed her half-finished plate away. "I feel so overwhelmed. Don't know how to handle Janie. Nor Andy. Do you think he wants a keepsake also?"

Letta rose from the table, cleared the plates, and put leftovers away. "You ain't got to handle Andy. He grown. Let him choose. Janie one to worry over. Her and that baby that's coming," Letta said. "A book, even if she can't read it, be okay. Books feel good."

"Well, what do you think of perfume? Eve always loved 'Joy'. Used it even toward the end."

"Perfume good. Janie likes smells." Letta continued clearing the kitchen. "She and her mother used to primp and talk and sit in there smelling that stuff. Missus Eve tell Janie how to dress and be a lady. How to use face creams and keep her hands soft. They be laughing and playing together. Them school gals come a time or two, talking and helping with all sorts of things."

Outside, Mutt barked with a series of cheerful woofs. Greying around the muzzle, he nonetheless retained his enthusiasm for announcing any visitor. Susan Pea's head jerked toward the porch. The mailman, on his rounds, made his way up the steps.

He clumped across porch boards and stuffed letters, store circulars, and grocery flyers into the box. He whistled as he continued his rounds. Mutt, apparently satisfied he'd defended his territory, resumed his napping position, head on paws. He fell asleep.

Stepping outside, Susan Pea retrieved the mail and returned to the kitchen. "Seems odd not to have Eve in the porch swing. Toward the end, it was one of her few pleasures."

"Yessum. Fact is, she make Major put that swing up when Janie started that high school. Said she sit there wait on her girl come home from school."

Letta continued puttering around, washing plates, wiping counters, and tidying up.

"I'll finish going through the clothes," Susan Pea said. "Really don't see anything else we should keep now that you mention it. Can you fold all this stuff and separate it into stacks? Maybe label where they should go? I still have jewelry, personal papers, and books to go through." She walked back into the library.

Letta stood silent, then nodded curtly.

An ancient rolltop desk had been in the library as long as Susan Pea could remember. It seemed more a part of the house than she. Eve had converted it into her own personal secretary shortly after she moved into the library.

Susan Pea rolled the top back and began sorting through pens, papers, and cards. The task loomed before her, at once tedious and necessary. She discarded a sheaf of medical reports, insurance notices, and articles on cancer. No sense keeping reports, especially with Eve gone. She pulled open a middle drawer and immediately noticed a small drawstring pouch. Her hands trembled slightly as she opened it. Inside, a single rope of pearls. They glowed with warmth akin to summer moonlight.

Eve had bought them during her one trip to New York. The salesperson had handed the necklace to Eve, who stood as if dreaming and allowed the iridescent orbs to trickle through her fingers, catching the light. She had paid for the necklace and wore it out of the store.

Remembering the shopping excursion, Susan Pea caught her breath, half-whispered, half-thought, "Even small irritants can be shaped by life into things of beauty." Her hand closed around the watery drops. "Save these for Janie." She carefully replaced them in the pouch and set it aside.

A small jewelry box, pushed back in the antique dresser, caught her attention. She opened it and examined the contents. Her hands shook as she handled each item, her mind spinning back through the years. A miniscule baby's ring. *Her* baby ring. An old-fashioned, emerald engagement ring, a gift from Major to Eve when they still loved. A silver bracelet she'd sent to Eve for her first wedding. Susan Pea, tears stinging her eyes, closed the box and set it aside for Janie.

Letta, finished with kitchen chores, walked into the room and placed boxes in a line under the window. In bold, block letters, she labeled each box and settled down to separate the clothing according to recipient. She worked silently, efficiently.

Susan Pea, intent on her tasks, did not look up. In a second drawer, Susan Pea carefully unfolded newspaper clippings: Articles about soldiers returning from a devastated 1945 Europe. The Pacific theater still in turmoil. Proliferation of newly formed suburbs and houses with picket fences. Women dismissed from factory jobs as the men came home, status as housewives resumed. A baby boom. The beginning of Korea. John Kennedy's presidential election. A few articles on Vietnam as a sleeping dragon. Clippings lovingly placed in protective clear sleeves, reflecting Eve's concerns.

She handed the stack to Letta. "Let's set these aside for Janie and Andy later. They might like to know what it was like for Eve when the men came back."

Susan Pea sighed aloud. "I'm in way over my head. Thank goodness you're here to take care of the house and help with this weeding." She stretched her back and rolled her shoulders, face wrinkling into a frown. She sat in the desk chair, sighed, and resumed shuffling through the items.

Letta, paused with her folding, spoke quietly. "You still needs plan for taking care for that woman-child and her baby. You need think on takin' care of Butlers and Butler doings *without* me. I got my own need caring."

"Oh, Letta, you've always been here. You're part of the household." Susan Pea waved her hand dismissively, barely glancing at the woman.

"I ain't funning with you." Letta frowned, looked directly at Susan Pea to make sure she was understood. "My man gone. I a widow with two children I need raise up." Face deeply furrowed, she turned back to her task, all the while mumbling under her breath.

"Missus Eve too kind a soul. This here family chewed her up right quick. My bottle tree ain't powerful enough to help her, it never able do her no good."

Susan Pea blinked rapidly at Letta. The full weight of the woman's words descended, and she thought of drowning.

The dark energy that followed Major settled on the two women. They retreated into separate thoughts. The hall clock ticked too loud. The house creaked and groaned with age and accrued sadness.

Finally, Susan Pea exhaled and began shifting through letters from friends on plain and pastel stationery and book reviews snipped from the newspaper. She found a slim volume of haiku by Bashō, possibly a keepsake for Janie, despite being print and not braille. Janie apparently knew most of it by heart anyway.

Susan Pea placed several books aside for Andy—Wallace Stevens, Robert Frost, and William Carlos Williams. Rummaging further in the desk drawer, she found a Shaeffer writing set. Three special books and a pen would be easy for him to carry as he moved from duty station to duty station. She placed the stack of items aside for his consideration.

Carefully, she skimmed scattered cards and letters, bundled the most personal and potentially treasured into a stack for Andy and Janie to read together later. Two slim volumes of poetry, her favorites, caught her eye. She put them aside for herself. Picking through Eve's things resembled a bad dream. Susan Pea could no longer separate real from what was not. Her mind danced from joy to anger to limbo, flittering along the limits of reality. She closed her eyes a moment, then resumed her task.

The two women worked in silence, moved about carefully.

After several minutes, Susan Pea looked at her companion and spoke softly. "Letta, do you want a keepsake?" Hands quiet for a moment, she paused and regarded the housekeeper.

Letta smiled to herself and responded in a soft, accented voice. "Naw. I done settle with Missus Eve earlier."

"Oh. When did she do that?"

Letta straightened and said calmly, "Some time back. Missus Eve said she wanted me to have something." She nodded to herself, reflected on the personal gift, and then continued separating clothes for church groups and middle school kids. As an afterthought, she added, "Missus Eve give me a gold broach that's got curlicues. Got small diamonds and one them yeller stones. She says it called amber. She let me choose one of her Sunday meeting church jackets. Dress, too."

"That sounds nice," Susan Pea said. She sat a long time, reflected on her bond with Letta and on Eve's relationship with both. Events had left each wounded in turn while time knitted them together. Sighing, Susan Pea returned to her task.

On the bottom of the open drawer, Susan Pea found a manila envelope. An address in the upper left corner identified Boswell Laboratory, Atlanta as sender, addressed to Major Jacob Butler at his office.

Curious, she opened the metal clasp and pulled out papers—a cover letter, standard business format, and a laboratory blood-grouping analysis stamped "original." She read quickly, opened her mouth, and snapped it close.

"Letta, look here. Have you ever seen this before?" Susan Pea's lips pressed into a tight thin line. She frowned. The envelope trembled in her hands as she extended it toward Letta.

Glancing up from her separating chore, Letta nodded. She spoke in a carefully modulated voice. "Yessum. Major comes home one day and give it to me right after Mr. Andy joined Army. Tell me show it to Missus Eve. She reads. Next time he come here, they fight—screaming and hollering. I hear her pop him. She crying. They both get to cussing. He leave house. He take up living in that town apartment again." Her face was blank.

"What apartment?"

"That one he rented when that first Mrs. Butler here," Letta explained.

"Where was Janie?"

"At school. She come home, no Major. She axed questions. Missus Eve don't tell her what happened. Janie and Missus Eve go to hollering at each other. I seen their mother-daughter hissy fits before, but this time it bad. That when I know'd Janie got feelings for Major."

"Feelings? What do you mean?"

"She says her mama don't understand. Say all them stories about him and first Missus Butler lies. She tells her mother Major's misunderstood."

"Misunderstood. Really? What else?"

"Missus Eve start crying. Janie say her mama too cold. Major tell her, he can't get no baby, cause she cold. Say he need spice."

"What?" Susan Pea sat numb, felt her face draining. "He's up to something. I knew it after I caught him and Janie in the kitchen, but I was not certain what. Damn it all."

Letta leaned toward Susan Pea conspiratorially, lowered her voice. "I only tell what that blind girl say. That when Missus Eve slap Janie straight across her face."

Susan Pea stood, unsure what to do next, began to pace the room.

Her voice rose to a screech. "Don't ever tell anyone that. Ever! Do you hear me? That's almost an admission that old cock was banging Janie." She whirled and paced around the room, fingers on her forehead.

Easing back, Letta shook her head. "Ain't never told nobody 'bout that fight except you. Ain't gonna neither. But I tell you this—Major not jumping that girl's bones. Anybody in that little gal's panties, it that cracker Wes." She leaned forward and said, "I know not to speak ill of departed. 'Specially no white person. I ain't got no more to say, but mark my words, bad things coming down. Cost of sin be high."

"Does this drama have no end? Damn both their souls."

Letta watched as Susan Pea stormed out. The Pontiac's tires threw gravel in the air.

CHAPTER FORTY-ONE
MAJOR BUTLER

Without knocking, Susan Pea barged into Major's office, door bouncing off the wall as she slapped the manila folder on his desk. She snarled at Thomas, in the process of taking dictation.

"Out!" She thumbed an abrupt gesture toward the door. "Major and I have something to discuss." Air in the room changed color.

Pen and pad held awkwardly, Thomas blinked. He looked at Major, who nodded toward the reception area. Gathering a raft of papers, he stood and left.

As soon as the door closed, Major leaned back in the heavy, leather chair. It grumbled, protesting his movement.

Meticulously groomed, he wore a tweed jacket and pressed shirt, collar open. After the bloody mud of Europe, he swore he'd be clean every day.

"Sister, dearest," Major said, "it's unwise to get yourself so worked up in this heat. You might have a stroke. Of course, it's always a pleasure to see you in my office, but please, there are no family privileges here.

Next time, *call.* Make an appointment." He frowned, bent forward to glance at the report.

Susan Pea stabbed the folder with her forefinger and leaned across the desk toward Major. "Since this letter is addressed to you, I believe you know exactly what it contains. My personal guess is you ordered and paid for that report."

"Ah, yes. One of several types of reports I've had to fool with, sweet sister. You see, my first wife was not strictly accurate when she told stuff, but none of what she told was a lie either." He grunted. Displeasure writ on his face, wrinkles deepening.

"I'm curious, how did you get the first Mrs. Butler—Mrs. Lacy Anderson Butler—to consent to a blood test?" Susan Pea's voice dripped with sarcasm.

He rose from the desk, stepped to the sideboard, and poured two fingers of whiskey. Sipping it neat, he stood before the windows, his back to her. "This is my town. I have made it grow this last decade. There's a daily shuffling of cars, noise, people, especially on workdays. All this bustle and crowding marks the growth I've created. Guided."

Slow and deliberate, Major turned toward Susan Pea, his face blank.

"But you came to discuss this report. Yes," he said, "it is interesting. Straight forward and dry, like most reports. The detective reports were livelier. As to my methods, my first wife was young and foolish. She assured me, despite her philandering, that Andy was mine. In fact, as a show of good faith, I allowed her to name him Joshua Anderson Butler. My name, her maiden name, and the Butler moniker."

Susan Pea angled her head to the side. *"You allowed?"*

"As it turned out, she called him Andy, her pet nickname." Major sipped his whiskey and continued in a dry tone. "Oddly enough, Andrew was the name of a favorite among her many paramours. She also called *him* Andy. Interesting, don't you think?" He had waxed foolish when that bit of information reached his ears.

Outside, on the street, a woman struggled with a baby and stroller. She dinged the car door next to her, and finally managed to get baby and stroller out safely. The engine of another vehicle revved, backed out several parking spaces away. Scattered voices drifted up, too indistinct to be intelligible.

Susan Pea crossed arms over her bosom. "Go on."

"By the time that boy—Andy, as we *all* called him— was five, that harlot fell into her old habits. I consented to continue the marriage only if Andy proved to be mine. You see, she had grown accustomed to the pleasures of gentrified living. Was eager to maintain her living style. I don't think I need explain further. Especially since you hold some of those same tastes in common." He briefly held his shot glass to the light, watched it glow amber, and turned away.

"Why spend all these years allowing untrue gossip?" Susan Pea asked. "He's your son. Not a stray dog. For chrissake, he'll carry the Butler name as your heir."

"This is none of your business. It's between me and him since the former Mrs. Butler is out of the picture."

The sounds outside grated, muffled with his back turned.

Susan Pea's voice rose a notch. She caught herself and struggled to speak in a normal tone, pronouncing each word deliberately. "Yes, it is my business. Believe it or not, I have claim here. I'm your sister. His aunt. A Butler daughter. No question about my legitimacy."

"Does it really matter? I've made a man out of Andy. Hadn't been for me, he'd be in some small-town, turnip-patch law firm married to the local punch, narrow between the eyes from a shallow gene pool. As it stands, he has a solid career in the military."

"You abhor the military. Besides, it wasn't his choice. He might have been happier in a turnip-patch town, raising snotty nose kids. Maybe serve on the school board or run for mayor. You preempted those choices, made the decisions for him."

"What do you want from me?" He turned abruptly, clunked the glass on his desk. "After dear old daddy went to his reward, there was nothing left. What we have here, *I* worked for and snatched from the poorhouse door. I supported you in that liberal, rabbit-hole hotel. Sent tuition to that college. Allowed you to have your loathsome ways in the big city."

"I'd call that restitution for a guilty conscience," Susan Pea said.

Major still faced her, knocked back the whiskey in a single motion. "My dear, in case you've forgotten, there's rot in this family. You know, one of those father-to-son things, *ad nauseum*. Including any daughters." He turned away from her, stared out the window. "I helped our sweet daddy cross over the proverbial river. Another hand did the deed, but my deaf ear failed to call any attention to the events. He lies peaceful with our other relatives. And, I might add, *your acquiescence* helped."

Voice raspy with guilt, Susan Pea spat out the words. "Ironic, isn't it, he was hunting alone." She dropped into a chair, twisted her hands, and looked at the old man's portrait on the wall.

"Not ironic. Opportune, I'd say." Major walked to the credenza, refilled his whiskey, and whirled it around in the glass.

"Convenient you had witnesses as to your whereabouts. Or was it simply influence?" she said.

"Had it not been for my *influence*," he said, "you'd be tricking up and down the redneck Riviera, catering to tour groups. Sweet sister, remember, I hold the purse strings to the family fortune. To your lifestyle."

"You are despicable. But we've both known that for a long time. Point is, Andy's your son. What do you intend to do about him?"

"He has his own life. We're two separate people. Besides, I have my plans. Now take this report and stuff it..." he paused, raised an eyebrow, "in the bottom drawer where you found it. I've got work to do. Like any other good *businessman* in this town."

Susan's mouth dropped open. She blinked. Finally, she stood and stepped forward to grip the edge of Major's desk, her knobby knuckles protruding from the effort.

"You've lived long past your time. But, as it stands, your son may be on trial for murder. A murder he did not commit."

"I've declined to take the case. You know I cannot enter this fray."

"Your finger is in every pie from north Georgia to Savannah, and all the way down to the Florida line. Don't get pious on me and say you don't have influence. You may not be directly involved but *you know who is.* You have connections. *If* you didn't hire the hit on Wes, you can find out who pulled the trigger. Better yet, you could pinpoint why. Or is that too close to home?"

"Wes got what he deserved." Spittle droplets hung in the air. Major leaned toward Susan Pea, face twisted. "He was common. Arrogant to boot." His upper lip curling, Major straightened to his full height.

Susan Pea stared at Major, her jaw muscles bulging. "But he didn't deserve to die. Things could have been handled another way."

"And him with Janie? What was that—ambition or lust?" He snorted harshly. "Most likely *both.*"

"Is your jealousy poking its nasty head up?" Susan Pea asked.

"No, dear sister." Major placed his glass on the desk. "While I'll admit temptation, there was no action on my part." He inclined his head slightly, reflecting on the previous incident in the kitchen. "I repeat, temptation, but nothing further."

"Lack of opportunity? Or did Wes simply get there first and knock you out of the saddle?"

He picked the glass up, took a sip, and strode to the window. "You are *not* the only one dear old daddy scarred. Abuse seems to be our family gift to each other. Remember, sister dear, the Butler name has fewer smudges because I have chosen to pull it out of the muck and apply a coat of whitewash."

He faced Susan Pea, a sneer played across his lips. He had been deeply incented by the family's alcoholism, loss of the family fortune. Major did not relish poverty. Not after the war. Remembered again the ridicule by his father, his uncle. Their thinly disguised masochistic discipline. Their bullying until he morphed into what he detested.

"Really? Your treatment of Wes and Letta are no doubt shining examples of your kindness?" Susan Pea blinked hard, her lips quivered.

"You mean white trash and a Black woman? I paid them for their work. I treated them well. They got more than they deserved." Major resumed his seat behind the desk radiating his warped racist thinking, political graft. No doubt, his sister had left Georgia for those reasons. She had crawled back seeking family status, a place in society. He had pegged her right—a daughter of the South with debts coming due.

Susan Pea shuddered, clenching, and loosening her fists.

"And while you're counting people sucking on my tit," Major said, "do remember Eve and her sightless whelp." He gulped his drink, set the empty glass down, picked up the manila envelope, and handed it back to his sister. "Close the door politely when you leave. *Please*." He arched an eyebrow.

She leaned across the desk as if in a fog and took the envelope. Turning toward the door, she stumbled slightly, caught herself, and walked out.

Major slumped down into his chair, overpowered by unnatural forces. He wanted another drink. But, limbs heavy, he felt too tired to walk to the credenza for a refill. Usually, a shot of whiskey sharpened the world. Lately, it pushed him further into a quagmire. He stretched his hand before his face, fingers splayed, and felt memories drip through like water. Time had passed as a will-o-the-wisp. Dreams strained his reality and floated away deeply bruised.

He reminisced on all he had done. A good brother. A good father. Maybe even a good husband. Had built his community, protected it. His family, his town simply did not understand how he made their lives better, easier. His sister lacking any appreciation of his struggle—and its cost. The town ungrateful. Now he stood on the brink of too many deaths. Somehow, his life was fraying apart, thread by thread.

CHAPTER FORTY-TWO
LETTA DAVIS

WEEKS BEFORE JOHN'S ARMY discharge and his return home, Merry, his young sister, had been raped. She had stayed to help her teacher with several slow readers and was late starting home. Several men drove by as she walked, hung out the truck window, and hollered. An open truck door. Secluded piney woods. One thing happened, and another. Merry dumped on the road. Dirty, bleeding, and shocked.

Mose Jones and his wife found her, took her home. Letta sank to the floor at the sight of her daughter. Gathering the girl in her arms, Letta rocked back and forth, their hearts cracking open, crumbling. Rape. Even the word tore into Letta's insides, left hateful shreds behind.

"My baby, my baby," Letta said. "We gonna take care of this. We make it through this. We make it." She hummed a lullaby even as Merry sank into a troubled, nightmare-laced sleep. The community midwife did what she could to ease Merry's pain. Word spread and neighbors gathered, formed a protective circle in the small house. Tears flowed until the folks were exhausted.

Letta had held her daughter throughout night, petted her hair, stroked her arms, and whispered in her ear. Hummed softly and rocked her. She wiped sweat off the girl's face, kissed her head.

"Big brother on his way home. He gets here, that when debits be paid off. We take care my baby girl. We make everything balance soon."

Friends and womenfolk stayed with mother and daughter, their men clustered outside, until morning. Hearts heavy, they had drifted away to their day jobs. Finally, at last, the part-time preacher left for his hospital janitorial job. Those with night jobs came, rotating in, offering their support and caring.

Weeks later, when John arrived, Letta met him at the door. Her words were peremptory, to the point.

"What you telling me?! You saying my sister done had that filth on her?!" John bellowed in his mother's face. "What the holy hell?"

Letta shook her head, sank into a nearby chair, and sobbed, unable to talk further.

John grabbed a kitchen chair and slammed it through the window, banging the wood shutter off its hinges. He swept his arm across the table, knocked glasses and fruit jars asunder.

Mose Jones and his wife, the preacher, and a few others, knowing Letta's news would impact John harshly, had gathered before he arrived home. With his rampage, they backed away, screamed for him to stop.

John whirled toward the kitchen pantry, grabbed his pappy's ancient shotgun propped behind the door, fumbled for shells.

Letta struggled to stand in his way. "You got to stop. This not helping Merry. Not helping. They kill you where you stand, they see that old gun." She lurched forward, locked her hands around the barrel, and held on.

Face distorted and with a guttural roar, John brandished the gun as he stormed outside, cussed, spittle flying, eyes wild.

Finally, through their collective weight, the men pinned his arms and forcibly restrained his helpless rage. Mose Jones pulled the shotgun from John's hands.

Immobilized, John slumped, as if the strings holding him upright had been cut. He sank to his knees. His years enduring mistreatment in the Army, the jagged return home, and the helplessness at Merry's abuse boiled over. He cried.

Letta gathered his head in her arms and rocked. "We work through this. Don't do no more killing right now. We got to help Merry first. We help her then think on putting this right."

John sobbed in impotence, cried out his hurt, his anger until his body shook.

Mose Jones took the gun, propped it on the porch, gimped toward John, and knelt next to him. "Listen here, you listen!" He thumped John's chest hard with his forefinger. "I come along when them devils finish they meanness. They take off, strutting like roosters. They be in a slime-green pickup. I know'd that truck cause it got they hood tied down with bungee cord. I know them. *They common Lee Town trash.*"

Grabbing John's shirt, Letta jerked at him, stuck her face next to him. "You let this go now. Take care Merry first. We fix them others later." She looked around the circle, at the grief-streaked faces, at neighbors surrounding them, listened as he choked on tears.

He struggled to control himself, to regain a balance. Acting on impulse out of rage could get him killed. Gradually, John stopped struggling. Letta wiped his tears and cleaned his nose with her apron..

Letta bent close to John's face, spoke with gravel in her voice. "I hold memory of my man and what they done to him. Taste like bitterness way back in my throat. I still got to set things right for him. Now they hurt my Merry. Two debts need repaying. I never hit another human being long as I lived. Never planned no harm to another." She took a deep breath and held it before she spoke. "But I'll set it right 'fore I leave this place." Her anger bubbled out in shades of purple shadows.

Still at last, John spoke in a deadly, calm voice, now entirely controlled. He had a dark edge that frightened Letta. "I know, Momma, we can't let this go. I'm a man and I do what's right for my sister. And my pappy."

"Yes, son, you a man. We mindful 'bout your pappy and sister. Soon. But not today."

"Soon. Not today," he repeated.

Hours later, with most folks gone, Letta and John watched Merry in her restless sleep. They talked long into the night.

John grew quiet, face tense, and jaws clenched. His anger checked, focused, he held his momma's hand. After long minutes, he dropped her hand, stood, and walked to the bedroom to look at Merry sleeping. He returned to Letta, sat down, and said, "Tell me all you know."

"It be Mose Jones that brought her home. One other our men helped him. His wife help." Letta's voice had a ragged edge.

"Mose tells a man with green truck, hood strapped down, done it." John's demeanor morphed from his earlier outrage to cold calculation, eyes narrowed and body taut.

From the fertile soil of hate, they plotted, knowing the cost would be high. Together, he and his momma pushed the wheels of vengeance into motion.

LETTA RECOGNIZED John's new Army skills, his love of weapons. She listened as he vowed not to allow these men to go unpunished. Vowed to set his pappy's death on the scales for justice.

Grief-stricken, she shook her head. "Can't undo all the harm them white crackers put on us. Lord says wages of sin be blood. We take care this with help of the Lord." Letta gritted her teeth and drew a deep breath.

"Lord's gonna work through me this time." John clenched his big hands into fists. "I make a promise, I don't break it. And I promise Merry's wrong gonna be set right. Pappy's, too."

He stalked outside to the porch, lit a cigarette, and stood smoking. He held his smoke in a cupped hand until it burned down to a nub. Taking a last quick puff, he crushed it on the porch with his boot, toed it off onto the dirt.

A week slipped past. A Black man, especially an unemployed one fresh from the Army, became a convenient scapegoat for any altercation or infraction in the county, no matter the stimulating event. Or any facts.

Deeply haunted, John took a job to cover his decision to stay. Swallowing rage for the present, he turned eyes toward the sawmill, as his pappy before him. He needed to come and go without raising suspicion. Needed planning time. Needed money for any travel north. The sawmill job could provide those things.

From that vantage point, John plotted. He bought a long gun. Caressed it. Felt its terrible weight.

The mill was the last thing Letta wanted for John. Although sawmills had changed from cut-out-and-get-out mentality to one of tree plantation and plywood products over the years, it continued as tough, dangerous work. Logs required bucking and delimbing before they could be loaded on trucks for the mills.

Nonetheless, she understood his terrible choice and nodded her consent. Always, the looming specter of Major floated before them as John turned toward the mill. The straw boss set him bucking logs.

Nights after work, reeking of sawdust and sweat, rage gnawed at John's soul. It smelled of sulfur. They worked him five days before allowing him to check in with the dour woman responsible for payroll.

"Can't authorize pay for those earlier days because you on probation," she said.

"Ain't nobody said no nothing about probation. You steal a week's free work. Ain't no probation."

"Following rules is all," she said.

"Rules for everybody or only folks my color?"

The boss stood by, listened to the back and forth. "You want this job or not?" Chewing on a stem of grass and fanning gnats, he gave a bored take-it-or-leave-it shrug, adding, "Only give you a job because of your pappy. He was a good worker. Got sloppy, though. Too bad 'bout his accident." He propped his heavy frame against a windowsill.

John stood silent with his hat in hand, stared across the lumberyard, and finally mumbled, "Yessah." He thumped the hat on his leg, stared at the floorboards a moment, raised his eyes, and looked the man square in the face. "I only come back cause of my momma. She needs my help."

The man nodded twice and stood silent, still chewing on the dry grass stem. "I'll overlook your smart mouth, the disrespect you showing me, seeing as how you recent back outta Vietnam. I got a son in the Army, too. I reckon you earned something. I only overlook what you say this one time. No more. You're a *hired hand, boy*." The foreman flicked the grass stem aside. "Go on now," he said, flapped his hand dismissively, and walked back into the mill office. The screen door bounced closed behind him.

Pre-dawn the next day, John appeared for work, carefully arranged his face into a blank slate. He arrived before the giant cutting blade screamed awake and threw sawdust into the air. Each day for the following weeks, John came early, carefully arranging his demeanor and actions to reflect an earnest work ethic.

Always, nights after work, reeking of sawdust and sweat, rage gnawed at John's soul. It smelled of sulfur.

Evenings were consumed covertly watching Lee Town, the comings and goings of the people, their habits.

Over the next weeks, humidity rose with the sun. The wind laid by. Gnats swarmed around the eyes of those arriving for the workday. Heat smothered the countryside. Sweat dried and crusted white on the plowing mules. Hens stopped laying. Milk cows dried up. People mopped their faces with wet rags, stood under shade trees, and hoped for relief, however faint.

Folks, regardless of color, allowed themselves license for any touchiness, opining the heat was the devil's tool, made them all irritable, and caused strange things to happen.

The too-hot Bainbridge days melted, one day into the next. Vine ripe tomatoes, watermelons freshly picked, and ears of sweet corn coaxed neighbors into sharing over church cookouts. Gossip, exchanged along with food at the cookouts, became an essential connection.

Mostly the community slogged through work, felt the day's sweaty arms hold them close. Evenings with its shallow coolness and iced tea, gave them a certain relief from their grinding days. For others, homebrew alleviated the summer heat until saturation left the drinker disoriented and sloppy.

John wiped his forehead with his handkerchief and cursed under his breath. Careful to avoid too much of anything, he swore off bootleg corn. Pappy had followed that demon. John would not.

Sometimes John hunted with his long gun, adding to the family table. Sometimes he stalked the swamps and honed his marksmanship skills. He caressed the rifle as he would a woman—and loved it with more fidelity.

And, always, he knew the whereabouts of the green truck, its hood held down with a bungee cord.

CHAPTER FORTY-THREE
MIDNIGHT

Late one Saturday, two bubbas stinking of beer lurched from Johnny Reb's to their pickup and drove, green hood rattling against a bungee cord, to a clapboard house on the edge of town. Swinging out of the vehicle, they stumbled toward the structure.

A figure stood in the shadows, listened to the men's drunken banter. He had watched them before, knew them for brothers. Knew from local gossip their meanness crossed the Black-white line with almost equal frequency. Complaints, some official and others spoken in undertones, circulated.

They climbed out of the still dieseling truck. One slapped a mosquito, leaving a red smear on his arm. He flicked the smashed body off his fingers.

"You one stupid sumbitch. Stop messin' round and git inside. I'm tired." His companion stopped, peed on a yard post, rezipped, and reeled onto the open porch, bouncing slightly off the wooden supports. Steading himself, he stepped inside, sagged down on a bench near the kitchen wall, and, head drooping forward, snored hoarsely.

"Turn on the goddamn light." He pulled the dangling light cord. A single, bare bulb lit the area, weakly filled the room, dribbled out the window to the near edge of the porch. The man scratched his mosquito bite. Unsteady, he stood a moment, plunked down heavily at the table, slumped forward. Slobbering, he dozed off, spittle pooling near his open mouth.

Still, among the tall weeds in the back alley, a smoke held in a cupped hand, glowed briefly with a short pull. A man's shadow moved to the open porch. Gently, as if handling a kitten, the figure tucked the cigarette behind the sticks in a matchbook, placed it atop oil-soaked rags piled on the edge, and faded back into the shadows.

Faintly, a flame fretted on the porch among the rags, grew stronger, flared, gnawed at the greasy strips, and spread slowly to the brittle structure. Sparks jumped into the dark with a malevolent ferocity. Smoke roiled up.

One man staggered out of the kitchen, coughing, turned, and, apparently confused, swayed back inside. Heat exploded windows, spewed glass shards outward.

The sound of a cartridge jacked into a chamber was lost in the dark.

Inside, the second man rose from the table, stumbled across the room, and stood in the door frame, only to be shoved backwards as if by an unseen hand. A sound like a bursting pine knot resonated.

Puzzled, the man looked down as red blossomed across his chest. He touched the wetness, wiped his fingers together, and, sighing, fell backward onto the floor. His leg twitched, stopped. He did not move again.

Night shadows shifted in the flames, glinted off an ejected cartridge as an elegant hand picked up the spent shell and stuffed it into a pocket. Another cartridge chambered, the sound sharp.

Ceiling beams began a sluggish collapse. Wall uprights fell inward and obliquely covered the bodies. Smoke undulated skyward in thick columns, vanished into the night's ink.

An obscure apparition among the alley weeds and stunted trees walked away.

The derelict structure collapsed, surrendered the souls therein to the inferno.

Lee Town's volunteer fire department, interrupted during their Saturday night poker, arrived late. Although the house was almost consumed, they uncoiled their hoses and focused water on nearby buildings.

Neighbors gathered to watch the final smoldering crossbeams and collapsed debris. Charred flesh lay in blackened hunks, limbs mostly gone, greasy odors rising toward the dawn. Ash floated in the air. Adjacent structures scorched, but intact.

The volunteers commented on the shame of it all. Bleached-out women stood in clusters, muttered among themselves, worry criss-crossing their faces. Men gathered, passed a jug.

"Those two brothers went to hell in a handbasket after their mother died. I'll bet she's rolling over in her grave," one said.

"She was a good woman. Tried hard with them boys, but she couldn't never get them in hand once her husband passed. They sold white dog all over the county. Chased after women."

Several voiced agreement.

"She let 'em sell that stuff. Made 'em give her the money. She was as much to blame as them."

"She shoulda spoke out to keep those boys from chasing after so many skirts. Shoulda taught them better."

"She weren't never able to keep them boys corralled."

"They're too lazy to keep things picked up. Their mama would've fussed about that."

"Plum lucky they didn't set the whole damn town on fire with their drinking and hooligan ways."

Standing in groups, men talked, scratched at their crotches, and chewed tobacco while passing the jug hand to hand.

"They ought to know better than leave a pile of old, greasy stuff out on the porch," a woman said.

"Musta used them rags for cleaning engine parts."

"No disrespect, but these two ain't no real loss no how."

"You right about that. Ain't no loss."

"Except I'll miss the shine they sold."

"Still, it was strange," an emaciated woman said. She held a toddler on her hip. "The place burned down not long after they raped that gal from the quarters."

"Naw. That weren't proved."

"Hell no, but everybody know'd they done it. They known to lift skirts ever chance they got. They done too much talking."

"They done more'n one. Weren't always Black neither. Good many folks holding hard feelings 'ward them."

Rubbing smoke from their eyes, the crowd fell silent as they passed the last of the jug and watched the smoldering timbers.

"Wait a gall-dern minute. You reckon we ought to question that soldier boy? He some kind kin to that gal."

A man extended his hand for the jug, took a swig, and made a sour face as he downed the liquid. "Lordy, but this stuff's raw. Who cooked it anyway?" He passed the jug along. "Heard tell that soldier feller was one of them sharpshooters with the Army. You know, over in 'Nam."

"That ain't right. He was a cook."

"Naw. My brother says he's hard-core Army. Maybe a Ranger. Y'all can tell their kind by the way they walk."

"You mean to say, he can handle a gun?"

"No telling what the hell he learnt."

Sheriff stepped forward, gestured with his hands. "Whoa, boys. Stop right there. Settle down. Let's not get your britches pulled up your crack and start a mob here. Law's my business. I can take care of this." He shifted and resettled his holster and belt. Glaring at the circle of men, he looked each in the face. "Y'all go on home. I know how to handle these people. I need something from y'all, I'll do the calling."

Another man passed the whiskey to a companion, and swiped his nose across his sleeve. The group shifted away from the residual heat and moved away from drifting smoke. They continued emptying the jug and slowly broke up.

Finally, a younger mother sighed and said, "I got to get back to the house. Make sure them babies still sleeping. I left 'em alone."

Several other women nodded, clutched clothing tighter, and slouched toward sweaty bedrooms and unattended children. Men guzzled the last of the shine and drifted off to talk in small clusters before making their way home through junk-filled yards. Sunday morning church was only a few hours away. Plenty of time to tell what they knew after the preaching was finished.

As the people drifted off, Sheriff fell into step with the fire chief, clapped him on the back. "I'll call the coroner come get these two. Probably be later tomorrow morning. He'll not relish picking up the pieces. My deputies can keep an eye on this till he gets here."

"Guess they was too drunk to get out," Chief said. He gestured toward the burned-out structure.

"Reckon they musta been." Sheriff waved his hand toward the smoldering heap. "Whole thing's kinda strange. Maybe an accidental fire. Then again, maybe not."

"Does seem odd. Hard to say what happened. I come back tomorrow and investigate then. In daylight." Fire chief shook his head. "Gonna be a mess to unravel."

"Yeah, best do this work in daylight. Can't do nothing more tonight."

Sheriff turned and, mumbling to no one in particular, walked to his patrol car. "There might be other mischief, but those two boys not gonna be involved. They knocked out of the game for good."

He cranked the car and pulled out of the dirt driveway, still mulling over night's events. He turned on his flashing lights and accelerated toward town.

CHAPTER FORTY-FOUR
LETTA DAVIS

Monday morning after the fire, Letta stood a long moment glaring out the window as Major stamped toward the house.

Crows croaked, pumped up and down in a pine tree nearby. They flew low as Major approached. Letta nodded, recognized harbinger value of crow sisters.

She wanted her children safe. Planned the route north over and over. A chain of car rides. Bus tickets bought two counties over. Passage on a train with seats as hard as living. Conjurer woman had been right. Her incantations swelled into fruition. Swallowing her thoughts, Letta kneaded biscuit dough, rolled it out as Major entered the kitchen.

"You folks got a boil going on down on the southside," he said. "Seems a Lee Town bootlegger and his brother died in a house fire Saturday night. Talk has it that one of y'all set it going."

Letta continued working the dough, did not look up.

"I'll admit those two were worthless hog wash," Major said, "but we can't have some darkie setting fires and killing white men under *any* circumstances." He poured himself a mug of coffee, added a hit from his flask, and peered at Letta. "You know anything about it?" He blew across the cup, watched his housekeeper with narrowed eyes.

"Naw, sah." She carefully averted her face, gripped wooden biscuit cutter, cut rounds, and placed them on a baking sheet. She cleared her throat, rearranged cutouts for better browning.

"They were trash and probably deserved it. But, your kind can't be deciding that. You best be sure, I hear *everything* that goes on in this county. Eventually."

She swallowed a choking fear rising from her stomach, climbing into her throat. She coughed. "Only thing I know, ain't none of my people gonna kill no white man. Especially my John." She paused, swallowed her fear. "'Less he have a cause can't be overlooked."

"Really? What would that *possibility* be?" Major leaned back beside the kitchen counter, his posture arrogant.

She did not look at him, held the wooden cutter, an heirloom connection to her family. Her thoughts spun wildly. He shifted and moved close, smell of whiskey surrounding him. Cold prickles crawled up her arms. She kept her head down, looked at the baking sheet.

"I asked you—what could be so important?"

She flinched at his tone and spoke in a strained voice. "Man's family important. Our men got they pride. Got they love, too." She placed the wooden cutter on the stove, shifted away from him, wiped her hand down her apron sides, smeared flour, her chest heaving. Her determination not to allow this honkey devil any further information surged with every heartbeat. She strained to breath normally, felt a weariness in her joints. She worked her mouth, trying to find enough moisture to speak. "Got nothing more to say. Damnation following us. *Both* us." She clinched her jaw, shaken she had spoken so bold, and looked him in the eyes.

Major watched her with contempt, then deliberately, slowly smacked her hard across the face.

Surprised, her entire body spun away. She slumped, caught herself on the sink, and glowered at her tormentor. For a moment, she stood rigid, rage heating her face, understanding that Major held power for this place while she knew an ancient strength of warrior queens, knew stealth, patience, and capability of haints. Without speaking, she slowly bowed her head and looked down.

"If you have something to tell me, best spit it out straight. Right now." He leaned over and wiped his hand on a dish towel. "You know, if I tell him, sheriff and his helpers will go through the quarters shack-by-shack." Like fighting cocks, his words sprung at her, spittle flying. "Any sonofabitch even looks sideways at them, they'll beat him, until he begs to die—before they'll throw *him* in county lock-up for 'disrupting the peace.' Hear me real good, woman. Best tell what you know. Whole family will suffer if *anything* is found." He turned his back on her and added another splash of whiskey to his coffee.

Casually, as if at an afternoon church social, he slipped the flask back into his pocket, blew across his mug, and sipped the dark liquid. Steam floated up in thin spirals, dissipating in kitchen sunlight.

"Since that house you and your whelps are living in is mine, I have some control over *when* it gets searched." A thin, hard smile played along Major's lips, his voice gruff. "For sure, Letta, it *will* get searched. Only question is *when*." He sat the mug down, took the flask out, and titling his head back, swilled directly from the container.

"Yessah." She stared at the floor. "Ain't sure whose rules is right. Still, I always try to see you a fair man." Pulling herself erect, she looked him straight on. "Right got no color. You law. You supposed to be fair."

Major cocked his head, admired her courage. His voice carried a note of respect. "Well, I do consider myself fair," he said. "Especially if someone owns up before things get too far out of hand. Before they get in a tangle." He watched her face grow darker, her eyes narrow in anger, and then roll white with fear.

Silently, she cursed him, a reverse blessing asking haints to heap brimstone on him for eternity. *Don't let nobody even offer him a thimble of water.* She stared down at her feet.

"You do a fine job taking care of this house," Major said. "But that was back a few years. Lately, since that sister of mine has started living here, you've become an aggravation."

She squared her shoulders, looked into time.

He shifted against the counter. "I know some y'all been sneaking out to catch bus north these last years. Running from obligations here. Running from debt. Running from the law. I grew up hearing that stuff. Still hear about y'all sneaking off. No one ever gave anyone permission to go."

"People don't need no permission to leave a place. They free." Her answer curt, Letta continued to mentally comb through her plans. With this recent turn of events, she had to push their leaving forward. It unnerved her. Made her doubt herself.

"Not if they owe a debt to a landowner or a merchant," Major said. "Like me letting you live rent free in that cabin. Why, if I charged rent retroactively, you'd be in real debt. But I feel generous today. If—*if*—I could be assured of a housekeeper for my daughter—my stepdaughter Janie—so long as she lives here, I might offer some intervention. I need someone dependable. And loyal. Discreet. Someone that can keep her mouth shut." He paused. "I can *suggest* sheriff not worry too much about this fracas. Especially since those boys were hog swill and crossed line once too often. Tell him to count whole thing off to a random fire. An *accidental* fire. Have him question a few down in the quarters. Be *late* getting to my property." He paused, sat his mug on the counter. "I can talk to sheriff as a gesture to you, since you've worked for my family for so many years. You might say, as a thank you payment from a *kindly* boss man." He cocked an eyebrow, smiled without warmth.

The hall clock chimed. Somewhere in the house, a limb scratched a window screen. Sunlight shimmered on the floor. Major yawned. He picked up the coffee mug, added another splash from his flask, and drank.

Letta swayed, fought anger throbbing across her soul and plunging into her bowels. "Them white men put their hands on my daughter." Muscles in her jaw throbbed, stood out against her face.

"I know," he said, "and I'm regretful of that, but still, that was weeks ago. I'd thought y'all would have forgotten that little incident by now." Major watched Letta's face for any twitch or eye flicker.

Black-white divide in Bainbridge, dating from the early 1600s, was *still* a *living* entity.

Letta willed herself silent. *Forgotten? Little incident? Gotta hold on.* She gripped the biscuit cutter in both hands, her knuckles growing pale from strain.

"Simple fact is," Major said, "we can't have *you* people taking things into your own hands. Y'all need to know your place. Learn to keep to it."

She turned to the sink and swallowed hard to keep from gagging. "That what you gonna trade? You leave my daughter to live with that filth those men put on her? Make me do cooking? Scrubbing toilets? You acting like you doing some kinda charity. That ain't right. It ain't Christian." Her voice was low, barely audible. "Running off to see that Albany woman ain't Chrisitan, neither."

"Eve's dead."

"Yessah." She swallowed, stared down to avoid meeting his gaze. "Still, ain't seem right." Her legs trembled, she placed a hand on the table to steady herself. Her mind reeled remembering long days enduring remarks, times she neglected her own children because of Butler demands. Time swirled around her, hot with vengeance until she could not hear, could not think. She swallowed. Tried to still her thoughts.

"Strong talk for one in your position." His lips curled into a mirthless line. "Would it be more reasonable to consider my offer of protected work a trade? You know, one type of work for another? Especially since not everyone in town *understands* about family."

Eyes scrunched, lines in her face deepened, anger and fear gnawed at her innards. She worked her lips and mouth together, fighting dryness—and her urge to claw his face, exact revenge.

"You know as well as I," Major said, "that if this man, this *Black* man protecting his family, is caught, town people would want to take care of him on their own instead of a trial. Help save taxpayer's money, so to speak." Lips pulled into a thin acerbic line, he watched her face over the cup rim as he drank. "I do consider myself fair. Willing to overlook a man's skin color in the interest of justice."

She flinched. Screams, words rang in her ears. Beaten, bloodied, wasted, ravaged, shot to death—violence reverberated against her entire body. Any lawless act, because of skin color, scared her. Even scared whites. Plain and simple, it was mob murder sanctioned by the larger society.

"Of course, I could tell sheriff I know of a certain young Black girl who was raped. Know her brother, fresh out of Army, has got a set of skills that he might use to exact his own justice," he said. "See what happens when common folks demand he question your son. What's his name? John? Eventually sheriff might figure it out, and town will scream for blood. You know how these people are." He shrugged a shoulder. "You've been a solid and discrete housekeeper. I'd like to keep you on. Cabin rent free and all. Think about it."

Letta heard Major, heard words, viscerally understood an implied threat. She stood silent, not trusting her voice. Then, she stood ramrod straight and looked directly at him. "Don't seem right to me."

"What's a better word that would please you?" Major walked toward the stove and refilled his mug from the coffee pot. "Let's be generous with each other—let's settle on calling this a trade."

Bile rose in her mouth, threatened to gag her. She willed her body still, face blank. Fear radiated off her in malodorous waves. His voice raked across her. For the moment, he held the power. She swallowed several times—and nodded.

Major spoke evenly. "I'll tell sheriff not to search my cabin and interrogate my housekeeper just yet. Have him wait until Tuesday. I might be able to protect this man's family if that man somehow left town." He raised an eyebrow and placed his mug on the table.

Her eyes flashed wide, whites showing, anger rising.

"Coffee's still a mite weak. Take care of that will you." Putting a cigar in his mouth, he strode out of the kitchen. Outside, he paused and lit it.

Letta stood at the sink until the soapy dishwater grew cold. *Oh, my dear Jesus. Save my Merry. Protect my sons.*

She did not turn until she heard Janie bustling around upstairs. Mumbling low, she shook her head. "Got no choice. Them rednecks touched my daughter, my Merry. Elijah exposed to Major now that Wes was gone. John working under them crackers. They won't allow nothing, especially no second chance. I got keep my children from being run to ground. I tolerate this. For now."

She turned, pulled her apron off, and set the breakfast table, breathing in quick gasps. Fear and anger coursed through her. No choice but to keep steady, to bear up. Northern route in place. Conjure woman had outlined the escape, leaving only the exact departure date unsaid. Could she do this?

CHAPTER FORTY-FIVE
LETTA DAVIS

ANXIOUS, Letta waited until Susan Pea left the house to take Janie to school. Major was forcing her hand with his threats. She needed to act now, push the wheels into motion.

She scurried out to the kennels. Elijah should be there alone. "Elijah!" Fear laced her voice. She was powerless to hide it. "Elijah," she called.

He popped out of the larger barn and stepped into the shadows to meet her. She grabbed his face, held him, fingers digging into his cheeks, and fiercely hissed in his ear.

"It's time for John and Merry to go. *Now*. Run home and pull one of them bottles off my tree. One that got a long neck. Lay it down in that porch rocker. Make sure that chair set back sideways against wall and neck pointed north."

Her grip dug deeper into Elijah's cheeks until he squirmed. "Momma, you hurt me. Let go."

"You listen hard, or I skin you alive." She loosened her grip, spoke fiercely. "This be what we talked over. Remember? Get that gunnysack under bed we done packed. Take them boiled eggs, a few turnips we pulled up, and leftover bread near the stove. Wrap everything up in one of them kitchen towels. Put in a butcher knife."

"Okay, Momma. I remember." Elijah fidgeted from one foot to the other.

"You get clothes for your own self."

Elijah's eyes widened, he stopped moving. "You send me away, Momma? We ain't talked on this."

Letta took a deep breath and glanced around the kennels and down the road. Her voice high and anxious, she continued talking. "Bad things a'brewing. Ain't got no choice." She grabbed his shoulder and pulled him closer.

"Go in that hen house, get that Luzianne coffee tin. Third nest from that corner."

"Our saved-up money? All of it?"

Letta paused a heartbeat. "Y'all gonna need it. Long way north."

"Yes, Momma," He gasped, the ruthlessness of the last days hitting him hard.

"Tie everything up. Hide that gunny under the back step. Be sure it don't show."

She released him, watched his face, and leaned forward to pinch his cheeks again. "You understand me?" Her voice was sharp, harsh. "Major ain't gonna want us leaving. White folks never have liked us leaving. But we free people."

Elijah's eyes widened, narrowed into slits, his heart pounding. He solemnly leaned toward his mother. "Yes, Momma, I understand. I can do it. I know how go round them peckerwoods."

"Fetch Merry from her auntie's. You and Merry wait at the house for your brother. Hide in that corn crib. I'll go get John. Be ready to leave when he come."

She hugged the gangly youngster against her, kissed the top of his head. Holding him slightly away from her, she said, "Don't muddle this up. Them rednecks got meanness on their mind. Don't let nobody see you." She gave him another long hug and nudged him toward the barn opening.

The boy stumbled, caught himself, and eyes wide, said, "Yes, Momma. I can do this." He disappeared at a run.

She ran into the house, flung her apron on a chair, not caring what Susan Pea might think when she returned and found the house empty.

"Lord, let my John, Elijah, and Merry go. My babies walking through the valley of the shadow of death. They walking to the promised land of the north. Let them go. Like you let them Israelites go." Her heart thumping, she strode out the back door.

She bent and touched a long neck blue bottle, silently called the Old Ones, stood, and broke into a trot toward the sawmill.

Her way to the sawmill curled past the rot and decay of the town. She followed the footpath winding through the pines to the quarters, along the weed-choked drainage ditch. Past houses faded to gray with wooden window shutters hanging slack. Around potholes dotting the road. Wrecked cars propped up on blocks. Yards swept bare and concrete hard. Folks turned blind eyes at her passing, not wanting to know her mission, allowing ignorance to be their protection.

Even at a quarter-mile distance, she could hear the mill's saw blade whine, teeth bite into the logs, shattering the afternoon as clean as it cut the pine boards. Sweet, scented clouds of wood dust floated on the air.

Memory of her man's death still plagued her. The untruth of it made her tremble. The whole thing, explained away with accusations of drunkenness, made her heartsick. She missed him, recognized he had done his best. She vowed not to lose another family member to Major and his mill.

Letta had consulted with conjure woman weeks prior. Her children to go first, she'd follow later. She and John figured timing in detail according to her directions, careful not to call attention to family or raise questions within community.

The Lee Town fire pushed their careful plans ahead faster than planned. She hated Major for his devil's bargain, but still, it allowed her to warn John. Give him hours to collect thoughts and run. They'd use the same plan, only needed to move faster. She'd *make* it work.

A thunderstorm built to the east, clouds roiling and changing like living beings. Pine needles whooshed in dark waves, whispering of harm. Overhead, a crow flew north, roadkill in its beak. Acknowledging omens of death and blood, Letta trotted faster toward the mill.

At lumberyard's edge, she stopped. Cut pine and oak odors rose. Saws howled, ripped the day apart, until, thankfully, the afternoon lunch whistle shrilled, and the great circular blade slowed to a stop.

Sidling through ragweed toward stacked lumber and water well on the backside, she shuffled, neck bent, poking in weeds as if looking for something. Her head pounded. Sweat beaded in her neck creases, stained her dress around the armholes. In the noon hustle, no one paid her any attention.

Old Mose Jones limped past, carrying a water-filled bucket for workers. She caught his glance and, arms at her side, curled her fingers inward, signaling him to take a message. He nodded slightly and continued his hobble toward the main work shed.

White workers in the shed shouted at Mose to hurry, bring the damn water. They were working men, not no shuffling old fool. Greedy, they drank and poured water over their head and arms, using the entire bucket, rinsing off work grime before they settled in the shade to eat lunch. They joked among themselves, ignored Moses, and ate their sandwiches. Obligated to get a second bucket for his fellow Black workers, Mose limped to the hand pump, his shirt sleeves without buttons, flapped with up-and-down strokes. His too big feet poked out of slits cut in the leather. Bucket full, he walked back, sloshing water with every step.

Letta stood behind a tree until Mose drew close, paused, set the buckets down, and hands on his hips, arched his back, easing his gimp-leg. Fiercely, she whispered. "Tell John. Time come early. Follow blue bottle."

Mose wiped his face with a rag, picked up his bucket, and hobbled toward other workers grouped under a scrub pine. Wood dust outlined their bodies. Sweat trickled from their necks, left damp streaks down their backs, shirt cloth stuck to their bodies. Loosely grouped, they joked and drank water from the old dipper as Mose offered it.

Next to John, he stopped, set his water bucket down, and wiped his neck and face with a bandana. He muttered softly, stuffed it in his hip pocket, paused only seconds longer than usual.

Eyes straight ahead, no expression, John drank. Finished, he blinked at Mose and slightly inclined his head. Mose continued his water rounds.

Letta faded back into the woods, slipped into tree shadows, and started home.

STILL RAW BECAUSE of abuse to his sister, John stayed hyperalert and cautious. He had arms thick as tree trunks and a capacity for endurance. He'd protect his mother, siblings, and himself, get everyone North on will and strength alone.

The straw boss dozed unaware, hand on his brown water bottle, occasionally fanned flies off his face or slapped at a mosquito. John's fellows quietly continued, their unseeing eyes turned away. Disparate parts of the crew finished lunch and sprawled out to rest.

John rose and stretched. He nudged his lunch bucket aside with his foot, picked up his jacket, and walked into the woods to relieve himself.

With lunch break ended, a shrill whistle sounded across yard. Men gathered their belongs and prepared to work through the humid afternoon.

Mose stooped, picked up John's lunch tin. He'd take it to Letta.

CHAPTER FORTY-SIX
MAJOR BUTLER

MAJOR, more tired than he remembered being in a long time, rubbed his head, fingers massaging his temples. Physically, he had slowed, could not recall when dread had settled so heavily across him. Now he struggled to forget how it sprang up and straddled his shoulders for days, weeks at a time.

He rose from behind his desk and poured a scotch, neat, hoping to ward off his headache. He stood at the window, watching office workers make their way across town square and eventually homeward. How many times had his own father stood in this very spot and watched over the town?

The first Butler patriarch had bequeathed his son a timber empire dating back to 1850. Under the crush of the first world war, Spanish flu epidemic, and northern migration of the South's cheap labor force, his father and the old guard began an unacknowledged crumbling.

Major sighed ruefully at the irony of a German Irish family aspiring to higher status as vintners, only to collapse under drink's power. Great grandfather pulled up roots and grapevines to transplant them in Georgia's red clay. His status and power had grown, until his death among pines in an assumed hunting mishap. Major's father and uncle pillaged the family fortune, drank it dry, and each in turn, had died with alcohol fumes rising above their caskets.

Questionable investments, a fondness for gambling, and brown water drained Butler coffers, albeit slowly. Whiskey their signature odor. Major smiled ruefully at the absurdity, took another sip of scotch.

Briefly, after World War II, with soldiers returning home, the economy twisted as Korea raged, political divisiveness grew, and social changes were spawned, sending shock waves through the social landscape. The European killing fields had tainted him deeply. Familial betrayal had filled him with overflowing wrath.

A light tap on the door snatched him back to the present. His clerk Thomas stuck his head in. "Is there anything further you need tonight?"

"No, Thomas. I'm fine."

"I hope I'm not being presumptuous, but you look tired." He stood quietly for a moment and spoke in a neutral voice. He had worked for Major for twenty-five years. Still, he did not think them close and thus unsure of changes he saw in his employer.

Major responded as if from a distance. "You know, I loved her back then. She was a flash of excitement and energy I'd never had before." He part-chuckled and part-snorted. "Yes, sir, my first Mrs. Butler was a fireball."

Thomas stood inside the open door. He did not respond, undecided if Major was speaking to him or simply reminiscing aloud.

Major continued. "She loved Army life. Moving every year or two, especially new towns, social obligations, people. Relished that constant flow of fodder for her bed." Major smiled ruefully and spoke, his voice slightly above a whisper. "She loved those early days. But when I resigned my commission and returned here to take over the mill, things changed. Since there was nothing here but local, small-town stuff, my power to fascinate evaporated." He paused and sipped his drink. "If I'm honest with myself, I bored her."

Thomas shifted from foot-to-foot, held the doorknob in one hand. "I see."

"I guess if I'd been smart," Major said, "I'd have noticed the roving tendencies earlier. She was quite a vixen." He laughed aloud. "I rather enjoyed that side of her. Up to a point."

Thomas, palms sweaty, remained silent.

"But, plain truth hurts. She had Andy. At that time, I could never be sure if he was mine or not."

"Sir, is there something you're trying to tell me?" Thomas, still uneasy, shifted and glanced around the room.

"No, Thomas, I'm just ruminating over the past." Major turned to the window and watched foot traffic cross the town square below. He exuded confidence with a veneer of evil. The war years created a certain callousness, and, although he'd been accused of a cold-blooded murder while serving, he reordered facts until his life went on, no matter who or what happened.

His voice husky, he continued. "When she and I reconciled, town chinwags had already decided I was not Andy's father."

"Yes, sir." Thomas fidgeted, toyed with keys in his pocket. He wiped a line of perspiration off his upper lip.

Major crossed to the credenza and refreshed his drink. The tawny liquid darkened as the room slowly lost light.

"You remember when my old man died in that hunting accident, don't you?"

"No, sir. I was finishing law school. I heard about it from town gossips." Thomas looked askance at Major.

"When I came home from war, that old fool had drunk up every-thing," Major said. "I could barely salvage that godforsaken sawmill."

"Yes, sir." Thomas, hands in his jacket, listened, his face expressionless.

"But *I pulled it together*. Sold timber acres but kept mill control. Whatever they cut had to come back to me for processing. At *my* mill, *my* prices."

"I didn't know that." Thomas cocked his head to the side and continued. "As it is, about a third of the town works for you. Others support those that you employ. Town's lucky." Thomas, adept at stroking Major's ego, shifted yet again.

"Whole damn South crumbling. Sharecroppers and Blacks running north. Whites stomping them at slightest provocation. No wonder those pitiful fools ran like rabbits." Major turned to face Thomas more directly. "Anyway, what was it you needed?"

"Only stepped in to say good night, sir." Thomas said.

"Seems ironic," Major said, ignoring the comment. "We were wine butlers in the old country. Now seems juice of the vine has done us in." Major thought ruefully of the absurdity, took another swallow of scotch. "You have been a steady sounding board. Not afraid to speak your mind to me. I've appreciated that."

"Thank you, sir. Is there anything further?" Thomas pressed his question, his desire to leave growing.

"No, Thomas, you go on." Major sighed, looked at his clerk. "I need to stay awhile. I've got a few things to straighten out yet." He bent to light a cigar and inhaled, pulling on the stogie until his cheeks were deeply concave. He picked a flake of tobacco off his tongue and flicked it toward the ashtray.

Thomas paused, nodded. "Yes, sir. Call me if you need something. Otherwise, I'll be here Wednesday."

"Thank you, Thomas."

Stopping a moment, he stared at Major, positive he never remembered Major saying "thank you." Ever. But perhaps he had simply forgotten. Carefully, he pulled the door closed behind him.

His father had handled things hard. Major had inherited those hard ways. Andy hadn't been quite as hard until Major had forced a hardness into him.

Major sat in his huge chair, leaned back, smoked, poured another scotch. Loneliness settled in, lodged along his spine, made him twist to relieve tension in his shoulders. A sense of having botched everything settled. Eve. Janie. Andy. Susan Pea, too. He'd *loved* them all—enough to kill.

That half-assed county sheriff will eventually figure it out. Sordid details will flare into the open for town to pick over. Gossip mill will run amuck. He pulled on the cigar, flicked his finger across the ashes, watched them land next to the ashtray.

He'd run the lumber business, always made a profit. Maybe a little rough on coloreds. Especially Letta's man. Sure, maybe he could've stopped that *accident,* but man was a whipping boy and a drunk. Besides, he knew too much about Mrs. Butler number one. An example was needed and he was it. Major thumped the cigar again.

He made room for Letta's older boy John when he came back from the service. Paid him meager wages. You can't be too good to Blacks. Even if they did serve in the war. They expect better wages, but what the hell? Things can get out of control. Office empty, Major continued to reminisce. Letta had tolerated cruelty and phoniness within the household. No natter about his first wife. As housekeeper, she deserved credit for raising Andy, helped Eve and Janie adjust. Even when Letta's daughter Merry got raped, she did not utter a word to that genteel white community. A good woman, no matter her color. He had given her a place to live after her husband's accident. The rent free shack a bond for her discretion.

Still, he expected her and her boys to understand their place. And *keep it.*

Major fingered his glass and propped his feet on the desk. Hell, his desk cost more than a year's salary of even any *white mill* worker. Those living in the quarters understood the score. Anger pushed them to the boiling point. Sheriff needed to handle those little problems a bit faster. And better.

Letta's eyes always bored through Major. She was deferential in his presence—and properly anxious. Other times, he glimpsed her anger, deep down, smoldering below the surface. Guilt fluttered into his thinking, a rather troublesome gnat.

Those Lee Towners should have been fired for their man-mischief. Thankfully, now, at no great loss, they're both dead. Expendable trash. He mouthed the phrase again- expendable trash.

Rising from the chair, Major fixed himself a third drink. By the time he finished, streetlights were fully lit, and music gushed from the Southern Comfort Grill. Happy hour customers either drifted away or stayed and grew rowdier. Early diners met friends and selected Mario's Italian Kitchen or the Last Cowboy Steakhouse, both self-proclaimed gourmet restaurants, for their evening gatherings. People enjoyed downtown. Especially the park with its Confederate war statue.

He had guided his backwater town into a more modern future. Growth and small-town prestige his doing. Susan Pea and Andy lived well cushioned lives and social standing as a direct result of Major's efforts.

Provisions for Janie's education and her future grew out of Eve's insistence that Major bequeath her Butler name and money. At least in part.

A copy of her mother, Major found Janie still pulled at him. He struggled to tamp those feelings down. Despite his anger at Susan Pea, he had to admit she saved him from any action toward Janie.

Janie's pregnancy changed family dynamics. Major had taken care of that little mess rather expeditiously. He considered himself justified in his handling of circumstances.

He downed last of his drink and stubbed out the cigar. September shadows inched across the office and nestled into corners. Somehow, the gloom soothed him. Made hard less hard, less visible. Fall winds were arriving, scuttling leaves across streets and down alleyways, piling into corners, covering things up.

Scotch allowed him to feel regret without falling into despondency. He spoke aloud to the room, the desk, the town.

"I'm a *good* man. Why can't people see this?"

CHAPTER FORTY-SEVEN
SHERIFF

THE FALL HEAT carried less humidity than the earlier summer months. Nonetheless, the back of Sheriff's shirt was sweat stained, damp from sitting in the car on the drive over from the old Decatur County Courthouse to the Butler mansion.

Parked in the driveway, cruiser sported a thin layer of dust which covered the state logo, a round image proclaiming "Wisdom, Justice, Moderation."

"Lucky you recovered that dog of yours." Sheriff hooked his thumbs in his service belt and stood deferentially near the mansion porch steps.

"Otto? Yeah, I'm glad we got him back." Major bit the end of his cigar, spat it out, and watched Sheriff's face through the match flame as he lit up. "Man that brought Otto home has worked for me a time or two. He is what you call a sometime employee." Rolling the cigar between his fingers, Major raised one eyebrow. "He recognized that shorthair right off. Realized dog belonged to my kennel. I'll chalk all that off to sheer luck."

Sheriff nodded, turned slightly to watch the road, and nodded again. "Seems sort of strange for Wes to take the dog and later show up dead in his own pickup. Rifle shot to the head. Seems almost as if he was trying to steal it but got caught. And it was your man—your some-time employee—that found him?"

Major's cheeks hollowed as he took another pull on his cigar. He tipped his head back and blew smoke straight up. "As I said, sheer luck." He stood a moment as if thinking, thumped ashes off. "But I'm glad to get my dog back. I'll try him this season. If he does well, I'll sell him for a profit. Course, it'll be a difficult season without Wes. Man was a damn good trainer. Knew exactly how to find those coveys. How to work dogs. He seemed to talk to them in their language."

Sheriff shifted his weight from one leg to the other and back again. "We arrested your son Andy for auto theft based on your complaint. Had a bit of a bureaucratic scuffle over that."

"I'm appreciative of your trouble," Major said. He took another long pull and blew smoke toward Sheriff.

"Later on, we found Wes dead."

Major looked at the tip of his cigar. "Go on. Finish what you're thinking."

"Everything seemed to fit that your son did the shooting."

"There's question as to whether he's my son or not," Major said, took another pull on his cigar. "What else?"

Sheriff narrowed his eyes. "Turns out we had to let him go. Since he's Army, he's confined to his base until we get this killing stuff untangled."

"Well, Sheriff, I did speculate he might have had cause to shoot my trainer. Andy was prone to act before thinking." Major rolled the cigar around with his fingers. "He threatened Wes. I'm not sure why. You know how young studs are." His expression mild, Major looked at Sheriff. "Wes had most of the men in the county after his hide because of some woman or straying wife. Lots of husbands glad to see him gone."

"Well, truth be told, we suspected Wes might have been complicit in that rape a few months back, too. One involving your housekeeper's daughter. He might have withheld knowledge of a crime. But, before we could get an investigation going, that fire over in Lee Town happened. Couple of men got caught in it. Died."

"That's bad business for everyone. But I don't recall Wes or anyone here being involved." Major flicked a shred of tobacco off his finger, watched Sheriff's face. He vaguely considered Letta's oldest son John sneaking out of town. And her daughter. Another expendable one that disappeared same time as the older son. Poof. Gone. Like they never even lived.

"It all seemed to me kinda odd that you didn't help that old woman out," Sheriff said. "At least tried to find out who was involved with her girl. What with her being your housekeeper for so many years, it seems logical you'd want to help."

"Didn't you talk with that son of hers? Ask him what was going on?"

Sheriff took his hat off and wiped sweat off his face. "By the time we got around to it, he'd disappeared. Especially since we put off getting to him by at least a full twenty-four hours. At *your* request." He replaced his hat. "That old woman said she didn't know what happened to her boy. Kept telling us he stole her egg money. Took off. We couldn't make sense out of what she was talking about."

Major stepped off the porch. "Sheriff, how long have you known me? You got something on your mind, say it straight out."

"Well, I'm sort of thinking out loud," he said. "Wes had a checkered past. Somehow involved with your dog disappearing. Then there has been a lot of loose talk from townspeople about your stepdaughter."

"Meaning...?" Major straightened, eyes narrowed. He pulled again on the cigar.

"Got a secondhand report of a scuffle between your son and Wes—seems suspicious, especially since, shortly afterwards, he turns up murdered. Then a house fire and two dead white men. That Black soldier, raped gal, both disappeared so quick like." Sheriff replaced his hat. "Seems to circle around you in one way or another. You told everything?"

"Well, seems to me a lot of loose talk and speculation by gossips," Major said. "Folks scuffle back and forth all the time. Townspeople might need to be reminded hearsay doesn't stand up in court."

"I know the law. It's up to me to keep order in this county," Sheriff's tone grew prickly, sweat glistening off his upper lip.

"Sheriff, you don't mean to imply anyone in my household is responsible for anything, do you?" Major's comments were at once confusing and evasive.

"Well, sir, you where one to call in that report on Andy." Sheriff's tone took on an exasperated note. "Now, here you are telling me that it was all an error in communication. That you never intended to imply a problem." Sheriff glared at Major and eyed the cool of the porch.

Standing on the porch edge, Major declined to invite Sheriff to step into the shade. "Andy was too smart to be out looking for an unproven dog. The fact kennels were in disarray is what got him suspicious."

"Too much happening over the past year looks bad for the county. Town can't be expected to grow with all these killings and such." Sheriff hitched his duty belt higher on his hips. The leather creaked.

Major stepped off the porch toward the man, guiding him with an encircling arm gesture to the patrol car. The vehicle appeared forlorn, even embarrassed, crouched on gravel, dust tainted, engine still ticking with heat from the drive. The radio squawked. Sheriff leaned toward the window, listened. The message was routine, of no consequence.

"Lucky for all of us," Major said, "stuff always gets taken care of in the end. I'm sure your office will get it straightened out." He smiled, opened the car door wider. "In fact, your office has a knack for untangling things that *need* to be untangled. I'm sure you'll reach the *right* decision in this case."

Sheriff swallowed hard, tossed his hat on the car seat, slid inside.

Major closed the door, leaned down and spoke through the open window. "How's the re-election campaign coming along? Those things are a nuisance, coming up so frequent. I'll be sending in a bit more than my usual donation next week. Donations always help the winning candidate." He patted the car door and stepped back.

Sheriff turned the key. The engine jumped to life. He sat a moment and clenched his teeth. "Much obliged." Easing the car around the circular driveway, he slowed past the kennels, ducked to get a better view through the window.

Otto stood on his hind legs, front feet against the gate. He whined, head swiveled as sheriff rolled pass. Turning, the dog hopped onto the pine bench, and stretched out, head on his paws. Gunner, lengthwise on his bench, was already napping.

"Only witness—a dog who can't tell me nothing." Sheriff shook his head, drove out.

On the road, he picked up speed toward town.

CHAPTER FORTY-EIGHT
LETTA DAVIS

WEDNESDAYS WERE TRADITIONALLY clothes-wash days in the Butler household. A routine that varied with the seasons for as long as Letta could remember. Summertime clothes dried on the line. Rainy and cold months, Letta used the clothes drier.

With this late fall day, she took bedsheets, sundry clothing, and towels off the clothesline, knowing Susan Pea stood watching from the back porch. Letta dropped various items in a laundry basket. With the last sheet, she turned and, with a certain weariness, climbed the porch steps with the sun-dried items.

Inside the utility room, she pulled items from the basket one at a time, smoothed and folded towels, underwear, bras, stacking them carefully in small piles, hung shirts to be ironed later. She paused, massaged her work-roughened hands, scaley from years of dishes, scrubbing floors, and cleaning toilets. Hands cracked from summer days of gardening, pulling weeds. Her toes poked out of cuts in her wear-hardened shoes, too-big feet throbbing, and her day only half over.

Reflecting on prior years, she had stumbled home to her children and her man after work. Tired, but grateful for her time away from the mansion. She and her man had stood up proper before a preacher, gone to bother of getting a license at the courthouse. He said her sassy ways gave him strength. She knew a man didn't marry a woman unless he loved her. The memories warmed her, still brought joy. Those days, his muscles had rippled beneath sweat-greased skin, elegant and exciting. She'd burned from his lust—her lust—stoking it into passionate, sweat-filled nights leaving them breathless. With time, their fire burned down, and Letta's passion flickered, become an ash-covered pyre. Her man sagged under his mill workdays.

She didn't put blame on him for easing his brutal days with a moonshine-filled soda pop bottle. Tolerated Friday nights laced too tight with juke joint music and, sometimes, a whiff of another woman's musk. Forgave him the rusted out '59 Cadillac, barely running when he bought it. Held her tongue when beans and hog neckbones were all the children ate for supper. Said nothing when kids passed clothes and cardboard-sole-patched shoes from one to the next. Letta reckoned her husband had been a good man, doing his best for family, worn down but never quitting.

Somehow the two families, Butlers and her own family, the Davises, leaked into the same pool of need, of caring. Letta remembered mornings and family bustle with Susan Pea and Andy trundled off to school. Afternoons spent in basketball practice and family dinner to prepare. Shared conversations. Laughing over the same incident. Until Susan Pea left.

Years in between glowed red with ire, grey with collapsed hope, dark with animosity. Sometimes yellow with joy. With Eve's cancer came additional work, heightened caring for Janie, and tangled needs for Andy. Her own children, growing into adulthood, required more attention. Then, Susan Pea had returned.

Letta moved the laundry basket aside, stacked piles of jumbled magazines on an odd table to make room for her to fold fresh sheets. She stared at Susan Pea across the heap, took a deep breath. "I'm leaving."

Susan Pea lit a cigarette and tossed the almost empty pack onto a chair. "You've hinted at leaving before." She took a drag, squinted to keep smoke out of her eyes. "Be careful. It's hard out there. Besides, we need you here."

"My children already gone on. They get settled good and then I go."

Hair on Susan Pea's arms prickled up into chicken skin. She blinked, realized this announcement, this time, serious. "You can't leave. Not now." Her voice rose. She stared at Letta a minute then said, "Why not move into the mansion? It's safer and we've got room."

Surprised, Letta eyed Susan Pea.

"You've been the anchor in this family my entire life," Susan Pea said. "You're practically my mother. How can you leave?" Grimacing, she took a second deep drag.

"With that first Mrs. Butler," Letta said, "I lived with more screaming fits, hitting, and aggravation between them two than I even care to remember, much less tell. Andy crying, fighting at school. First Mrs. disappears. Maybe run off. Maybe not."

"Of course, she ran off. Who wouldn't?" Susan Pea blew smoke toward the ceiling. "Are you thinking something else could have happened?"

Letta paused, narrowed her eyes, shuddered, and continued folding.

"Well?" Susan Pea said.

Letta humphed. "Don't reckon I know nothing. Major tells me, keep my mouth closed. Especially no talking on that first missus."

She continued to fold sheets and pillowcases, grimaced remembering when Mose Jones had come with word of the death of her husband. How, many days later, Major came by and growled, "You keep working, take care of Eve, Janie, big house. Live in that shack for free. Keep your mouth shut." He had pointed a finger at her. Never allowed any sympathy in his voice, never uttered a word of condolence.

Letta stopped folding. "I stay. Like he says." Setting the folded sheet down, she paused, appeared to be considering the offer to move. She fingered her wedding band, thought about all her husband had endured at Major's hand. Living in the mansion smacked of sacrilege. "Thank you for the offer, but I need stay where I am." Letta sucked her teeth and half-turned away.

Susan Pea crushed her cigarette out. "What on earth will you do? Who do you know? Where will you live?"

"I'll go live with my people," Letta said.

"Your people? I always thought you were one of us." Susan Pea's voice quivered.

"Never been, nor will ever be, one of y'all. You only see *Butler* problems. *Butler* wants. You look at me, you see *hired help*. Don't see no woman with a life, a family. Y'all don't see her crying, nor do no caring if she be happy or been up all night with her own sick babies. Her worrying about her man sucking down brown water. Nah, you only worry about breakfast. Who's gonna clean up Butler dirt. Plant the garden. Take care this old house."

Astonished, Susan Pea's face collapsed. "I live my life with someone and have only a vague awareness of her. Does skin color make that much difference? This is a *nightmare*, a horror movie." Her breath came in gasps. She crushed her cigarette out and fumbled for another, took a draw, her cheeks concave.

Letta's voice took on a hard edge. "Burying my man not like what y'all done for Missus Eve. My John not allowed to come for his pappy's homegoing. We treated different. Major says no sense getting *town folks* stirred up. Be quiet about my man."

The two women stood silent, neither looking at the other, knowing they stood on opposite sides of a chasm. Recognized wrong and hurt done to everyone. Realized they were shoulder to shoulder. Now Major happened to be the only bridge available—missing planks, rusty nails, and frayed rope notwithstanding.

"Major think free rent gonna make up for my man?" Letta said. "What does he know about doing right? He thinks I can't see his true self. Don't understand him." She stopped folding, stacked several towels in the basket. "He wrong."

Susan Pea shot Letta a quick look, lowered her eyes, and flicked ashes off her cigarette onto the utility room floor.

Letta glanced down at the ashes, sighed, turned away, and continued. "Major treat Missus Eve like queen till he find out she can't have no baby. Then he out looking again. He messing with a kept woman while he got a cancer wife and blind girl living under his roof. Him trying to play *good* husband."

Susan Pea thumped more ashes off. Missed the ash tray, her hand unsteady. "I've only been home four months, and I've already buried my sister-in-law and assumed care of my niece—and her expecting." Her voice rose an octave. "Andy's under scrutiny for murder. Goddamn Major." Panic seeped into her bones. "Letta, I can't handle this alone. I need you." She stubbed her cigarette out, ashes dusting the small table. "I can't do all the work around here. You're at least needed for that."

"For work? What happened to that there anchor? What about almost you mother?" Letta stretched her arms wide, holding sheets, lined up corners, and folded. "I ain't always been a wrinkled up old woman. You folks never appreciate that. You only want next day's *work*." Letta glared at Susan Pea. "But I got my own life."

Resentment edged into Susan Pea's voice. "Your life? What about me? How will I manage? What? You must stay and help me." She lit another cigarette. The tip flared bright.

"No," Letta said. "I played deaf in this house for the last time. I seen my last meanness here. Changed my last tangled-up sheet with man-dirt." She stood tall, frowning at Susan Pea, offered only a blank face. "I know how Major treat us folks. He throw dark meat out to any snarling pack come around when there be trouble. He sling chum under wheels if necessary. I been down this chunked-up road too many times. *My people* travel it, too." Letta folded another sheet, stacked them neatly together.

"This is a catastrophe," Susan Pea said, her mouth dry, eyes growing glassy.

Somewhere in the house, floorboards creaked, groaning from the years. Wind caught a loose screen and banged it against the outside. The striped cat waltzed in and rubbed against Letta's legs several times, sashayed out as quiet as it had entered.

"Missus Eve passed." Letta leaned in and whispered. "Man who planted that seed in her daughter's belly done showed up dead, too. Major maybe one that got rid of that Lee Town trash. Haints growing spiteful."

Susan Pea spoke sharp, in disbelief. "You can't believe Major had anything to do with that killing. He was in town when Wes was shot."

"Took a week to find that body," Letta felt distain at whites refusing to see what was clear. "Understand this, that man knows how to make things happen and leave his hands looking clean."

Susan Pea sat dumbfounded.

Letta picked up an armload of folded laundry, started out of the room, stopped in the doorway. "Major take care things his way."

"You don't know what you're talking about," Susan Pea said, her voice rising toward hysteria. She rubbed her forehead as if to banish what she knew to be true.

"Mr. Andy in Army—studying on best way to kill people. *Kill people.*

One at a time. How that something to be proud of? Killing?" Letta turned brooding eyes toward Susan Pea.

Susan Pea swallowed and turned away, not wanting to face possibilities.

Letta spoke low and rough. "Given a chance, you run. Leave me holding this here wore-out gunny sack. Nobody got no hold on me. I telling you cause your thoughts be like mine. They same. Soon's Major gone, we free."

"What the hell?' Susan Pea's voice shook with skepticism. "Major's not leaving. What are you talking about?"

Like the fierce queens of her ancestors, Letta stood tall and defiant. Her lips a thin line, she looked directly into Susan Pea's face. "Was a time a Black person couldn't even look no white in their eyes. Never use front door. Always served last—out back."

Susan Pea blinked several times.

"I been thinking on leaving a long time," Letta said. "I got one last chore need doing. I late getting to it, but time done come ripe."

The scent of sun-and-wind-dried clothes filled the utility room. Light dappled through the window. Somewhere inside, boards complained as they scraped together.

"Come this weekend, I'm gone to Cleveland," Letta said, her voice steady. "Noonday bus. Open daylight. Ever thing I gotta do here be finished by Saturday."

Outside sounds floated through the window screen. Dust motes twirled in the air. Summer flexed its muscles a last time as autumn tiptoed forward. Changing season meant winter was riding hard in their direction, and, with it, a time of cold and rest.

"Have you told Janie?" Susan Pea broke the silence.

"I tell her before I leave. Do it my own way." Letta's voice resonated with pain. "Missus Eve done set up that bird man. He talk funny, but he be good." As if exhausted, she nodded to herself. With the girl's potential move to the university, Letta had fulfilled her obligations to those she cared about.

Susan Pea paced back and forth, tears stinging her eyes. "I can't live here in this festering town forever. I have *my life*, too." She slumped down in a chair. "I'm afraid."

"Y'all strong. I cared about Missus Eve, but she gone, at peace. I fond of Janie, but she growed up, finding her own way." Gesturing, Letta continued explaining. "Y'all two—you and Andy—always been independent, making you own way." Letta waved her hand around the room, motioned toward outside. "None this my concern no more. Bottle tree still here. Think on what it says."

"Major may not see it the same way," Susan Pea said.

Letta's shoulders stiffened, she thrust her chin forward and crushed folded clothes against her chest. "He got all he's gonna get from me. Any debt he thinks I owe him been settled. Besides, boatman already waiting on him. Man *wants* to go."

"What boatman?" Susan Pea blinked, shook her head, puzzled at unexpected references. All her life, she had lived in Major's shadow often under his thumb. Letta had voiced Susan Pea's thoughts about Major. *Wants to go.* Sighing, she acknowledged years of angst.

"Boatman Missus Eve and Major done read 'bout." Sadness resonated in Letta's voice. She stood silent a moment, stepped through the doorway, and went about putting laundry away, never breaking stride or looking back. Her shuffle, in diminishing notes, came back faintly until only stillness reverberated in the old mansion.

Outside, the bottle tree tinkled softly in an afternoon breeze. A delicate fragrance of dying leaves hung in the air. Heat slowly released its hold as the sun began its descent. Night coolness crept forward on kitten claws. The years had rolled by too quick, yet stretched on endlessly.

CHAPTER FORTY-NINE
MAJOR BUTLER

MAJOR'S LINCOLN hummed smooth as he pulled into the Butler driveway. He cut the engine, swung the car door open, and climbed out. It was his custom to store his hunting gear at the mansion. Likewise, he left the jeep pickup, with its patina of dust, in the driveway available for his next outing.

Regular as clockwork, Fridays, about daylight, he came around to work dogs. With cooling weather and hunt season approaching, his ritual became as conscientious as Sunday homilies: tramp into the kitchen, drink two full mugs of coffee, change into field gear, and select a gun.

Even with Wes gone, he maintained the habit.

Major prowled fields, tramped creek byways, and checked on well-being of game birds. Checked more frequently as the season approached. When Wes was alive, he sometimes accompanied Major. But mostly not. Major favored going alone, used that time to focus on guns and shooting.

At the sound of the Lincoln, Letta watched from the kitchen window before moving away. For thirty years she'd perked a pot of coffee just for him. This day, only a half a pot, exactly what he would drink before heading out to the field.

She spooned grounds into the basket and, hands shaking, added extra from a small tin she had tucked into her pocket earlier. Strong coffee. She set the pot on the stove burner, replaced coffee can in the cupboard, dropped the tin back into her pocket.

He paused on the porch and rummaged around a few minutes. Apparently finding what he needed, he clumped into the kitchen, threw his sports coat on a straight back chair.

"Coffee ready?" His bulk filled the kitchen, voice gravelly, harsh.

"Yessah." She poured a mug, set it on the table, and turned back to her stove.

He picked up the mug, blew across the steaming liquid, waited, and then slurped a mouthful. "Did you change brands on me? Mite stout this morning."

"Nah, sah. No brand change. I make it special today. Know you want it strong. Specially when you hunting." Letta crossed the kitchen and ran a sink of dishwater. "It don't suit you, I make a fresh pot." Her hands shook. She slipped them into soapy water to hide the trembling. She took several deep breaths and began to wash up the biscuit makings.

He drank silently, looked at Letta again, nodded slightly, and walked into the knotty pine-paneled hallway. He sat on an antique church pew placed snug against the wall. Grunting, he slipped off his shoes, pulled on hunt boots, laced gaiters up his ankles and legs, and stood. In two steps, he crossed the hallway and opened the glass-front antique gun cabinet. A metallic odor of oil and cedar lining coiled out.

A basic 30-30 Remington for deer, bolt action. A 26-inch barrel five-shot Winchester. A 20-gauge pump, easy to swing forward on flying dove. A repeating Ruger 10/22 with slight recoil for small game. A finely balanced, special edition Browning side-by-side shotgun. A hunt scene depicting a field pointer and flying quail engraved on the stock. Burled wood lent it elegance. Eve had given it to him one anniversary—while she still loved.

Hoisting the 12-gauge Browning, he closed the cabinet and relocked it. He caressed the stock, rubbed his finger across the engraving, smiled, and drank the last of the coffee. He stared at the dregs, looked up at Letta. Nodded.

Mutt sat on full alert, aware of the pre-hunt preparation ritual. Gun. Box of shells. Heavy shirt against the chill. Day-glow vest on top. Orange cap on the peg next to the door. Easy to don on his way out.

Major gestured for a second coffee, stood a long moment, faced his housekeeper. "Time for me to go." He raised the cup, as if in a toast, and drank half.

"Yessah." Bowing her head, Letta fingered her apron pocket and turned away.

Opening the back door, he grabbed his hunt cap and clucked to Mutt. The dog danced ahead across the porch, tongue lolling out and ears cocked. The light began to shift from the thin dawn hours to early tangerine streaks. It held the promise of an uncommon beginning.

Parked near the barn, dog crates in the bed and gun rack across the rear window, sat the jeep pickup. Mutt sashayed to the vehicle and shifted back and forth on his feet before the door, whining.

Major opened the door. Shotgun placed in the rack, box of shells on the seat, he turned to the dog. "Come, Mutt. In." He gestured toward the seat. The dog bounced several times and scrambled in.

Stumbling slightly, Major placed his hand on the jeep door. Straightening, he zipped the jacket up, adjusted his cap, and stepped into the cab. Scooting Mutt over to the passenger side, he took a slow, deep breath, and turned the ignition.

The engine coughed several cranks, finally caught, and burped dark exhaust smoke. Major jerked the vehicle into gear. Sputtering, it lurched down the driveway, bumped onto the street, stalled slightly at the traffic light, and finally ran smoothly as Major turned onto the asphalt county road.

He drove steadily toward Frog Bottom slightly too fast, crossing the center line several times. Vision blurring, heart pounding, he eased off the accelerator at the crossroads and palmed the wheel into a nondescript two-pump gas station. He rubbed his forehead, frowned, and swallowed hard.

A florid, overweight man lumbered toward him wearing deeply stained bib overalls. Grease ringed his fingernails, hands grimy.

"Top off the tank and check the oil." Major spoke with authority and disdain. He stepped out, left the door open, stretched, and spat a wad of phlegm on the gravel. Mutt shifted on the truck seat but did not jump out.

The man waved a sullen, freckled-face boy toward a bucket of dirty water holding a brush. "I git the gas. You wash that there windshield."

The boy moved like winter molasses toward his task.

"Y'all gonna be huntin' today?" Man's voice was flat, with a deep twang.

Major did not respond.

"Feller lives down road tells it, them bobwhites thick as fleas over near Flint River." Man inserted the nozzle in the jeep, clicked gas pump on.

"That right?" Major said. "I might mosey over. See what Mutt can hustle up. Haven't decided."

"He ain't one your regular hunt dogs. He gonna do any good?"

"He's what I need today." Major barely glanced at him.

"Too much tramping around might git them birds spooked. They ain't stay around if'n you go scare 'em too early."

"Not your business."

"Yessah." He turned back to his pump gas chore.

Major stared off into space. He needed to tune up his hand-eye coordination, think about birds, get ready for the full season.

The sullen boy finished the windshield, moved the soapy wash bucket aside, and walked away. Major handed a crisp ten to the man.

With infinite slowness, he trundled into the store, returned with five dollars and two quarters change.

Major placed the bills in his money clip, climbed in, pushed coins toward the dusty glove compartment, and slammed the door. He sat, rubbed his eyes, and finally cranked the jeep. Shaking his head slightly, he pulled onto the paved road and drove toward Frog Bottom.

He spoke to Mutt and rubbed his eyes. "Seems I'm seeing double today."

At the turnoff, he rattled down the dirt track to a weedy area, pulled in, and cut the engine. He got out and, swaying slightly, walked to the passenger side, signaled Mutt down, and propped himself against the seat edge. Leaning down, he dry-heaved.

Dawn glistened across the field. An earthbound cloud hovered above grass, then dissolved. Songbirds twittered. Farther afield, a bobwhite called. Another answered. Morning coolness settled and a spider web floated past, glinting with dew. For a moment, silence fell. The bird chorus rose a second time, a full-throated requiem, gracing a new day.

Mutt shifted at Major's feet and whined. He patted the dog's head absently, realized he felt unsteady. Decided he'd cut the day short. Maybe he'd feel better later. He held onto the jeep door and leaned into the cab, wrestled the shotgun off the back rack. Propped against the vehicle, he loaded the gun and stuffed extra shells into his pocket. He fumbled, dropped several into the grass and, leaning down, slowly picked up three shells. He puzzled over them, rolled them around in his hand, tested his dexterity, and finally stuffed them into his vest.

Braced against the door, random thoughts trickled through his head. First wife, a bit wild, gone. Second one—pick of the litter—dead of cancer. Lee Town trash out of the way. Wes shot. Letta in her place. Susan Pea needing to be forced back into her nether world. That'd leave Janie, alone.

He snapped the shotgun closed, slammed the jeep door, and walked toward a pine stand. Mutt sniffed along ahead. They crossed the switch grass field and headed toward the wooded strip on the north end.

Major stumbled in rough ground, caught himself, took a deep breath. Jeep fumes must have affected him more than he realized. He shook his head and turned parallel to the trees, lurched toward the river. A sagging fence marked the area boundary. He stared at the deadfall, the debris tangled in the wire.

"I forgot this damn fence." He noted broken limbs and dried grass, rusted wire, yawning gaps. Overwhelmed with a need to cross, Major bent down, looked closer. He spat on the ground, then righted himself, realized his legs seemed wooden, hard to control. The shotgun felt too heavy.

Carefully, he used the butt of the shotgun to push the wire barrier down and climb over. Toe of his boot caught in the debris. Part-falling and part-climbing the fence, he landed on his backside. He sat there, legs askew, uncertain. His foot twitched. Bile rose in his throat with a bitter aftertaste. He drooled spittle, belched, smelled carrots. He maneuvered his back against a post, spat again, and wiped his mouth on his sleeve. His heart hammering against his ribs, he heard someone calling.

I'm coming.

Silence. Again, a sound, rising and falling, as if from a distance. A woman's voice? Was it familiar or did it simply give that impression? Maybe it was those birds... hard to tell.

Slowly, with great care, he pulled out his flask, took a deep swig, licked his lips, and replaced it in his vest. His legs jerked. A shadow stretched across his boots. The wind picked up.

Sweating, Major turned his face toward the gust and shivered. Numbness crawled from his feet to his knees, legs, and, inch-by-inch, moved toward his thighs. His heart pounded uncontrollably. He sucked in his breath.

I'm coming, said the voice.

His hand touched the shotgun, fence post solid against his back, braced him. The shadow crept to his waist, lingered near his chest. Grimacing, he gazed across the creek, grasses, and into pines. Heard fiddle music, watched Old Scratch dance toward him, laughing, clicking his heels. Birds sang a choral dirge. Insects buzzed somber and mournful.

The woman's voice called again, *Come. Take my hand. I'll help you into the boat.*

A booming noise reverberated. An invisible force shoved him hard into the post. Things felt too close, yet distant, abandoned. Puzzled, he stared at his hand. At the gun. Felt wetness weep out of his chest.

Mutt crawled beside Major, licked his face, settled into a sedge grass clump a few feet away, and whimpered. Figures drew near, cavorted with abandon.

Major slumped, a puppet with strings cut, drooping against the post. Listing slightly, he raised his head and stared toward the trees, listened to whispers, his eyes unblinking.

If only things had been different. If only he had been able to love. If only regret had not accumulated. Figures grew more distinct. Fiddle music rose. Hum of voices grew louder. If only...

Come with me. The woman's voice. *It's time.*

"I'm coming." He twisted under the weight of crumbled memories. Lost dreams dissolved as if breath on a cold morning. He stared at a crow on the edge of the woods, watched it take flight.

Silence.

CHAPTER FIFTY
LETTA DAVIS

WITH WORK-CHAPPED HANDS, Letta removed her apron, laid it across the back porch rail. She slipped a Sunday jacket over her plaid, cotton dress, adjusted the amber pin.

Saturday morning dawned clear as a mockingbird's trill. Rain that had graced the town during the night dripped off leaves in multicolored crystals, pausing before plunging to earth. Stooping slightly, she picked up a cardboard suitcase, one end dented and fraying apart. She started out of the yard, paused, and looked at her blue bottle tree, took a square bottle off, a smallish, apothecary one, used for some medicine or other. She rolled it around in her palm, held it to the sun, and felt its brilliance. Carefully, she placed it in her pocket. For protection. And remembrance.

She curtsied to the Chinaberry tree with its summer shade and fall berries. Listened to a flicker drum at hidden insects. She grinned at the one-eyed ginger cat, a sassy survivor, as he strolled across the yard to another place.

Turning, she looked down the road toward the tin-can town, sorted through her memories. Pink azaleas in the spring. Languid afternoons shelling peas and pine trees sighing in the wind. Taste of salty boiled peanuts and vine-ripe tomatoes. Witness oak weeping moss strings. All-day gospel sings, dinner on the ground, sweetness of her church people with their cache of gentleness, shaping experiences by what got shed and what got kept. Children laughing as they played tag. Felt her man's love. Recognized again *division* and *interdependence* between her people and white town folk. Understood summer heat as the devil's device.

Letta's walk to the Greyhound bus station took twenty minutes. She did not move fast, but at her normal pace to avoid drawing attention. Arriving sweaty, she stood quietly at the ticket window underneath a faded sign, "For Coloreds Only." Still above the ticket window, still readable after all the years.

"I take a ticket one way to Cleveland. Ohio."

Agent's tone and manner unmistakably condescending. "I know Cleveland is in Ohio." He stared at Letta, held her ticket behind the glass, slightly out of reach. He fidgeted a minute and then asked, "You Butler housekeeper?"

"That's right, Butler housekeeper for Missus Eve afore she passed. I'm going to visit my son. Done told I'm going." She shifted her feet, felt discomfort under the man's stare, anger at his questions. She pushed her money closer to him across the counter. "Don't need no permission." She did not offer any additional comment. She only had to hold her tongue a little longer, not respond further to the agent.

"I need to double check you not running out on obligations." He looked at her a moment, glanced around the area. Seeing no one to ask, he finally shrugged, picked up the rumpled bills, and scraped coins into the cash drawer. He pushed the ticket toward her. Carefully, he moved his hands to the far edges of the clerk window, beyond her touch.

Letta picked the ticket up, stood a moment. *Color don't rub off. Only thing come off is spitefulness.* She turned toward her bus.

Those first days when Susan Pea came home to help Missus Eve with her cancer and the callousness in Major's soul grew, Letta worried about her own adult son, wanted him to find a woman and build a family. She touched the blue bottle in her pocket and wished for a woman that understood country living. A woman that knew how love and hate are woven together in a single cord. A woman that could understand violence of a place sobbing humidity and moss strings. A woman who had seen strange fruit dangling up high and pushed back against it. Understood how caring can cross color lines. Letta caressed her bottle. Felt its warmth. Heard the conjure woman's words: *He wants to go.*

Being ignored hurts the soul, diminishes a person. But it can be useful, too. Heat keeps people worrying about their malicious, hidden ways. Sweat glosses over everything. Excuses lust and hate and even love. Makes people leak out their kindness, their giving, and their caring till ain't no more left. They look up and here comes truth, dressed shabby, like some unwelcomed third cousin on your stepdaddy's side. Tired, she sat on her suitcase, hoping it wouldn't collapse.

Driver stood by the door, collected tickets. Several sailors in white uniforms climbed on before her, headed to Birmingham they said. An elderly, gray-tinted couple teetered up the steps to the third row of seats. A tattooed hippy and his girlfriend with twig-size arms swung aboard, walked down the aisle, took seats midway back. Driver tossed their baggage onto his waiting northbound bus.

She continued twisting her wedding band and watched fellow passengers. Diesel odors made her sneeze.

With white passengers settled, the driver, sweat beading on his bald head, gestured at Letta. "Where you going?"

"Cleveland. Live with my sons. Got a daughter there, too." She looked him straight on without blinking, her back erect.

He paused a moment, suspicious of her brazen attitude, and squinched his eyes. "You not leaving some church lady without kitchen help, are you? Not ducking out on rent?"

"Nah."

He took the ticket, examined it closely.

She stared off down the street, waited for the ticket, spoke slow. "Done finished ever thing. Nuthin' more I *needs* doing."

He shrugged, punched the ticket, and handed it back.

She nodded, stuffed it in her pocket next to the blue bottle.

He stepped aside.

She climbed the steps, chose a place in the back, settled against stained cushions, grateful the morning was giving way to the afternoon. The bus was scheduled out at one o'clock.

Passengers shifted, made settling noises, and spoke to each other in muted voices. The sun stood at its noonday zenith. Letta's thoughts played across the years, the people. She willed the bus to depart before she lost courage, or someone decided against her going.

Driver climbed on board and closed the doors with a pneumatic belch. Twisting the steering wheel, he glanced in the rear-view mirror at his passengers, backed the rig out, and swung onto the street moving north.

CHAPTER FIFTY-ONE
SHERIFF

Saturday dawned still dripping after the nighttime rain, began to dry in the afternoon sun. It had been a busy morning for Sheriff with routine traffic problems—weekend rush to kids' baseball games, a fender bender near the grocery store, a request for help with keys locked inside a car—usual stuff.

Now, damn it all to hell and back, Susan Pea had called, worried about Major gone hunting on Friday and not back yet. Got a dog missing, too. He'd sent deputies to follow up while he finished working a last-minute car-pedestrian collision.

A half-hour later, his radio squawked again. He keyed the mic, dreading any message before he answered.

"We found him, Sheriff. Over near Flint River. Sitting up against a fence post. Eyes wide open. Dead."

"What the dickens?"

"Not only that, but he's *still warm*. Well, sort of. Soaking wet from that rain, too."

"Damn it. Warm, you say? How are we going to explain this?"

Sheriff keyed his mic off, ran his fingers through his hair, sat silent, and keyed on again. "I'm out on the highway headed toward Frog Bottom Creek. I'll circle back your way to the river. Coroner been out?"

"No, sir," deputy replied. "We called you first. See how you want to handle this. Me and Henry still out here."

"Go ahead and call the coroner. I'll be there before him anyway."

"Right," deputy responded. "Reckon why Major ended up way over here?"

"Now how in hell's name am I supposed to know?" Sheriff said. "Y'all stay put till I get there. Don't move nothing. Leave the dang place exactly like you found it." Sheriff flipped on the cruiser lights and siren, made a U-turn, and accelerated toward county south.

CHAPTER FIFTY-TWO
SUSAN PEA BUTLER

IT WAS mid-Saturday afternoon before Sheriff pulled into the Butler driveway. Susan Pea stepped out on the porch to meet him. He parked and climbed out of the cruiser.

"Did you find him?"

"Yes, Miss Butler, we found him. Him and that dog."

"Where?"

"At Flint River. Near that stand of persimmon and live oaks, close to that old fence line."

"Flint River? I thought he usually hunted Frog Bottom Creek. Especially when he went alone." Susan Pea stared past his shoulder toward the road. She twisted her hands, stuffed them in her pants pockets, and looked at him again. "Well? What else?" Her voice rose a notch.

Sheriff fumbled with his hat, hands twitching while he scuffed his boot toe across driveway gravel. "Damn it all, I hate to bring this news."

"Well, you've brought it. Tell the rest." She folded her arms across her chest and looked at him wordlessly.

"He must have tried to climb over a fence next to the river. There was a mess of deadfall tangled around that wire. The gun got caught or his foot got snagged or something happened. Anyway, we found him there. He was sitting next to a post, kinda like he was waiting on somebody. Eyes wide open."

Susan Pea blinked twice and shook her head. "Doesn't make sense. He has hunted there and knows the fields, knows his guns. Knows how to cross deadfall. Especially with a loaded gun. What could possibly have happened?" Her heart pounded so hard she was sure Sheriff could hear it. Panic climbed into her throat.

"Stuff must've been slippery, what with rain last night. Could be he slipped."

Mouth agape, Susan repeated, "Slipped? He was out hunting yesterday morning. Didn't rain until late last night. He couldn't have slipped because it was not wet at that time."

"Well, I don't rightly know. Maybe it was rotten limbs. Could be happened after raining. Don't rightly know."

"I thought you knew how to handle this kind of thing. Thought you could put two and two together." She swiveled her head as she glanced down the road, toward the kennels, and back to Sheriff. "My good Lord."

"Well, we *just* found him." His voice rose in a defensive arc. "Haven't had time to really investigate yet. Wanted to let you know before you heard it from someone else."

"Well, you've done that." She continued to glare at him, then glanced away. "What about Mutt?"

"Found that dog next to the path in some high sedge."

"He's not a bird dog. He's a porch dog. Janie's dog. Why would he take Mutt and not pointers if he were hunting?"

"Can't answer that," Sheriff said. "Dog kept shaking and whining. Cowered down, like he seen devil himself." He held his hat by the brim, moved it around in his hand, looked down at the ground, and raised his head to meet her eyes again. "Like I said, we found Major kinda sitting there, you know, propped against that post. Musta tried to climb that broke-down fence. Shotgun right there beside him. One barrel empty. Awful lot of blood around. Despite rain." He shifted. "Nice gun. Had a scene of a hunt along one side. You know, a dog and birds flying."

Susan Pea gasped, covered her mouth with her hand. "Eve gave him that gun." She stood still, tears welling, swallowed her thoughts, and turned away. Her vision blurred as she cried in deep gulps, tears coursing down her cheeks, shoulders shaking. Finally, she stopped, wiped her nose on her shirttail hem, and turned around to face Sheriff again. "Go on. Tell the rest."

"Shot got him in the side of his chest," he said. "Musta bled out since shot didn't seem to have killed him right off. No telling how long that took. Might'a saved him if we'd found him sooner. Still had his finger in that trigger guard."

Susan Pea dropped her hand, dry-coughed. "Almost sounds as if he shot himself." Her voice rose. "Why would he do that?"

Suicide brought shame on a family. Especially since their father had died under strange circumstances. Her hand slid slowly down from her mouth to her throat. She swallowed her scream rising toward the air, held the porch railing, felt her knees close to buckling.

Sheriff stood silent.

"Oh, Lord, this is too strange, unreal." Susan Pea's eyes darted wildly around the yard. She continued to sag against the porch railing.

"Beg your pardon, Miss Butler," Sheriff grew testy, "but we just got started on this. How should I know why he went there? Never understood what went on in that man's mind, anyway. Got to let the coroner finish up his investigation and tell us what he thinks happened."

Hands shaking, Susan Pea frowned and rubbed her temples. "Odd he should take Janie's dog, use the gun Eve gave him, and hunt a place he rarely goes. Be so clumsy about climbing a fence."

She silently rolled the word "dead" around in her mouth, tasted its bitterness. Smelled sulfur.

"Your maid say anything about him this morning?"

"No. She did not." Susan Pea's knuckles strained against her pallid skin as she gripped the porch railing. "In fact, I've not seen her. Took the bus for Ohio early today. Cleveland, I think she said. Told me days ago she was leaving."

"You tell her okay to leave?"

Susan Pea stiffened. "She's hired help, but she *is* a free woman. I'm not Major, marionetting everyone everywhere. Besides, it's 1970 and I think Johnson took care of that issue back in 1964." Hands on her hips, she stood glaring, silently paused a moment, swallowed. "Letta's headed north to her sons, her daughter. Said she plans to live up there."

"Well, probably don't matter. Her kind won't tell if they do know anything. Let it go. She's only the housekeeper."

"She's always been *more* than a housekeeper," Susan Pea said. "I only wish I had understood that earlier. She's a good woman."

Sheriff blinked at her and put his hat on. He turned to go, then stopped. "One other thing. We found two quarters on the seat. A gas receipt was thrown there, too. Had a name on it. Looked like 'Sharon.' You reckon that's some woman he knew? You know anyone by that name?"

"No, I don't know a Sharon." Susan Pea shook her head, swallowed several times.

Sheriff stood, a blank stare on his face. "I can't recall anyone called Sharon around here by that name either."

Susan Pea frowned at Sheriff and continued shaking her head.

"Well, in all honesty, we couldn't tell if it was a 'C' or an 'S.' Didn't make sense."

Susan Pea stood, fingers clenching the rail, aching, and turning white. Her mouth set in a grim line. She swallowed, her throat contracting with the effort. Words, thoughts, materialized: *He wants to go. Meanness stops with his death. Freedom comes after he's gone. Janie going to the university. Letta leaving for the north. Everything on my shoulders.*

She took a deep breath and said, "I'd be grateful if you don't say any more than you must. Please ask your deputies and the coroner to do the same."

"Miss Butler, I expect them two—my deputies—done already told everybody that will listen. Don't know about the coroner." Sheriff frowned, uncertain what he should do. "I'll tell 'em to hold their tongues, but I reckon word's already spreading. You know how small-town people love to talk."

She turned away, twisted back, and spoke, her voice cracking, "Janie's at her piano teacher this afternoon. I'll pick her up. Tell her what's happened." Susan Pea took several steps toward the front door and paused again. "You don't mind, get in touch with Andy. Army, 1st Ranger Battalion. I expect you know how to get in touch with boys in the service."

"Yes, ma'am. I'll get started on that."

Susan Pea felt her mouth go dry, blinked eye moisture away, and slowly realized Sheriff was speaking to her again. "What?"

He cleared his throat. "County coroner will have final say on what caused his death."

"Yes, of course." Susan Pea stared off across the yard and down the tree-lined street, teeth clinched. "An accident. You hear? An accident. Point is, he's dead. Best that you don't say anything about details. No need to tell more."

Sheriff nodded acquiescence. He placed his hat on his head and turned. "Hate to bring this up now, but you'll need to come down to the station tomorrow. Sign some paperwork."

He frowned, looked at the ground, then said, "I'm real sorry all this happened so soon after Mrs. Butler's passing." He touched the brim of his hat, then stepped into the cruiser, and guided it slowly toward town. No siren. No lights.

Susan Pea watched the patrol car until it disappeared down the drive and onto the road. The sound gradually diminished, leaving her standing alone.

Unfocused, she shuddered as if waking from a nightmare. Her mouth dry, she barely croaked aloud, "It wasn't an 'S.' Not Sharon. He meant Charon."

Goosebumps settled over her forearms. Major and Eve had once read Dante's *Divine Comedy* together, a favorite to discuss. They talked about the various circles of hell, degrees of sinning, punishment, and heaven. About boatman Charon rowing souls to purgatory for two coins, usually placed on the eyes of the departed. The custom lost through the centuries with its in and out of cultures, river names changing until... until it became a euphemism for the passage between life and the next worlds. He and Eve had shared the book before things turned sour. He must have placed the coins in the truck and left the scribbled name coincidentally *before* he went hunting, an odd action.

She shivered slightly in the breeze, felt alone, wiped mucus off her nose. For the second time in her life, *acquiescence* around a death took center stage. She blinked and stared at Eve's empty porch rocker. A breeze pushed against the chair, moving it slightly, as if a person had settled down for the afternoon.

Susan Pea rubbed her head, braced her shoulder against the porch post. She had wanted him dead. Had deliberated about what would happen with him gone. Had disliked him. Had even hated him. He was her brother. Somewhere caring or love or something was mixed in. Now that he no longer lived, what was she meant to feel—guilt? Relief? Anger? Caring? Did *thoughts* have that much power? An overwhelming sense of aloneness descended, shrouded her body.

She sat on the porch step and wept until she felt weak and tired and drained. The shadows lengthened and turned from dusk-colored to leaden. She stood, held the railing to steady herself, and blew her nose on her shirttail.

A stillness settled. The wind laid by, as if respectful of a life passed, albeit a blighted one. A spectral crow flew low, a town crier with news for the other side.

Susan Pea's mind pulsated over past days, over her relationship with Eve and Letta, over Major. Mostly, she rummaged over her time ahead with Janie.

At the edge of the yard, the ornamental bottle tree, Tiny Blue, sparkled in the sun's late rays. Susan Pea needed to pick up her niece. Tell her. The thought made her nauseous. She swallowed, took a deep breath.

Stepping off the porch, she brushed Tiny Blue on her way to the Pontiac. Soft tinkling sounds and haint voices rose, lingered. Drawn by a long-neck bottle pointing due north, she caressed it, felt its heat. Eyes swollen from crying, Susan Pea opened the car door, climbed inside.

CHAPTER FIFTY-THREE
FUNERAL

As SELF-CENTERED as Major had been in life, there was no need for further pretentious events. The funeral had been a small intimate affair with only the closest people and themselves in attendance.

"There must be a lot of flowers. I can smell lilies," Janie said. "Maybe carnations, too. What colors are they?" Her voice, like water over pebbles, had a calming quality.

"They're white." Susan Pea squeezed Janie's hand, released it, and leaned her forearms on the iron fence.

Janie stepped forward, her hand fluttering in front of her until it rested on the fence. "White. Like a taste of sugar. Or feel of smooth paper. And, maybe like *pure* thoughts. All good symbols. Can that be right?"

"I don't know." Susan Pea took Janie's hand again.

They were silent a few moments, lost in separate thoughts.

Janie shifted her feet. "I don't hear anybody. We're alone."

"Yes," responded Susan Pea.

They stood for a time, listened to the low buzz of traffic, felt the sun's heat. On the yard fringes, the sound of voices drifted across the graves.

"I loved him," Susan Pea said. "When we were children, I loved him. But, even then, he was a bully."

They stood close, holding separate thoughts. Shadows crept long across the graveyard. A chorus of insects rose. Outside the iron fence, city sounds floated free, stained the peace of the sleeping.

Susan Pea shifted. "I wished him dead. I thought about it so often, it was hard to separate what I did from what I didn't. Letta told me thoughts have power." Her shoulders slumped. She rubbed her head. "I often wondered how my life would have changed if he had shown me some *caring,* however insignificant."

"You mustn't talk like that. You said no one really knows what happened out there. Nor how." Janie's voice had taken on a deeper quality. "I think he did the best he knew how."

Somehow, in intervening weeks with Eve gone, Wes's death, and now Major's, Susan Pea had seen Janie begin a slow maturing. She laced her fingers in Janie's hand and leaned over to kiss her forehead. "You're right. I'll have to live with everything as it is. We both will."

Off in the distance, a crow began a raucous cawing, pumping up and down on a limb, calling to the other side. Wind kicked up and leaves crab-walked across cemetery ground, unpretentious spirits on their way to a gathering. Each soul struggling alone.

The two women held hands, walked from heat and into shade of the oaks lining the area. Janie's pregnancy bloomed noticeably, juxtaposed as it was even against Susan Pea's round figure.

EPILOGUE

The Butler mansion was sold and sub-divided into apartments. The town eventually absorbed the kennels and training field, converting them into a modest housing development.

The blue bottle tree was stripped, branches broken up, and burned in toney fireplaces. Haints roamed free. The conjure woman faded into shadows.

Janie told Pieter DeGroot about Wes. He simply said, "Birth fathers are not always loving," He kissed her on the cheek and added, "I'm *grootpapa* and I love this baby. Besides, you are only one in Bainbridge who can pronounce Pieter correctly." She smiled, remembered Wes's struggle to define himself, be independent. He had *chosen* her. She was unexpected and held potential for a different life.

The two women, aunt and niece, had moved to state university in the fall quarter along with baby Hope Evangeline Butler. They lived in a two-bedroom house perched on the edge of campus. Mutt and the striped cat shared the cottage.

Susan Pea served as nanny during Janie's workday and whenever she and Pieter travelled their lecture circuit. He continued to live in his apartment, but often turned up for dinner, saying it was a grandfather's right to drop by.

By 1974, Janie and Pieter, with their parallel careers, gained modest recognition as a research team. They spoke at regional conferences and symposia. He strutted about, pride glowing, relishing his status as a chosen grandfather. Janie's confidence as a mother and researcher blossomed. Since she wasn't troubled by sight, some things were easier for her and also more complex. She redefined herself, but continued to use the name Butler.

Eventually, Susan Pea found a fragile inner peace caring for her niece. As auntie, she took long campus walks, carefully guided the stroller across lawns and down sidewalks. They often sat under a tree with Mutt, his muzzle turning greyer each year. Susan Pea bounced Hope and cooed to her, both laughing in dappled shade while the old dog napped.

She stayed in touch with her New York friends, especially Theresa Scalia, but never traveled north again. Nor did they venture south.

Sometimes on moon-dark nights, Letta reflected on her affection for the South, sometimes felt it turn to animosity. On such nights, she held her blue bottle until it grew warm and thought about Old Ones. Her children married, had their families, and found a measure of peace. She lived to see her grandchildren. After Letta left, the unloved wooden structure where she had lived gave up and fell inward. Summer hogweeds and curtains of Virginia creeper devoured it. Crows congregated nearby during the day and told of different realms.

Didn't matter how Major died. Could have been murder. Could have been an accident. Or maybe, God forbid, suicide. Didn't matter— he was still dead.

With the Civil Rights Movement and Vietnam fading, people

looked away, eyes glazing over, while their paltry lives undulated in waves of good, bad, and indifferent.

New people moved into Bainbridge, most unaware of the family's story. Those who did remember declined to disturb sleeping souls.

Only the ancient oak with its scarred bark, moss strings, and crooked branches continued to mark the Georgia landscape and bear witness.

Hometowns mark a person, making them at one and the same time carefree and crippled. Sometimes, to survive, leaving that place called home is the best option.

ACKNOWLEDGMENTS

My family, born and bred, in the deep South, gave me an appreciation for people, animals, and places. My stepdaddy, a dirt farmer, raised hogs and tobacco along the South Georgia-North Florida strip between Jacksonville, Valdosta, and Panama City. Mother was a history teacher in the local high school and stood as a steadfast pillar, shaping my values and shortcomings. My maternal grandfather was a car salesman, not always straightforward, who also traded in bird dogs, horses, and mules. He loved bird hunting, fishing, and roaming the countryside. Occasionally, he took me along. My beloved uncles and aunts were storytellers, drinkers, and smokers, each a product of their time.

Thank you goes to my critique groups: Ozark Mountain Guild of Writers guided by the Pen-L Publishing team of Duke and Kim Pennell. Special appreciation to the Writers Guild of Arkansas with Dr. Maeve Maddox and Raymona Anderson, both strong group anchors. I thank all the group members, individually and collectively.

Specific thanks to Lia Wu and the publishing team at Ozark Hollow Press. They have collectively shaped my book into more than I could have alone.

Gratitude to beta readers Amy Matthews, master English teacher; reader extraordinaire Audley Hall; and, artist/author Ken Landrum, now deceased, for their comments and gift of time. Appreciation to artist Graham Hawks for his bottle tree and house sketch. Recognition to my friends who have cheered me one through the years. I treasure and thank each.

No book is the product of a single person.

ABOUT THE AUTHOR

Nancy Hartney's Southern roots dig into the sweat-soaked hardscrabble farm on which she was raised. Her second novel, *The Blue Bottle Tree*, is set during the summer of 1970. It is a tale of racial divide, revenge, and roots that stare into the eyes of her people, careworn with living, grasping for understanding, doing the best they know how.

Her debut collection of short stories, ***Washed in the Water: Tales from the South***, earned the President's Award and named Best Book of the Year Fiction 2014 by Ozarks Writers League (MO). Her second collection of short stories, ***If the Creek Don't Rise: Tales from the South*** has been met with critical acclaim. Both books feature original sketches by artist Susan Raymond. *Kirkus Reviews* says of her first novel, ***If You Walk Long Enough***, "Realistic, sharply descriptive, and movingly observant writing."

Nancy lives in the Arkansas Ozarks but along the way has worked with differently abled individuals in Texas and California, taught grade school in Texas, enjoyed a stint with international students at the University of Arkansas, and been employed as a librarian. Animals or birds, sometimes both, appear in her tales—a writing quirk. She still considers sweet tea her beverage of choice.

Her work has appeared in various literary journals, magazines, and other publications.

Find her at **NancyHartney.net** and on Facebook at **Nancy Hartney Author.**